DOVER · THRIFT · EDITIONS

Great Irish Short Stories

EDITED BY

EVAN BATES

DOVER PUBLICATIONS, INC.
Mineola, New York

DOVER THRIFT EDITIONS

GENERAL EDITOR: PAUL NEGRI

EDITOR OF THIS VOLUME: EVAN BATES

Bibliographical Note

This Dover edition, first published in 2004, is a new selection of twelve short stories reprinted from the sources on p. vii. A new introductory Note has been specially prepared for this edition.

Library of Congress Cataloging-in-Publication Data

Great Irish short stories / edited by Evan Bates.
     p. cm. — (Dover thrift editions)
   ISBN 0-486-43788-4 (pbk.)
    1. Short stories, English—Irish authors. 2. Ireland—Social life and customs—
Fiction. I. Bates, Evans. II. Series.

PR8876.G74 2004
823'.01089417—dc22

                                                                      2004055277

Manufactured in the United States of America
Dover Publications, Inc., 31 East 2nd Street, Mineola, N.Y. 11501

Note

Frank O'Connor, one of the most important practitioners of the Irish short story as well as one of the genre's most profound critics, has suggested that short stories thrive under particular social conditions—circumstances very different from those that produce novels:

> The novel by its very nature presupposes a group, a social system that can absorb the lonely figure. The short story is the art form that deals with the individual when there is no longer a society to absorb him, and when he is compelled to exist, as it were, by his own inner light.[1]

Ireland in the nineteenth and early twentieth centuries, with its rural population and relatively fragmented cultural life, lent itself to short-story writing. The country's complicated relationship with England and the English language added to the estrangement that fueled this literature. O'Connor maintains that Irish intellectuals, unlike their American and European counterparts, never believed that organized society could function beneficially for all its members and they thus assumed a permanent role outside the community. The short story's form, with its limited point of view and its plot often comprising a single event, corresponded to their social sentiments.[2]

---

[1] Frank O'Connor, *The Mirror in the Roadway; a Study of the Modern Novel* (Freeport, N.Y.: Books for Libraries Press, 1970).

[2] Frank O'Connor. *The Lonely Voice, A Study of the Short Story* (Cleveland, Ohio: World Publishing, 1963).

Other critics propose more fundamental sources for Ireland's short-story tradition. Most often cited is the country's rich national culture of oral storytelling. Practiced over centuries, the storyteller's art served to transmit history and genealogy between generations.

Another scholar has idiosyncratically suggested that the Irish have a particular taste for art on a small scale, mentioning that they have been called "a nation of miniaturists in perfection in the arts." He cites the Tara brooch, the Ardagh chalice, the memorable tune, the exquisite oratory, and, in literature, the lyric poem, the one-act play, and of course, the short story, as examples.[3]

This volume presents a diverse selection of Irish short literature spanning two centuries. It begins with the early-nineteenth-century work of Maria Edgeworth and William Carleton, generally considered to be the beginning of Irish prose fiction in English. Following the century through to the Irish Literary Revival—an attempt by Lady Gregory, Standish O'Grady, and other intellectuals to resurrect the folklore and mythology of Ireland's past—the collection touches upon the supernatural (J. Sheridan Le Fanu's "Green Tea"), the mystical (Yeats's "Tables of the Law"), and the humorous (Somerville and Ross's "Lisheen Races, Second-Hand"). The modern Irish short story begins with George Moore's "Home Sickness" and is followed by works from many of the twentieth century's most significant writers: James Stephens, James Joyce, Daniel Corkery, Seumas O'Kelly, and, closer to the present, Liam O'Flaherty.

---

[3] Richard J. Thompson, *Everlasting Voices: Aspects of the Modern Irish Short Story*, (Troy, N.Y.: Whitston Press, 1989).

Bibliographical Sources

Edgeworth, Maria, "The Limerick Gloves." Excerpted from *Popular Tales*. London: George Routledge and Sons, n.d.

Carleton, William, "The Donagh; or, The Horse-Stealers." Excerpted from *Traits and Stories of the Irish Peasantry, 2nd Series*. Dublin: W. F. Wakeman, 1833.

Le Fanu, J. Sheridan, "Green Tea." Excerpted from *In a Glass Darkly*. London: R. Bentley and Son, 1886.

O'Grady, Standish H., "Death of Fergus." Excerpted from *Silva Gadelica: A Collection of Tales in Irish, Vol. 2*. Edited and translated by Standish H. O'Grady. London: Williams and Norgate, 1892.

Yeats, W. B., "The Tables of the Law." Excerpted from *The Tables of the Law and The Adoration of the Magi*. London: Privately printed by R. Clay & Sons, Ltd., 1897.

Somerville, E. Œ. and Martin Ross, "Lisheen Races, Second-Hand." Excerpted from *Some Experiences of an Irish R. M.* London: Longmans, Green, and Co., 1910.

Augusta, Isabella, Lady Gregory, "The Only Son of Aoife." Excerpted from *Cuchulain of Muirthemne: The Story of the Men of the Red Branch of Ulster*. (4th ed.). London: John Murray, 1911.

Moore, George, "Home Sickness." Excerpted from *The Untilled Field*. Philadelphia: J. B. Lippincott Company, 1903.

Stephens, James, "The Blind Man." Excerpted from *Here Are Ladies*. London: Macmillan and Co., Ltd., 1913.

Joyce, James, "The Dead." Excerpted from *Dubliners*. London: Grant Richards, 1914.

Corkery, Daniel, "The Ploughing of Leaca-na-Naomh." Excerpted from *A Munster Twilight and The Hounds of Banba*. Dublin: The Talbot Press Ltd., n.d.

O'Kelly, Seumas, "The Weaver's Grave." Excerpted from *The Golden Barque and The Weaver's Grave*. New York and London: G. P. Putnam's Sons, 1920.

O'Flaherty, Liam, "The Pedlar's Revenge." Excerpted from *The Pedlar's Revenge and Other Stories*. Dublin: Wolfhound Press, 1976.

Contents

Great Irish
Short Stories

THE LIMERICK GLOVES

Maria Edgeworth

I

Surmise is often partly True and partly False.

IT was Sunday morning, and a fine day in autumn; the bells of Hereford Cathedral rang, and all the world, smartly dressed, were flocking to church.

"Mrs. Hill! Mrs. Hill! Phœbe! Phœbe! There's the cathedral bell, I say, and neither of you ready for church, and I a verger," cried Mr. Hill, the tanner, as he stood at the bottom of his own staircase.

"I'm ready, papa," replied Phœbe; and down she came, looking so clean, so fresh, and so gay, that her stern father's brows unbent, and he could only say to her, as she was drawing on a new pair of gloves,

"Child, you ought to have had those gloves on before this time of day."

"Before this time of day!" cried Mrs. Hill, who was now coming down stairs, completely equipped—"before this time of day! She should know better, I say, than to put on those gloves at all—more especially when going to the cathedral."

"The gloves are very good gloves, as far as I see," replied Mr. Hill. "But no matter now; it is more fitting that we should be in proper time in our pew, to set an example, as becomes us, than to stand here talking of gloves and nonsense."

He offered his wife and daughter each an arm, and set out for the cathedral; but Phœbe was too busy drawing on her new gloves, and her mother was too angry at the sight of them, to accept of Mr. Hill's courtesy.

"What I say is always nonsense, I know, Mr. Hill," resumed the matron; "but I can see as far into a millstone as other folks. Was it not I that first gave you a hint of what became of the great dog that we lost out of our tan-yard last winter? And was it not I who first took notice to you, Mr. Hill, verger as you are, of the hole under the foundation of the cathedral? Was it not, I ask you, Mr. Hill?"

"But, my dear Mrs. Hill, what has all this to do with Phœbe's gloves?"

"Are you blind, Mr. Hill? Don't you see that they are Limerick gloves?"

"What of that?" said Mr. Hill, still preserving his composure, as it was his custom to do as long as he could when he saw his wife was ruffled.

"What of that, Mr. Hill! why don't you know that Limerick is in Ireland, Mr. Hill?"

"Will all my heart, my dear."

"Yes, and with all your heart, I suppose, Mr. Hill, you would see our cathedral blown up, some fair day or other, and your own daughter married to the person that did it, and you a verger, Mr. Hill?"

"God forbid!" cried Mr. Hill, and he stopped short and settled his wig. Presently recovering himself, he added, "But, Mrs. Hill, the cathedral is not yet blown up, and our Phœbe is not yet married."

"No; but what of that, Mr. Hill? Forewarned is forearmed, as I told you before your dog was gone; but you would not believe me, and you see how it turned out in that case, and so it will in this case, you'll see, Mr. Hill."

"But you puzzle and frighten me out of my wits, Mrs. Hill," said the verger, again settling his wig. "*In that case, and in this case!* I can't understand a syllable of what you've been saying to me this half-hour. In plain English, what is there the matter about Phœbe's gloves?"

"In plain English, then, Mr. Hill, since you can understand nothing else, please to ask your daughter Phœbe who gave her those gloves. Phœbe, who gave you those gloves?"

"I wish they were burnt," said the husband, whose patience could endure no longer. "Who gave you these cursed gloves, Phœbe?"

"Papa," answered Phœbe, in a low voice, "they were a present from Mr. Brian O'Neill."

"The Irish glover!" cried Mr. Hill, with a look of terror.

"Yes," resumed the mother; "very true, Mr. Hill, I assure you. Now, you see, I had my reasons."

"Take off the gloves directly, I order you, Phœbe," said her father, in his most peremptory tone. "I took a moral dislike to that Mr. Brian O'Neill the first time I ever saw him. He's an Irishman, and that's enough, and too much, for me. Off with the gloves, Phœbe! When I order a thing, it must be done."

Phœbe seemed to find some difficulty in getting off the gloves, and gently urged that she could not well go into the cathedral without them. This objection was immediately removed, by her mother's pulling from her pocket a pair of mittens, which had once been brown, and once been whole, but which were now rent in sundry places; and which, having been long stretched by one who was twice the size of Phœbe, now hung in huge wrinkles upon her well-turned arms.

"But, papa," said Phœbe, "why would we take a dislike to him because he is an Irishman? Cannot an Irishman be a good man?"

The verger made no answer to this question; but, a few seconds after it was put to him, observed that the cathedral bell had just done ringing; and as they were now got to the church door, Mrs. Hill, with a significant look at Phœbe, remarked that it was no proper time to talk or think of good men or bad men, or Irishmen, or any men, especially for a verger's daughter.

We pass over in silence the many conjectures that were made by several of the congregation concerning the reason why Miss Phœbe Hill should appear in such a shameful shabby pair of gloves on Sunday. After service was ended, the verger went, with great mystery, to examine the hole under the foundation of the cathedral; and Mrs. Hill repaired, with the grocer's and the stationer's ladies, to take a walk in the Close; where she boasted to all her female acquaintance, whom she called her friends, of her maternal discretion in prevailing upon Mr. Hill to forbid her daughter Phœbe to wear the Limerick gloves.

II

Words ill understood are among our worst Misfortunes.

In the mean time Phœbe walked pensively homeward, endeavouring to discover why her father should take a mortal dislike to a man at first sight, merely because he was an Irishman; and why her mother had talked so much of the great dog which had been lost last year out of the tanyard, and of the hole under the foundation of the cathedral? What has all this to do with my Limerick gloves? thought she. The more she thought the less connection she could perceive between these things; for, as she had not taken a dislike to Mr. Brian O'Neill at first sight, because he was an Irishman, she could not think it quite reasonable to suspect him of making away with her father's dog, nor yet of a design to blow up the Hereford Cathedral. As she was pondering upon these matters, she came within sight of the ruins of a poor woman's house, which, a few months before this time, had been burnt down. She recollected that her first acquaintance with her lover began at the time of this fire; and she thought that the courage and humanity he showed, in exerting himself to save this unfortunate woman and her children, justified her notion of the possibility that an Irishman might be a good man.

The name of the poor woman whose house had been burnt down was Smith; she was a widow, and she now lived at the extremity of a narrow lane, in a wretched habitation. Why Phœbe thought of her with more concern than usual at this instant we need not examine, but she did; and, reproaching herself for having neglected it for some weeks past, she resolved to go directly to see the widow Smith, and to give her a crown which she had long had in her pocket, with which she had intended to have bought play-tickets.

It happened that the first person she saw in the poor widow's kitchen was the identical Mr. O'Neill.

"I did not expect to see anybody here but you, Mrs. Smith," said Phœbe, blushing.

"So much the greater the pleasure of the meeting;—to me, I mean, Miss Hill," said O'Neill, rising, and putting down a little boy, with whom he had been playing. Phœbe went on talking to the poor woman, and after slipping the crown into her hand, said she would call again.

O'Neill, surprised at the change in her manner, followed her when she left the house, and said, "It would be a great misfortune to me to have done anything to offend Miss Hill, especially if I could not conceive how or what it was, which is my case at this present speaking;" and, as the spruce glover spoke, he fixed his eyes upon Phœbe's ragged gloves.

She drew them up in vain, and then said, with her natural simplicity and gentleness, "You have not done anything to offend me, Mr. O'Neill, but you are some way or other displeasing to my father and mother, and they have forbid me to wear the Limerick gloves."

"And sure Miss Hill would not be after changing her opinion of her humble servant, for no reason in life but because her father and mother, who have taken a prejudice against him, are a little contrary."

"No," replied Phœbe; "I should not change my opinion without any reason; but I have not had time yet to fix my opinion of you, Mr. O'Neill."

"To let you know a piece of my mind then, my dear Miss Hill," resumed he, "the more contrary they are, the more pride and joy it would give me to win and wear you, in spite of 'em all; and if without a farthing in your pocket, so much the more I should rejoice in the opportunity of proving to your dear self, and all else whom it may consarn, that Brian O'Neill is no Irish fortune-hunter, and scorns them that are so narrow-minded as to think that no other kind of cattle but these fortune-hunters can come out of all Ireland. So, my dear

Phœbe, now we understand one another, I hope you will not be paining my eyes any longer with the sight of these odious brown bags, which are not fit to be worn by any Christian's arms, to say nothing of Miss Hill's, which are the handsomest, without any compliment, that ever I saw; and, to my mind, would become a pair of Limerick gloves beyond anything; and I expect she'll show her generosity and proper spirit by putting them on immediately."

"You expect, sir!" repeated Miss Hill, with a look of more indignation than her gentle countenance had ever before been seen to assume. "Expect! If he had said hope," thought she, "it would have been another thing; but expect! what right has he to expect?"

Now Miss Hill, unfortunately, was not sufficiently acquainted with the Irish idiom to know that to *expect* in Ireland is the same thing as to *hope* in England; and, when her Irish admirer said "I expect," he meant only in plain English "I hope." But thus it is that a poor Irishman, often for want of understanding the niceties of the English language, says the rudest when he means to say the civillest things imaginable.

Miss Hill's feelings were so much hurt by this unlucky "I expect," that the whole of his speech, which had before made some favourable impression upon her, now lost its effect, and she replied with proper spirit, as she thought, "You expect a great deal too much, Mr. O'Neill, and more than ever I gave you reason to do. It would be neither pleasure nor pride to me to be won and worn, as you were pleased to say, in spite of them all, and to be thrown, without a farthing in my pocket, upon the protection of one who expects so much at first setting out. So I assure you, sir, whatever you may expect, I shall not put on the Limerick gloves."

Mr. O'Neill was not without his share of pride and proper spirit. Nay, he had, it must be confessed, in common with some others of his countrymen, an improper share of pride and spirit. Fired by the lady's coldness, he poured forth a volley of reproaches, and ended by wishing, as he said, a good morning, for ever and ever, to one who could change her opinion point blank, like the weathercock. "I am, Miss, your most obedient, and I expect you'll never think any more of poor Brian O'Neill and the Limerick gloves."

If he had not been in too great a passion to observe anything, poor Brian O'Neill would have found out that Phœbe was not a weathercock; but he left her abruptly, and hurried away, imagining all the while that it was Phœbe, and not himself, who was in a rage. Thus, to the horseman who is galloping at full speed, the hedges, trees, and houses, seem rapidly to recede, whilst, in reality, they never move from their places,—it is he that flies from them, and not they from him.

III

Endeavours to be consistent often lead to Obstinacy in Error.

On Monday morning, Miss Jenny Brown, the perfumer's daughter, came to pay Phœbe a morning visit, with a face of busy joy.

"So, my dear," said she, "fine doings in Hereford! But what makes you look so downcast? To be sure you are invited, as well as the rest of us?"

"Invited where?" cried Mrs. Hill, who was present, and who could never endure to hear of an invitation in which she was not included. "Invited where, pray, Miss Jenny?"

"La! have not you heard? Why, we all took it for granted that you and Miss Phœbe would have been the first and foremost to have been asked to Mr. O'Neill's ball."

"Ball!" cried Mrs. Hill, and luckily saved Phœbe, who was in some agitation, the trouble of speaking. "Why, this is a mighty sudden thing; I never heard a tittle of it before."

"Well, this is really extraordinary! And, Phœbe, have not you received a pair of Limerick gloves?"

"Yes, I have," said Phœbe; "but what then? What have my Limerick gloves to do with the ball?"

"A great deal," replied Jenny. "Don't you know that a pair of Limerick gloves is, as one may say, a ticket to this ball? for every lady that has been asked has had a pair sent to her along with the card; and I believe as many as twenty, beside myself, have been asked this morning."

Jenny then produced her new pair of Limerick gloves, and, as she tried them on, and showed how well they fitted, she counted up the names of the ladies who, to her knowledge, were to be at this ball. When she had finished the catalogue, she expatiated upon the grand preparations which it was said the widow O'Neill, Mr. O'Neill's mother, was making for the supper, and concluded by condoling with Mrs. Hill, for her misfortune in not having been invited. Jenny took her leave, to get her dress in readiness; "for," added she, "Mr. O'Neill has engaged me to open the ball, in case Phœbe does not go; but I suppose she will cheer up and go, as she has a pair of Limerick gloves as well as the rest of us."

There was a silence for some minutes after Jenny's departure, which was broken by Phœbe, who told her mother that early in the morning a note had been brought to her, which she had returned unopened, because she knew, from the handwriting of the direction, that it came from Mr. O'Neill.

We must observe that Phœbe had already told her mother of her meeting with this gentleman at the poor widow's; and of all that had passed between them afterwards. This openness, on her part, had softened the heart of Mrs. Hill, who was really inclined to be good-natured, provided people would allow that she had more penetration than any one else in Hereford. She was moreover a good deal piqued and alarmed by the idea that the perfumer's daughter might rival and outshine her own. Whilst she had thought herself sure of Mr. O'Neill's attachment to Phœbe, she had looked higher; especially as she was persuaded, by the perfumer's lady, to think that an Irishman could not be a good match: but now she began to suspect that the perfumer's lady had changed her opinion of Irishmen, since she did not object to her own Jenny's leading up the ball at Mr. O'Neill's.

All these thoughts passed rapidly in the mother's mind; and, with her fear of losing an admirer for her Phœbe, the value of that admirer suddenly rose in her estimation. Thus, at an auction, if a lot is going to be knocked down to a lady, who is the only person that has bid for it, even she feels discontented, and despises that which nobody covets; but if, as the hammer is falling, many voices answer to the question, "Who bids more?" then her anxiety to secure the prize suddenly rises; and, rather than be outbid, she will give far beyond its value."

"Why, child," said Mrs. Hill, "since you have a pair of Limerick gloves, and since certainly that note was an invitation to us to this ball; and since it is much more fitting that you should open the ball than Jenny Brown; and since, after all, it was very handsome and genteel of the young man to say he would take you without a farthing in your pocket, which shows that those were misinformed who talked of him as an Irish adventurer; and since we are not certain 'twas he made away with the dog, although he said its barking was a great nuisance; and since, if he did not kill or entice away the dog, there is no great reason to suppose he was the person who made the hole under the foundation of the cathedral, or that he could have such a wicked thought as to blow it up; and since he must be in a very good way of business to be able to afford giving away four or five guineas' worth of Limerick gloves, and balls and suppers; and since, after all, it is no fault of his to be an Irishman, I give it as my vote and opinion, my dear, that you put on your Limerick gloves and go to this ball; and I'll go and speak to your father, and bring him round to our opinion; and then I'll pay the morning visit I owe to the widow O'Neill, and make up your quarrel with Brian. Love-quarrels are easy to make up, you know; and then we shall have things all upon velvet again; and Jenny Brown need not come, with her hypocritical condoling face, to us any more."

After running this speech glibly off, Mrs. Hill, without waiting to hear a syllable from poor Phœbe, trotted off in search of her consort. It was not, however, quite so easy a task, as his wife expected it would be, to bring Mr. Hill round to her opinion. He was slow in declaring himself of any opinion; but, when once he had said a thing, there was but little chance of altering his notions. On this occasion, Mr. Hill was doubly bound to his prejudice against our unlucky Irishman; for he had mentioned, with great solemnity, at the club which he frequented, the grand affair of the hole under the foundation of the cathedral; and his suspicions that there was a design to blow it up. Several of the club had laughed at this idea; others, who supposed that Mr. O'Neill was a Roman Catholic, and who had a confused notion that a Roman Catholic *must* be a very wicked dangerous person, thought that there might be a great deal in the verger's suggestions; and observed that a very watchful eye ought to be kept upon this Irish glover, who had come to settle at Hereford nobody knew why, and who seemed to have money at command nobody knew how.

The news of this ball sounded to Mr. Hill's prejudiced imagination like the news of a conspiracy. "Ay! ay!" thought he; "the Irishman is cunning enough! But we shall be too many for him: he wants to throw all the good sober folks of Hereford off their guard, by feasting and dancing, and carousing, I take it; and so to perpetrate his evil designs when it is least suspected: but we shall be prepared for him! Fools as he takes us plain Englishmen to be, I warrant."

In consequence of these most shrewd cogitations, our verger silenced his wife with a peremptory nod, when she came to persuade him to let Phœbe put on the Limerick gloves, and go to the ball.

"To this ball she shall not go; and I charge her not to put on those Limerick gloves, as she values my blessing," said Mr. Hill. "Please to tell her so, Mrs. Hill, and trust to my judgment and discretion in all things, Mrs. Hill. Strange work may be in Hereford yet: but I'll say no more, I must go and consult with knowing men, who are of my own opinion."

He sallied forth, and Mrs. Hill was left in a state which only those who are troubled with the disease of excessive curiosity can rightly comprehend or compassionate. She hied back to Phœbe, to whom she announced her father's answer; and then went gossiping to all her female acquaintance in Hereford, to tell them all that she knew, and all that she did not know; and to endeavour to find out a secret where there was none to be found.

IV

The Certainties of Suspicion are always doubtful, and often ridiculous.

There are trials of temper in all conditions; and no lady, in high or low life, could endure them with a better grace than Phœbe.

Whilst Mr. and Mrs. Hill were busied abroad, there came to see Phœbe one of the widow Smith's children. With artless expressions of gratitude to Phœbe, this little girl mixed the praises of O'Neill, who, she said, had been the constant friend of her mother, and had given her money every week since the fire happened. "Mammy loves him dearly, for being so good-natured," continued the child; "and he has been good to other people as well as to us."

"To whom?" said Phœbe.

"To a poor man, who has lodged for these few days past next door to us," replied the child; "I don't know his name rightly, but he is an Irishman; and he goes out a-haymaking in the daytime, along with a number of others. He knew Mr. O'Neill in his own country, and he told mammy a great deal about his goodness."

As the child finished these words, Phœbe took out of a drawer some clothes, which she had made for the poor woman's children, and gave them to the little girl. It happened that the Limerick gloves had been thrown into this drawer; and Phœbe's favourable sentiments of the giver of those gloves were revived by what she had just heard, and by the confession Mrs. Hill had made, that she had no reasons, and but vague suspicions, for thinking ill of him. She laid the gloves perfectly smooth, and strewed over them, whilst the little girl went on talking of Mr. O'Neill, the leaves of a rose which she had worn on Sunday.

Mr. Hill was all this time in deep conference with those prudent men of Hereford who were of his own opinion about the perilous hole under the cathedral. The ominous circumstance of this ball was also considered, the great expense at which the Irish glover lived, and his giving away gloves; which was a sure sign he was not under any necessity to sell them, and consequently a proof that, though he pretended to be a glover, he was something wrong in disguise. Upon putting all these things together, it was resolved, by these overwise politicians, that the best thing that could be done for Hereford, and the only possible means of preventing the immediate destruction of its cathedral, would be to take Mr. O'Neill into custody. Upon recollection, however, it was perceived that there were no legal grounds on which he could be attacked. At length, after consulting an attorney, they devised what they thought an admirable mode of proceeding.

Our Irish hero had not that punctuality which English tradesmen usually observe in the payment of bills: he had, the preceding year, run up a long bill with a grocer in Hereford; and, as he had not at Christmas cash in hand to pay it, he had given a note, payable six months after date. The grocer, at Mr. Hill's request, made over the note to him; and it was determined that the money should be demanded, as it was now due, and that, if it was not paid directly, O'Neill should be that night arrested. How Mr. Hill made the discovery of this debt to the grocer agree with his former notion, that the Irish glover had always money at command, we cannot well conceive; but anger and prejudice will swallow down the grossest contradictions without difficulty.

When Mr. Hill's clerk went to demand payment of the note, O'Neill's head was full of the ball which he was to give that evening. He was much surprised at the unexpected appearance of the note: he had not ready money by him to pay it; and, after swearing a good deal at the clerk, and complaining of this ungenerous and ungentleman-like behaviour in the grocer and the tanner, he told the clerk to be gone, and not to be bothering him at such an unseasonable time; that he could not have the money then, and did not deserve to have it all.

This language and conduct were rather new to the English clerk's mercantile ears. We cannot wonder that it should seem to him, as he said to his master, more the language of a madman than a man of business. This want of punctuality in money transactions, and this mode of treating contracts as matters of favour and affection, might not have damned the fame of our hero in his own country, where such conduct is, alas! too common; but he was now in a kingdom where the manners and customs are so directly opposite, that he could meet with no allowance for his national faults. It would be well for his countrymen if they were made, even by a few mortifications, somewhat sensible of this important difference in the habits of Irish and English traders, before they come to settle in England.

But, to proceed with our story. On the night of Mr. O'Neill's grand ball, as he was seeing his fair partner, the perfumer's daughter, safely home, he felt himself tapped on the shoulder by no friendly hand. When he was told that he was the king's prisoner, he vociferated, with sundry strange oaths which we forbear to repeat, "No, I am not the king's prisoner! I am the prisoner of that shabby rascally tanner, Jonathan Hill. None but he would arrest a gentleman in this way, for a trifle not worth mentioning."

Miss Jenny Brown screamed when she found herself under the protection of a man who was arrested; and what between her screams and his oaths, there was such a disturbance that a mob soon collected.

Among this mob there was a party of Irish haymakers, who, after returning late from a harvest-home, had been drinking in a neighbouring alehouse. With one accord they took part with their countryman, and would have rescued him from the civil officers, with all the pleasure imaginable, if he had not fortunately possessed sufficient sense and command of himself to restrain their party-spirit, and to forbid them, as they valued his life and reputation, to interfere, by word or deed, in his defence.

He then despatched one of the haymakers home to his mother, to inform her of what had happened, and to request that she would get somebody to be bail for him as soon as possible, as the officers said they could not let him out of their sight till he was bailed by substantial people, or till the debt was discharged.

The widow O'Neill was just putting out the candles in the ball-room when this news of her son's arrest was brought to her. We pass over Hibernian exclamations. She consoled her pride by reflecting that it would certainly be the most easy thing imaginable to procure bail for Mr. O'Neill in Hereford, where he had so many friends who had just been dancing at his house; but to dance at his house she found was one thing, and to be bail for him quite another. Each guest sent excuses; and the widow O'Neill was astonished at what never fails to astonish everybody when it happens to themselves.

"Rather than let my son be detained in this manner for a paltry debt," cried the widow, "I'd sell all I have, within half an hour, to a pawnbroker."

It was well no pawnbroker heard this declaration: she was too warm to consider economy. She sent for a pawnbroker, who lived in the same street; and after pledging goods to treble the amount of the debt, she obtained ready money for her son's release.

O'Neill, after being in custody for about an hour and a half, was set at liberty upon the payment of his debt. As he passed by the cathedral, in his way home, he heard the clock strike; and he called to a man, who was walking backwards and forwards in the churchyard, to ask whether it was two or three that the clock struck. "Three," answered the man; "and as yet all is safe."

O'Neill, whose head was full of other things, did not stop to inquire the meaning of these last words. He little suspected that this man was a watchman, whom the over-vigilant verger had stationed there to guard the Hereford cathedral from his attacks. O'Neill little guessed that he had been arrested merely to keep him from blowing up the cathedral this night. The arrest had an excellent effect upon his mind, for he was a young man of good sense: it made him resolve to retrench his expenses in time,—to live more like a glover, and less like a gentleman,—and to aim more at establishing credit, and less at gaining popularity. He found from experience that good friends will not pay bad debts.

V

Conjecture is an Ignis Fatuus, *that by seeming to light may dangerously mislead.*

On Thursday morning our verger rose in unusually good spirits, congratulating himself upon the eminent service he had done to the city of Hereford by his sagacity in discovering the foreign plot to blow up the cathedral, and by his dexterity in having the enemy held in custody at the very hour when the dreadful deed was to have been perpetrated. Mr. Hill's knowing friends further agreed it would be necessary to have a guard that should sit up every night in the churchyard, and that as soon as they could, by constantly watching the enemy's motions, procure any information which the attorney should deem sufficient grounds for a legal proceeding, they should lay the whole business before the mayor.

After arranging all this most judiciously and mysteriously with the friends who were exactly of his own opinion, Mr. Hill laid aside his dignity of verger, and assuming his other character of a tanner, proceeded to his tan-yard. What was his surprise and consternation when he beheld his great rick of oak bark levelled to the ground! The pieces of bark were scattered far and wide,—some over the close, some over the fields, and some were seen swimming upon the water. No tongue, no pen, no muse can describe the feelings of our tanner at this spectacle!—feelings which became the more violent from the absolute silence which he imposed on himself upon this occasion. He instantly decided in his own mind that this injury was perpetrated by O'Neill, in revenge for his arrest, and went privately to the attorney to inquire what was to be done on his part to secure legal vengeance.

The attorney, unluckily,—or at least as Mr. Hill thought unluckily,— had been sent for, half an hour before, by a gentleman, at some distance from Hereford, to draw up a will, so that our tanner was obliged to postpone his legal operations.

We forbear to recount his return, and how many times he walked up and down the close to view his scattered bark, and to estimate the damage that had been done to him. At length that hour came which usually suspends all passions by the more imperious power of appetite,—the hour of dinner,—an hour of which it was never needful to remind Mr. Hill by watch, clock, or dial; for he was blessed with a punctual appetite, and powerful as punctual; so powerful, indeed, that it often excited the spleen of his more genteel or less hungry wife.

"Bless my stars, Mr. Hill," she would oftentimes say, "I am really downright ashamed to see you eat so much; and when company is to dine with us, I do wish you would take a snack, by way of a damper, before dinner, that you may not look so prodigious famishing and ungenteel."

Upon this hint, Mr. Hill commenced a practice, to which he ever afterwards religiously adhered, of going, whether there was to be company or no company, into the kitchen regularly every day, half an hour before dinner, to take a slice from the roast or the boiled before it went up to table. As he was this day, according to his custom, in the kitchen, taking his snack, by way of a damper, he heard the housemaid and the cook talking about some wonderful fortune-teller, whom the housemaid had been consulting. This fortune-teller was no less a personage than the

successor to Bampfylde Moore Carew, king of the gipsies, whose life and
adventures are probably in many, too many, of our readers' hands.
Bampfylde the Second, king of the gipsies, assumed this title in hopes of
becoming as famous, or as infamous, as his predecessor. He was now
holding his court in a wood, near the town of Hereford; and numbers of
servant-maids and apprentices went to consult him; nay, it was whispered
that he was resorted to, secretly, by some whose education might have
taught them better sense.

Numberless were the instances which our verger heard in his kitchen
of the supernatural skill of this cunning man; and whilst Mr. Hill ate his
snack with his wonted gravity, he revolved great designs in his secret soul.
Mrs. Hill was surprised several times during dinner to see her consort put
down his knife and fork and meditate.

"Gracious me, Mr. Hill, what can have happened to you this day?
What can you be thinking of, Mr. Hill, that can make you forget what
you have upon your plate?"

"Mrs. Hill," replied the thoughtful verger, "our grandmother Eve had
too much curiosity; and we all know it did not lead to any good. What
I am thinking of will be known to you in due time, but not now, Mrs.
Hill; therefore, pray, no questions, or teazing, or pumping. What I think,
I think; what I say, I say; what I know, I know; and that is enough for you
to know at present: only this, Phœbe,—you did very well not to put on
the Limerick gloves, child. What I know, I know. Things will turn out
just as I said from the first. What I say, I say; and what I think, I think;
and this is enough for you to know at present."

Having finished dinner with this solemn speech, Mr. Hill settled himself
in his arm-chair, to take his after-dinner's nap; and he dreamed of blowing
up cathedrals, and of oak bark floating upon the waters; and the cathedral
was, he thought, blown up by a man dressed in a pair of woman's Limerick
gloves; and the oak bark turned into mutton-steaks, after which his great
dog Jowler was swimming; when, all on a sudden, as he was going to beat
Jowler for eating the bark transformed into mutton-steaks, Jowler became
Bampfylde the Second, king of the gipsies; and putting a horsewhip with
a silver handle into Hill's hand, commanded him, three times, in a voice as
loud as the towncrier's, to have O'Neill whipped through the market-place
of Hereford; but, just as he was going to the window to see this whipping,
his wig fell off and he awoke.

It was difficult, even for Mr. Hill's sagacity, to make sense of this dream;
but he had the wise art of always finding in his dreams something that
confirmed his waking determinations. Before he went to sleep, he had
half resolved to consult the king of the gipsies in the absence of the
attorney; and his dream made him now wholly determine upon this
prudent step. From Bampfylde the Second, thought he, I shall learn for

certain who made the hole under the cathedral, who pulled down my rick of bark, and who made away with my dog Jowler; and then I shall swear examinations against O'Neill, without waiting for attorneys. I will follow my own way in this business: I have always found my own way best.

So, when the dusk of the evening increased, our wise man set out towards the wood to consult the cunning man. Bampfylde the Second, king of the gipsies, resided in a sort of hut made of the branches of trees. The verger stooped, but did not stoop low enough, as he entered this temporary palace; and whilst his body was almost bent double, his peruke was caught upon a twig. From this awkward situation he was relieved by the consort of the king; and he now beheld, by the light of some embers, the person of his gipsy majesty, to whose sublime appearance this dim light was so favourable, that it struck a secret awe into our wise man's soul; and, forgetting Hereford cathedral, and oak bark, and Limerick gloves, he stood for some seconds speechless. During this time the queen very dexterously disencumbered his pocket of all superfluous articles. When he recovered his recollection, he put, with great solemnity, the following queries to the king of the gipsies, and received the following answers:—

"Do you know a dangerous Irishman, of the name of O'Neill, who has come, for purposes best known to himself, to settle at Hereford?"

"Yes, we know him well."

"Indeed! And what do you know of him?"

"That he is a dangerous Irishman."

"Right! And it was he, was it not, that made away with my dog Jowler, that used to guard the tan-yard?"

"It was."

"And who was it that pulled down, or caused to be pulled down, my rick of oak-bark?"

"It was the person that you suspect."

"And was it the person whom I suspect that made the hole under the foundation of our Cathedral?"

"The same, and no other."

"And for what purpose did he make that hole?"

"For a purpose that must not be named," replied the king of the gipsies, nodding his head in a mysterious manner.

"But it may be named to me," cried the verger, "for I have found it out, and I am one of the vergers, and is it not fit that a plot to blow up the Hereford cathedral should be known *to* me and *through* me?"

> "Now, take my word,
> Wise man of Hereford,
> None in safety may be,
> Till the *bad man* doth flee."

These oracular verses, pronounced by Bampfylde with all the enthusiasm of one who was inspired, had the desired effect upon our wise
man, and he left the presence of the king of the gipsies with a prodi-
giously high opinion of his majesty's judgment, and of his own, fully
resolved to impart the next morning to the mayor of Hereford his
important discoveries.

VI

Falsehood and Folly usually confute themselves.

Now it happened that, during the time Mr. Hill was putting the forego-
ing queries to Bampfylde the Second, there came to the door or entrance
of the audience-chamber an Irish haymaker, who wanted to consult the
cunning man about a little leathern purse which he had lost, whilst he
was making hay in a field near Hereford. This haymaker was the same
person who, as we have related, spoke so advantageously of our hero
O'Neill, to the widow Smith. As this man, whose name was Paddy
M'Cormack, stood at the entrance of the gipsies' hut, his attention was
caught by the name of O'Neill, and he lost not a word of all that passed.
He had reason to be somewhat surprised at hearing Bampfylde assert it
was O'Neill who had pulled down the rick of bark. "By the holy poker,"
said he to himself, "the old fellow now is out there. I know more o' that
matter than he does, no offence to his majesty; he knows no more of my
purse, I'll engage now, than he does of this man's rick of bark and his
dog: so I'll keep my tester in my pocket, and not be giving it to this king
o' the gipsies, as they call him, who, as near as I can guess, is no better
than a cheat. But there is one secret which I can be telling this conjurer
himself; he shall not find it such an easy matter to do all what he thinks;
he shall not be after running an innocent countryman of my own, whilst
Paddy M'Cormack has a tongue and brains."

Now, Paddy M'Cormack had the best reason possible for knowing
that Mr. O'Neill did not pull down Mr. Hill's rick of bark; it was
M'Cormack himself who, in the heat of his resentment for the insulting
arrest of his countryman in the streets of Hereford, had instigated his
fellow-haymakers to this mischief; he headed them, and thought he was
doing a clever, spirited action.

There is a strange mixture of virtue and vice in the minds of the lower
class of Irish, or rather a strange confusion in their ideas of right and
wrong, from want of proper education. As soon as poor Paddy found out
that his spirited action of pulling down the rick of bark was likely to be
the ruin of his countryman, he resolved to make all the amends in his
power for his folly; he went to collect his fellow-haymakers, and per-

suaded them to assist him this night in rebuilding what they had pulled down.

They went to this work when everybody except themselves, as they thought, was asleep in Hereford. They had just completed the stack, and were all going away except Paddy, who was seated at the very top finishing the pile, when they heard a loud voice cry out, "Here they are! Watch! watch!"

Immediately all the haymakers who could ran off as fast as possible. It was the watch who had been sitting up at the cathedral who gave the alarm. Paddy was taken from the top of the rick, and lodged in the watch-house till morning. "Since I'm to be rewarded this way for doing a good action, sorrow take me," said he, "if they catch me doing another the longest day I ever live."

Happy they who have in their neighbourhood such a magistrate as Mr. Marshal. He was a man who, to an exact knowledge of the duties of his office, joined the power of discovering truth from the midst of contradictory evidence; and the happy art of soothing, or laughing, the angry passions into good humour. It was a common saying in Hereford—that no one ever came out of Justice Marshal's house as angry as he went into it.

Mr. Marshal had scarcely breakfasted, when he was informed that Mr. Hill, the verger, wanted to speak to him on business of the utmost importance. Mr. Hill, the verger, was ushered in; and with gloomy solemnity, took a seat opposite to Mr. Marshal.

"Sad doings in Hereford, Mr. Mayor—sad doings, sir."

"Sad doings? Why, I was told we had merry doings in Hereford;—a ball the night before last, as I heard."

"So much the worse, Mr. Marshal; so much the worse: as those think with reason that see as far into things as I do."

"So much the better, Mr. Hill," said Mr. Marshal, laughing; "so much the better: as those think with reason that see no farther into things than I do."

"But, sir," said the verger, still more solemnly, "this is no laughing matter, nor time for laughing, begging your pardon, Mr. Mayor. Why, sir, the night of that diabolical ball, our Hereford cathedral, sir, would have been blown up,—blown up from the foundation,—if it had not been for me, sir!"

"Indeed, Mr. Verger! And pray how, and by whom, was the cathedral to be blown up; and what was there diabolical in this ball?"

Here Mr. Hill let Mr. Marshal into the whole history of his early dislike to O'Neill, and his shrewd suspicions of him the first moment he saw him in Hereford. He related in the most prolix manner all that the reader knows already, and concluded by saying that, as he was now certain of his facts, he was come to swear examinations against this villainous Irishman, who, he hoped, would be speedily brought to justice, as he deserved.

"To justice he shall be brought, as he deserves," said Mr. Marshal; "but before I write, and before you swear, will you have the goodness to inform me how you have made yourself as certain as you evidently are, of what you call your facts?"

"Sir, that is a secret," replied our wise man, "which I shall trust to you alone;" and he whispered into Mr. Marshal's ear that his information came from Bampfylde the Second, king of the gipsies.

Mr. Marshal instantly burst into laughter; then composing himself, said, "My good sir, I am really glad that you have proceeded no farther in this business; and that no one in Hereford, besides myself, knows that you were on the point of swearing examinations against a man on the evidence of Bampfylde the Second, king of the gipsies. My dear sir, it would be a standing joke against you to the end of your days. A grave man, like Mr. Hill; and a verger too! Why, you would be the laughing-stock of Hereford!"

Now Mr. Marshal well knew the character of the man to whom he was talking, who, above all things on earth, dreaded to be laughed at. Mr. Hill coloured all over his face, and pushing back his wig by way of set-tling it, showed that he blushed not only all over his face but all over his head.

"Why, Mr. Marshal, sir," said he, "as to my being laughed at, it is what I did not look for; there being men in Hereford, to whom I have men-tioned that hole in the cathedral, who have thought it no laughing mat-ter, and who have been precisely of my own opinion thereupon."

"But did you tell these gentlemen that you had been consulting the king of the gipsies?"

"No, sir, no: I can't say that I did."

"Then, I advise you, keep your own counsel, as I will."

Mr. Hill, whose imagination wavered between the hole in the cathe-dral and his rick of bark on one side, and between his rick of bark and his dog Jowler on the other, now began to talk of the dog, and now of the rick of bark; and when he had exhausted all he had to say upon these subjects, Mr. Marshal gently pulled him towards the window, and putting a spy-glass into his hand, bid him look towards his own tan-yard, and tell him what he saw. To his great surprise, Mr. Hill saw his rick of bark rebuilt. "Why, it was not there last night," exclaimed he, rubbing his eyes. "Why, some conjurer must have done this."

"No," replied Mr. Marshal, "no conjurer did it; but your friend Bampfylde the Second, king of the gipsies, was the cause of its being rebuilt; and here is the man who actually pulled it down, and who actu-ally rebuilt it.

As he said these words, Mr. Marshal opened the door of an adjoining room, and beckoned to the Irish haymaker, who had been taken into custody about an hour before this time. The watch who took Paddy had called at Mr. Hill's house to tell him what had happened, but Mr. Hill was not then at home.

VII

*Our Mistakes are our very selves; we therefore
combat for them to the last.*

It was with much surprise that the verger heard the simple truth from this poor fellow; but no sooner was he convinced that O'Neill was innocent as to this affair, than he recurred to his other ground of suspicion, the loss of his dog.

The Irish haymaker now stepped forward, and with a peculiar twist of the hips and shoulders, which those only who have seen it can picture to themselves, said, "Please your honour's honour, I have a little word to say too about the dog."

"Say it then," said Mr. Marshal.

"Please your honour, if I might expect to be forgiven, and let off for pulling down the jontleman's stack, I might be able to tell him what I know about the dog."

"If you can tell me anything about my dog," said the tanner, "I will freely forgive you for pulling down the rick; especially as you have built it up again. Speak the truth now: did not O'Neill make away with the dog?"

"Not at-all at-all, plase your honour," replied the haymaker: "and the truth of the matter is, I know nothing of the dog, good or bad; but I know something of his collar, if your name, plase your honour, is Hill, as I take it to be?"

"My name is Hill; proceed," said the tanner, with great eagerness. "You know something about the collar of my dog Jowler."

"Plase your honour, this much I know, any way, that it is now, or was the night before last, at the pawnbroker's there, below in town; for, plase your honour, I was sent late at night (that night that Mr. O'Neill, long life to him! was arrested), to the pawnbroker's for a Jew, by Mrs. O'Neill, poor cratur! she was in great trouble that same time."

"Very likely," interrupted Mr. Hill: "but go on to the collar; what of the collar?"

"She sent me,—I'll tell you the story, plase your honour, *out of the face.* She sent me to the pawnbroker's, for the Jew; and it being so late at night, the shop was shut, and it was with all the trouble in life that I got into the house any way; and when I got in, there was none but a slip of a boy up; and he set down the light that he had in his hand, and ran up the stairs to awaken his master; and whilst he was gone, I just made bold to look round at what sort of a place I was in, and at the old clothes, and rags, and scraps; and there was a sort of a frieze trusty."

"A trusty!" said Mr. Hill; "what is that, pray?"

"A big coat sure, plase your honour: there was a frieze big coat lying in a corner, which I had my eye upon, to trate myself to; I having, as I then thought, money in my little purse enough for it. Well, I won't trouble your honour's honour with telling of you now how I lost my purse in the field, as I found after: but about the big coat, as I was saying, I just lifted it off the ground, to see would it fit me; and as I swung it round, something plase your honour hit me a great knock on the shins: it was in the pocket of the coat, whatever it was, I knew; so I looks into the pocket to see what was it, plase your honour, and out I pulls a hammer, and a dog-collar; it was a wonder, both together, they did not break my shins entirely: but its no matter for my shins now: so before the boy came down, I just, out of idleness, spelt out to myself the name that was upon the collar; there were two names, plase your honour; and out of the first there was so many letters hammered out I could make nothing of it, at-at at-all; but the other name was plain enough to read any way, and it was Hill, plase your honour's honour, as sure as life: Hill, now."

This story was related in tones, and with gestures, which were so new and strange, to English ears and eyes, that even the solemnity of our verger gave way to laughter. Mr. Marshal sent a summons for the pawn-broker, that he might learn from him how he came by the dog-collar. The pawnbroker, when he found from Mr. Marshal that he could by no other means save himself from being committed to prison, for receiving stolen goods, knowing them to be stolen, confessed that the collar had been sold to him by Bampfylde the Second, king of the gipsies.

A warrant was immediately despatched for his majesty; and Mr. Hill was a good deal alarmed, by the fear of its being known in Hereford, that he was on the point of swearing examinations against an innocent man, upon the evidence of a dog-stealer and a gipsy.

Bampfylde the Second made no sublime appearance, when he was brought before Mr. Marshal: nor could all his astrology avail him upon this occasion. The evidence of the pawnbroker was so positive, as to the fact of his having sold to him the dog-collar, that there was no resource left for Bampfylde but an appeal to Mr. Hill's mercy. He fell on his knees, and confessed that it was he who stole the dog; which used to bark at him at night so furiously that he could not commit certain petty depre-dations, by which, as much as by telling fortunes, he made his livelihood.

"And so," said Mr. Marshal, with a sternness of manner which till now he had never shown, "to screen yourself, you accused an innocent man; and by your vile arts would have driven him from Hereford, and have set two families for ever at variance, to conceal that you had stolen a dog."

The king of the gipsies was, without further ceremony, committed to the house of correction. We should not omit to mention that, on searching his hut, the Irish haymaker's purse was found; which some of his majesty's train had emptied. The whole set of gipsies decamped, upon the news of the apprehension of their monarch.

VIII

Good Sense and Good Humour are the best Peace-makers.

Mr. Hill stood in profound silence, leaning upon his walking-stick, whilst the committal was making out for Bampfylde the Second. The fear of ridicule was struggling with the natural positiveness of his temper; he was dreadfully afraid that the story of his being taken in by the king of the gipsies would get abroad, and at the same time he was unwilling to give up his prejudice against the Irish glover.

"But, Mr. Mayor," cried he, after a long silence, "the hole under the foundation of our cathedral has never been accounted for; that is, was, and ever will be, an ugly mystery to me; and I never can have a good opinion of this Irishman till it is cleared up; nor can I think the cathedral in safety."

"What," said Mr. Marshal, with an arch smile, "I suppose, the verses of the oracle still work upon your imagination, Mr. Hill. They are excellent of their kind—I must have them by heart, in order that, when I am asked the reason why Mr. Hill has taken an aversion to an Irish glover, I may be able to repeat them:—

> 'Now, take my word,
> Wise man of Hereford,
> None in safety may be
> Till the bad man doth flee.' "

"You'll oblige me, Mr. Mayor," said the verger, "if you would never repeat those verses, sir, nor mention in any company the affair of the king of the gipsies."

"I will oblige you," replied Mr. Marshal, "if you will oblige me. Will you tell me, honestly, whether, now that you find this Mr. O'Neill is neither a dog-killer nor a puller down of bark-ricks, you feel that you could forgive him for being an Irishman, if the mystery, as you call it, of the hole under the cathedral is cleared up?"

"But that is not cleared up, I say, sir," cried Mr. Hill, striking his walking-stick forcibly upon the ground with both his hands. "As to the matter of his being an Irishman, I have nothing to say to it; I am not saying anything about that, for I know we are all born where it pleases God, and an Irishman may be as good as another. I know that much, Mr. Marshal; and I am not one of those illiberal-minded, ignorant people that cannot abide a man that was not born in England. Ireland is now in his Majesty's dominions, I know very well, Mr. Mayor; and I have no manner of doubt, as I said before, that an Irishman born may be as good, almost, as an Englishman born."

"I am glad," said Mr. Marshal, "to hear you speak almost as reasonably as an Englishman born, and as every man ought to speak; and I am convinced that you have too much English hospitality to persecute an inoffensive stranger, who comes amongst us trusting to our justice and good-nature."

"I would not persecute a stranger, God forbid, Mr. Mayor," replied the verger, "if he was, as you say, inoffensive."

"And if he was not only inoffensive, but ready to do every service in his power to those who are in want of his assistance, we should not return evil for good, should we?"

"That would be uncharitable, to be sure; and, moreover, a scandal," said the verger.

"Then," said Mr. Marshal, "will you walk with me as far as the widow Smith's, the poor woman whose house was burnt last winter? This haymaker, who lodged near her, can show us the way to her present abode."

During his examination of Paddy M'Cormack, who would tell his whole history, as he called it, *out of the face,* Mr. Marshal heard several instances of the humanity and goodness of O'Neill, which Paddy related to excuse himself for that warmth of attachment to his cause that had been manifested so injudiciously by pulling down the rick of bark in revenge for the arrest. Amongst other things, Paddy mentioned his countryman's goodness to the widow Smith; Mr. Marshal was determined, therefore, to see whether he had in this instance spoken the truth; and he took Mr. Hill with him, in hopes of being able to show him the favourable side of O'Neill's character.

Things turned out just as Mr. Marshal expected. The poor widow and her family, in the most simple and affecting manner, described the distress from which they had been relieved by the good gentleman and lady. The lady was Phœbe Hill, and the praises that were bestowed upon Phœbe were delightful to her father's ear, whose angry passions had now all subsided.

The benevolent Mr. Marshal seized the moment when he saw Mr. Hill's heart was touched, and exclaimed, "I must be acquainted with this Mr. O'Neill. I am sure we people of Hereford ought to show some hospitality to a stranger who has so much humanity. Mr. Hill, will you dine with him to-morrow at my house?"

Mr. Hill was just going to accept of this invitation, when the recollection of all he had said to his club, about the hole under the cathedral, came across him, and drawing Mr. Marshal aside, he whispered, "But, sir, sir, that affair of the hole under the cathedral has not been cleared up yet."

At this instant, the widow Smith exclaimed, "Oh! here comes my little Mary," one of her children who came running in; "this is the little girl, sir, to whom the lady has been so good. Make your curtsey, child. Where have you been all this while?"

"Mammy," said the child, "I've been showing the lady my rat."

"Lord bless her! Gentlemen, the child has been wanting me this many a day to go and see this tame rat of hers, but I could never get time, never; and I wondered, too, at the child's liking such a creature. Tell the gentlemen, dear, about your rat. All I know is, that let her have but never such a tiny bit of bread for breakfast or supper, she saves a little of that for this rat of hers; she and her brothers have found it out somewhere by the cathedral."

"It comes out of a hole under the wall of the cathedral," said one of the elder boys; "and we have diverted ourselves watching it, and sometimes we have put victuals for it, and so it has grown in a manner tame like."

Mr. Hill and Mr. Marshal looked at one another during this speech, and the dread of ridicule again seized on Mr. Hill, when he apprehended that, after all he had said, the mountain might at last bring forth—a rat. Mr. Marshal, who instantly saw what passed in the verger's mind, relieved him from this fear by refraining even from a smile on this occasion. He only said to the child, in a grave manner, "I am afraid, my dear, we shall be obliged to spoil your diversion. Mr. Verger, here, cannot suffer rat-holes in the cathedral; but to make you amends for the loss of your favourite, I will give you a very pretty little dog, if you have a mind."

The child was well pleased with this promise, and at Mr. Marshal's desire she then went along with him and Mr. Hill to the cathedral, and they placed themselves at a little distance from that hole which had created so much disturbance. The child soon brought the dreadful enemy to light; and Mr. Hill, with a faint laugh, said, "I'm glad it's no worse; but there were many in our club who were of my opinion; and if they had not suspected O'Neill, too, I am sure I should never have given you so much trouble, Mr. Mayor, as I have done this morning. But I hope, as the club know nothing about that vagabond, that king of the gipsies, you will not let any one know anything about the prophecy and all that? I am sure I am very sorry to have given you so much trouble, Mr. Mayor."

Mr. Marshall assured him that he did not regret the time which he had spent in endeavouring to clear up all these mysteries and suspicions, and Mr. Hill gladly accepted his invitation to meet O'Neill at his house the next day. No sooner had Mr. Marshal brought one of the parties to reason and good humour than he went to prepare the other for a reconciliation. O'Neill and his mother were both people of warm but forgiving tempers; the arrest was fresh in their minds; but when Mr. Marshal represented to them the whole affair, and the verger's prejudices, in a humourous light, they joined in the good-natured laugh, and O'Neill declared that for his part he was ready to forgive and to forget everything, if he could but see Miss Phœbe in the Limerick gloves.

Phœbe appeared the next day at Mr. Marshal's in the Limerick gloves; and no perfume ever was so delightful to her lover as the smell of the rose-leaves in which they had been kept.

Mr. Marshal had the benevolent pleasure of reconciling the two families. The tanner and the glover of Hereford became, from bitter enemies, useful friends to each other, and they were convinced by experience that nothing could be more for their mutual advantage than to live in union.

THE DONAGH; OR, THE HORSE-STEALERS

William Carleton

CARNMORE, one of those small villages that are to be found in the out-skirts of many parishes in Ireland, whose distinct boundaries are lost in the contiguous mountain wastes, was situated at the foot of a deep gorge, or pass, overhung by two bleak hills, from the naked sides of which the storm swept over it without discomposing the peaceful little nook of cabins that stood below. About a furlong farther down were two or three farmhouses, inhabited by a family named Cassidy, men of simple, inof-fensive manners and considerable wealth. They were, however, acute and wise in their generation; intelligent cattle dealers, on whom it would have been a matter of some difficulty to impose an unsound horse, or a cow older than was intimated by her horn-rings, even when conscien-tiously dressed up for sale by the ingenious aid of the file or burning-iron. Between their houses and the hamlet rose a conical pile of rocks, loosely heaped together, from which the place took its name of Carnmore.

About three years before the time of this story there came two men with their families to reside in the upper village, and the house which they chose as a residence was one at some distance from those which composed the little group we have just been describing. They said their name was Meehan, although the general report went that this was not true; that the name was an assumed one, and that some dark mystery, which none could penetrate, shrouded their history and character. They were certainly remarkable men. The elder, named Anthony, was a dark, black-browed person, stern in his manner, and atrociously cruel in his disposition. His form was herculean, his bones strong and hard as iron, and his sinews stood out in undeniable evidence of a life hitherto spent in severe toil and exertion, to bear which he appeared to an amazing degree capable. His brother Denis was a small man, less savage and daring in his character, and consequently more vacillating and cautious than Anthony; for the points in which he resembled him were superinduced upon his natural disposition by the close connection that subsisted between them, and by the identity of their former pursuits in life, which, beyond doubt, had been such as could not bear investigation.

The old proverb of "birds of a feather flock together" is certainly a true one, and in this case it was once more verified. Before the arrival of these men in the village there had been five or six bad characters in the neighbourhood, whose delinquencies were pretty well-known. With these persons the strangers, by that sympathy which assimilates with congenial good or evil, soon became acquainted; and although their intimacy was as secret and cautious as possible, still it had been observed and was known; for they had frequently been seen skulking together at daybreak or in the dusk of evening.

It is unnecessary to say that Meehan and his brother did not mingle much in the society of Carnmore. In fact, the villagers and they mutually avoided each other. A mere return of the common phrases of salutation was generally the most that passed between them: they never entered into that familiarity which leads to mutual intercourse and justifies one neighbour in freely entering the cabin of another, to spend a winter's night or a summer's evening in amusing conversation. Few had ever been in the house of the Meehans since it became theirs. Nor were the means of their subsistence known. They led an idle life, had no scarcity of food, were decently clothed, and never wanted money—circumstances which occasioned no small degree of conjecture in Carnmore and its vicinity.

Some said they lived by theft; others, that they were coiners; and there were many who imagined, from the diabolical countenance of the elder brother, that he had sold himself to the devil, who, they affirmed, set his mark upon him, and was his paymaster. Upon this hypothesis several were ready to prove that he had neither breath nor shadow: they had seen him, they said, standing under a hedgerow of elder—that unholy tree which furnished wood for the cross, and on which Judas hanged himself—yet, although it was noonday in the month of July, his person threw out no shadow. Worthy souls! because the man stood in the shade at the time. But with these simple explanations Superstition had nothing to do, although we are bound, in justice to the reverend old lady, to affirm that she was kept exceedingly busy in Carnmore. If a man had a sick cow, she was elf-shot; if his child became consumptive, it had been overlooked, or received a blast from the fairies; if the whooping cough was rife, all the afflicted children were put three times under an ass; or when they happened to have the "mumps," were led before sunrise to a south-running stream, with a halter hanging about their necks, under an obligation of silence during the ceremony. In short, there could not possibly be a more superstitious spot than that which these men of mystery had selected for their residence. Another circumstance which caused the people to look upon them with additional dread was their neglect of mass on Sundays and holidays, though they avowed themselves Roman Catholics. They did not, it is true, join in the dances, drinking matches, football, and other sports with which the Carnmore folk celebrated the Lord's Day; but they scrupled not, on the other hand, to mend their garden ditch or mold a row of cabbages on the Sabbath—a circumstance for which two or three of the Carnmore boys were, one Sunday evening when tipsy, well-nigh chastising them. Their usual manner, however, of spending that day was by sauntering lazily about the fields, or stretching themselves supinely on the sunny side of the hedges, their arms folded into their bosoms, and their hats lying over their faces to keep off the sun.

In the meantime, loss of property was becoming quite common in the neighbourhood. Sheep were stolen from the farmers, and cows and horses from the more extensive graziers in the parish. The complaints against the authors of these depredations were loud and incessant. Watches were set, combinations for mutual security formed, and subscriptions to a considerable amount entered into, with a hope of being able, by the temptation of a large reward, to work upon the weakness or cupidity of some accomplice to betray the gang of villains who infested the neighbourhood. All, however, was in vain: every week brought some new act of plunder to light, perpetrated upon such unsuspecting persons as had hitherto escaped the notice of the robbers; but no trace could be discovered of the perpetrators. Although theft had from time to time been committed upon a small scale before the arrival of the Meehans in the village, yet it was undeniable that since that period the instances not only multiplied, but became of a more daring and extensive description. They arose in a gradual scale from the hen-roost to the stable; and with such ability were they planned and executed, that the people, who in every instance identified Meehan and his brother with them, began to believe and hint that, in consequence of their compact with the devil, they had power to render themselves invisible. Common fame, who can best treat such subjects, took up this and never laid it aside until, by narrating several exploits which Meehan the elder was said to have performed in other parts of the kingdom, she wound it up by roundly informing the Carnmorians that having been once taken prisoner for murder, he was caught by the leg when half through a hedge, but that being most wickedly determined to save his neck, he left the leg with the officer who took him, shouting out that it was a new species of legbail; and yet he moved away with surprising speed upon two of as good legs as any man in his Majesty's dominions might wish to walk off upon from the insinuating advances of a bailiff or a constable!

The family of the Meehans consisted of their wives, and three children, two boys and a girl—the former were the offspring of the younger
brother, and the latter of Anthony. It has been observed, with truth and
justice, that there is no man, how hardened and diabolical soever in his
natural temper, who does not exhibit to some particular object a peculiar species of affection. Such a man was Anthony Meehan. That sullen
hatred which he bore to human society, and that inherent depravity of
heart which left the trail of vice and crime upon his footsteps, were flung
off his character when he addressed his daughter Anne. To him her voice
was like music. To her he was not the reckless villain, treacherous and
cruel, which the helpless and unsuspecting found him, but a parent kind
and indulgent as ever pressed an only and beloved daughter to his bosom.
Anne was handsome: had she been born and educated in an elevated
rank in society, she would have been softened by the polish and luxury
of life into perfect beauty; she was, however, utterly without education.
As Anne experienced from her father no unnatural cruelty, no harshness,
nor even indifference, she consequently loved him in return; for she
knew that tenderness from such a man was a proof of parental love rarely
to be found in life. Perhaps she loved not her father the less on perceiving that he was proscribed by the world—a circumstance which might
also have enhanced in his eyes the affection she bore him. When Meehan
came to Carnmore she was sixteen; and as that was three years before the
incident occurred on which we have founded this narrative, the reader
may now suppose her to be about nineteen; an interesting country girl
as to person, but with a mind completely neglected, yet remarkable for
an uncommon stock of good nature and credulity.

About the hour of eleven o'clock one winter's night in the beginning
of December, Meehan and his brother sat moodily at their hearth. The
fire was of peat which had recently been put down, and from between
the turf the ruddy blaze was shooting out in those little tongues and gusts
of sober light which throw around the rural hearth one of those charms
which make up the felicity of domestic life. The night was stormy, and
the wind moaned and howled along the dark hills beneath which the
cottage stood. Every object in the house was shrouded in a mellow shade,
which afforded to the eye no clear outline, except around the hearth
alone, where the light brightened into a golden hue, giving the idea of
calmness and peace. Anthony Meehan sat on one side of it, and his
daughter opposite him, knitting. Before the fire sat Denis, drawing shapes
in the ashes for his own amusement.

"Bless me," said he, "how sthrange it is!"

"What is?" inquired Anthony, in his deep and grating tones.

"Why, thin, it is sthrange!" continued the other, who, despite of the
severity of his brother, was remarkably superstitious—"a coffin I made in

the ashes three times runnin'! Isn't it very quare, Anne?" he added, addressing the niece.

"Sthrange enough, of a sartinty," she replied, being unwilling to express before her father the alarm which the incident, slight as it was, created in her mind; for she, like the uncle, was subject to such ridiculous influences. "How did it happen, uncle?"

"Why, thin, no way in life, Anne; only, as I was thryin' to make a shoe, it turned out a coffin on my hands. I thin smoothed the ashes, and began agin, an' sorra bit of it but was a coffin still. Well, says I, I'll give you another chance—here goes once more; an', as sure as a gun's iron, it was a coffin the third time! Heaven be about us, it's odd enough!"

"It would be little matther you were nailed down in a coffin," replied Anthony fiercely; "the world would have little loss. What a pitiful, cowardly rascal you are—afraid o' your own shadow afther the sun goes down, except I'm at your elbow! Can't you dhrive all them palavers out o' your head? Didn't the sargint tell us, an' prove to us, the time we broke the guardhouse, an' took Frinch lave o' the ridgment for good, that the whole o' that, an' more along wid it, is all priestcraft?"

"I remember he did, sure enough. I dunna where the same sargint is now, Tony? About no good, anyway, I'll be bail. Howsomever, in regard o' that, why doesn't yourself give up fastin' from the mate of a Friday?"

"Do you want me to sthretch you on the hearth?" replied the savage, whilst his eyes kindled into fury, and his grim visage darkened into a Satanic expression. "I'll tache you to be puttin' me through my catechiz about atin' mate. I may manage that as I plase; it comes at first cost, anyhow; but no cross-questions to me about it, if you regard your health!"

"I must say for you," replied Denis reproachfully, "that you're a good warrant to put the health astray upon us of an odd start: we're not come to this time o' day widout carryin' somethin' to remember you by. For my own part, Tony, I don't like such tokens; an' moreover, I wish you had resaved a thrifle o' larnin', espishily in the writin' line; for whenever we have any difference you're so ready to prove your opinion by settin' your mark upon me, that I'd rather, fifty times over, you could write it with pen an' ink."

"My father will give that up, uncle," said the niece. "It's bad for anybody to be fightin', but worst of all for brothers, that ought to live in peace and kindness. Won't you, father?"

"Maybe I will, dear, some o' these days, on your account, Anne; but you must get this creature of an uncle of yours to let me alone, an' not be aggravatin' me with his folly. As for your mother, she's worse; her tongue's sharp enough to skin a flint, and a batin' a day has little effect on her."

Anne sighed, for she knew how low an irreligious life, and the infamous society with which, as her father's wife, her mother was compelled to mingle, had degraded her.

"Well, but, Father, you don't set her a good example yourself," said Anne; "and if she scolds and drinks now, you know she was a different woman when you got her. You allow this yourself; and the crathur, the dhrunkest time she is, doesn't she cry bittherly, remimberin' what she has been. Instead of one batin' a day, Father, thry no batin' a day, an' maybe it'll turn out betther than thumpin' an' smashin' her, as you do."

"Why, thin, there's thruth an' sinse in what the girl says, Tony," observed Denis.

"Come," replied Anthony, "whatever she may say, I'll suffer none of your interference. Go an' get us the black bottle from the place: it'll soon be time to move. I hope they won't stay too long."

Denis obeyed this command with great readiness, for whisky in some degree blunted the fierce passions of his brother and deadened his cruelty, or, rather, diverted it from minor objects to those which occurred in the lawless perpetration of his villainy.

The bottle was got; and in the meantime the fire blazed up brightly. The storm without, however, did not abate, nor did Meehan and his brother wish that it should. As the elder of them took the glass from the hands of the other, an air of savage pleasure blazed in his eyes, on reflecting that the tempest of the night was favorable to the execution of the villainous deed on which they were bent.

"More power to you!" said Anthony, impiously personifying the storm. "Sure, that's one proof that God doesn't throuble His head about what we do, or we would not get such a murtherin' fine night as is in it, anyhow. That's it! blow an' tundher away, an' keep yourself an' us as black as hell, sooner than we should fail in what we intind! Anne, your health, *acushla!*[1]—Yours, Dinny! If you keep your tongue off o' me, I'll neither make nor meddle in regard o' the batin' o' you."

"I hope you'll stick to that, anyhow," replied Denis. "For my part, I'm sick and sore o' you everyday in the year. Many another man would put salt wather between himself and yourself, sooner nor become a batin'-stone for you, as I have been. Few would bear it when they could mend themselves."

"What's that you say?" replied Anthony, suddenly laying down his glass, catching his brother by the collar, and looking him, with a murderous scowl, in the face. "Is it thrachery you hint at?—eh? sarpent, is it thrachery you mane?" and as he spoke he compressed Denis's neck between his powerful hands until the other was black in the face.

Anne flew to her uncle's assistance, and with much difficulty succeeded in rescuing him from the deadly grip of her father, who exclaimed,

---

[1] Gaelic *a chuisle,* "O pulse [of my heart]."

as he loosed his hold, "You may thank the girl, or you'd not spake, nor dare to spake, about crossin' the salt wather or lavin' me in a desateful way agin. If I ever suspect that a thought of thrachery comes into your heart, I'll do for you; and you may carry your story to the world I'll send you to."

"Father, dear, why are you so suspicious of my uncle?" said Anne. "Sure, he's a long time livin' with you, an' goin' step for step in all the danger you meet with. If he had a mind to turn out a Judas agin you, he might a done it long agone; not to mintion the throuble it would bring on his own head, seein' he's as deep in everything as you are."

"If that's all that throubling you," replied Denis, trembling, "you may make yourself asy on the head of it. But well I know 'tisn't that that's on your mind; 'tis your own conscience; but, sure, it's not fair nor rasonable for you to vent your evil thoughts on me!"

"Well, he won't," said Anne; "he'll quit it; his mind's throubled, an', dear knows, it's no wondher it should. Och, I'd give the world wide that his conscience was lightened of the load that's upon it! My mother's lameness is nothing'; but the child, poor thing! An' it was only widin three days of her lyin'-in. Och, it was a cruel sthroke, father! An' when I seen its little innocent face, dead, an' me widout a brother, I thought my heart would break, thinkin' upon who did it!" The tears fell in showers from her eyes, as she added, "Father, I don't want to vex you, but I wish you to feel sorry for that at laste. Oh, if you'd bring the priest, an' give up sich coorses, father dear, how happy we'd be, an' how happy yourself ud be!"

Conscience for a moment started from her sleep, and uttered a cry of guilt in his spirit; his face became ghastly, and his eyes full of horror; his lips quivered, and he was about to upbraid his daughter with more harshness than usual, when a low whistle, resembling that of a curlew, was heard at a chink of the door. In a moment he gulped down another glass of spirits, and was on his feet: "Go, Denis, an' get the arms," said he, "while I let them in."

On opening the door, three men entered, having their greatcoats muffled about them, and their hats slouched. One of them, named Kenny, was a short villain, but of a thick-set, hairy frame. The other was known as "the Big Mower," in consequence of his following that employment every season, and of his great skill in performing it. He had a deep-rooted objection against permitting the palm of his hand to be seen; a reluctance which common fame attributed to the fact of his having received on that part the impress of a hot iron, in the shape of the letter T, not forgetting to add that T was the hieroglyphic for Thief. The villain himself affirmed it was simply the mark of a cross, burned into it by a blessed friar, as a charm against St. Vitus's dance, to which he had been subject. The people, however, were rather sceptical, not of the friar's power to cure that malady, but of the fact of his ever having moved a limb under it; and they concluded with telling him, good-humoredly enough, that, notwithstanding the charm, he was destined to die "wid the threble of it in his toe." The third was a noted pedlar called Martin, who, under pretense of selling tape, pins, scissors, &c., was very useful in "setting" such premises as this virtuous fraternity might, without much risk, make a descent upon.

"I thought yees would outstay your time," said the elder Meehan, relapsing into his determined hardihood of character; "we're ready, hours agone. Dick Rice gave me two curlew an' two patrich[2] calls today. Now pass the glass among yees while Denny brings the arms. I know there's danger in this business, in regard of the Cassidys livin' so near us. If I see anybody afut, I'll use the curlew call; an' if not, I'll whistle twice on the patrich one, an' yees may come an. The horse is worth aighty guineas if he's worth a shillin'; an' we'll make sixty of him ourselves."

For some time they chatted about the plan at contemplation, and drank freely of the spirits, until at length the impatience of the elder Meehan at the delay of his brother became ungovernable. His voice deepened into tones of savage passion as he uttered a series of blasphemous curses against this unfortunate butt of his indignation and malignity. At length he rushed out furiously to know why he did not return; but on reaching a secret excavation in the mound against which the house was built, he found, to his utter dismay, that Denis had made his escape by an artificial passage scooped out of it to secure themselves a retreat in case of surprise or detection. It opened behind the house among a clump of blackthorn and brushwood, and was covered with green turf in such a manner as to escape the notice of all who were not acquainted with the secret. Meehan's face, on his return, was worked up into an expression truly awful.

"We're sold!" said he; "but stop, I'll tache the thraithur what revinge is!"

In a moment he awoke his brother's two sons, and dragged them by the neck, one in each hand, to the hearth.

"Your villain of a father's off," said he, "to betray us. Go an' folly him—bring him back, an' he'll be safe from me; but let him become a stag agin us, an' if I should hunt you both into the bowels of the airth, I'll send yees to a short account. I don't care that," and he snapped his fingers—"ha, ha!—no, I don't care that for the law; I know how to dale with it when it comes! An' what's the stuff about the other world but priestcraft and lies!"

---

[2] Partridge.

"Maybe," said the Big Mower, "Denis is gone to get the foreway of us, an' to take the horse himself. Our best plan is to lose no time, at all events; so let us hurry, for fraid the night might happen to clear up."

"He!" said Meehan, "he go alone! No; the miserable wretch is afeared of his own shadow. I only wondher he stuck to me so long; but, sure, he wouldn't, only I bate the courage in, and the fear out of him. You're right, Brian," said he, upon reflection; "let us lose no time, but be off. Do yees mind?" he added to his nephews; "did yees hear me? If you see him, let him come back, an' all will be berrid; but if he doesn't, you know your fate;" saying which, he and his accomplices departed amid the howling of the storm.

The next morning Carnmore, and indeed the whole parish, was in an uproar; a horse, worth eighty guineas, had been stolen in the most daring manner from the Cassidys, and the hue-and-cry was up after the thief or thieves who took him. For several days the search was closely maintained, but without success: not the slightest trace could be found of him or them. The Cassidys could very well bear to lose him; but there were many struggling farmers, on whose property serious depredations had been committed, who could not sustain their loss so easily. It was natural, under these circumstances, that suspicion should attach to many persons, some of whom had but indifferent characters before, as well as to several who certainly had never deserved suspicion. When a fortnight or so had elapsed, and no circumstances transpired that might lead to discovery, the neighbors, including those who had principally suffered by the robberies, determined to assemble upon a certain day at Cassidy's house, for the purpose of clearing themselves, on oath, of the imputations thrown out against some of them as accomplices in the thefts. In order, however, that the ceremony should be performed as solemnly as possible, they determined to send for Father Farrell and Mr. Nicholson, a magistrate, both of whom they requested to undertake the task of jointly presiding upon this occasion; and that the circumstance should have every publicity, it was announced from the altar by the priest on the preceding Sabbath, and published on the church gate in large legible characters, ingeniously printed with a pen by the village schoolmaster.

In fact, the intended meeting and the object of it were already notorious; and much conversation was held upon its probable result, and the measures which might be taken against those who should refuse to swear. Of the latter description there was but one opinion, which was that their refusal in such a case would be tantamount to guilt. The innocent were anxious to vindicate themselves from suspicion; and as the suspected did not amount to more than a dozen, of course the whole body of the people, including the thieves themselves, who applauded it as loudly as the others, all expressed their satisfaction at the measures about to be adopted. A day was therefore appointed on which the inhabitants of the neighborhood, particularly the suspected persons, should come to assemble at Cassidy's house, in order to have the characters of the innocent cleared up, and the guilty made known.

On the evening before this took place were assembled in Meehan's cottage the elder Meehan and the rest of the gang, including Denis, who had absconded on the night of the theft.

"Well, well, Denny," said Anthony who forced his rugged nature into an appearance of better temper that he might strengthen the timid spirit of his brother against the scrutiny about to take place on the morrow— perhaps, too, he dreaded him—"Well, well, Denny, I thought, sure enough, that it was some new piece of cowardice came over you. Just think of him," he added, "shabbin' off, only because he made, with a bit of a rod, three strokes in the ashes that he thought resembled a coffin!— ha, ha, ha!"

This produced a peal of derision at Denis's pusillanimous terror.

"Ay!" said the Big Mower, "he was makin' a coffin, was he? I wondher it wasn't a rope you drew, Denny. If any here dies in the coil, it will be the greatest coward, an' that's yourself."

"You may all laugh," replied Denis, "but I know such things to have a manin'. When my mother died, didn't my father—the heavens be his bed—see a black coach about a week before it? an' sure, from the first day she tuck ill, the dead-watch was heard in the house every night. And what was more nor that, she kept warm until she went into her grave; an' accordingly didn't my sisther Shibby die within a year afther?"

"It's no matther about thim things," replied Anthony; "it's thruth about the dead-watch, my mother keepin' warm, an' Shibby's death, anyway. But on the night we tuck Cassidy's horse I thought you were goin' to betray us; I was surely in a murdherin' passion, an' would have done harm, only things turned out as they did."

"Why," said Denis, "the thruth is, I was afeard some of us would be shot, an' that the lot would fall on myself; for the coffin, thinks I, was sent as a warnin'. How-and-ever, I spied about Cassidy's stable till I seen that the coast was clear; so whin I heard the low cry of the patrich that Anthony and I agreed on, I joined yees."

"Well, about tomorrow," observed Kenny—"ha, ha, ha!—there'll be lots o' swearin'. Why, the whole parish is to switch the primer; many a thumb and coat cuff will be kissed in spite of priest or magistrate. I remember once, whin I was swearin' an *alibi* for long Paddy Murray, that suffered for the M'Gees, I kissed my thumb, I thought, so smoothly that no one would notish it; but I had a keen one to dale with, so says he, 'You know, for the matther o' that, my good fellow, that you have your thumb to kiss everyday in the week,' says he; 'but you might salute the book out o' dacency and good manners—not,' says he, 'that you an' it are strangers aither; for, if I don't mistake, you're an ould hand at swearin' *alibis.*' At all evints, I had to smack the book itself, and it's I and Barney Green and Tim Casserly that did swear stiffly for Paddy; but the thing was too clear agin him; so he suffered, poor fellow, an' died right game, for he said over his dhrop—ha, ha, ha!—that he was as innocent o' the murdher as a child unborn; and so he was in one sinse, bein' afther gettin' absolution."

"As to thumb-kissin'," observed the elder Meehan, "let there be none of it among us tomorrow; if we're caught at it, 'twould be as bad as stayin' away altogether. For my part, I'll give it a smack like a pistol shot—ha, ha, ha!"

"I hope they won't bring the priest's book," said Denis. "I haven't the laste objection agin payin' my respects to the magistrate's paper, but somehow I don't like tastin' the priest's in a falsity."

"Don't you know," said the Big Mower, "that whin a magistrate's present it's ever an' always only the Tistament by law that's used. I myself wouldn't kiss the mass-book in a falsity."

"There's none of us sayin' we'd do it in a lie," said the elder Meehan; "an' it's well for thousands that the law doesn't use the priest's book; though, afther all, aren't there books that say religion's all a sham? I think myself it is; for if what they talk about justice an' Providence is thrue, would Tom Dillon be transported for the robbery we committed at Bantry? Tom, it's true, was an ould offender; but he was innocent of that, anyway. The world's all chance, boys, as Sargint Eustace used to say, and whin we die there's no more about us; so that I don't see why a man mightn't was well switch the priest's book as any other, only that somehow a body can't shake the terror of it off o' them."

"I dunna, Anthony, but you an' I ought to curse that sargint; only for him we mightn't be as we are, sore in our conscience, an' afeard of every fut we hear passin'," observed Denis.

"Spake for your own cowardly heart, man alive," replied Anthony; "for my part, I'm afeared o' nothin'. Put round the glass, and don't be nursin' it there all night. Sure, we're not so bad as the rot among the sheep, nor the black leg among the bullocks, nor the staggers among the horses, anyhow; an' yet they'd hang us up only for bein' fond of a bit o' mate—ha, ha, ha!"

"Thrue enough," said the Big Mower, philosophizing. "God made the beef and the mutton, and the grass to feed it; but it was man made the ditches. Now we're only bringin' things back to the right away that Providence made them in, when ould times were in it, manin' before ditches war invinted—ha, ha, ha!"

"'Tis a good argument," observed Kenny, "only that judge and jury would be a little delicate in actin' up to it; an' the more's the pity. Howsomever, as Providence made the mutton, sure it's no harm for us to take what He sends."

"Ay, but," said Denis—

> "God made man, an' man made money;
> God made bees, an' bees made honey;
> God made Satan, an' Satan made sin;
> An' God made a hell to put Satan in.

Let nobody say there's not a hell; isn't it there plain from Scripthur?"

"I wish you had Scripthur tied about your neck!" replied Anthony. "How fond of it one o' the greatest thieves that ever missed the rope is! Why, the fellow could plan a roguery with any man that ever danced the hangman's hornpipe, an' yit he be's repatin' bits an' scraps of ould prayers, an' charms, an' stuff. Ay, indeed! Sure, he has a varse out o' the Bible that he thinks can prevint a man from bein' hung up any day!"

While Denny, the Big Mower, and the two Meehans were thus engaged in giving expression to their peculiar opinions, the pedlar held a conversation of a different kind with Anne.

With the secrets of the family in his keeping, he commenced a rather penitent review of his own life, and expressed his intention of abandoning so dangerous a mode of accumulating wealth. He said he thanked Heaven that he had already laid up sufficient for the wants of a reasonable man; that he understood farming and the management of sheep particularly well; that it was his intention to remove to a different part of the kingdom and take a farm; and that nothing prevented him from having done this before but the want of a helpmate to take care of his establishment. He added that his present wife was of an intolerable temper and a greater villain by fifty degrees than himself. He concluded by saying that his conscience twitched him night and day for living with her, and that, by abandoning her immediately, becoming truly religious, and taking Anne in her place, he hoped, he said, to atone in some measure for his few errors.

Anthony, however, having noticed the earnestness which marked the pedlar's manner, suspected him of attempting to corrupt the principles of his daughter, having forgotten the influence which his own opinions were calculated to produce upon her heart.

"Martin," said he, "'twould be as well you ped attintion to what we're sayin' in regard o' the trial tomorrow, as to be palaverin' talk into the girl's ear that can't be good comin' from your lips. Quit it, I say, quit it! *Corp an duowol*[3]—I won't allow such proceedings!"

---

[3] Would-be phonetic Gaelic for "Devil take you" or "Devil take me."

"Swear till you blister your lips, Anthony," replied Martin; "as for me, bein' no residenthur, I'm not bound to it; an' what's more, I'm not suspected. 'Tis settin' some other bit o' work for yees I'll be, while you're all clearin' yourselves from stealin' honest Cassidy's horse. I wish we had him safely disposed of in the manetime, an' the money for him an' the other beasts in our pockets."

Much more conversation of a similar kind passed between them upon various topics connected with their profligacy and crimes. At length they separated for the night, after having concerted their plan of action for the ensuing scrutiny.

The next morning, before the hour appointed arrived, the parish, particularly the neighborhood of Carnmore, was struck with deep consternation. Labor became suspended, mirth disappeared, and every face was marked with paleness, anxiety, and apprehension. If two men met, one shook his head mysteriously, and inquired from the other, "Did you hear the news?"

"Ay! ay! the Lord be about us all! I did; an' I pray God it may lave the counthry as it came to it!"

"Oh, an' that it may, I humbly make supplication this day!"

If two women met, it was with similar mystery and fear. "Vread, do you know what's at the Cassidys'?"

"Whisht, *ahagur!* I do; but let what will happen, sure it's best for us to say nothin'."

"Say!—the blessed Virgin forbid! I'd cut my hand off o' me afore I'd spake a word about it; only that—"

"Whisht, woman!—for mercy's sake—don't—"

And so they would separate, each crossing herself devoutly.

The meeting at Cassidy's was to take place that day at twelve o'clock; but about two hours before the appointed time, Anne, who had been in some of the other houses, came into her father's, quite pale, breathless, and trembling.

"Oh!" she exclaimed, with clasped hands, whilst the tears fell fast from her eyes, "we'll be lost—ruined! Did yees hear what's in the neighborhood wid the Cassidys?"

"Girl," said the father, with more severity than he had ever manifested to her before, "I never yit ris my hand to you, but *ma corp an duowol,* if you open your lips, I'll fell you where you stand. Do you want that cowardly uncle o' yours to be the manes o' hangin' your father? Maybe that was one o' the lessons Martin gave you last night?" And as he spoke he knit his brows at her with that murderous scowl which was habitual to him. The girl trembled, and began to think that since her father's temper deepened in domestic outrage and violence as his crimes multiplied, the sooner she left the family the better. Every day indeed diminished that species of instinctive affection which she had entertained towards him, and this in proportion as her reason ripened into a capacity for comprehending the dark materials of which his character was composed.

"What's the matter now?" inquired Denis, with alarm. "Is it anything about us, Anthony?"

"No, 'tisn't," replied the other, "anything about us! What ud it be about us for? 'Tis a lyin' report that some cunnin' knave spread, hopin' to find out the guilty. But hear me, Denis, once for all: we're going to clear ourselves—now listen, an' let my words sink deep into your heart— if you refuse to swear this day, no matther what's put into your hand, you'll do harm—that's all—have courage, man; but should you cow, you're coorse will be short; an' mark, even if *you* escape me, your sons won't. I have it all planned; an' *corp an duowol!* thim you won't know from Adam will revinge me if I'm taken up through your unmanliness."

"Twould be betther for us to lave the counthry," said Anne. "We might slip away as it is."

"Ay," said the father, "an' be taken by the neck afore we'd get two miles from the place! No, no, *girsha*[4]; it's the safest way to brazen thim out. Did you hear me, Denis?"

Denis started, for he had been evidently pondering on the mysterious words of Anne, to which his brother's anxiety to conceal them gave additional mystery. The coffin, too, recurred to him; and he feared that the death shadowed out by it would in some manner or other occur in the family. He was, in fact, one of those miserable villains with but half a conscience—that is to say, as much as makes them the slaves of the fear which results from crime, without being the slightest impediment to their committing it. It was no wonder he started at the deep, pervading tones of his brother's voice, for the question was put with ferocious energy.

On starting, he looked with vague terror on his brother, fearing, but not comprehending, his question.

"What is it, Anthony?" he inquired.

"Oh, for that matter," replied the other, "nothin' at all. Think of what I said to you, anyhow: swear through thick an' thin, if you have a regard for your own health or for your childher. Maybe I had betther repate it agin for you," he continued, eyeing him with mingled hatred and suspicion. "Denis, as a friend I bid you mind yourself this day, an' see you don't bring aither of us into throuble."

There lay before the Cassidys' houses a small flat of common, trodden into rings by the young horses they were in the habit of training. On this

---

[4] Gaelic *geirrseach,* "girl."

level space were assembled those who came, either to clear their own character from suspicion, or to witness the ceremony. The day was dark and lowering, and heavy clouds rolled slowly across the peaks of the surrounding mountains; scarcely a breath of air could be felt; and as the country people silently approached, such was the closeness of the day, their haste to arrive in time, and their general anxiety, either for themselves or their friends, that almost every man on reaching the spot might be seen taking up the skirts of his *cothamore,* or "big coat" (the peasant's handkerchief), to wipe the sweat from his brow; and as he took off his dingy woollen hat, or *caubeen,* the perspiration rose in strong exhalations from his head.

"Michael, am I in time?" might be heard from such persons as they arrived. "Did this business begin yit?"

"Full time, Larry; myself's here an hour ago, but no appearance of anything as yit. Father Farrell an' Squire Nicholson are both in Cassidy's, waitin' till they're all gother, whin they'll begin to put thim through their facins. You hard about what they've got?"

"No; for I'm only on my way home from the berril of a *cleaveen*[5] of mine, that we put down this morning' in Tullyard. What is it?"

"Why, man alive, it's through the whole parish inready!" He then went on, lowering his voice to a whisper, and speaking in a tone bordering on dismay.

The other crossed himself, and betrayed symptoms of awe and astonishment, not unmingled with fear.

"Well," he replied, "I dunna whether I'd come here if I'd known that; for, innocent or guilty, I wouldn't wish to be near it. Och, may God pity thim that's to come acrass it, espishly if they dare to do it in a lie!"

"They needn't, I can tell yees both," observed a third person, "be a hair afeard of it, for the best rason livin', that there's no thruth at all in the report, nor the Cassidys never thought of sindin' for anything o' the kind. I have it from Larry Cassidy's own lips, an' he ought to know best."

The truth is that two reports were current among the crowd: one, that the oath was to be simply on the Bible; and the other, that a more awful means of expurgation was to be resorted to by the Cassidys. The people, consequently, not knowing which to credit, felt the most painful of all sensations—uncertainty.

During the period which intervened between their assembling and the commencement of the ceremony, a spectator, interested in contemplating the workings of human nature in circumstances of deep interest, would have had ample scope for observation. The occasion was to them

---

[5] Gaelic *cliamhain,* "a relative by marriage."

a solemn one. There was little conversation among them; for when a man is wound up to a pitch of great interest, he is seldom disposed to relish discourse. Every brow was anxious, every cheek blanched, and every arm folded: they scarcely stirred, or when they did, only with slow, abstracted movements, rather mechanical than voluntary. If an individual made his appearance about Cassidy's door, a sluggish stir among them was visible, and a low murmur of a peculiar character might be heard; but on perceiving that it was only some ordinary person, all subsided again into a brooding stillness that was equally singular and impressive.

Under this peculiar feeling was the multitude when Meehan and his brother were seen approaching it from their own house. The elder, with folded arms, and hat pulled over his brows, stalked grimly forward, having that remarkable scowl upon his face which had contributed to establish for him so diabolical a character. Denis walked by his side, with his countenance strained to inflation—a miserable parody of that sullen effrontery which marked the unshrinking miscreant beside him. He had not heard of the ordeal, owing to the caution of Anthony, but notwithstanding his effort at indifference, a keen eye might have observed the latent anxiety of a man who was habitually villainous and naturally timid.

When this pair entered the crowd, a few secret glances, too rapid to be noticed by the people, passed between them and their accomplices. Denis, on seeing them present, took fresh courage, and looked with the heroism of a blusterer upon those who stood about him, especially whenever he found himself under the scrutinizing eye of his brother. Such was the horror and detestation in which they were held, that on advancing into the assembly the persons on each side turned away and openly avoided them; eyes full of fierce hatred were bent on them vindictively; and "curses, not loud, but deep," were muttered with an indignation which nothing but a divided state of feeling could repress within due limits. Every glance, however, was paid back by Anthony with interest from eyes and black shaggy brows tremendously ferocious; and his curses, as they rolled up half-smothered from his huge chest, were deeper and more diabolical by far than their own. He even jeered at them; but there was something truly appalling in the dark gleam of his scoff which threw them at an immeasurable distance behind him in the power of displaying on the countenance the worst of human passions.

At length Mr. Nicholson, Father Farrell, and his curate, attended by the Cassidys and their friends, issued from the house; two or three servants preceded them, bearing a table and chairs for the magistrate and priests, who, however, stood during the ceremony. When they entered one of the rings before alluded to, the table and chairs were placed in the center of it, and Father Farrell, as possessing most influence over the people, addressed them very impressively.

"There are," said he, in conclusion, "persons in this crowd whom we know to be guilty; but we will have an opportunity of now witnessing the lengths to which crime, long indulged in, can carry them. To such people I would say, beware! for they know not the situation in which they are placed."

During all this time there was not the slightest allusion made to the mysterious ordeal which had excited so much awe and apprehension among them—a circumstance which occasioned many a pale, downcast face to clear up, and reassume its usual cheerful expression. The crowd now were assembled around the ring, and every man on whom an imputation had been fastened came forward, when called upon, to the table at which the priests and magistrate stood uncovered. The form of the oath was framed by the two clergymen, who, as they knew the reservations and evasions commonest among such characters, had ingeniously contrived not to leave a single loophole through which the consciences of those who belonged to this worthy fraternity might escape.

To those acquainted with Irish courts of justice there was nothing particularly remarkable in the swearing. Indeed, one who stood among the crowd might hear from those who were stationed at the greatest distance from the table such questions as the following:—

"Is the *thing* in it, Art?"

"No; 'tis nothin' but the law Bible, the magistrate's own one."

To this the querist would reply, with a satisfied nod of the head, "Oh, is that all? I heard they war to have *it*." On which he would push himself through the crowd until he reached the table, where he took his oath as readily as another.

"Jem Hartigan," said the magistrate to one of those persons, "are you to swear?"

"Faix, myself doesn't know, your honor: only that I hard them say that the Cassidys mintioned our names wid many other honest people; an' one wouldn't, in that case, lie under a false report, your honor, from any one, when we're as clear as them that never saw the light of anything of the kind."

The magistrate then put the book into his hand, and Jem, in return, fixed his eye, with much apparent innocence, on his face. "Now, Jem Hartigan," &c., &c., and the oath was accordingly administered. Jem put the book to his mouth, with his thumb raised to an acute angle on the back of it; nor was the smack by any means a silent one which he gave it (his thumb).

The magistrate set his ear with the air of a man who had experience in discriminating such sounds. "Hartigan," said he, "you'll condescend to kiss the book, sir, if you please; there's a hollowness in that smack, my good fellow, that can't escape me."

"Not kiss it, your honour? Why, by this staff in my hand, if ever a man kissed—"

"Silence, you impostor," said the curate; "I watched you closely, and am confident your lips never touched the book."

"My lips never touched the book! Why, you know I'd be sarry to conthradict either o' yees; but I was jist goin' to observe, wid simmission, that my own lips ought to know best; an' don't you hear them tellin' you that they did kiss it?" and he grinned with confidence in their faces.

"You double-dealing reprobate," said the parish priest, "I'll lay my whip across your jaws. I saw you, too, an' you did not kiss the book."

"By dad, an' maybe I did not, sure enough," he replied. "Any man may make a mistake unknownst to himself; but I'd give my oath, an' be the five crasses, I kissed it as sure as—however, a good thing's never the worse o' bein' twice done, gintlemen; so here goes, jist to satisfy yees," and placing the book near his mouth, and altering his position a little, he appeared to comply, though, on the contrary, he touched neither it nor his thumb. "It's the same thing to me," he continued, laying down the book with an air of confident assurance—"it's the same thing to me if I kissed it fifty times over, which I'm ready to do if that doesn't satisfy yees."

As every man acquitted himself of the charges brought against him, the curate immediately took down his name. Indeed, before the "clearing" commenced, he requested that such as were to swear would stand together within the ring, that after having sworn, he might hand each of them a certificate of the fact, which they appeared to think might be serviceable to them, should they happen to be subsequently indicted for the same crime in a court of justice. This, however, was only a plan to keep them together for what was soon to take place.

The detections of thumb-kissing were received by those who had already sworn, and by several in the outward crowd, with much mirth. It is but justice, however, to many of those assembled, to state that they appeared to entertain a serious opinion of the nature of the ceremony, and no small degree of abhorrence against those who seemed to trifle with the solemnity of an oath.

Standing on the edge of the circle, in the innermost row, were Meehan and his brother. The former eyed, with all the hardness of a stoic, the successive individuals as they passed up to the table. His accomplices had gone forward, and to the surprise of many who strongly suspected them, in the most indifferent manner "cleared" themselves, in the trying words of the oath, of all knowledge of and participation in the thefts that had taken place.

The grim visage of the elder Meehan was marked by a dark smile, scarcely perceptible; but his brother, whose nerves were not so firm, appeared somewhat confused and distracted by the imperturbable villainy of the perjurers.

At length they were called up. Anthony advanced slowly but collectedly to the table, only turning his eye slightly about to observe if his brother accompanied him. "Denis," said he, "which of us will swear first? You may." For as he doubted his brother's firmness, he was prudent enough, should he fail, to guard against having the sin of perjury to answer for, along with those demands which his country had to make for his other crimes. Denis took the book, and cast a slight glance at his brother, as if for encouragement. Their eyes met, and the darkened brow of Anthony hinted at the danger of flinching in this crisis. The tremor of his hand was not, perhaps, visible to any but Anthony, who, however, did not overlook this circumstance. He held the book, but raised not his eye to meet the looks of either the magistrate or the priests; the color also left his face as with shrinking lips he touched the Word of God in deliberate falsehood. Having then laid it down, Anthony received it with a firm grasp, and whilst his eye turned boldly in contemptuous mockery upon those who presented it, he impressed it with the kiss of a man whose depraved conscience seemed to goad him only to evil. After "clearing" himself he laid the Bible upon the table with the affected air of a person who felt hurt at the imputation of theft, and joined the rest with a frown upon his countenance and a smothered curse upon his lips.

Just at this moment a person from Cassidy's house laid upon the table a small box covered with black cloth; and our readers will be surprised to hear that if fire had come down visibly from heaven, greater awe and fear could not have been struck into their hearts or depicted upon their countenances. The casual conversation, and the commentaries upon the ceremony they had witnessed, instantly settled into a most profound silence, and every eye was turned towards it with an interest absolutely fearful.

"Let," said the curate, "none of those who have sworn depart from within the ring until they once more clear themselves upon this," and as he spoke he held it up. "Behold!" said he, "and tremble—behold THE DONAGH!!!"

A low murmur of awe and astonishment burst from the people in general, whilst those within the ring, who, with few exceptions, were the worst characters in the parish, appeared ready to sink into the earth. Their countenances, for the most part, paled into the condemned hue of guilt; many of them became almost unable to stand; and altogether, the state of trepidation and terror in which they stood was strikingly wild and extraordinary.

The curate proceeded: "Let him now who is guilty depart; or if he wishes, advance and challenge the awful penalty annexed to perjury upon THIS! Who has ever been known to swear falsely upon the Donagh without being visited by a tremendous punishment, either on the spot, or in twenty-four hours after his perjury? If we ourselves have not seen such instances with our own eyes, it is because none liveth who dare incur such a dreadful penalty; but we have heard of those who did, and of their awful punishment afterwards. Sudden death, madness, paralysis, self-destruction, or the murder of someone dear to them, are the marks by which perjury on the Donagh is known and visited. Advance now, ye who are innocent; but let the guilty withdraw, for we do not desire to witness the terrible vengeance which would attend a false oath upon the DONAGH. Pause, therefore, and be cautious! for if this grievous sin be committed, a heavy punishment will fall, not only upon you, but upon the parish in which it occurs!"

The words of the priest sounded to the guilty like the death sentence of a judge. Before he had concluded, all, except Meehan and his brother and a few who were really innocent, had slunk back out of the circle into the crowd. Denis, however, became pale as a corpse, and from time to time wiped the large drops from his haggard brow. Even Anthony's cheek, despite of his natural callousness, was less red; his eyes became disturbed; but by their influence he contrived to keep Denis in sufficient dread to prevent him from mingling, like the rest, among the people. The few who remained along with them advanced, and notwithstanding their innocence, when the Donagh was presented, and the figure of Christ and the Twelve Apostles displayed in the solemn tracery of its rude carving, they exhibited symptoms of fear. With trembling hands they touched the Donagh, and with trembling lips kissed the crucifix, in attestation of their guiltlessness of the charge of which they had been accused.

"Anthony and Denis Meehan, come forward," said the curate, "and declare your innocence of the crimes with which you are charged by the Cassidys and others."

Anthony advanced; but Denis stood rooted to the ground; on perceiving which the former sternly returned a step or two, and catching him by the arm with an admonitory grip that could not easily be misunderstood, compelled him to proceed with himself step by step to the table. Denis, however, could feel the strong man tremble, and perceive that although he strove to lash himself into the energy of despair, and the utter disbelief of all religious sanction, yet the trial before him called every slumbering prejudice and apprehension of his mind into active power. This was a death blow to his own resolution, or, rather, it confirmed him in his previous determination not to swear on the Donagh, except to acknowledge his guilt, which he could scarcely prevent himself from doing, such was the vacillating state of mind to which he felt himself reduced.

When Anthony reached the table, his huge form seemed to dilate by his effort at maintaining the firmness necessary to support him in this awful struggle between conscience and superstition on the one hand, and guilt, habit, and infidelity on the other. He fixed his deep, dilated eyes upon the Donagh in a manner that betokened somewhat of irresolution; his countenance fell; his color came and went, but eventually settled in a flushed red; his powerful hands and arms trembled so much that he folded them to prevent his agitation from being noticed; the grimness of his face ceased to be stern, while it retained the blank expression of guilt; his temples swelled out with the terrible play of their blood vessels; his chest, too, heaved up and down with the united pressure of guilt and the tempest which shook him within. At length he saw Denis's eye upon him, and his passions took a new direction: he knit his brows at him with more than usual fierceness, ground his teeth, and with a step and action of suppressed fury he placed his foot at the edge of the table, and bowing down under the eye of God and man, took the awful oath on the mysterious Donagh in a falsehood! When it was finished a feeble groan broke from his brother's lips. Anthony bent his eye on him with a deadly glare; but Denis saw it not. The shock was beyond his courage—he had become insensible.

Those who stood at the outskirts of the crowd, seeing Denis apparently lifeless, thought he must have sworn falsely on the Donagh, and exclaimed, "He's dead! Gracious God! Denis Meehan's struck dead by the Donagh! He swore in a lie, and is now a corpse!" Anthony paused, and calmly surveyed him as he lay with his head resting upon the hands of those who supported him. At this moment a silent breeze came over where they stood, and as the Donagh lay upon the table, the black ribbons with which it was ornamented fluttered with a melancholy appearance that deepened the sensations of the people into something peculiarly solemn and preternatural. Denis at length revived, and stared wildly and vacantly about him. When composed sufficiently to distinguish and recognize individual objects, he looked upon the gloomy visage and threatening eye of his brother, and shrunk back with a terror almost epileptical. "Oh!" he exclaimed, "save me!—save me from that man, and I'll discover all!"

Anthony calmly folded one arm into his bosom, and his lip quivered with the united influence of hatred and despair.

"Hould him!" shrieked a voice, which proceeded from his daughter— "hould my father, or he'll murdher him! Oh! oh! merciful Heaven!"

Ere the words were uttered she had made an attempt to clasp the arms of her parent, whose motions she understood; but only in time to receive from the pistol, which he had concealed in his breast, the bullet aimed at her uncle! She tottered; and the blood spouted out of her neck upon her father's brows, who hastily put up his hand and wiped it away, for it had actually blinded him.

The elder Meehan was a tall man, and as he stood elevated nearly a head above the crowd, his grim brows red with his daughter's blood—which, in attempting to wipe away, he had deeply streaked across his face—his eyes shooting fiery gleams of his late resentment, mingled with the wildness of unexpected horror—as he thus stood, it would be impossible to contemplate a more revolting picture of that state to which the principles that had regulated his life must ultimately lead, even in this world.

On perceiving what he had done, the deep working of his powerful frame was struck into sudden stillness, and he turned his eyes on his bleeding daughter with a fearful perception of her situation. Now was the harvest of his creed and crimes reaped in blood; and he felt that the stroke which had fallen upon him was one of those by which God will sometimes bare His arm and vindicate His justice. The reflection, however, shook him not; the reality of his misery was too intense and pervading, and grappled too strongly with his hardened and unbending spirit, to waste its power upon a nerve or a muscle. It was abstracted, and beyond the reach of bodily suffering. From the moment his daughter fell he moved not; his lips were half open with the conviction produced by the blasting truth of her death, effected prematurely by his own hand.

Those parts of his face which had not been stained with her blood assumed an ashy paleness, and rendered his countenance more terrific by the contrast. Tall, powerful, and motionless, he appeared, to the crowd, glaring at the girl, like a tiger anxious to join his offspring, yet stunned with the shock of the bullet which has touched a vital part. His iron-grey hair, as it fell in thick masses about his neck was moved slightly by the blast, and a lock which fell over his temple was blown back with a motion rendered more distinct by his statue-like attitude, immovable as death.

A silent and awful gathering of the people around this impressive scene intimated their knowledge of what they considered to be a judicial punishment annexed to perjury upon the Donagh. This relic lay on the table, and the eyes of those who stood within view of it, turned from Anthony's countenance to it, and again back to his bloodstained visage, with all the overwhelming influence of superstitious fear. Shudderings, tremblings, crossings, and ejaculations marked their conduct and feeling; for though the incident in itself was simply a fatal and uncommon one, yet they considered it supernatural and miraculous.

At length a loud and agonising cry burst from the lips of Meehan— "Oh, God!—God of heaven an' earth!—have I murdhered my daughter?" and he cast down the fatal weapon with a force which buried it some inches into the wet clay.

The crowd had closed upon Anne; but with the strength of a giant he flung them aside, caught the girl in his arms, and pressed her bleeding to his bosom. He gasped for breath. "Anne," said he,—"Anne, I am without hope, an' there's none to forgive me except you—none at all: from God to the poorest of His creatures, I am hated an' cursed by all except you! Don't curse me, Anne—don't curse me. Oh, isn't it enough, darlin', that my sowl is now stained with your blood, along with my other crimes? Oh, think, darlin', of my broken heart! In hell, on earth, an' in heaven, there's none to forgive your father but yourself!—NONE! NONE! Oh, what's comin' over me! I'm dizzy an' shiverin'! How cowld the day's got of a sudden! Hould up, *avourneen machree*[6]! I was a bad man; but to you, Anne, I was not as I was to every one! Darlin', oh, look at me with forgiveness in your eye; or, anyway, don't curse me! Oh! I'm far cowlder now! Tell me that you forgive me, *acushla oge machree!*[7]—*Manim asthee hu,*[8] darlin', say it. I DARN'T LOOK TO GOD! but oh! do you say the forgivin' word to your father before you die!"

"Father," said she, "I deserve this—it's only just. I had plotted with that divilish Martin to betray them all, except yourself, an' to get the reward; an' then we intended to go—an'—live at a distance—an' in wickedness—where we—might not be known. He's at our house—let him be—secured. Forgive me, father; you said so often that there was no thruth in religion—that I began to—think so. Oh!—God! have mercy upon me!" and with these words she expired.

Meehan's countenance, on hearing this, was overspread with a ghastly look of the most desolating agony; he staggered back, and the body of his daughter, which he strove to hold, would have fallen from his arms, had it not been caught by the bystanders. His eye sought out his brother, but not in resentment. "Oh! she died, but didn't say, 'I FORGIVE YOU!' Denis, bring me home—I'm sick—very sick—oh, but it's cowld—everything's reeling—cowld—cowld it is!" and as he uttered the last words he shuddered, fell down in a fit of apoplexy, never to rise again; and the bodies of his daughter and himself were both waked and buried together.

The result is brief. The rest of the gang were secured; Denis became approver, by whose evidence they suffered that punishment decreed by law to the crimes of which they had been guilty. The two events which we have just related of course added to the supernatural fear and reverence previously entertained for this terrible relic. It is still used as an ordeal of expurgation in cases of stolen property; and we are not wrong in asserting that many of those misguided creatures, who too frequently hesitate not to swear falsely on the Word of God, would suffer death itself sooner than commit a perjury on the Donagh.

---

[6] Darling of my heart.
[7] Young pulse of my heart.
[8] My life is in you.

GREEN TEA

J. Sheridan Le Fanu

PROLOGUE

Martin Hesselius, the German Physician

THOUGH carefully educated in medicine and surgery, I have never practised either. The study of each continues, nevertheless, to interest me profoundly. Neither idleness nor caprice caused my secession from the honourable calling which I had just entered. The cause was a very trifling scratch inflicted by a dissecting knife. This trifle cost me the loss of two fingers, amputated promptly, and the more painful loss of my health, for I have never been quite well since, and have seldom been twelve months together in the same place.

In my wanderings I became acquainted with Dr. Martin Hesselius, a wanderer like myself, like me a physician, and like me an enthusiast in his profession. Unlike me in this, that his wanderings were voluntary, and he a man, if not of fortune, as we estimate fortune in England, at least in what our forefathers used to term "easy circumstances." He was an old man when I first saw him; nearly five-and-thirty years my senior.

In Dr. Martin Hesselius, I found my master. His knowledge was immense, his grasp of a case was an intuition. He was the very man to inspire a young enthusiast, like me, with awe and delight. My admiration has stood the test of time and survived the separation of death. I am sure it was well-founded.

For nearly twenty years I acted as his medical secretary. His immense collection of papers he has left in my care, to be arranged, indexed and bound. His treatment of some of these cases is curious. He writes in two distinct characters. He describes what he saw and heard as an intelligent layman might, and when in this style of narrative he had seen the patient either through his own hall-door, to the light of day, or through the gates of darkness to the caverns of the dead, he returns upon the narrative, and in the terms of his art and with all the force and originality of genius, proceeds to the work of analysis, diagnosis and illustration.

Here and there a case strikes me as of a kind to amuse or horrify a lay reader with an interest quite different from the peculiar one which it may possess for an expert. With slight modifications, chiefly of language, and of course a change of names, I copy the following. The narrator is Dr. Martin Hesselius. I find it among the voluminous notes of cases which he made during a tour in England about sixty-four years ago.

It is related in series of letters to his friend Professor Van Loo of Leyden. The professor was not a physician, but a chemist, and a man who read history and metaphysics and medicine, and had, in his day, written a play.

The narrative is therefore, if somewhat less valuable as a medical record, necessarily written in a manner more likely to interest an unlearned reader.

These letters, from a memorandum attached, appear to have been returned on the death of the professor, in 1819, to Dr. Hesselius. They are written, some in English, some in French, but the greater part in German. I am a faithful, though I am conscious, by no means a graceful translator, and although here and there I omit some passages, and shorten others, and disguise names, I have interpolated nothing.

I

Dr. Hesselius Relates How He Met the Rev. Mr. Jennings

The Rev. Mr. Jennings is tall and thin. He is middle-aged, and dresses with a natty, old-fashioned, high-church precision. He is naturally a little stately, but not at all stiff. His features, without being handsome, are well formed, and their expression extremely kind, but also shy.

I met him one evening at Lady Mary Heyduke's. The modesty and benevolence of his countenance are extremely prepossessing.

We were but a small party, and he joined agreeably enough in the conversation. He seems to enjoy listening very much more than contributing to the talk; but what he says is always to the purpose and well said. He is a great favourite of Lady Mary's, who it seems, consults him upon many things, and thinks him the most happy and blessed person on earth. Little knows she about him.

The Rev. Mr. Jennings is a bachelor, and has, they say sixty thousand pounds in the funds. He is a charitable man. He is most anxious to be actively employed in his sacred profession, and yet though always tolerably well elsewhere, when he goes down to his vicarage in Warwickshire, to engage in the actual duties of his sacred calling, his health soon fails him, and in a very strange way. So says Lady Mary.

There is no doubt that Mr. Jennings' health does break down in, generally, a sudden and mysterious way, sometimes in the very act of officiating in his old and pretty church at Kenlis. It may be his heart, it may be his brain. But so it has happened three or four times, or oftener, that after proceeding a certain way in the service, he has on a sudden stopped short, and after a silence, apparently quite unable to resume, he has fallen into solitary, inaudible prayer, his hands and his eyes uplifted, and then pale as death, and in the agitation of a strange shame and horror, descended trembling, and got into the vestry-room, leaving his congregation, without explanation, to themselves. This occurred when his curate was absent. When he goes down to Kenlis now, he always takes care to provide a clergyman to share his duty, and to supply his place on the instant should he become thus suddenly incapacitated.

When Mr. Jennings breaks down quite, and beats a retreat from the vicarage, and returns to London, where, in a dark street off Piccadilly, he inhabits a very narrow house, Lady Mary says that he is always perfectly well. I have my own opinion about that. There are degrees of course. We shall see.

Mr. Jennings is a perfectly gentlemanlike man. People, however, remark something odd. There is an impression a little ambiguous. One thing which certainly contributes to it, people I think don't remember; or, perhaps, distinctly remark. But I did, almost immediately. Mr. Jennings has a way of looking sidelong upon the carpet, as if his eye followed the movements of something there. This, of course, is not always. It occurs now and then. But often enough to give a certain oddity, as I have said, to his manner, and in this glance travelling along the floor there is something both shy and anxious.

A medical philosopher, as you are good enough to call me, elaborating theories by the aid of cases sought out by himself, and by him watched and scrutinised with more time at command, and consequently infinitely more minuteness than the ordinary practitioner can afford, falls insensibly into habits of observation, which accompany him everywhere, and are exercised, as some people would say, impertinently, upon every subject that presents itself with the least likelihood of rewarding inquiry.

There was a promise of this kind in the slight, timid, kindly, but reserved gentleman, whom I met for the first time at this agreeable little evening gathering. I observed, of course, more than I here set down; but I reserve all that borders on the technical for a strictly scientific paper.

I may remark, that when I here speak of medical science, I do so, as I hope some day to see it more generally understood, in a much more comprehensive sense than its generally material treatment would warrant. I believe the entire natural world is but the ultimate expression of that spiritual world from which, and in which alone, it has its life. I believe that the essential man is a spirit, that the spirit is an organised substance, but as different in point of material from what we ordinarily understand by matter, as light or electricity is; that the material body is, in the most literal sense, a vesture, and death consequently no interruption of the living man's existence, but simply his extrication from the natural body—a process which commences at the moment of what we term death, and the completion of which, at furthest a few days later, is the resurrection "in power."

The person who weighs the consequences of these positions will probably see their practical bearing upon medical science. This is, however, by no means the proper place for displaying the proofs and discussing the consequences of this too generally unrecognized state of facts.

In pursuance of my habit, I was covertly observing Mr. Jennings, with all my caution—I think he perceived it—and I saw plainly that he was as cautiously observing me. Lady Mary happening to address me by my name, as Dr. Hesselius, I saw that he glanced at me more sharply, and then became thoughtful for a few minutes.

After this, as I conversed with a gentleman at the other end of the room, I saw him look at me more steadily, and with an interest which I thought I understood. I then saw him take an opportunity of chatting with Lady Mary, and was, as one always is, perfectly aware of being the subject of a distant inquiry and answer.

This tall clergyman approached me by-and-by; and in a little time we had got into conversation. When two people, who like reading, and know books and places, having travelled, wish to discourse, it is very strange if they can't find topics. It was not accident that brought him near me, and led him into conversation. He knew German and had read my Essays on Metaphysical Medicine which suggest more than they actually say.

This courteous man, gentle, shy, plainly a man of thought and reading, who moving and talking among us, was not altogether of us, and whom I already suspected of leading a life whose transactions and alarms were carefully concealed, with an impenetrable reserve from, not only the world, but his best beloved friends—was cautiously weighing in his own mind the idea of taking a certain step with regard to me.

I penetrated his thoughts without his being aware of it, and was careful to say nothing which could betray to his sensitive vigilance my suspicions respecting his position, or my surmises about his plans respecting myself.

We chatted upon indifferent subjects for a time but at last he said:

"I was very much interested by some papers of yours, Dr. Hesselius, upon what you term Metaphysical Medicine—I read them in German, ten or twelve years ago—have they been translated?"

"No, I'm sure they have not—I should have heard. They would have asked my leave, I think."

"I asked the publishers here, a few months ago, to get the book for me in the original German; but they tell me it is out of print."

"So it is, and has been for some years; but it flatters me as an author to find that you have not forgotten my little book, although," I added, laughing, "ten or twelve years is a considerable time to have managed without it; but I suppose you have been turning the subject over again in your mind, or something has happened lately to revive your interest in it."

At this remark, accompanied by a glance of inquiry, a sudden embarrassment disturbed Mr. Jennings, analogous to that which makes a young lady blush and look foolish. He dropped his eyes, and folded his hands together uneasily, and looked oddly, and you would have said, guiltily, for a moment.

I helped him out of his awkwardness in the best way, by appearing not to observe it, and going straight on, I said: "Those revivals of interest in a subject happen to me often; one book suggests another, and often sends me back a wild-goose chase over an interval of twenty years. But if you still care to possess a copy, I shall be only too happy to provide you; I have still got two or three by me—and if you allow me to present one I shall be very much honoured."

"You are very good indeed," he said, quite at his ease again, in a moment: "I almost despaired—I don't know how to thank you."

"Pray don't say a word; the thing is really so little worth that I am only ashamed of having offered it, and if you thank me any more I shall throw it into the fire in a fit of modesty."

Mr. Jennings laughed. He inquired where I was staying in London, and after a little more conversation on a variety of subjects, he took his departure.

II

The Doctor Questions Lady Mary and She Answers

"I like your vicar so much, Lady Mary," said I, as soon as he was gone. "He has read, travelled, and thought, and having also suffered, he ought to be an accomplished companion."

"So he is, and, better still, he is a really good man," said she. "His advice is invaluable about my schools, and all my little undertakings at Dawlbridge, and he's so painstaking, he takes so much trouble—you have no idea—wherever he thinks he can be of use: he's so good-natured and so sensible."

"It is pleasant to hear so good an account of his neighbourly virtues. I can only testify to his being an agreeable and gentle companion, and in addition to what you have told me, I think I can tell you two or three things about him," said I.

"Really!"

"Yes, to begin with, he's unmarried."

"Yes, that's right—go on."

"He has been writing, that is he *was,* but for two or three years perhaps, he has not gone on with his work, and the book was upon some rather abstract subject—perhaps theology."

"Well, he was writing a book, as you say; I'm not quite sure what it was about, but only that it was nothing that I cared for; very likely you are right, and he certainly did stop—yes."

"And although he only drank a little coffee here to-night, he likes tea, at least, did like it extravagantly."

"Yes, that's *quite* true."

"He drank green tea, a good deal, didn't he?" I pursued.

"Well, that's very odd! Green tea was a subject on which we used almost to quarrel."

"But he has quite given that up," said I.

"So he has."

"And, now, one more fact. His mother or his father, did you know them?"

"Yes, both; his father is only ten years dead, and their place is near Dawlbridge. We knew them very well," she answered.

"Well, either his mother or his father—I should rather think his father, saw a ghost," said I.

"Well, you really are a conjurer, Dr. Hesselius."

"Conjurer or no, haven't I said right?" I answered merrily.

"You certainly have, and it *was* his father: he was a silent, whimsical man, and he used to bore my father about his dreams, and at last he told him a story about a ghost he had seen and talked with, and a very odd story it was. I remember it particularly, because I was so afraid of him. This story was long before he died—when I was quite a child—and his ways were so silent and moping, and he used to drop in sometimes, in the dusk, when I was alone in the drawing-room, and I used to fancy there were ghosts about him."

I smiled and nodded.

"And now, having established my character as a conjurer, I think I must say good-night," said I.

"But how *did* you find out?"

"By the planets, of course, as the gipsies do," I answered, and so, gaily we said good-night."

Next morning I sent the little book he had been inquiring after, and a note to Mr. Jennings, and on returning late that evening, I found that he had called at my lodgings, and left his card. He asked whether I was at home, and asked at what hour he would be most likely to find me.

Does he intend opening his case, and consulting me "professionally," as they say? I hope so. I have already conceived a theory about him. It is supported by Lady Mary's answers to my parting questions. I should like much to ascertain from his own lips. But what can I do consistently with good breeding to invite a confession? Nothing. I rather think he meditates one. At all events, my dear Van L., I shan't make myself difficult of access; I mean to return his visit tomorrow. It will be only civil in return for his politeness, to ask to see him. Perhaps something may come of it. Whether much, little, or nothing, my dear Van L., you shall hear.

III

Dr. Hesselius Picks Up Something in Latin Books

Well, I have called at Blank Street.

On inquiring at the door, the servant told me that Mr. Jennings was engaged very particularly with a gentleman, a clergyman from Kenlis, his parish in the country. Intending to reserve my privilege, and to call again, I merely intimated that I should try another time, and had turned to go, when the servant begged my pardon, and asked me, looking at me a little more attentively than well-bred persons of his order usually do, whether I was Dr. Hesselius; and, on learning that I was, he said, "Perhaps then, sir, you would allow me to mention it to Mr. Jennings, for I am sure he wishes to see you."

The servant returned in a moment, with a message from Mr. Jennings, asking me to go into his study, which was in effect his back drawing-room, promising to be with me in a very few minutes.

This was really a study—almost a library. The room was lofty, with two tall slender windows, and rich dark curtains. It was much larger than I had expected, and stored with books on every side, from the floor to the ceiling. The upper carpet—for to my tread it felt that there were two or three—was a Turkey carpet. My steps fell noiselessly. The bookcases standing out, placed the windows, particularly narrow ones, in deep recesses. The effect of the room was, although extremely comfortable, and even luxurious, decidedly gloomy, and aided by the silence, almost oppressive. Perhaps, however, I ought to have allowed something for association. My mind had connected peculiar ideas with Mr. Jennings. I stepped into this perfectly silent room, of a very silent house, with a peculiar foreboding; and its darkness, and solemn clothing of books, for except where two narrow looking-glasses were set in the wall, they were everywhere, helped this somber feeling.

While awaiting Mr. Jennings' arrival, I amused myself by looking into some of the books with which his shelves were laden. Not among these, but immediately under them, with their backs upward, on the floor, I lighted upon a complete set of Swedenborg's "Arcana Cælestia," in the original Latin, a very fine folio set, bound in the natty livery which theology affects, pure vellum, namely, gold letters, and carmine edges. There were paper markers in several of these volumes, I raised and placed them, one after the other, upon the table, and opening where these papers were placed, I read in the solemn Latin phraseology, a series of sentences indicated by a pencilled line at the margin. Of these I copy here a few, translating them into English.

"When man's interior sight is opened, which is that of his spirit, then there appear the things of another life, which cannot possibly be made visible to the bodily sight." . . . .

"By the internal sight it has been granted me to see the things that are in the other life, more clearly than I see those that are in the world. From these considerations, it is evident that external vision exists from interior vision, and this from a vision still more interior, and so on." . . . .

"There are with every man at least two evil spirits." . . . .

"With wicked genii there is also a fluent speech, but harsh and grating. There is also among them a speech which is not fluent, wherein the dissent of the thoughts is perceived as something secretly creeping along within it."

"The evil spirits associated with man are, indeed from the hells, but when with man they are not then in hell, but are taken out thence. The place where they then are, is in the midst between heaven and hell, and is called the world of spirits—when the evil spirits who are with man, are in that world, they are not in any infernal torment, but in every thought and affection of man, and so, in all that the man himself enjoys. But when they are remitted into their hell, they return to their former state." . . . .

"If evil spirits could perceive that they were associated with man, and yet that they were spirits separate from him, and if they could flow in into the things of his body, they would attempt by a thousand means to destroy him; for they hate man with a deadly hatred." . . . .

"Knowing, therefore, that I was a man in the body, they were continually striving to destroy me, not as to the body only, but especially as to the soul; for to destroy any man or spirit is the very delight of the life of all who are in hell; but I have been continually protected by the Lord. Hence is appears how dangerous it is for man to be in a living consort with spirits, unless he be in the good of faith." . . . .

"Nothing is more carefully guarded from the knowledge of associate spirits than their being thus conjoint with a man, for if they knew it they would speak to him, with the intention to destroy him." . . . .

"The delight of hell is to do evil to man, and to hasten his eternal ruin."

A long note, written with a very sharp and fine pencil, in Mr. Jennings' neat hand, at the foot of the page, caught my eye. Expecting his criticism upon the text, I read a word or two, and stopped, for it was something quite different, and began with these words, *Deus misereatur mei*—"May God compassionate me." Thus warned of its private nature, I averted my eyes, and shut the book, replacing all the volumes as I had found them, except one which interested me, and in which, as men studious and solitary in their habits will do, I grew so absorbed as to take no cognisance of the outer world, nor to remember where I was.

I was reading some pages which refer to "representatives" and "correspondents," in the technical language of Swedenborg, and had arrived at a passage, the substance of which is, that evil spirits, when seen by other eyes than those of their infernal associates, present themselves, by "correspondence," in the shape of the beast *(fera)* which represents their particular lust and life, in aspect direful and atrocious. This is a long passage, and particularises a number of those bestial forms.

IV

Four Eyes Were Reading the Passage

I was running the head of my pencil-case along the line as I read it, and something caused me to raise my eyes.

Directly before me was one of the mirrors I have mentioned, in which I saw reflected the tall shape of my friend, Mr. Jennings, leaning over my shoulder, and reading the page at which I was busy, and with a face so dark and wild that I should hardly have known him.

I turned and rose. He stood erect also, and with an effort laughed a little, saying:

"I came in and asked you how you did, but without succeeding in awaking you from your book; so I could not restrain my curiosity, and very impertinently, I'm afraid, peeped over your shoulder. This is not your first time of looking into those pages. You have looked into Swedenborg, no doubt, long ago?"

"Oh dear, yes! I owe Swedenborg a great deal; you will discover traces of him in the little book on Metaphysical Medicine, which you were so good as to remember."

Although my friend affected a gaiety of manner, there was a slight flush in his face, and I could perceive that he was inwardly much perturbed.

"I'm scarcely yet qualified. I know so little of Swedenborg. I've only had them a fortnight," he answered, "and I think they are rather likely to make a solitary man nervous—that is, judging from the very little I have read—I don't say that they have made me so," he laughed; "and I'm so very much obliged for the book. I hope you got my note?"

I made all proper acknowledgments and modest disclaimers.

"I never read a book that I go with, so entirely, as that of yours," he continued. "I saw at once there is more in it than is quite unfolded. Do you know Dr. Harley?" he asked, rather abruptly.

In passing, the editor remarks that the physician here named was one of the most eminent who had ever practised in England.

I did, having had letters to him, and had experienced from him great courtesy and considerable assistance during my visit to England.

"I think that man one of the very greatest fools I ever met in my life," said Mr. Jennings.

This was the first time I had ever heard him say a sharp thing of anybody, and such a term applied to so high a name a little startled me.

"Really! and in what way?" I asked.

"In his profession," he answered.

I smiled.

"I mean this," he said: "he seems to me, one half, blind—I mean one half of all he looks at is dark—preternaturally bright and vivid all the rest; and the worst of it is, it seems *wilful*. I can't get him—I mean he won't—I've had some experience of him as a physician, but I look on him as, in that sense, no better than a paralytic mind, an intellect half dead. I'll tell you—I know I shall some time—all about it," he said, with a little agitation. "You stay some months longer in England. If I should be out of town during your stay for a little time, would you allow me to trouble you with a letter?"

"I should be only too happy," I assured him.

"Very good of you. I am so utterly dissatisfied with Harley."

"A little leaning to the materialistic school," I said.

"A *mere* materialist," he corrected me; "you can't think how that sort of thing worries one who knows better. You won't tell any one—any of my friends you know—that I am hippish; now, for instance, no one knows—not even Lady Mary—that I have seen Dr. Harley, or any other doctor. So pray don't mention it; and, if I should have any threatening of an attack, you'll kindly let me write, or, should I be in town, have a little talk with you."

I was full of conjecture, and unconsciously I found I had fixed my eyes gravely on him, for he lowered his for a moment, and he said:

"I see you think I might as well as tell you now, or else you are forming a conjecture; but you may as well give it up. If you were guessing all the rest of your life, you will never hit on it."

He shook his head smiling, and over that wintry sunshine a black cloud suddenly came down, and he drew his breath in, through his teeth as men do in pain.

"Sorry, of course, to learn that you apprehend occasion to consult any of us; but, command me when and how you like, and I need not assure you that your confidence is sacred."

He then talked of quite other things, and in a comparatively cheerful way and after a little time, I took my leave.

V

Dr. Hesselius is Summoned to Richmond

We parted cheerfully, but he was not cheerful, nor was I. There are certain expressions of that powerful organ of spirit—the human face—which, although I have seen them often, and possess a doctor's nerve, yet disturb me profoundly. One look of Mr. Jennings haunted me. It had seized my imagination with so dismal a power that I changed my plans for the evening, and went to the opera, feeling that I wanted a change of ideas.

I heard nothing of or from him for two or three days, when a note in his hand reached me. It was cheerful, and full of hope. He said that he had been for some little time so much better—quite well, in fact—that he was going to make a little experiment, and run down for a month or so to his parish, to try whether a little work might not quite set him up. There was in it a fervent religious expression of gratitude for his restoration, as he now almost hoped he might call it.

A day or two later I saw Lady Mary, who repeated what his note had announced, and told me that he was actually in Warwickshire, having resumed his clerical duties at Kenlis; and she added, "I begin to think that he is really perfectly well, and that there never was anything the matter, more than nerves and fancy; we are all nervous, but I fancy there is nothing like a little hard work for that kind of weakness, and he has made up his mind to try it. I should not be surprised if he did not come back for a year."

Notwithstanding all this confidence, only two days later I had this note, dated from his house off Piccadilly:

DEAR SIR,—I have returned disappointed. If I should feel at all able to see you, I shall write to ask you kindly to call. At present, I am too low, and, in fact, simply unable to say all I wish to say. Pray don't mention my name to my friends. I can see no one. By-and-by, please God, you shall hear from me. I mean to take a run into Shropshire, where some of my people are. God bless you! May we, on my return, meet more happily than I can now write.

About a week after this I saw Lady Mary at her own house, the last person, she said, left in town, and just on the wing for Brighton, for the London season was quite over. She told me that she had heard from Mr. Jenning's niece, Martha, in Shropshire. There was nothing to be gathered from her letter, more than that he was low and nervous. In those words, of which healthy people think so lightly, what a world of suffering is sometimes hidden!

Nearly five weeks had passed without any further news of Mr. Jennings. At the end of that time I received a note from him. He wrote:

"I have been in the country, and have had change of air, change of scene, change of faces, change of everything—and in everything—but *myself*. I have made up my mind, so far as the most irresolute creature on earth can do it, to tell my case fully to you. If your engagements will permit, pray come to me to-day, to-morrow, or the next day; but, pray defer as little as possible. You know not how much I need help. I have a quiet house at Richmond, where I now am. Perhaps you can manage to come to dinner, or to luncheon, or even to tea. You shall have no trouble in finding me out. The servant at Blank Street, who takes this note, will have a carriage at your door at any hour you please; and I am always to be found. You will say that I ought not to be alone. I have tried everything. Come and see."

I called up the servant, and decided on going out the same evening, which accordingly I did.

He would have been much better in a lodging-house, or hotel, I thought, as I drove up through a short double row of sombre elms to a very old-fashioned brick house, darkened by the foliage of these trees, which overtopped, and nearly surrounded it. It was a perverse choice, for nothing could be imagined more triste and silent. The house, I found, belonged to him. He had stayed for a day or two in town, and, finding it for some cause insupportable, had come out here, probably because being furnished and his own, he was relieved of the thought and delay of selection, by coming here.

The sun had already set, and the red reflected light of the western sky illuminated the scene with the peculiar effect with which we are all familiar. The hall seemed very dark, but, getting to the back drawing-room, whose windows command the west, I was again in the same dusky light.

I sat down, looking out upon the richly-wooded landscape that glowed in the grand and melancholy light which was every moment fading. The corners of the room were already dark; all was growing dim, and the gloom was insensibly toning my mind, already prepared for what was sinister. I was waiting alone for his arrival, which soon took place. The door communicating with the front room opened, and the tall figure of Mr. Jennings, faintly seen in the ruddy twilight, came, with quiet stealthy steps, into the room.

We shook hands, and, taking a chair to the window, where there was still light enough to enable us to see each other's faces, he sat down beside me, and, placing his hand upon my arm, with scarcely a word of preface began his narrative.

VI

How Mr. Jennings Met His Companion

The faint glow of the west, the pomp of the then lonely woods of Richmond, were before us, behind and about us the darkening room, and on the stony face of the sufferer—for the character of his face, though still gentle and sweet, was changed—rested that dim, odd glow which seems to descend and produce, where it touches, lights, sudden though faint, which are lost, almost without gradation, in darkness. The silence, too, was utter: not a distant wheel, or bark, or whistle from without; and within the depressing stillness of an invalid bachelor's house.

I guessed well the nature, though not even vaguely the particulars of the revelations I was about to receive, from that fixed face of suffering that so oddly flushed stood out, like a portrait of Schalken's, before its background of darkness.

"It began," he said, "on the 15th of October, three years and eleven weeks ago, and two days—I keep very accurate count, for every day is torment. If I leave anywhere a chasm in my narrative tell me.

"About four years ago I began a work, which had cost me very much thought and reading. It was upon the religious metaphysics of the ancients."

"I know," said I, "the actual religion of educated and thinking paganism, quite apart from symbolic worship? A wide and very interesting field."

"Yes, but not good for the mind—the Christian mind, I mean. Paganism is all bound together in essential unity, and, with evil sympathy, their religion involves their art, and both their manners, and the subject is a degrading fascination and the Nemesis sure. God forgive me!

"I wrote a great deal; I wrote late at night. I was always thinking on the subject, walking about, wherever I was, everywhere. It thoroughly infected me. You are to remember that all the material ideas connected with it were more or less of the beautiful, the subject itself delightfully interesting, and I, then, without a care."

He sighed heavily.

"I believe, that every one who sets about writing in earnest does his work, as a friend of mine phrased it, *on* something—tea, or coffee, or tobacco. I suppose there is a material waste that must be hourly supplied in such occupations, or that we should grow too abstracted, and the mind, as it were, pass out of the body, unless it were reminded often enough of the connection by actual sensation. At all events, I felt the want, and I supplied it. Tea was my companion—at first the ordinary black tea, made in the usual way, not too strong: but I drank a good deal, and increased its strength as I went on. I never experienced an uncomfortable symptom from it. I began to take a little green tea. I found the effect pleasanter, it cleared and intensified the power of thought so, I had come to take it frequently, but not stronger than one might take it for pleasure. I wrote a great deal out here, it was so quiet, and in this room. I used to sit up very late, and it became a habit with me to sip my tea—green tea—every now and then as my work proceeded. I had a little kettle on my table, that swung over a lamp, and made tea two or three times between eleven o'clock and two or three in the morning, my hours of going to bed. I used to go into town every day. I was not a monk, and, although I spent an hour or two in a library, hunting up authorities and looking out lights upon my theme, I was in no morbid state as far as I can judge. I met my friends pretty much as usual and enjoyed their society, and, on the whole, existence had never been, I think, so pleasant before.

"I had met with a man who had some odd old books, German editions in mediæval Latin, and I was only too happy to be permitted access to them. This obliging person's books were in the City, a very out-of-the-way part of it. I had rather out-stayed my intended hour, and, on coming out, seeing no cab near, I was tempted to get into the omnibus which used to drive past this house. It was darker than this by the time the 'bus had reached an old house, you may have remarked, with four poplars at each side of the door, and there the last passenger but myself got out. We drove along rather faster. It was twilight now. I leaned back in my corner next the door ruminating pleasantly.

"The interior of the omnibus was nearly dark. I had observed in the corner opposite to me at the other side, and at the end next the horses, two small circular reflections, as it seemed to me of a reddish light. They were about two inches apart, and about the size of those small brass buttons that yachting men used to put upon their jackets. I began to speculate, as listless men will, upon this trifle, as it seemed. From what centre did that faint but deep red light come, and from what—glass beads, buttons, toy decorations—was it reflected? We were lumbering along gently, having nearly a mile still to go. I had not solved the puzzle, and it became in another minute more odd, for these two luminous points, with a sudden jerk, descended nearer and nearer the floor, keeping still their relative distance and horizontal position, and then, as suddenly, they rose to the level of the seat on which I was sitting and I saw them no more.

"My curiosity was now really excited, and, before I had time to think,

I saw again these two dull lamps, again together near the floor; again they disappeared, and again in their old corner I saw them.

"So, keeping my eyes upon them, I edge quietly up my own side, towards the end at which I still saw these tiny discs of red.

"There was very little light in the 'bus. It was nearly dark. I leaned forward to aid my endeavour to discover what these little circles really were. They shifted position a little as I did so. I began now to perceive an outline of something black, and I soon saw, with tolerable distinctness, the outline of a small black monkey, pushing its face forward in mimicry to meet mine; those were its eyes, and I now dimly saw its teeth grinning at me.

"I drew back, not knowing whether it might not meditate a spring. I fancied that one of the passengers had forgot this ugly pet, and wishing to ascertain something of its temper, though not caring to trust my fingers to it, I poked my umbrella softly towards it. It remained immovable—up to it—*through* it. For through it, and back and forward it passed, without the slightest resistance.

"I can't, in the least, convey to you the kind of horror that I felt. When I had ascertained that the thing was an illusion, as I then supposed, there came a misgiving about myself and a terror that fascinated me in impotence to remove my gaze from the eyes of the brute for some moments. As I looked, it made a little skip back, quite into the corner, and I, in a panic, found myself at the door, having put my head out, drawing deep breaths of the outer air, and staring at the lights and trees we were passing, too glad to reassure myself of reality.

"I stopped the 'bus and got out. I perceived the man look oddly at me as I paid him. I dare say there was something unusual in my looks and manner, for I had never felt so strangely before."

VII

The Journey: First Stage

"When the omnibus drove on, and I was alone upon the road, I looked carefully round to ascertain whether the monkey had followed me. To my indescribable relief I saw it nowhere. I can't describe easily what a shock I had received, and my sense of genuine gratitude on finding myself, as I supposed, quite rid of it.

"I had got out a little before we reached this house, two or three hundred steps. A brick wall runs along the footpath, and inside the wall is a hedge of yew, or some dark evergreen of that kind, and within that again the row of fine trees which you may have remarked as you came.

"This brick wall is about as high as my shoulder, and happening to raise my eyes I saw the monkey, with that stooping gait, on all fours, walking or creeping, close beside me, on top of the wall. I stopped, looking at it with a feeling of loathing and horror. As I stopped so did it. It sat up on the wall with its long hands on its knees looking at me. There was not light enough to see it much more than in outline, nor was it dark enough to bring the peculiar light of its eyes into strong relief. I still saw, however, that red foggy light plainly enough. It did not show its teeth, nor exhibit any sign of irritation, but seemed jaded and sulky, and was observing me steadily.

"I drew back into the middle of the road. It was an unconscious recoil, and there I stood, still looking at it. It did not move.

"With an instinctive determination to try something—anything, I turned about and walked briskly towards town with askance look, all the time, watching the movements of the beast. It crept swiftly along the wall, at exactly my pace.

"Where the wall ends, near the turn of the road, it came down, and with a wiry spring or two brought itself close to my feet, and continued to keep up with me, as I quickened my pace. It was at my left side, so close to my leg that I felt every moment as if I should tread upon it.

"The road was quite deserted and silent, and it was darker every moment. I stopped dismayed and bewildered, turning as I did so, the other way—I mean, towards this house, away from which I had been walking. When I stood still, the monkey drew back to a distance of, I suppose, about five or six yards, and remained stationary, watching me.

"I had been more agitated than I have said. I had read, of course, as everyone has, something about 'spectral illusions,' as you physicians term the phenomena of such cases. I considered my situation, and looked my misfortune in the face.

"These affections, I had read, are sometimes transitory and sometimes obstinate. I had read of cases in which the appearance, at first harmless, had, step by step, degenerated into something direful and insupportable, and ended by wearing its victim out. Still as I stood there, but for my bestial companion, quite alone, I tried to comfort myself by repeating again and again the assurance, 'the thing is purely disease, a well-known physical affection, as distinctly as small-pox or neuralgia. Doctors are all agreed on that, philosophy demonstrates it. I must not be a fool. I've been sitting up too late, and I daresay my digestion is quite wrong, and, with God's help, I shall be all right, and this is but a symptom of nervous dyspepsia.' Did I believe all this? Not one word of it, no more than any other miserable being ever did who is once seized and riveted in this satanic captivity. Against my convictions, I might say my knowledge, I was simply bullying myself into a false courage.

"I now walked homeward. I had only a few hundred yards to go. I had forced myself into a sort of resignation, but I had not got over the sickening shock and the flurry of the first certainty of my misfortune.

"I made up my mind to pass the night at home. The brute moved close beside me, and I fancied there was the sort of anxious drawing toward the house, which one sees in tired horses or dogs, sometimes as they come toward home.

"I was afraid to go into town, I was afraid of any one's seeing and recognizing me. I was conscious of an irrepressible agitation in my manner. Also, I was afraid of any violent change in my habits, such as going to a place of amusement, or walking from home in order to fatigue myself. At the hall door it waited till I mounted the steps, and when the door was opened entered with me.

"I drank no tea that night. I got cigars and some brandy and water. My idea was that I should act upon my material system, and by living for a while in sensation apart from thought, send myself forcibly, as it were, into a new groove. I came up here to this drawing-room. I sat just here. The monkey then got upon a small table that then stood *there*. It looked dazed and languid. An irrepressible uneasiness as to its movements kept my eyes always upon it. Its eyes were half closed, but I could see them glow. It was looking steadily at me. In all situations, at all hours, it is awake and looking at me. That never changes.

"I shall not continue in detail my narrative of this particular night. I shall describe, rather, the phenomena of the first year, which never varied, essentially. I shall describe the monkey as it appeared in daylight. In the dark, as you shall presently hear, there are peculiarities. It is a small monkey, perfectly black. It had only one peculiarity—a character of malignity—unfathomable malignity. During the first year it looked sullen and sick. But this character of intense malice and vigilance was always underlying that surly languor. During all that time it acted as if on a plan of giving me as little trouble as was consistent with watching me. Its eyes were never off me. I have never lost sight of it, except in my sleep, light or dark, day or night, since it came here, excepting when it withdraws for some weeks at a time, unaccountably.

"In total dark it visible as in daylight. I do not mean merely its eyes. It is *all* visible distinctly in a halo that resembles a glow of red embers, and which accompanies it in all its movements.

"When it leaves me for a time, it is always at night, in the dark, and in the same way. It grows at first uneasy, and then furious, and then advances towards me, grinning and shaking, its paws clenched, and, at the same time, there comes the appearance of fire in the grate. I never have any fire. I can't sleep in the room where there is any, and it draws nearer and nearer to the chimney, quivering, it seems, with rage, and when its fury rises to the highest pitch, it springs into the grate, and up the chimney, and I see it no more.

"When first this happened, I thought I was released. I was now a new man. A day passed—a night—and no return, and a blessed week—a week—another week. I was always on my knees, Dr. Hesselius, always, thanking God and praying. A whole month passed of liberty, but on a sudden, it was with me again."

VIII

The Second Stage

"It was with me, and the malice which before was torpid under a sullen exterior, was now active. It was perfectly unchanged in every other respect. This new energy was apparent in its activity and its looks, and soon in other ways.

"For a time, you will understand, the change was shown only in an increased vivacity, and an air of menace, as if it were always brooding over some atrocious plan. Its eyes, as before, were never off me."

"Is it here now?" I asked.

"No," he replied, "it has been absent exactly a fortnight and a day— fifteen days. It has sometimes been away so long as nearly two months, once for three. Its absence always exceeds a fortnight, although it may be but by a single day. Fifteen days having past since I saw it last, it may return now at any moment."

"Is its return," I asked, "accompanied by any peculiar manifestation?"

"Nothing—no," he said. "It is simply with me again. On lifting my eyes from a book, or turning my head, I see it, as usual, looking at me, and then it remains, as before, for its appointed time. I have never told so much and so minutely before to any one."

I perceived that he was agitated, and looking like death, and he repeatedly applied his handkerchief to his forehead; I suggested that he might be tired, and told him that I would call, with pleasure, in the morning, but he said:

"No, if you don't mind hearing it all now. I have got so far, and I should prefer making one effort of it. When I spoke to Dr. Harley, I had nothing like so much to tell. You are a philosophic physician. You give spirit its proper rank. If this thing is real—"

He paused looking at me with agitated inquiry.

"We can discuss it by-and-by, and very fully. I will give you all I think," I answered, after an interval.

"Well—very well. If it is anything real, I say, it is prevailing, little by little, and drawing me more interiorly into hell. Optic nerves, he talked of. Ah! well—there are other nerves of communication. May God Almighty help me! You shall hear.

"Its power of action, I tell you, had increased. Its malice became, in a way, aggressive. About two years ago, some questions that were pending between me and the bishop having been settled, I went down to my parish in Warwickshire, anxious to find occupation in my profession. I was not prepared for what happened, although I have since thought I might have apprehended something like it. The reason of my saying so is this—"

He was beginning to speak with a great deal more effort and reluctance, and sighed often, and seemed at times nearly overcome. But at this time his manner was not agitated. It was more like that of a sinking patient, who has given himself up.

"Yes, but I will first tell you about Kenlis, my parish.

"It was with me when I left this place for Dawlbridge. It was my silent travelling companion, and it remained with me at the vicarage. When I entered on the discharge of my duties, another change took place. The thing exhibited an atrocious determination to thwart me. It was with me in the church—in the reading-desk—in the pulpit—within the communion rails. At last, it reached this extremity, that while I was reading to the congregation, it would spring upon the book and squat there, so that I was unable to see the page. This happened more than once.

"I left Dawlbridge for a time. I placed myself in Dr. Harley's hands. I did everything he told me. He gave my case a great deal of thought. It interested him, I think. He seemed successful. For nearly three months I was perfectly free from a return. I began to think I was safe. With his full assent I returned to Dawlbridge.

"I travelled in a chaise. I was in good spirits. I was more—I was happy and grateful. I was returning, as I thought, delivered from a dreadful hallucination, to the scene of duties which I longed to enter upon. It was a beautiful sunny evening, everything looked serene and cheerful, and I was delighted. I remember looking out of the window to see the spire of my church at Kenlis among the trees, at the point where one has the earliest view of it. It is exactly where the little stream that bounds the parish passes under the road by a culvert, and where it emerges at the road-side, a stone with an old inscription is placed. As we passed this point, I drew my head in and sat down, and in the corner of the chaise was the monkey.

"For a moment I felt faint, and then quite wild with despair and horror. I called to the driver, and got out, and sat down at the road-side, and prayed to God silently for mercy. A despairing resignation supervened. My companion was with me as I reentered the vicarage. The same persecution followed. After a short struggle I submitted, and soon I left the place.

"I told you," he said, "that the beast has before this become in certain ways aggressive. I will explain a little. It seemed to be actuated by intense and increasing fury, whenever I said my prayers, or even meditated prayer.

It amounted at last to a dreadful interruption. You will ask, how could a silent immaterial phantom effect that? It was thus, whenever I meditated praying; it was always before me, and nearer and nearer.

"It used to spring on a table, on the back of a chair, on the chimney-piece, and slowly to swing itself from side to side, looking at me all the time. There is in its motion an indefinable power to dissipate thought, and to contract one's attention to that monotony, till the ideas shrink, as it were, to a point, and at last to nothing—and unless I had started up, and shook off the catalepsy I have felt as if my mind were on the point of losing itself. There are other ways," he sighed heavily; "thus, for instance, while I pray with my eyes closed, it comes closer and closer, and I see it. I know it is not to be accounted for physically, but I do actually see it, though my lids are closed, and so it rocks my mind, as it were, and overpowers me, and I am obliged to rise from my knees. If you had ever yourself known this, you would be acquainted with desperation."

IX

The Third Stage

"I see, Dr. Hesselius, that you don't lose one word of my statement. I need not ask you to listen specially to what I am now going to tell you. They talk of the optic nerves, and of spectral illusions, as if the organ of sight was the only point assailable by the influences that have fastened upon me—I know better. For two years in my direful case that limitation prevailed. But as food is taken in softly at the lips, and then brought under the teeth, as the tip of the little finger caught in a mill crank will draw in the hand, and the arm, and the whole body, so the miserable mortal who has been once caught firmly by the end of the finest fibre of his nerve, is drawn in and in, by the enormous machinery of hell, until he is as *I* am. Yes, Doctor, as *I* am, for a while I talk to you, and implore relief, I feel that my prayer is for the impossible, and my pleading with the inexorable."

I endeavoured to calm his visibly increasing agitation, and told him that he must not despair.

While we talked the night had overtaken us. The filmy moonlight was wide over the scene which the window commanded, and I said:

"Perhaps you would prefer having candles. This light, you know, is odd. I should wish you, as much as possible, under your usual conditions while I make my diagnosis, shall I call it—otherwise I don't care."

"All lights are the same to me," he said; "except when I read or write, I care not if night were perpetual. I am going to tell you what happened about a year ago. The thing began to speak to me."

"Speak! How do you mean—speak as a man does, do you mean?"

"Yes; speak in words and consecutive sentences, with perfect coherence and articulation; but there is a peculiarity. It is not like the tone of a human voice. It is not by my ears it reaches me—it comes like a singing through my head.

"This faculty, the power of speaking to me, will be my undoing. It won't let me pray, it interrupts me with dreadful blasphemies. I dare not go on, I could not. Oh! Doctor, can the skill, and thought, and prayers of man avail me nothing!"

"You must promise me, my dear sir, not to trouble yourself with unnecessarily exciting thoughts; confine yourself strictly to the narrative of *facts;* and recollect, above all, that even if the thing that infests you be, you seem to suppose a reality with an actual independent life and will, yet it can have no power to hurt you, unless it be given from above: its access to your senses depends mainly upon your physical condition—this is, under God, your comfort and reliance: we are all alike environed. It is only that in your case, the *'paries,'* the veil of the flesh, the screen, is a little out of repair, and sights and sounds are transmitted. We must enter on a new course, sir,—be encouraged. I'll give to-night to the careful consideration of the whole case."

"You are very good, sir; you think it worth trying, you don't give me quite up; but, sir, you don't know, it is gaining such an influence over me: it orders me about, it is such a tyrant, and I'm growing so helpless. May God deliver me!"

"It orders you about—of course you mean by speech?"

"Yes, yes; it is always urging me to crimes, to injure others, or myself. You see, Doctor, the situation is urgent, it is indeed. When I was in Shropshire, a few weeks ago" (Mr. Jennings was speaking rapidly and trembling now, holding my arm with one hand, and looking in my face), "I went out one day with a party of friends for a walk: my persecutor, I tell you, was with me at the time. I lagged behind the rest: the country near the Dee, you know, is beautiful. Our path happened to lie near a coal mine, and at the verge of the wood is a perpendicular shaft, they say, a hundred and fifty feet deep. My niece had remained behind with me— she knows, of course nothing of the nature of my sufferings. She knew, however, that I had been ill, and was low, and she remained to prevent my being quite alone. As we loitered slowly on together, the brute that accompanied me was urging me to throw myself down the shaft. I tell you now—oh, sir, think of it!—the one consideration that saved me from that hideous death was the fear lest the shock of witnessing the occurrence should be too much for the poor girl. I asked her to go on and walk with her friends, saying that I could go no further. She made excuses, and the more I urged her the firmer she became. She looked doubtful and frightened. I suppose there was something in my looks or manner that alarmed her; but she would not go, and that literally saved me. You had no idea, sir, that a living man could be made so abject a slave of Satan," he said, with a ghastly groan and a shudder.

There was a pause here, and I said, "You *were* preserved nevertheless. It was the act of God. You are in His hands and in the power of no other being: be therefore confident for the future."

X

Home

I made him have candles lighted, and saw the room looking cheery and inhabited before I left him. I told him that he must regard his illness strictly as one dependent on physical, though *subtle* physical causes. I told him that he had evidence of God's care and love in the deliverance which he had just described, and that I had perceived with pain that he seemed to regard its peculiar features as indicating that he had been delivered over to spiritual reprobation. Than such a conclusion nothing could be, I insisted, less warranted; and not only so, but more contrary to facts, as disclosed in his mysterious deliverance from that murderous influence during his Shropshire excursion. First, his niece had been retained by his side without his intending to keep her near him; and, secondly, there had been infused into his mind an irresistible repugnance to execute the dreadful suggestion in her presence.

As I reasoned this point with him, Mr. Jennings wept. He seemed comforted. One promise I exacted, which was that should the monkey at any time return, I should be sent for immediately; and, repeating my assurance that I would give neither time nor thought to any other subject until I had thoroughly investigated his case, and that to-morrow he should hear the result, I took my leave.

Before getting into the carriage I told the servant that his master was far from well, and that he should make a point of frequently looking into his room.

My own arrangements I made with a view to being quite secure from interruption.

I merely called at my lodgings, and with a travelling-desk and carpet-bag, set off in a hackney carriage for an inn about two miles out of town, called "The Horns," a very quiet and comfortable house, with good thick walls. And there I resolved, without the possibility of intrusion or distraction, to devote some hours of the night, in my comfortable sitting-room, to Mr. Jennings' case, and so much of the morning as it might require.

(There occurs here a careful note of Dr. Hesselius' opinion upon the case, and of the habits, dietary, and medicines which he prescribed. It is curious—some persons would say mystical. But, on the whole, I doubt whether it would sufficiently interest a reader of the kind I am likely to meet with, to warrant its being here reprinted. The whole letter was plainly written at the inn where he had hid himself for the occasion. The next letter is dated from his town lodgings.)

I left town for the inn where I slept last night at half-past nine, and did not arrive at my room in town until one o'clock this afternoon. I found a letter in Mr. Jennings' hand upon my table. It had not come by post, and, on inquiry, I learned that Mr. Jennings' servant had brought it, and on learning that I was not to return until to-day, and that no one could tell him my address, he seemed very uncomfortable, and said his orders from his master were that he was not to return without an answer.

I opened the letter and read:

> DEAR DR. HESSELIUS.—It is here. You had not been an hour gone when it returned. It is speaking. It knows all that has happened. It knows everything—it knows you, and is frantic and atrocious. It reviles. I send you this. It knows every word I have written—I write. This I promised, and I therefore write, but I fear very confused, very incoherently. I am so interrupted, disturbed.
>
> Ever yours, sincerely yours,
> ROBERT LYNDER JENNINGS.

"When did this come?" I asked.

"About eleven last night: the man was here again, and has been here three times to-day. The last time is about an hour since."

Thus answered, and with the notes I had made upon his case in my pocket, I was in a few minutes driving towards Richmond, to see Mr. Jennings.

I by no means, as you perceive, despaired of Mr. Jennings' case. He had himself remembered and applied, though quite in a mistaken way, the principle which I lay down in my Metaphysical Medicine, and which governs all such cases. I was about to apply it in earnest. I was profoundly interested, and very anxious to see and examine him while the "enemy" was actually present.

I drove up to the somber house, and ran up the steps, and knocked. The door, in a little time, was opened by a tall woman in black silk. She looked ill, and as if she had been crying. She curtseyed, and heard my question, but she did not answer. She turned her face away, extending her hand towards two men who were coming down-stairs; and thus having, as it were, tacitly made me over to them, she passed through a side-door hastily and shut it.

The man who was nearest the hall, I at once accosted, but being now close to him, I was shocked to see that both his hands were covered with blood.

I drew back a little, and the man, passing downstairs, merely said in a low tone, "Here's the servant, sir."

The servant had stopped on the stairs, confounded and dumb at seeing me. He was rubbing his hands in a handkerchief, and it was steeped in blood.

"Jones, what is it? what has happened?" I asked, while a sickening suspicion overpowered me.

The man asked me to come up to the lobby. I was beside him in a moment, and, frowning and pallid, with contracted eyes, he told me the horror which I already half guessed.

His master had made away with himself.

I went upstairs with him to the room—what I saw there I won't tell you. He had cut his throat with his razor. It was a frightful gash. The two men had laid him on the bed, and composed his limbs. It had happened, as the immense pool of blood on the floor declared, at some distance between the bed and the window. There was carpet round his bed, and a carpet under his dressing-table, but none on the rest of the floor, for the man said he did not like a carpet on his bedroom. In this somber and now terrible room, one of the great elms that darkened the house was slowly moving the shadow of one of its great boughs upon this dreadful floor.

I beckoned to the servant, and we went downstairs together. I turned off the hall into an old-fashioned panelled room, and there standing, I heard all the servant had to tell. It was not a great deal.

"I concluded, sir, from your words, and looks, sir, as you left last night, that you thought my master was seriously ill. I thought it might be that you were afraid of a fit, or something. So I attended very close to your directions. He sat up late, till past three o'clock. He was not writing or reading. He was talking a great deal to himself, but that was nothing unusual. At about that hour I assisted him to undress, and left him in his slippers and dressing-gown. I went back softly in about half-an-hour. He was in his bed, quite undressed, and a pair of candles lighted on the table beside his bed. He was leaning on his elbow, and looking out at the other side of the bed when I came in. I asked him if he wanted anything, and he said No.

"I don't know whether it was what you said to me, sir, or something a little unusual about him, but I was uneasy, uncommon uneasy about him last night.

"In another half hour, or it might be a little more, I went up again. I did not hear him talking as before. I opened the door a little. The candles were both out, which was not usual. I had a bedroom candle, and I let the light in, a little bit, looking softly round. I saw him sitting in that chair beside the dressing-table with his clothes on again. He turned round and looked at me. I thought it strange he should get up and dress, and put out the candles to sit in the dark, that way. But I only asked him again if I could do anything for him. He said, No, rather sharp, I thought. I asked him if I might light the candles, and he said, 'Do as you like, Jones.' So I lighted them, and I lingered about the room, and he said, 'Tell me the truth, Jones; why did you come again—you did not hear anyone cursing?' 'No, sir,' I said, wondering what he could mean.

"'No,' said he, after me, 'of course, no;' and I said to him, 'Wouldn't it be well, sir, you went to bed? It's just five o'clock;' and he said nothing, but, 'Very likely; good-night, Jones.' So I went, sir, but in less than an hour I came again. The door was fast, and he heard me, and called as I thought from the bed to know what I wanted, and he desired me not to disturb him again. I lay down and slept for a little. It must have been between six and seven when I went up again. The door was still fast, and he made no answer, so I did not like to disturb him, and thinking he was asleep, I left him till nine. It was his custom to ring when he wished me to come, and I had no particular hour for calling him. I tapped very gently, and getting no answer, I stayed away a good while, supposing he was getting some rest then. It was not till eleven o'clock I grew really uncomfortable about him—for at the latest he was never, that I could remember, later than half-past ten. I got no answer. I knocked and called, and still no answer. So not being able to force the door, I called Thomas from the stables, and together we forced it, and found him in the shocking way you saw."

Jones had no more to tell. Poor Mr. Jennings was very gentle, and very kind. All his people were fond of him. I could see that the servant was very much moved.

So, dejected and agitated, I passed from that terrible house, and its dark canopy of elms, and I hope I shall never see it more. While I write to you I feel like a man who has but half waked from a frightful and monotonous dream. My memory rejects the picture with incredulity and horror. Yet I know it is true. It is the story of the process of a poison, a poison which excites the reciprocal action of spirit and nerve, and paralyses the tissue that separates those cognate functions of the senses, the external and the interior. Thus we find strange bed-fellows, and the mortal and immortal prematurely make acquaintance.

CONCLUSION

A Word for Those Who Suffer

My dear Van L———, you have suffered from an affection similar to that which I have just described. You twice complained of a return of it.

Who, under God, cured you? Your humble servant, Martin Hesselius.

Let me rather adopt the more emphasised piety of a certain good old French surgeon of three hundred years ago: "I treated, and God cured you."

Come, my friend, you are not to be hippish. Let me tell you a fact.

I have met with, and treated, as my book shows, fifty-seven cases of this kind of vision, which I term indifferently "sublimated," "precocious," and "interior."

There is another class of affections which are truly termed—though commonly confounded with those which I describe—spectral illusions. These latter I look upon as being no less simply curable than a cold in the head or a trifling dyspepsia.

It is those which rank in the first category that test our promptitude of thought. Fifty-seven such cases have I encountered, neither more nor less. And in how many of these have I failed? In no one single instance.

There is no one affliction of mortality more easily and certainly reducible, with a little patience, and a rational confidence in the physician. With these simple conditions, I look upon the cure as absolutely certain.

You are to remember that I had not even commenced to treat Mr. Jennings' case. I have not any doubt that I should have cured him perfectly in eighteen months, or possibly it might have extended to two years. Some cases are very rapidly curable, others extremely tedious. Every intelligent physician who will give thought and diligence to the task, will effect a cure.

You know my tract on "The Cardinal Functions of the Brain." I there, by the evidence of innumerable facts, prove, as I think, the high probability of a circulation arterial and venous in its mechanism, through the nerves. Of this system, thus considered, the brain is the heart. The fluid, which is propagated hence through one class of nerves, returns in an altered state through another, and the nature of that fluid is spiritual, though not immaterial, any more than, as I before remarked, light or electricity are so.

By various abuses, among which the habitual use of such agents as green tea is one, this fluid may be affected as to its quality, but it is more frequently disturbed as to equilibrium. This fluid being that which we have in common with spirits, a congestion found upon the masses of brain or nerve, connected with the interior sense, forms a surface unduly exposed, on which disembodied spirits may operate: communication is thus more or less effectually established. Between this brain circulation and the heart circulation there is an intimate sympathy. The seat, or rather the instrument of exterior vision, is the eye. The seat of interior vision is the nervous tissue and brain, immediately about and above the eyebrow. You remember how effectually I dissipated your pictures by the simple application of iced eau-de-cologne. Few cases, however, can be treated exactly alike with anything like rapid success. Cold acts powerfully as a repellant of the nervous fluid. Long enough continued it will even produce that permanent insensibility which we call numbness, and a little longer, muscular as well as sensational paralysis.

I have not, I repeat, the slightest doubt that I should have first dimmed and ultimately sealed that inner eye which Mr. Jennings had inadvertently opened. The same senses are opened in delirium tremens, and entirely shut up again when the overaction of the cerebral heart, and the prodigious nervous congestions that attend it, are terminated by a decided change in the state of the body. It is by acting steadily upon the body, by a simple process, that this result is produced—and inevitably produced—I have never yet failed.

Poor Mr. Jennings made away with himself. But that catastrophe was the result of a totally different malady, which, as it were, projected itself upon the disease which was established. His case was in the distinctive manner a complication, and the complaint under which he really succumbed, was hereditary suicidal mania. Poor Mr. Jennings I cannot call a patient of mine, for I had not even begun to treat his case, and he had not yet given me, I am convinced, his full and unreserved confidence. If the patient do not array himself on the side of the disease, his cure is certain.

DEATH OF FERGUS

Standish H. O'Grady

*The king of the Lepracanes' journey to Emania, and how
the death of Fergus mac Léide king of Ulidia was brought about.*

A RIGHTEOUS king, a maintainer of truth and a giver of just judgments, that had dominion over the happy *clanna Rudhraidhe* or "children of Rury": Fergus son of *Léide* son of Rury; and these are they that were his heroes and men of war: Eirgenn, Amergen *iurthunnach* or "the ravager," Conna Buie son of Iliach, and Dubthach son of Lughaid.

By that king a great feast was made in Emania, and it was ready, fit to be consumed, all set in order and well furnished forth; that very season and hour being the same also at which the king of the *Lupra* and *Lupracán* held a banquet: whose name was *Iubhdán* son of *Abhdaein*.

These are the names of the men of war that were Iubhdan's: Conan son of Ruiched, Gerrchu son of Gairid, and Righbeg son of Robeg; Luigin son of Luiged, Glunan son of Gabarn, Febal son of Feornin, and Cinnbeg son of Gnuman; together with Buan's son Brigbeg, Liran son of Luan, and Mether son of Mintan. To them was brought the strong man of the region of the Lupra and Lupracan, whose prize feat that he used to perform was the hewing down of a thistle at a single stroke; whereas it was a twelve men's effort of the rest of them to give him singly a wrestling-fall. To them was brought the king's presumptive successor: Beg that was son of Beg; the king's poet and man of art likewise: Esirt son of Beg son of Buaidghen, with the other notables of the land of the Lupra and Lupracan.

By these now that banquet-house was ordered according to qualities and to precedence: at one side Iubhdan was placed, having next to him on either hand *Bébhó* his wife, and his chief poet; at the other side of the hall and facing Iubhdan sat Beg son of Beg, with the notables and chiefs; the king's strong man too: Glomhar son of Glomradh's son Glas, stood beside the doorpost of the house. Now were the spigots drawn from the vats, the colour of those vats being a dusky red after the tint of red yew. Their carvers stood up to carve for them and their cupbearers to pour; and old ale, sleep-compelling, delicious, was served out to the throng so that on one side as on the other of the hall they were elevated and made huge noise of mirth.

At last Iubhdan, that was their king and the head of all their counsel, having in his hand the *corn breac* or "variegated horn" stood up; on the other hand, over against Iubhdan and to do him honour, stood up Beg son of Beg. Then the king, by this time affably inclining to converse, enquired of them saying: "have ye ever seen a king that was better than myself?" and they answered: "we have not." "Have ye ever seen a strong man better than my strong man?" "We have not." "Horses or men of battle have ye ever seen better than they which to-night are in this house?" "By our words," they made answer, "we never have." "I too," Iubhdan went on, "wage my word that it were a hard task forcibly to take out of this house to-night either captives or hostages: so surpassing are its heroes and men of battle, so many its lusty companions and men of might, so great the number of its fierce and haughty ones that are stuff out of which kings might fittingly be made."

All which when he had heard, the king's chief poet Esirt burst out a-laughing; whereupon Iubhdan asked: "Esirt, what moved thee to that laugh?" Said the poet: "I wot of a province that is in Ireland, and one man of them would lift hostages and captives from all four battalions that here ye muster of the Luchra." "Lay the poet by the heels," cried the king, "that vengeance be taken of him for his bragging speech!" So it was done; but Esirt said: "Iubhdan, this thy seizure of me will bear thee evil fruit; for in requital of the arrest thou shalt thyself be for five years captive in Emania, whence thou shalt not escape without leaving behind thee the rarest thing of all thy wealth and treasures. By reason of this seizure Cobthach Cas also, son of Munster's king, shall fall, and the king of Leinster's son Eochaid; whilst I myself must go to the house of Fergus son of Leide and in his goblet be set a-floating till I be all but drowned." Which said he indited:—

> "A great feast there is to-night in Emania, but a feast evil to
> women, and to men an evil one: jovial as be the crowds that now
> enjoy it, the end will be melancholy dismal gloom . . .

"An evil arrest is this thou hast made of me, O king," Esirt went on: "but grant me now a three-days' and three-nights' respite that I may

travel to Emania and to the house of Leide's son Fergus, to the end that
if there I find some evident token by which thou shalt recognise truth to
be in me I may bring the same hither; or if not, then do to me that thou
wilt."

Then Esirt, his bonds being loosed, rose and next to his white skin put
on a smooth and glossy shirt of delicate silk. Over that he donned his
gold-broidered tunic and his scarlet cloak, all fringed and beautiful, in
soft folds flowing: the scarlet being of the land of the Finn, and the fringe
of pale gold in varied pattern. Betwixt his feet and the earth he set his
two dainty shoes of the white bronze, overlaid with ornament of gold.
After assumption of his white bronze poet's wand and his silken hood he
set out, choosing the shortest way and the straightest course, nor are we
told how he fared until he came to Emania and at the gate of the place
shook his poet's rod.

The gate-keeper when at the sound he was come forth beheld there
a tiny man, extraordinary comely and of a most gallant carriage, in
respect of whom the close-cropped grass of the green was so long that
it reached to his knee, aye, and to the thick of his thigh. At sight of him
wonder fell upon the gate-keeper; and he entered into the house, where
to Fergus and to the company he declared the matter. All enquired
whether he [Esirt] were less than Aedh: this Aedh being Ulster's poet,
and a dwarf that could stand on full-sized men's hands; but the gate-
keeper said: "upon Aedh's palm he, by my word, would have room
enough." Hereupon the guests with pealing laughter desired to see him:
each one deeming the time to be all too long till he should view Esirt
and, after seeing him, speak with him. Then upon all sides both men and
women had free access to him, but Esirt cried: "huge men that ye are, let
not your infected breaths so closely play upon me! but suffer yon small
man that is the least of you to approach me; who, little though he be
among you, would yet in the land where I dwell be accounted of great
stature." Into the great house therefore, and he standing upon his palm,
the poet Aedh bore him off.

Fergus, when he had sought him tidings who he might be, was
answered: "I am Esirt son of Beg son of Buaidghen: chief poet, bard and
rhymer, of the Luchra and Lupracan." The assembly were just then in
actual enjoyment of the feast, and a cup-bearer came to Fergus: "give to
the little man that is come to me," said the king. Esirt replied: "neither of
your meat will I eat, nor of your liquor will I drink." "By our word,"
quoth Fergus, "seeing thou art a flippant and a mocking fellow, it were
but right to drop thee into the beaker, where at all points round about
thou shouldst impartially quaff the liquor." At which hearing the cup-
bearer closed his hand on Esirt and popped him into the goblet, in which
upon the surface of the liquor that it contained he floated round, and:

"ye poets of Ulster," he vociferated, "much desirable knowledge and instruction there is which, upon my conscience, ye sorely need to have of me, yet ye suffer me to be drowned!"

With fair satin napkins of great virtue and with special silken fabrics he being now plucked out was cleaned spick and span, and Fergus enquired: "of what impediment spakest thou a while since as hindering thee that thou shouldst not share our meat?" "That will I e'en tell thee," the little man replied: "but let me not incur thy displeasure." "Thou shalt not," promised the king: "only resolve me the whole impediment." Then Esirt said [and Fergus answered him]:—

> *E.* "With poet's sharp-set words never be angered, Fergus; thy stern hard utterance restrain, nor against me take unjustifiable action" *F.* "O wee man of the seizure . . ."
> *E.* "Judgments lucid and truthful, if they be those to which thou dost provoke me: then I pronounce that thou triflest with thy steward's wife, while thine own foster-son ogles thy queen. Women fair-haired and accomplished, rough kings of the ordinary kind [i.e. mere chieftains]: how excellent soever be the form of these, 'tis not on them the former let their humour dwell [i.e. when a genuine king comes in their way]" *F.* "Esirt, thou art in truth no child, but an approved man of veracity; O gentle one, devoid of reproach, no wrath of Fergus shalt thou know!"

The king went on: "my share of the matter, by my word, is true; for the steward's wife is indeed my pastime, and all the rest as well therefore I the more readily take to be a verity." Then said Esirt: "now will I partake of thy meat, for thou hast confessed the evil; do it then no more." Here the poet waxing cheerful and of good courage went on: "upon my own lord I have made a poem which, were it your pleasure, I would declaim to you." Fergus answered: "we would esteem it sweet to hear it," and Esirt began:—

> "A king victorious, and renowned and pleasant, is Iubhdan son of Abhdaein: king of *magh Life,* king of *magh faithlenn.* His is a voice clear and sweet as copper's resonance, like the blood-coloured rowan-berry is his cheek; his eye is bland as it were a stream of mead, his colour that of the swan or of the river's foam. Strong he is in his yellow-haired host, in beauty and in cattle he is rich; and to brave men he brings death when he sets himself in motion. A man that loves the chase, active, a generous feast-giver; he is head of a bridle-wearing army, he is tall, proud and imperious. His is a solid squadron of grand headlong horses, of bridled horses rushing torrent-like; heads with smooth adornment of golden locks are on the warriors of the Luchra. All the men are comely, the women all

light-haired; over that land's noble multitude Iubhdan of truthful utterance presides. There the fingers grasp silver horns, deep notes of the timpan are heard; and how great soever be the love that women are reputed to bear thee [Fergus], 'tis surpassed by the desire that they feel for Iubhdan."

The lay ended Ulster equipped him with abundance of good things, till each heap of these as they lay there equalled their tall men's stature. "This on my conscience," quoth Esirt, "is indeed a response that is worthy of right men; nevertheless take away those treasures: of which I conceive that I have no need, seeing that in my lord's following is no man but possesses substance sufficient." Ulster said however: "we pledge our words that, as we never would have taken back aught though we had given thee our very wives and our kine, even so neither will we take again that we now have given thee." "Then divide ye the gifts, bards and professors of Ulster!" Esirt cried: "two thirds take for yourselves, and the other bestow on Ulster's horseboys and jesters."

So to the end of three days and three nights Esirt was in Emania, and he took his leave of Fergus and of Ulster's nobles. "I will e'en go with thee," said Ulster's poet and man of science, Aedh: that used to lie in their good warriors' bosoms, yet by Esirt's side was a giant; for this latter could stand upon Aedh's palm. Esirt said: "'tis not I that will bid thee come: for were I to invite thee, and kindness to be shewn thee in the sequel, thou wouldst say 'twas but what [by implication] had been promised thee; whereas if such be not held out to thee and thou yet receive the same thou wilt by grateful."

Out of Emania the pair of poets now went their way and, Aedh's step being the longer, he said: "Esirt thou art a poor walker." This one then took such a fit of running that he was an arrow's flight in front of Aedh, who said again: "between those two extremes lies the golden mean." "On my word," retorted Esirt, "that is the one category in which since I am among you I have heard mention made of the golden mean!" On they went then till they gained *tráigh na dtréinfhear* or "strand of the strong men" in Ulster: "and what must we do now?" Aedh asked here. "Travel the sea over her depths," said the other. To Aedh objecting: "never shall I come safe out of that [trial]," Esirt made answer: "seeing that I compassed the task 'twere strange that thou shouldst fail." Then Aedh vented a strain and Esirt answered him:—

A. "In the vast sea how shall I contrive? O generous Esirt, the wind will bear me down to the merciless wave [on which] though I mount upwards yet [none the less] shall I perish in the end" *E.* "To fetch thee fair Iubhdan's horse will come, get thee upon him and cross the stammering sea: an excellent horse truly and of surpassing colour, a king's valued treasure, good on sea as upon land. A beautiful horse that will carry thee away: sit on him nor be troubled; go, trust thyself to him."

They had been no long time there when something they marked which, swiftly careering, came towards them over the billows' crests. "Upon itself be the evil that it brings," Aedh cried, and to Esirt asking: "what seest thou?" answered: "a russet-clad hare I see." But Esirt said: "not so—rather is it Iubhdan's horse that comes to fetch thee." Of which horse the fashion was this: two fierce flashing eyes he had, an exquisite pure crimson mane, with four green legs and a long tail that floated in wavy curls. His [general] colour was that of prime artificers' gold-work, and a gold-encrusted bridle he bore withal. Esirt bestriding him said: "come up beside me, Aedh;" but again the latter objected: "nay, poet, to do thee alone a skiff's office his capacity is all too scant." "Aedh, cease from fault-finding: for ponderous as may be the wisdom that is in thee, yet will he carry us both."

They both being now mounted on the horse traversed the combing seas, the mighty main's expanse and Ocean's great profound, until in the end they, undrowned and without mishap, reached *magh faithlenn,* and there the Luchra people were before them in assembly. "Esirt approaches," they cried, "and a giant bears him company!" Then Iubhdan went to meet Esirt, and gave him a kiss: "but poet," said he, "wherefore bringest thou this giant to destroy us?" "No giant is he, but Ulster's poet and man of science, and the king's dwarf. In the land whence he comes he is the least, so that in their great men's bosoms he lies down and, as it were an infant, stands on the flat of their hands. For all which he is yet such that before him ye would do well to be careful of yourselves." They further asking: "what is his name?" were told that he was called 'poet Aedh.' "Alack man," they cried to Esirt," thy giant is huge indeed!"

Next, Esirt addressing Iubhdan said: "on thee, Iubhdan, I lay bonds which true warriors may not brook that in thine own person thou go to view the region out of which we come, and that of the 'lord's porridge' which for the king of Ulster is made to-night thou be the first man to make trial."

Then Iubhdan, in grief and faint of spirit, proceeded to confer with Bebo his wife: he told her how that by Esirt he was laid under bonds, and bade her bear him company. "That will I," she said: "but in that Esirt was cast into prison thou didst unjustly." So they mounted Iubhdan's golden horse and that same night made good their way to Emania, where they entered unperceived into the place. "Iubhdan," said Bebo, "search the town for the porridge spoken of by Esirt, and let us depart again before the people of the place shall rise."

They gained the inside of the palace and there found Emania's great cauldron, having in it the remnant of the "people's porridge." Iubhdan drew near, but might by no means reach it from the ground. "Get thee upon thy horse," said Bebo, "and from the horse upon the cauldron's rim." This he did but, the porridge being too far down and his arm too short, could not touch the shank of the silver ladle that was in the cauldron; whereupon he making a downward effort his foot slipped, and up to his very navel he fell into the cauldron; in which as though all existing iron gyves had been upon him he now found himself fettered and tethered both hand and foot. "Long thou tarriest, dark man!" Bebo cried to him (for Iubhdan was thus: hair he had that was jet-black and curled, his skin being whiter than foam of wave and his cheeks redder than the forest's scarlet berry: whereas—saving him only—all the Luchra people had hair that was ringletted indeed, but of a fair and yellow hue; hence then he was styled "dark man"). Bebo sang now, Iubhdan answering her:—

> *She.* "O dark man, and O dark man! dire is the strait in which thou art: to-day it is that the white horse must be saddled, for the sea is angry and the tide at flood" *He.* "O fair-haired woman, and O woman with fair hair! gyves hold me captive in a viscous mass nor, until gold be given for my ransom, shall I ever be dismissed. O Bebo, and O Bebo! morn is at hand, thou therefore flee away: fast in the doughy remnant sticks my leg, if here thou stay thou art but foolish, O Bebo!" *She.* "Rash word it was, 'twas a rash word, that in thy house thou utteredst: that but by thine own good pleasure none under the sun might hold thee fast, O man!" *He.* Rash was the word, the word was rash, that in my house I uttered: a year and a day I must be now, and neither man nor woman of my people see!"

"Bebo," cried Iubhdan, "get thee away, and to the Luchraland take back that horse." "Never say it," she answered: "of a surety I will not depart until I see what turn things shall take for thee."

The dwellers in the town when they were now risen anon lighted on Iubhdan in the porridge cauldron, out of which he could not frame to escape; in which plight when they saw him the people sent up a mighty roar of a laughter, then picked Iubhdan out of the cauldron and carried him off to Fergus. "My conscience," said the king, "this is not the tiny man that was here before: seeing that, whereas the former little fellow had fair hair, this one hath a black thatch. What art thou at all, mannikin, and out of what region come?" Iubhdan made answer: "I am of the Luchra-folk, over the which it is I that am king; this woman that ye see by me is my wife, and queen over the Luchra: her name is Bebo, and I have never told a lie." "Let him be taken out," cried Fergus, "and put with the common rabble of the household—guard him well!" Iubhdan was led out accordingly. . . . Said Iubhdan: "but if it may please thee to show me some favour, suffer me no longer to be among yonder loons, for the great men's breaths do all infect me; and my word I pledge that till by Ulster and by thee it be licensed I will never leave you." Fergus said: "could I but think that, thou shouldst no more be with the common varlets." Iubhdan's reply was: "never have I overstepped, nor ever will transgress, my plighted word."

Then he was conducted into a fair and privy chamber that Fergus had, where one that was a servant of trust to the king was set apart to minister to him. "An excellent retreat indeed is this," he said, "yet is my own retreat more excellent than it"; and he made a lay:—

> "In the land that lies away north I have a retreat, the ceiling of which is of the red gold, and the floor all of silver. Of the white bronze its lintel is, and its threshold of copper; of light-yellow bird-plumage is the thatch on it I ween. Golden are its candelabra, holding candles of rich light and gemmed over with rare stones, in the fair midst of the house. Save myself only and my queen, none that belongs to it feels sorrow now; a retinue is there that ages not, that wears wavy yellow tresses. There every man is a chess-player, good company is there that knows no stint: against man or woman that seeks to enter it the retreat is never closed."

Fer dédh or 'man of smoke' the fire-servant, as in Iubhdan's presence he kindled a fire, threw upon it a woodbine that twined round a tree, together with somewhat of all other kinds of timber, and this led Iubhdan to say: "burn not the king of trees, for he ought not to be burnt; and wouldst thou, Ferdedh, but act by my counsel, then neither by sea nor by land shouldst thou ever be in danger." Here he sang a lay:—

> "O man that for Fergus of the feasts dost kindle fire, whether afloat or ashore never burn the king of woods. Monarch of Innisfail's forests the woodbine is, whom none may hold captive; no feeble sovereign's effort is it to hug all tough trees in his embrace. The pliant woodbine if thou burn, wailings for misfortune will abound; dire extremity at weapons' points or drowning in great waves will come after. Burn not the precious apple-tree of spreading and low-sweeping bough: tree ever decked in bloom of white, against whose fair head all men put forth the hand. The surly blackthorn is a wanderer, and a wood that the artificer burns not; throughout his body, though it be scanty, birds in their flocks warble. The noble willow burn not, a tree sacred to poems; within his

bloom bees are a-sucking, all love the little cage. The graceful tree
with the berries, the wizards' tree, the rowan, burn; but spare the
limber tree: burn not the slender hazel. Dark is the colour of the
ash: timber that makes the wheels to go; rods he furnishes for horse-
men's hands, and his form turns battle into flight. Tenterhook
among woods the spiteful briar is, by all means burn him that is so
keen and green; he cuts, he flays the foot, and him that would
advance he forcibly drags backward. Fiercest heat-giver of all timber is green oak, from him none may escape unhurt: by partiality
for him the head is set on aching and by his acrid embers the eye is
made sore. Alder, very battle-witch of all woods, tree that is hottest
in the fight—undoubtingly burn at thy discretion both the alder
and the whitethorn. Holly, burn it green; holly, burn it dry: of all
trees whatsoever the critically best is holly. Elder that hath tough
bark, tree that in truth hurts sore: him that furnishes horses to the
armies from the *sídh* burn so that he be charred. The birch as well,
if he be laid low, promises abiding fortune: burn up most sure- and
certainly the stalks that bear the constant pods. Suffer, if it so please
thee, the russet aspen to come headlong down: burn, be it late or
early, the tree with the palsied branch. Patriarch of long-lasting
woods is the yew, sacred to feasts as is well known: of him now build
ye dark-red vats of goodly size. Ferdedh, thou faithful one, wouldst
thou but do my behest: to thy soul as to thy body, O man, 'twould
work advantage!"

After this manner then, and free of all supervision, Iubhdan abode in
the town; while to them of Ulster it was recreation of mind and body to
look at him and to listen to his words. . . .

Again, Iubhdan went to the house of a certain soldier of the king's
soldiers that chanced to fit on him new brogues that he had: discoursing
as he did so, and complaining, of their soles that were too thin. Iubhdan
laughed. The king asked: "Iubhdan, why laughst thou thus?" "Yon fellow
it is that provokes my laughter, complaining of his brogues while for his
own life he makes no moan. Yet, thin as be those brogues, he never will
wear them out." Which was true for Iubhdan, seeing that before night
that man and another one of the king's people fought and killed each
other. . . .

Yet another day the household disputed of all manner of things, how
they would do this or that, but never said: "if it so please God." Then
Iubhdan laughed and uttered a lay:—

> "Man talks but God sheweth the event; to men all things are but
> confusion, they must leave them as God knoweth them to be. All
> that which Thou, Monarch of the elements, hast ordained must be
> right; He, the King of kings, knows all that I crave of thee, Fergus.

No man's life, however bold he be, is more than the twinkling of an eye; were he a king's son he knoweth not whether it be truth that he utters of the future."

Iubhdan now tarried in Emania until such time as the Luchra-folk, being seven battalions strong, came to Emania's green in quest of him; and of these no single one did, whether in height or in bulk, exceed another. Then to Fergus and to Ulster's nobles that came out to confer with them they said: "bring us our king that we may redeem him, and we will pay for him a good ransom." Fergus asked: "what ransom?" "Every year, and that without ploughing, without sowing, we will cover this vast plain with a mass of corn." "I will not give up Iubhdan," said the king. "To-night we will do thee a mischief." "What mischief?" asked the king. "All Ulster's calves we will admit to their dams, so that by morning time there shall not in the whole province be found the measure of one babe's allowance of milk." "So much ye will have gained," said Fergus, "but not Iubhdan."

This damage accordingly they wrought that night; then at morn returned to the green of Macha and, with promise of making good all that they had spoiled, again required Iubhdan. Fergus refusing them however they said: "this night we will do another deed of vengeance: we will defile the wells, the rapids, and the river-mouths of the whole province." But the king answered: "that is but a puny mischief" (whence the old saw "dirt in a well") "and ye shall not have Iubhdan."

They having done this came again to Emania on the third day and demanded Iubhdan. Fergus said: "I will not give him." "A further vengeance we will execute upon thee." "What vengeance is that?" "To-night we will burn the millbeams and the kilns of the province." "But ye will not get Iubhdan," quoth the king.

Away they went and did as they had threatened, then on the fourth day repaired to Emania and clamoured for Iubhdan. Said Fergus: "I will not deliver him." We will execute vengeance on thee." "What vengeance?" "We will snip the ears off all the corn that is in the province." "Neither so shall ye have Iubhdan." This they did, then returned to Emania on the fifth day and asked for Iubhdan. Fergus said: "I will not yield him."

"Yet another vengeance we will take of thee." "What vengeance?" "Your women's hair and your men's we will e'en shave to such purpose that they shall for ever be covered with reproach and shame." Then Fergus cried: "if ye do that, by my word I will slay Iubhdan!" But here this latter said: "that is not the right thing at all; rather let me be enlarged, that in person I may speak with them and bid them first of all to repair such mischief as they have wrought, and then be gone."

At sight of Iubhdan they then, as taking for granted that the license accorded him must needs be in order to his departure with them, sent up a mighty shout of triumph. Iubhdan said however: "my trusty people, get you gone now, for I am not suffered to go with you; all that which ye have spoiled make good also, neither spoil anything more for, if ye do so, I must die." They thereupon, all gloomy and dejected, went away; a man of them making this ditty:—

"A raid upon thee we proclaim this night, O Fergus owner of many strong places! from thy standing corn we will snip the ears, whereby thy tables will not benefit. In this matter we have already burnt your kilns, your millbeams too we have all consumed; your calves we have most accurately and universally admitted to their dams. Your men's hair we will crop, and all locks of your young women: to your land it shall be a disfigurement, and such shall be our mischief's consummation. White be thy horse till time of war, thou king of Ulster and of warriors stout! but crimsoned be his trappings when he is in the battle's press. May no heat inordinate assail thee, nor inward flux e'er seize thee, nor eye-distemper reach thee during all thy life: but Fergus, not for love of thee! Were it not Iubhdan here whom Fergus holds at his discretion, the manner of our effecting our depredations would have been such that the disgrace incurred by the latter would have shown his refusal to be an evil one."

"And now get you hence," said Iubhdan: "for Esirt has prophesied of me that before I shall have abandoned here the choicest one of all my precious things I may not return."

So till a year's end all but a little he dwelt in Emania, and then said to Fergus: "of all my treasures choose thee now a single one, for so thou mayest. My precious things are good too"; and in a lay he proceeded to cast them up:—

"Take my spear, O take my spear, thou, Fergus, that hast enemies in number! in battle 'tis a match for an hundred, and a king that holds it will have fortune among hostile points. Take my shield, O take my shield, a good price it is for me, Fergus! be it stripling or be it grey-beard, behind his shelter none may wounded be. My sword, and O my sword! in respect of a battle-sword there is not in a prince's hand throughout all Innisfail a more excellent thing of price. Take my cloak, O take my cloak, the which if thou take it will be ever new! my mantle is good, Fergus, and for thy son and grandson will endure. My shirt, and O my shirt! whoe'er he be that in time to come may be within its weft—my grandsire's father's wife, her hands they were that spun it. Take my belt, O take my belt! gold and silver appertain to a knowledge of it; sickness will not lay hold on him that is encircled by it, nor on skin encompassed by my girdle. My helmet, O my helmet, no prize there is more admirable! no man that on his scalp shall assume it will ever be obnoxious to reproach of baldness. Take my tunic, O my tunic take, well-fitting silken garment! the which though for an hundred years it were on one, yet were its crimson none the worse. My cauldron, O my cauldron, a special rare thing for its handy use! though they were stones that should go into my cauldron, yet would it turn them out meat befitting princes. My vat, and O my vat! as compared with other vats of the best, by any that shall bathe in him life's stage is traversed thrice. Take my mace, O take my mace, no better treasure canst thou choose! in time of war, in sharp set-to, nine heads besides thine own it will protect. Take my horse-rod, O my horse-rod take: rod of the yellow horse so fair to see! let but the whole world's women look at thee [with that rod in thy hand and] in thee will centre all their hottest love. My timpan, O my timpan endowed with string-sweetness, from the red sea's borders! within its wires resides minstrelsy sufficing to delight all women of the universe. Whosoe'er should in the manner of tuning up my timpan be suddenly put to the test, if never hitherto he had been a man of art yet would the instrument of itself perform the minstrel's function. Ah how melodious is its martial strain, and its low cadence ah how sweet! all of itself too how it plays, without a finger on a single string of all its strings. My shears, and O my shears, that Barran's smith did make! of them that take it into their hands every man will secure a sweetheart. My needle, O my needle, that is made of the *eanach's* gold! . . . Of my swine two porkers take! they will last thee till thy dying day; every night they may be killed, yet within the watch will live again. My halter, O my halter! whoe'er should be on booty bent, though 'twere a black cow he put into it incontinently she would become a white one. Take my shoes, my shoes O take, brogues of the white bronze, of virtue marvellous! alike they travel land and sea, happy the king whose choice shall fall on these!"

"Fergus," said Iubhdan, "from among them all choose thee now one precious thing, and let me go."

But this was now the season and the hour when from his adventure poet Aedh returned; and him the professors presently examined touching Iubhdan's house, his household, and the region of the Luchra. Concerning all which Aedh forthwith began to tell them, inditing a lay:—

"A wondrous enterprise it was that took me away from you, our poets, to a populous fairy palace with a great company of princes and with men minute. Twelve doors there are to that house of roomy beds and [window] lighted sides; 'tis of vast marble [blocks], and in every doorway doors of gold. Of red, of yellow and green, of azure and of blue its bedclothes are; its authority is of ancient date: warriors' cooking-places it includes, and baths. Smooth are its terraces of the egg-shells of Iruath; pillars there are of crystal, columns of silver and of copper too. Silk and satin, silk and satin, bridles . . . ; its authority is of ancient date: warriors' cooking-places it includes, and chess-boards. Reciting of romances, of the Fian-lore, was there every day; singing of poems, instrumental music, the mellow blast of horns, and concerted minstrelsy. A noble king he is: Iubhdan son of Abhdaein, of the yellow horse; he is one whose form undergoes no change, and who needs not to strive after wis-dom. Women are there, that in pure pellucid loch disport them-selves: satin their raiment is, and with each one of them a chain of gold. As for the king's men-at-arms, that wear long tresses, hair ringletted and glossy: men of the mould ordinary with the Luchra can stand upon those soldiers' palms. Bebo—Iubhdan's blooming queen—an object of desire—never is the white-skinned beauty without three hundred women in her train. Bebo's women—'tis little they chatter of evil or of arrogance; their bodies are pure white, and their locks reach to their ankles. The king's chief poet, Esirt son of Beg son of Buaidghen: his eye is blue and gentle, and less than a doubled fist that man of poems is. The poet's wife—to all things good she was inclined; a lovely woman and a wonderful: she could sleep in my rounded glove. The king's cupbearer—in the banquet-hall a trusty man and true: well I loved Feror that could lie within my sleeve. The king's strong man—Glomhar son of Glomradh's son Glas, stern doer of doughty deeds: he could fell a thistle at a sweep. Of those the king's confidentials, seventeen 'swans' [i.e. pretty girls] lay in my bosom; four men of them in my belt and, all unknown to me, among my beard would be another. They (both fighting men and erudites of that *sídh*) would say to me, and the public acclamation ever was: 'enormous Aedh, O very giant!' Such, O Leide's son of forests, vast, such is my adventure: of a verity there is a wondrous thing befallen me.'

Of those matters then—of all Iubhdan's treasures—Fergus made choice, and his choice was Iubhdan's shoes. This latter therefore, leaving them his blessing and taking theirs, bade Fergus and the nobles of Ulster farewell (Ulster grieving for his departure) and with him the story henceforth has no more to do.

As regards Fergus however, this is why he picked out Iubhdan shoes: he with a young man of his people walking a day hard by Lochrury, they entered into the loch to bathe; and the monster that dwelt in the loch— the *sinech* of Lochrury—was aware of them. Then she shaking herself till the whole loch was in great and tempestuous commotion reared herself on high as it had been a solid arc hideous to behold, so that in extent she equalled the rainbow of the air. They both marking her towards them swam for the shore, she in pursuit with mighty strokes that in bursting deluge sent the water spouting from her sides. Fergus suffered his attendant to gain the land before himself, whereby the monster's breath impinging on the king turned him into a crooked and distorted squint-eyed being, with his mouth twisted round to his very poll. But he knew not that he was so; neither dared any enquire of him what it might be that had wrought this [change] in him, nor venture to leave a mirror in the one house with him.

The young man however told all the matter to his wife and the woman showed it to Fergus's wife, to the queen. When therefore anent precedence in use of the bath-stone there was a falling-out between the king and queen, the king giving her the fist broke a tooth in her head; whereupon anger seized the queen, and she said: "to avenge thyself on the *sinech* of Lochrury that dragged thy mouth round to thy poll would become thee better than to win bloodless victories of women." Then to Fergus she brought a mirror, and he looking upon his image said: "the woman's words are true for her, and to this complexion it is indeed the *sinech* of Lochrury that hath brought me." And hence it was that before all Iubhdan's other precious wares Fergus had taken his shoes.

In their ships and in their galleys the whole province of Ulster, accompanying Fergus, now gathered together to Lochrury. They entering the loch gained its centre; the monster rose and shook herself in such fashion that of all the vessels she made little bits and, as are the withered twigs beneath horses' feet, so were they severally comminuted and, or ever they could reach the strand, all swamped.

Fergus said to Ulster: "bide ye here and sit you all down, that ye may witness how I and the monster shall deal together." Then he being shod with Iubhdan's shoes leaped into the loch, erect and brilliant and brave, making for the monster. At sound of the hero's approach she bared her teeth as does a wolf-dog threatened with a club; her eyes blazed like two great torches kindled, suddenly she put forth her sharp claw's jagged array, bowed her neck with the curve of an arch and clenched her glittering tusks, effacing [i.e. throwing back] her ears hideously, till her whole semblance was one of gloomy cruel fury. Alas for any in this world that should be fated to do battle with that monster: huge-headed long-fanged portent that she was! The fearsome and colossal creature's form was this: a crest and mane she had of coarse hair, a mouth that yawned, deep-sunken eyes; on either side thrice fifty flippers, each armed with as many claws recurved; a body impregnable. Thrice fifty feet her extended altitude; round as an apple she was in contraction, but in bulk equalled some notable hill in its rough garb of furze.

When the king sighted her he charged, instant, impetuous, and as he went he made this *rosg* or "rhapsody":—

"The evil is upon me that was presaged . . ."

Then both of them, seeking the loch's middle part, so flogged it that the salmon of varied hue leaped and flung themselves out upon the shore because that in the water they found no resting-place, for the white bottom-sand was churned up to the surface. Now as the loch whiter than new milk, anon all turned to crimson froth of blood. At last the beast, in figure like some vast royal oak, rose on the loch and before Fergus fled. The hero-king pressing her plied her with blows so stalwart and so deadly that she died; and with the sword that was in his hand, with the *caladcholg,* best blade that was then in Ireland, he hewed her all in pieces. To the loch's port where Ulster sat he brought her heart; but if he did, his own wounds were as many [as hers] and than his skin no sieve could be more full of holes. To such pitch truly the beast had given him the tooth, that he brought up his very heart's red blood and hardly might make utterance, but groaned aloud.

As for Ulster, they took no pleasure to view the fight, but said the while that were it upon land the king and the beast had striven they would have succoured him, and that right valiantly. Then Fergus made a lay:—

> "My soul this night is full of sadness, my body mangled cruelly; red Lochrury's beast hath pushed sore through my heart. Iubhdan's shoes have brought me through undrowned; with sheeny spear and with the *caladcholg* I have fought a hardy fight. Upon the *sinech* I have avenged my deformity—a signal victory this. Man! I had rather death should snatch me than to live on misshapen. Great Eochaid's daughter Ailinn it is that to mortal combat's lists compelled me; and 'tis I assuredly that have good cause to sorrow for the shape imposed on me by Iubhdan."

He went on: "Ulster! I have gotten my death; but lay ye by and preserve this sword, until of Ulidia there come after me one that shall be a fitting lord for him; whose name also shall be Fergus: Ros Rua's son Fergus.

Then lamentably and in tears Ulster stood over Fergus; poet Aedh too, the king's bard, came and standing over him mourned for Fergus with this quatrain:—

> "By you now be dug Fergus's grave, the great monarch's, grave of Leide's son; calamity most dire it is that by a foolish petty woman's words he is done to death!"

Answering whom Fergus said:—

"By you be laid up this sword wherewith 'the iron-death' is wrought; here after me shall arise one with the name of Fergus. By you be this sword treasured, that none other take it from you; my share of the matter for all time shall be this: that men shall rehearse the story of the sword."

So Fergus's soul parted from his body: his grave was dug, his name written in the Ogham, his lamentation-ceremony all performed; and from the monumental stones [*uladh*] piled by Ulster this name of *Uladh* [Ulster] had its origin.

Thus far the Death of Fergus and the Luchra-people's doings.

THE TABLES OF THE LAW

W. B. Yeats

I

"WILL you permit me, Aherne," I said, "to ask you a question, which I have wanted to ask you for years, and have not asked because we have grown nearly strangers? Why did you refuse the biretta, and almost at the last moment? When you and I lived together, you cared neither for wine, women, nor money, and had thoughts for nothing but theology and mysticism." I had watched through dinner for a moment to put my question, and ventured now, because he had thrown off a little of the reserve and indifference which, ever since his last return from Italy, had taken the place of our once close friendship. He had just questioned me, too, about certain private and almost sacred things, and my frankness had earned, I thought, a like frankness from him.

When I began to speak he was lifting a glass of that wine which he could choose so well and valued to little; and while I spoke, he set it slowly and meditatively upon the table and held it there, its deep red light dyeing his long delicate fingers. The impression of his face and form, as they were then, is still vivid with me, and is inseparable from another and fanciful impression: the impression of a man holding a flame in his naked hand. He was to me, at that moment, the supreme type of our race, which, when it has risen above, or is sunken below, the formalisms of half-education and the rationalisms of conventional affirmation and denial, turns away, unless my hopes for the world and for the Church have made me blind, from practicable desires and intuitions towards desires so unbounded that no human vessel can contain them, intuitions so immaterial that their sudden and far-off fire leaves heavy darkness about hand and foot. He had the nature, which is half monk, half soldier of fortune, and must needs turn action into dreaming, and dreaming into action; and for such there is no order, no finality, no contentment in this world. When he and I had been students in Paris, we had belonged to a little group which devoted itself to speculations about alchemy and mysticism. More orthodox in most of his beliefs than Michael Robartes, he had surpassed him in a fanciful hatred of all life, and this hatred had found expression in the curious paradox—half borrowed from some fanatical monk, half invented by himself—that the beautiful arts were sent into the world to overthrow nations, and finally life herself, by sowing everywhere unlimited desires, like torches thrown into a burning city. This idea was not at the time, I believe, more than a paradox, a plume of the pride of youth; and it was only after his return to Ireland that he endured the fermentation of belief which is coming upon our people with the reawakening of their imaginative life.

Presently he stood up, saying, "Come, and I will show you why; you at any rate will understand," and taking candles from the table, he lit the way into the long paved passage that led to his private chapel. We passed between the portraits of the Jesuits and priests—some of no little fame—his family had given to the Church; and engravings and photographs of pictures that had especially moved him; and the few paintings his small fortune, eked out by an almost penurious abstinence from the things most men desire, had enabled him to buy in his travels. The photographs and engravings were from the masterpieces of many schools; but in all the beauty, whether it was a beauty of religion, of love, or of some fantastical vision of mountain and wood, was the beauty achieved by temperaments which seek always an absolute emotion, and which have their most continual, though not most perfect, expression in the legends and vigils and music of the Celtic peoples. The certitude of a fierce or gracious fervour in the enraptured faces of the angels of Francesca, and in the august faces of the sibyls of Michaelangelo; and the incertitude, as of souls trembling between the excitement of the spirit and the excitement of the flesh, in wavering faces from frescoes in the churches of Siena, and in the faces like thin flames, imagined by the modern symbolists and Pre-Raphaelites, had often made that long, grey, dim, empty, echoing passage become to my eyes a vestibule of eternity.

Almost every detail of the chapel, which we entered by a narrow Gothic door, whose threshold had been worn smooth by the secret worshippers of the penal times, was vivid in my memory; for it was in this chapel that I had first, and when but a boy, been moved by the mediaevalism which is now, I think, the governing influence in my life. The only thing that seemed new was a square bronze box which stood upon the altar before the six unlighted candles and the ebony crucifix, and was like those made in ancient times of more precious substances to hold the sacred books. Aherne made me sit down on an oak bench, and having bowed very low before the crucifix, took the bronze box from the altar, and sat down beside me with the box upon his knees.

"You will perhaps have forgotten," he said, "most of what you have read about Joachim of Flora, for he is little more than a name to even the well-read. He was an abbot in Cortale in the twelfth century, and is best known for his prophecy, in a book called *Expositio in Apocalypsin,* that the Kingdom of the Father was past, the Kingdom of the Son passing, the Kingdom of the Spirit yet to come. The Kingdom of the Spirit was to be a complete triumph of the Spirit, the *spiritualis intelligentia* he called it, over the dead letter. He had many followers among the more extreme Franciscans, and these were accused of possessing a secret book of his called the *Liber inducens in Evangelium aeternum.* Again and again groups of visionaries were accused of possessing this terrible book, in which the freedom of the Renaissance lay hidden, until at last Pope Alexander IV. had it found and cast into the flames. I have here the greatest treasure the world contains. I have a copy of that book; and see what great artists have made the robes in which it is wrapped. This bronze box was made by Benvenuto Cellini, who covered it with gods and demons, whose eyes are closed to signify an absorption in the inner light." He lifted the lid and took out a book bound in leather, covered with filigree work of tarnished silver. "And this cover was bound by one of the binders that bound for Canevari; while Giulio Clovio, an artist of the later Renaissance, whose work is soft and gentle, took out the beginning page of every chapter of the old copy, and set in its place a page surmounted by an elaborate letter and a miniature of some one of the great whose example was cited in the chapter; and wherever the writing left a little space elsewhere, he put some delicate emblem or intricate pattern."

I took the book in my hands and began turning over the gilded, many-coloured pages, holding it close to the candle to discover the texture of the paper.

"Where did you get this amazing book?" I said. "If genuine, and I cannot judge by this light, you have discovered one of the most precious things in the world."

"It is certainly genuine," he replied. "When the original was destroyed, one copy alone remained, and was in the hands of a lute-player of Florence, and from him it passed to his son, and so from generation to generation until it came to the lute-player who was father to Benvenuto Cellini, and from him it passed to Giulio Clovio, and from Giulio Clovio to a Roman engraver; and then from generation to generation, the story of its wandering passing on with it, until it came into the possession of the family of Aretino, and so Giulio Aretino, an artist and worker in metals, and student of the cabalistic reveries of Pico della Mirandola. He spent many nights with me at Rome, discussing philosophy; and at last I won his confidence so perfectly that he showed me this, his greatest treasure; and, finding how much I valued it, and feeling that he himself was growing old and beyond the help of its teaching, he sold it to me for no great sum, considering its great preciousness."

"What is the doctrine?" I said. "Some mediaeval straw-splitting about the nature of the Trinity, which is only useful to-day to show how many things are unimportant to us, which once shook the world?"

"I could never make you understand," he said with a sigh, "that nothing is unimportant in belief, but even you will admit that this book goes to the heart. Do you see the tables on which the commandments were written in Latin?" I looked to the end of the room, opposite to the altar, and saw that the two marble tablets were gone, and that two large empty tablets of ivory, like large copies of the little tablets we set over our desks, had taken their place. "It has swept the commandments of the Father away," he went on, "and displaced the commandments of the Son by the commandments of the Holy Spirit. The first book is called *Fractura Tabularum*. In the first chapter it mentions the names of the great artists who made them graven things and the likeness of many things, and adored them and served them; and the second the names of the great wits who took the name of the Lord their God in vain; and that long third chapter, set with the emblems of sanctified faces, and having wings upon its borders, is the praise of breakers of the seventh day and wasters of the six days, who yet lived comely and pleasant days. Those two chapters tell of men and women who railed upon their parents, remembering that their god was older than the god of their parents; and that which has the sword of Michael for an emblem commends the kings that wrought secret murder and so won for their people a peace that was *amore somnoque gravata et vestibus versicoloribus,* "heavy with love and sleep and many-coloured raiment"; and that with the pale star at the closing has the lives of the noble youths who loved the wives of others and were transformed into memories, which have transformed many poorer hearts into sweet flames; and that with the winged head is the history of the robbers who lived upon the sea or in the desert, lives which it compares to the twittering of the string of a bow, *nervi stridentis instar;* and those two last, that are fire and gold, and devoted to the satirists who bore false witness against their neighbours and yet illustrated eternal wrath, and to those that have coveted more than other men wealth and women, and have thereby and therefore mastered and magnified great empires.

"The second book, which is called *Straminis Deflagratio,* recounts the conversations Joachim of Flora held in his monastery at Cortale, and afterwards in his monastery in the mountains of La Sila, with travellers and pilgrims, upon the laws of many countries; how chastity was a virtue and robbery a little thing in such a land, and robbery a crime and unchastity a little thing in such a land; and of the persons who had flung themselves upon these laws and become *decussa veste Dei sidera,* stars shaken out of the raiment of God.

"The third book, which is the close, is called *Lex Secreta,* and describes the true inspiration of action, the only Eternal Evangel; and ends with a vision, which he saw among the mountains of La Sila, of his disciples sitting throned in the blue deep of the air, and laughing aloud, with a laughter that was like the rustling of the wings of Time: *Coelis in coeruleis ridentes sedebant discipuli mei super thronos: talis erat risus, qualis temporis pennati susurrus.*"

"I know little of Joachim of Flora," I said, "except that Dante set him in Paradise among the great doctors. If he held a heresy so singular, I cannot understand how no rumours of it came to the ears of Dante; and Dante made no peace with the enemies of the Church."

"Joachim of Flora acknowledged openly the authority of the Church, and even asked that all his published writings, and those to be published by his desire after his death, should be submitted to the censorship of the Pope. He considered that those whose work was to live and not to reveal were children and that the Pope was their father; but he taught in secret that certain others, and in always increasing numbers, were elected, not to live, but to reveal that hidden substance of God which is colour and music and softness and a sweet odour; and that these have no father but the Holy Spirit. Just as poets and painters and musicians labour at their works, building them with lawless and lawful things alike, so long as they embody the beauty that is beyond the grave, these children of the Holy Spirit labour at their moments with eyes upon the shining substance on which Time has heaped the refuse of creation; for the world only exists to be a tale in the ears of coming generations; and terror and content, birth and death, love and hatred, and the fruit of the Tree, are but instruments for that supreme art which is to win us from life and gather us into eternity like doves into their dove-cots.

"I shall go away in a little while and travel into many lands, that I may know all accidents and destinies, and when I return, will write my secret law upon those ivory tablets, just as poets and romance-writers have written the principles of their art in prefaces; and will gather pupils about me that they may discover their law in the study of my law, and the Kingdom of the Holy Spirit be more widely and firmly established."

He was pacing up and down, and I listened to the fervour of his words and watched the excitement of his gestures with not a little concern. I had been accustomed to welcome the most singular speculations, and had always found them as harmless as the Persian cat, who half closes her meditative eyes and stretches out her long claws, before my fire. But now I would battle in the interests of orthodoxy, even of the commonplace; and yet could find nothing better to say than: "It is not necessary to judge every one by the law, for we have also Christ's commandment of love."

He turned and said, looking at me with shining eyes:

"Jonathan Swift made a soul for the gentlemen of this city by hating his neighbour as himself."

"At any rate, you cannot deny that to teach so dangerous a doctrine is to accept a terrible responsibility."

"Leonardo da Vinci," he replied, "has this noble sentence: "The hope and desire of returning home to one's former state is like the moth's desire for the light; and the man who with constant longing awaits each new month and new year, deeming that the things he longs for are ever too late in coming, does not perceive that he is longing for his own destruction." How then can the pathway which will lead us into the heart of God be other than dangerous? Why should you, who are no materialist, cherish the continuity and order of the world as those do who have only the world? You do not value the writers who will express nothing unless their reason understands how it will make what is called the right more easy; why, then, will you deny a like freedom to the supreme art, the art which is the foundation of all arts? Yes, I shall send out of this chapel saints, lovers, rebels, and prophets: souls that will surround themselves with peace, as with a nest made with grass; and others over whom I shall weep. The dust shall fall for many years over this little box; and then I shall open it; and the tumults which are, perhaps, the flames of the Last Day shall come from under the lid."

I did not reason with him that night, because his excitement was great and I feared to make him angry; and when I called at his house a few days late, he was gone and his house was locked up and empty. I have deeply regretted my failure both to combat his heresy and to test the genuineness of his strange book. Since my conversion I have indeed done penance for an error which I was only able to measure after some years.

II

I was walking along one of the Dublin quays, on the side nearest the river, about ten years after our conversation, stopping from time to time to turn over the works upon an old bookstall, and thinking, curiously enough, of the terrible destiny of Michael Robartes, and his brotherhood, when I saw a tall and bent man walking slowly along the other side of the quay. I recognised, with a start, in a lifeless mask with dim eyes, the once resolute and delicate face of Owen Aherne. I crossed the quay quickly, but had not gone many yards before he turned away, as though he had seen me, and hurried down a side street; I followed, but only to lose him among the intricate streets on the north side of the river. During the next few weeks I inquired of everybody who had once known him, but he had made himself known to nobody; and I knocked, without result, at the door of his old house; and had nearly persuaded myself that I was mistaken, when I saw him again in a narrow street behind the Four Courts, and followed him to the door of his house.

I laid my hand on his arm; he turned quite without surprise; and indeed it is possible that to him, whose inner life had soaked up the outer life, a parting of years was a parting from forenoon to afternoon. He stood holding the door half open, as though he would keep me from entering; and would perhaps have parted from me without further words had I not said: "Owen Aherne, you trusted me once, will you not trust me again, and tell me what has come of the ideas we discussed in this house ten years ago?—but perhaps you have already forgotten them."

"You have a right to hear," he said, "for since I have told you the ideas, I should tell you the extreme danger they contain, or rather the boundless wickedness they contain; but when you have heard this we must part, and part for ever, because I am lost, and must be hidden!"

I followed him through the paved passage, and saw that its corners were choked with dust and cobwebs; and that the pictures were grey with dust and shrouded with cobwebs; and that the dust and cobwebs which covered the ruby and sapphire of the saints on the window had made it very dim. He pointed to where the ivory tablets glimmered faintly in the dimness, and I saw that they were covered with small writing, and went up to them and began to read the writing. It was in Latin, and was an elaborate casuistry, illustrated with many examples, but whether from his own life or from the lives of others I do not know. I had read but a few sentences when I imagined that a faint perfume had begun to fill the room, and turning round asked Owen Aherne if he were lighting the incense.

"No," he replied, and pointed where the thurible lay rusty and empty on one of the benches; as he spoke the faint perfume seemed to vanish, and I was persuaded I had imagined it.

"Has the philosophy of the *Liber inducens in Evangelium aeternum* made you very unhappy?" I said.

"At first I was full of happiness," he replied, "for I felt a divine ecstasy, an immortal fire in every passion, in every hope, in every desire, in every dream; and I saw, in the shadows under leaves, in the hollow waters, in the eyes of men and women, its image, as in a mirror; and it was as though I was about to touch the Heart of God. Then all changed and I was full of misery; and in my misery it was revealed to me that man can only come to that Heart through the sense of separation from it which we call sin, and I understood that I could not sin, because I had discovered the law of my being, and could only express or fail to express my being, and I understood that God has made a simple and an arbitrary law that we may sin and repent!"

He had sat down on one of the wooden benches and now became silent, his bowed head and hanging arms and listless body having more of dejection than any image I have met with in life or in any art. I went and stood leaning against the altar, and watched him, not knowing what I should say; and I noticed his black closely-buttoned coat, his short hair, and shaven head, which preserved a memory of his priestly ambition, and understood how Catholicism had seized him in the midst of the vertigo he called philosophy; and I noticed his lightless eyes and his earth-coloured complexion, and understood how she had failed to do more than hold him on the margin; and I was full of an anguish of pity.

"It may be," he went on, "that the angels who have hearts of the Divine Ecstasy, and bodies of the Divine Intellect, need nothing but a thirst for the immortal element, in hope, in desire, in dreams; but we whose hearts perish every moment, and whose bodies melt away like a sigh, must bow and obey!"

I went nearer to him and said, "Prayer and repentance will make you like other men."

"No, no," he said, "I am not among those for whom Christ died, and this is why I must be hidden. I have a leprosy that even eternity cannot cure. I have seen the whole, and how can I come again to believe that a part is the whole? I have lost my soul because I have looked out of the eyes of the angels."

Suddenly I saw, or imagined that I saw, the room darken, and faint figures robed in purple, and lifting faint torches with arms that gleamed like silver, bending above Owen Aherne; and I saw, or imagined that I saw, drops, as of burning gum, fall from the torches, and a heavy purple smoke, as of incense, come pouring from the flames and sweeping about us. Owen Aherne, more happy than I who have seen half initiated into the Order of the Alchemical Rose, or protected perhaps by his great piety, had sunk again into dejection and listlessness, and saw none of these things; but my knees shook under me, for the purple-robed figures were less faint every moment, and now I could hear the hissing of the gum in the torches. They did not appear to see me, for their eyes were upon Owen Aherne; now and again I could hear them sigh as though with sorrow for his sorrow, and presently I heard words which I could not understand except that they were words of sorrow, and sweet as though immortal was talking to immortal. Then one of them waved her torch, and all the torches waved, and for a moment it was as though some great bird made of flames had fluttered its plumage, and a voice cried as from far up in the air, "He has charged even his angels with folly, and they also bow and obey; but let your heart mingle with our hearts, which are wrought of Divine Ecstasy, and your body with our bodies, which are wrought of Divine Intellect." And at that cry I understood that the Order of the Alchemical Rose was not of this earth, and that it was still seeking over this earth for whatever souls it could gather within its glittering net; and when all the faces turned towards me, as I saw the mild eyes and the unshaken eyelids, I was full of terror, and thought they were about to fling their torches upon me, so that all I held dear, all that bound me to spiritual and social order, would be burnt up, and my soul left naked and shivering among the winds that blow from beyond this world and from beyond the stars; and then a voice cried, "Why do you fly from our torches that were made out of the trees under which Christ wept in the Garden of Gethsemane? Why do you fly from our torches that were made out of sweet wood, after it had perished from the world?"

It was not until the door of the house had closed behind my flight, and the noise of the street was breaking on my ears, that I came back to myself and to a little of my courage; and I have never dared to pass the house of Owen Aherne from that day, even though I believe him to have been driven into some distant country by the spirits whose name is legion, and whose throne is in the indefinite abyss, and whom he obeys and cannot see.

LISHEEN RACES, SECOND-HAND

E. Œ. Somerville and Martin Ross

IT may or may not be agreeable to have attained the age of thirty-eight, but, judging from old photographs, the privilege of being nineteen has also its drawbacks. I turned over page after page of an ancient book in which were enshrined portraits of the friends of my youth, singly, in David and Jonathan couples, and in groups in which I, as it seemed to my mature and possibly jaundiced perception, always contrived to look the most immeasurable young bounder of the lot. Our faces were fat, and yet I cannot remember ever having been considered fat in my life; we indulged in low-necked shirts, in "Jemima" ties with diagonal stripes; we wore coats that seemed three sizes too small, and trousers that were three sizes too big; we also wore small whiskers.

I stopped at last at one of the David and Jonathan memorial portraits. Yes, here was the object of my researches; this stout and earnestly romantic youth was Leigh Kelway, and that fatuous and chubby young person seated on the arm of his chair was myself. Leigh Kelway was a young man ardently believed in by a large circle of admirers, headed by himself and seconded by me, and for some time after I had left Magdalen for Sandhurst, I maintained a correspondence with him on large and abstract subjects. This phase of our friendship did not survive; I went soldiering to India, and Leigh Kelway took honours and moved suitably on into politics, as is the duty of an earnest young Radical with useful family connections and an independent income. Since then I had at intervals seen in the papers the name of the Honourable Basil Leigh Kelway mentioned as a speaker at elections, as a writer of thoughtful articles in the reviews, but we had never met, and nothing could have been less expected by me than the letter, written from Mrs. Raverty's Hotel, Skebawn, in which he told me he was making a tour in Ireland with

Lord Waterbury, to whom he was private secretary. Lord Waterbury was at present having a few days' fishing near Killarney, and he himself, not being a fisherman, was collecting statistics for his chief on various points connected with the Liquor Question in Ireland. He had heard that I was in the neighbourhood, and was kind enough to add that it would give him much pleasure to meet me again.

With a stir of the old enthusiasm I wrote begging him to be my guest for as long as it suited him, and the following afternoon he arrived at Shreelane. The stout young friend of my youth had changed considerably. His important nose and slightly prominent teeth remained, but his wavy hair had withdrawn intellectually from his temples; his eyes had acquired a statesmanlike absence of expression, and his neck had grown long and bird-like. It was his first visit to Ireland, as he lost no time in telling me, and he and his chief had already collected much valuable information on the subject to which they had dedicated the Easter recess. He further informed me that he thought of popularising the subject in a novel, and therefore intended to, as he put it, "master the brogue" before his return.

During the next few days I did my best for Leigh Kelway. I turned him loose on Father Scanlan; I showed him Mohona, our champion village, that boasts fifteen public-houses out of twenty buildings of sorts and a railway station; I took him to hear the prosecution of a publican for selling drink on a Sunday, which gave him an opportunity of studying perjury as a fine art, and of hearing a lady, on whom police suspicion justly rested, profoundly summed up by the sergeant as "a woman who had th' appairance of having knocked at a back door."

The net result of these experiences has not yet been given to the world by Leigh Kelway. For my own part, I had at the end of three days arrived at the conclusion that his society, when combined with a note-book and a thirst for statistics, was not what I used to find it at Oxford. I therefore welcomed a suggestion from Mr. Flurry Knox that we should accompany him to some typical country races, got up by the farmers at a place called Lisheen, some twelve miles away. It was the worst road in the district, the races of the most grossly unorthodox character; in fact, it was the very place for Leigh Kelway to collect impressions of Irish life, and in any case it was a blessed opportunity of disposing of him for the day.

In my guest's attire next morning I discerned an unbending from the rôle of cabinet minister towards that of sportsman; the outlines of the note-book might be traced in his breast pocket, but traversing it was the strap of a pair of field-glasses, and his light grey suit was smart enough for Goodwood.

Flurry was to drive us to the races at one o'clock, and we walked to Tory Cottage by the short cut over the hill, in the sunny beauty of an

April morning. Up to the present the weather had kept me in a more or less apologetic condition; any one who has entertained a guest in the country knows the unjust weight of responsibility that rests on the shoulders of the host in the matter of climate, and Leigh Kelway, after two drenchings, had become sarcastically resigned to what I felt he regarded as my mismanagement.

Flurry took us into the house for a drink and a biscuit, to keep us going, as he said, till "we lifted some luncheon out of the Castle Knox people at the races," and it was while we were thus engaged that the first disaster of the day occurred. The dining-room door was open, so also was the window of the little staircase just outside it, and through the window travelled sounds that told of the close proximity of the stable-yard; the clattering of hoofs on cobble stones, and voices uplifted in loud conversation. Suddenly from this region there arose a screech of the laughter peculiar to kitchen flirtation, followed by the clank of a bucket, the plunging of a horse, and then an uproar of wheels and galloping hoofs. An instant afterwards Flurry's chestnut cob, in a dogcart, dashed at full gallop into view, with the reins streaming behind him, and two men in hot pursuit. Almost before I had time to realise what had happened, Flurry jumped through the half-opened window of the dining-room like a clown at a pantomime, and joined in the chase; but the cob was resolved to make the most of his chance, and went away down the drive and out of sight at a pace that distanced every one save the kennel terrier, who sped in shrieking ecstasy beside him.

"Oh merciful hour!" exclaimed a female voice behind me. Leigh Kelway and I were by this time watching the progress of events from the gravel, in company with the remainder of Flurry's household. "The horse is desthroyed! Wasn't that the quare start he took! And all in the world I done was to slap a bucket of wather at Michael out the windy, and 'twas himself got it in place of Michael!"

"Ye'll never ate another bit, Bridgie Dunnigan," replied the cook, with the exulting pessimism of her kind. "The Master'll have your life!"

Both speakers shouted at the top of their voices, probably because in spirit they still followed afar the flight of the cob.

Leigh Kelway looked serious as we walked on down the drive. I almost dared to hope that a note on the degrading oppression of Irish retainers was shaping itself. Before we reached the bend of the drive the rescue party was returning with the fugitive, all, with the exception of the kennel terrier, looking extremely gloomy. The cob had been confronted by a wooden gate, which he had unhesitatingly taken in his stride, landing on his head on the farther side with the gate and the cart on top of him, and had arisen with a lame foreleg, a cut on his nose, and several other minor wounds.

"You'd think the brute had been fighting the cats, with all the scratches and scrapes he has on him!" said Flurry, casting a vengeful eye at Michael, "and one shaft's broken and so is the dashboard. I haven't another horse in the place; they're all out at grass, and so there's an end of the races!"

We all three stood blankly on the hall-door steps and watched the wreck of the trap being trundled up the avenue.

"I'm very sorry you're done out of your sport," said Flurry to Leigh Kelway, in tones of deplorable sincerity; "perhaps, as there's nothing else to do, you'd like to see the hounds—?"

I felt for Flurry, but of the two I felt more for Leigh Kelway as he accepted this alleviation. He disliked dogs, and held the newest views on sanitation, and I knew what Flurry's kennels could smell like. I was lighting a precautionary cigarette, when we caught sight of an old man riding up the drive. Flurry stopped short.

"Hold on a minute," he said; "here's an old chap that often brings me horses for the kennels; I must see what he wants."

The man dismounted and approached Mr. Knox, hat in hand, towing after him a gaunt and ancient black mare with a big knee.

"Well, Barrett," began Flurry, surveying the mare with his hands in his pockets, "I'm not giving the hounds meat this month, or only very little."

"Ah, Master Flurry," answered Barrett, "it's you that's pleasant! Is it give the like o' this one for the dogs to ate! She's a vallyble strong young mare, no more than shixteen years of age, and ye'd sooner be lookin' at her goin' under a side-car than eatin' your dinner."

"There isn't as much meat on her as 'd fatten a jackdraw," said Flurry, clinking the silver in his pockets as he searched for a matchbox. "What are you asking for her?"

The old man drew cautiously up to him.

"Master Flurry," he said solemnly, "I'll sell her to *your* honour for five pounds, and she'll be worth ten after you give her a month's grass."

Flurry lit his cigarette; then he said imperturbably, "I'll give you seven shillings for her."

Old Barrett put on his hat in silence, and in silence buttoned his coat and took hold of the stirrup leather. Flurry remained immovable.

"Master Flurry," said old Barrett suddenly, with tears in his voice, "you must make it eight, sir!"

"Michael!" called out Flurry with apparent irrelevance, "run up to your father's and ask him would he lend me a loan of his side-car."

Half-an-hour later we were, improbable as it may seem, on our way to Lisheen races. We were seated upon an outside-car of immemorial age, whose joints seemed to open and close again as it swung in and out of the ruts, whose tattered cushions stank of rats and mildew, whose wheels staggered and rocked like the legs of a drunken man. Between the shafts jogged the latest addition to the kennel larder, the eight-shilling mare. Flurry sat on one side, and kept her going at a rate of not less than four miles an hour; Leigh Kelway and I held on to the other.

"She'll get us as far as Lynch's anyway," said Flurry, abandoning his first contention that she could do the whole distance, as he pulled her on to her legs after her fifteenth stumble, "and he'll lend us some sort of a horse, if it was only a mule."

"Do you notice that these cushions are very damp?" said Leigh Kelway to me, in a hollow undertone.

"Small blame to them if they are!" replied Flurry. "I've no doubt but they were out under the rain all day yesterday at Mrs. Hurly's funeral."

Leigh Kelway made no reply, but he took his note-book out of his pocket and sat on it.

We arrived at Lynch's at a little past three, and were there confronted by the next disappointment of this disastrous day. The door of Lynch's farmhouse was locked, and nothing replied to our knocking except a puppy, who barked hysterically from within.

"All gone to the races," said Flurry philosophically, picking his way round the manure heap. "No matter, here's the filly in the shed here. I know he's had her under a car."

An agitating ten minutes ensued, during which Leigh Kelway and I got the eight-shilling mare out of the shafts and the harness, and Flurry, with our inefficient help, crammed the young mare into them. As Flurry had stated that she had been driven before, I was bound to believe him, but the difficulty of getting the bit into her mouth was remarkable, and so also was the crab-like manner in which she sidled out of the yard, with Flurry and myself at her head, and Leigh Kelway hanging on to the back of the car to keep it from jamming in the gateway.

"Sit up on the car now," said Flurry when we got out on to the road; "I'll lead her on a bit. She's been ploughed anyway; one side of her mouth's as though as a gad!"

Leigh Kelway threw away the wisp of grass with which he had been cleaning his hands, and mopped his intellectual forehead; he was very silent. We both mounted the car, and Flurry, with the reins in his hand, walked beside the filly, who, with her tail clasped in, moved onward in a succession of short jerks.

"Oh, she's all right!" said Flurry, beginning to run, and dragging the filly into a trot; "once she gets started——" Here the filly spied a pig in a neigh-bouring field, and despite the fact that she had probably eaten out of the same trough with it, she gave a violent side spring, and broke into a gallop.

"Now we're off!" shouted Flurry, making a jump at the car and clambering on; "if the traces hold we'll do!"

The English language is powerless to suggest the view-halloo with which Mr. Knox ended his speech, or to do more than indicate the rigid anxiety of Leigh Kelway's face as he regained his balance after the pre-liminary jerk, and clutched the back rail. It must be said for Lynch's filly that she did not kick; she merely fled, like a dog with a kettle tied to its tail, from the pursuing rattle and jingle behind her, with the shafts buf-feting her dusty sides as the car swung to and fro. Whenever she showed any signs of slackening, Flurry loosed another yell at her that renewed her panic, and thus we precariously covered another two or three miles of our journey.

Had it not been for a large stone lying on the road, and had the filly not chosen to swerve so as to bring the wheel on top of it, I dare say we might have got to the races; but by an unfortunate coincidence both these things occurred, and when we recovered from the consequent shock, the tire of one of the wheels had come off, and was trundling with cumbrous gaiety into the ditch. Flurry stopped the filly and began to laugh; Leigh Kelway said something startlingly unparliamentary under his breath.

"Well, it might be worse," Flurry said consolingly as he lifted the tire on to the car; "we're not half a mile from a forge."

We walked that half-mile in funereal procession behind the car; the glory had departed from the weather, and an ugly wall of cloud was ris-ing up out of the west to meet the sun; the hills had darkened and lost colour, and the white bog cotton shivered in a cold wind that smelt of rain.

By a miracle the smith was not at the races, owing, as he explained, to his having "the toothaches," the two facts combined producing in him a morosity only equalled by that of Leigh Kelway. The smith's sole com-ment on the situation was to unharness the filly, and drag her into the forge, where he tied her up. He then proceeded to whistle viciously on his fingers in the direction of a cottage, and to command, in tones of thunder, some unseen creature to bring over a couple of baskets of turf. The turf arrived in process of time, on a woman's back, and was arranged in a circle in a yard at the back of the forge. The tire was bedded in it, and the turf was with difficulty kindled at different points.

"Ye'll not get to the races this day," said the smith, yielding to a sar-donic satisfaction; "the turf's wet, and I haven't one to do a hand's turn for me." He laid the wheel on the ground and lit his pipe.

Leigh Kelway looked pallidly about him over the spacious empty land-scape of brown mountain slopes patched with golden furze and seamed with grey walls; I wondered if he were as hungry as I. We sat on stones opposite the smouldering ring of turf and smoked, and Flurry beguiled the smith into grim and calumnious confidences about every horse in the country. After about an hour, during which the turf went out three times, and the weather became more and more threatening, a girl with a red petticoat over her head appeared at the gate of the yard, and said to the smith:

"The horse is gone away from ye."

"Where?" exclaimed Flurry, springing to his feet.

"I met him walking wesht the road there below, and when I thought to turn him he commenced to gallop."

"Pulled her head out of the headstall," said Flurry, after a rapid survey of the forge. "She's near home by now."

It was at this moment that the rain began; the situation could scarcely have been better stage-managed. After reviewing the position, Flurry and I decided that the only thing to do was to walk to a public-house a couple of miles farther on, feed there if possible, hire a car, and go home.

It was an uphill walk, with mild generous raindrops striking thicker and thicker on our faces; no one talked, and the grey clouds crowded up from behind the hills like billows of steam. Leigh Kelway bore it all with egregious resignation. I cannot pretend that I was at heart sympathetic, but by virtue of being his host I felt responsible for the breakdown, for his light suit, for everything, and divined his sentiment of horror at the first sight of the public-house.

It was a long, low cottage, with a line of dripping elm-trees overshadowing it; empty cars and carts round its door, and a babel from within made it evident that the racegoers were pursuing a gradual homeward route. The shop was crammed with steaming countrymen, whose loud brawling voices, all talking together, roused my English friend to his first remark since we had left the forge.

"Sure, Yeates, we are not going into that place?" he said severely; "those men are all drunk."

"Ah, nothing to signify!" said Flurry, plunging in and driving his way through the throng like a plough. "Here, Mary Kate!" he called to the girl behind the counter, "tell your mother we want some tea and bread and butter in the room inside."

The smell of bad tobacco and spilt porter was choking; we worked our way through it after him towards the end of the shop, intersecting at every hand discussions about the races.

"Tom was very nice. He spared his horse all along, and then he put into him—""Well, at Goggin's corner the third horse was before the second, but he was goin' wake in himself." "I tell ye the mare had the hind leg fasht in the fore." "Clancy was dipping in the saddle." "'Twas a dam nice race whatever—"

We gained the inner room at last, a cheerless apartment, adorned with sacred pictures, a sewing-machine, and an array of supplementary tumblers and wineglasses; but, at all events, we had it so far to ourselves. At intervals during the next half-hour Mary Kate burst in with cups and plates, cast them on the table and disappeared, but of food there was no sign. After a further period of starvation and of listening to the noise in the shop, Flurry made a sortie, and, after lengthy and unknown adventures, reappeared carrying a huge brown teapot, and driving before him Mary Kate with the remainder of the repast. The bread tasted of mice, the butter of turf-smoke, the tea of brown paper, but we had got past the critical stage. I had entered upon my third round of bread and butter when the door was flung open, and my valued acquaintance, Slipper, slightly advanced in liquor, presented himself to our gaze. His bandy legs sprawled consequently, his nose was redder than a coal of fire, his prominent eyes rolled crookedly upon us, and his left hand swept behind him the attempt of Mary Kate to frustrate his entrance.

"Good-evening to my vinerable friend, Mr. Flurry Knox!" he began, in the voice of a town crier, "and to the Honourable Major Yeates, and the English gintleman!"

This impressive opening immediately attracted an audience from the shop, and the doorway filled with grinning faces as Slipper advanced farther into the room.

"Why weren't ye at the races, Mr. Flurry?" he went on, his roving eye taking a grip of us all at the same time; "sure the Miss Bennetts and all the ladies was asking where were ye."

"It'd take some time to tell them that," said Flurry, with his mouth full; "but what about the races, Slipper? Had you good sport?"

"Sport is it? Divil so pleasant an afternoon ever you seen," replied Slipper. He leaned against a side table, and all the glasses on it jingled. "Does your honour know O'Driscoll?" he went on irrelevantly. "Sure you do. He was in your honour's stable. It's what we were all sayin'; it was a great pity your honour was not there, for the likin' you had to Driscoll."

"That's thrue," said a voice at the door.

"There wasn't one in the Barony but was gethered in it, through and fro," continued Slipper, with a quelling glance at the interrupter; "and there was tints for sellin' porther, and whisky as pliable as new milk, and boys goin' round the tints outside, feeling for heads with the big ends of their blackthorns, and all kinds of recreations, and the Sons of Liberty's piffler and dhrum band from Skebawn; though faith! there was more of thim runnin' to look at the races than what was playin' in it; not to mintion different occasions that the bandmasther was atin' his lunch within in the whisky tint."

"But what about Driscoll?" said Flurry.

"Sure it's about him I'm tellin' ye," replied Slipper, with the practised orator's watchful eye on his growing audience. "'Twas within in the same whisky tint meself was, with the bandmasther and a few of the lads, an' we buyin' a ha'porth o' crackers, when I seen me brave Driscoll landin' into the tint, and a pair o' thim long boots on him; him that hadn't a shoe nor a stocking to his foot when your honour had him picking grass out o' the stones behind in your yard. 'Well,' says I to meself, 'we'll knock some spoort out of Driscoll!'

"'Come here to me, acushla!' says I to him; 'I suppose it's some way wake in the legs y'are,' says I, 'an' the docthor put them on ye the way the people wouldn't thrample ye!'

"'May the divil choke ye!' says he, pleasant enough, but I knew by the blush he had he was vexed.

"'Then I suppose 'tis a left-tenant colonel y'are,' says I; 'yer mother must be proud out o' ye!' says I, 'an' maybe ye'll lend her a loan o' thim waders when she's rinsin' yer bauneen in the river!' says I.

"'There'll be work out o' this!' says he, lookin' at me both sour and bitther.

"'Well indeed, I was thinkin' you were blue moulded for want of a batin',' says I. He was for fightin' us then, but afther we had him pacificated with about a quarther of a naggin o' sperrits, he told us he was goin' ridin' in a race.

"'An' what'll ye ride?' says I.

"'Owld Bocock's mare,' says he.

"'Knipes!' says I, sayin' a great curse; 'is it that little staggeen from the mountains; sure she's somethin' about the one age with meself,' says I. 'Many's the time Jamesy Geoghegan and meself used to be dhrivin' her to Macroom with pigs an' all soorts,' says I; 'an' is it leppin' stone walls ye want her to go now?'

"'Faith, there's walls and every vari'ty of obstackle in it,' says he.

"'It'll be the best o' your play, so,' says I, 'to leg it away home out o' this.'

"'An' who'll ride her, so?' says he.

"'Let the divil ride her,' says I."

Leigh Kelway, who had been leaning back seemingly half asleep, obeyed the hypnotism of Slipper's gaze, and opened his eyes.

"That was now all the conversation that passed between himself and meself," resumed Slipper, "and there was no great delay afther that till they said there was a race startin' and the dickens a one at all was goin' to ride only two, Driscoll, and one Clancy. With that then I seen Mr. Kinahane, the Petty Sessions clerk, goin' round clearin' the coorse, an' I gethered a few o' the neighbours, an' we walked the fields hither and over till we seen the most of th' obstackles.

"'Stand aisy now by the plantation,' says I; 'if they get to come as far as this, believe me ye'll see spoort,' says I, 'an' 'twill be a convanient spot to encourage the mare if she's anyway wake in herself,' says I, cuttin' somethin' about five foot of an ash sapling out o' the plantation.

"'That's yer sort!' says owld Bocock, that was thravellin' the racecoorse, peggin' a bit o' paper down with a thorn in front of every lep, the way Driscoll 'd know the handiest place to face her at it.

"Well, I hadn't barely thrimmed the ash plant—"

"Have you any jam, Mary Kate?" interrupted Flurry, whose meal had been in no way interfered with by either the story or the highly-scented crowd who had come to listen to it.

"We have no jam, only thraycle, sir," replied the invisible Mary Kate.

"I hadn't the switch barely thrimmed," repeated Slipper firmly, "when I heard the people screechin', an' I seen Driscoll an' Clancy comin' on, leppin' all before them, an' owld Bocock's mare bellusin' an' powdherin' along, an' bedad! whatever obstackle wouldn't throw *her* down, faith, she'd throw *it* down, an' there's the thraffic they had in it.

"'I declare to me sowl,' says I, 'if they continue on this way there's a great chance some one o' thim 'll win,' says I.

"'Ye lie!' says the bandmasther, bein' a thrifle fulsome after his luncheon.

"'I do not,' says I, 'in regard of seein' how soople them two boys is. Ye might observe,' says I, 'that if they have no convanient way to sit on the saddle, they'll ride the neck o' the horse till such time as they gets an occasion to lave it,' says I.

"'Arrah, shut yer mouth!' says the bandmasther; 'they're puckin' out this way now, an' may the divil admire me!' says he, 'but Clancy has the other bet out, and the divil such leatherin' and beltin' of owld Bocock's mare ever you seen as what's in it!' says he.

"Well, when I seen them comin' to me, and Driscoll about the length of the plantation behind Clancy, I let a couple of bawls.

"'Skelp her, ye big brute!' says I. 'What good's in ye that ye aren't able to skelp her?'"

The yell and the histrionic flourish of his stick with which Slipper delivered this incident brought down the house. Leigh Kelway was sufficiently moved to ask me in an undertone if "skelp" was a local term.

"Well, Mr. Flurry, and gintlemen," recommenced Slipper, "I declare to ye when owld Bocock's mare heard thim roars she sthretched out her neck like a gandher, and when she passed me out she give a couple of grunts, and looked at me as ugly as a Christian.

"'Hah!' says I, givin' her a couple o' dhraws o' th' ash plant across the butt o' the tail, the way I wouldn't blind her; 'I'll make ye grunt!' says I, 'I'll nourish ye!'

"I knew well she was very frightful of th' ash plant since the winter Tommeen Sullivan had her under a sidecar. But now, in place of havin' any obligations to me, ye'd be surprised if ye heard the blaspheemious expressions of that young boy that was ridin' her; and whether it was over-anxious he was, turnin' around the way I'd hear him cursin', or whether it was some slither or slide came to owld Bocock's mare, I dunno, but she was bet up agin the last obstackle but two, and before ye could say 'Schnipes,' she was standin' on her two ears beyond in th' other field! I declare to ye, on the vartue of me oath, she stood that way till she reconnoithered what side would Driscoll fall, an' she turned about then and rolled on him as cosy as if he was meadow grass!"

Slipper stopped short; the people in the doorway groaned appreciatively; Mary Kate murmured "The Lord save us!"

"The blood was dhruv out through his nose and ears," continued Slipper, with a voice that indicated the cream of the narration, "and you'd hear his bones crackin' on the ground! You'd have pitied the poor boy."

"Good heavens!" said Leigh Kelway, sitting up very straight in his chair.

"Was he hurt, Slipper?" asked Flurry casually.

"Hurt is it?" echoed Slipper in high scorn; "killed on the spot!" He paused to relish the effect of the *dénouement* on Leigh Kelway. "Oh, divil so pleasant an afthernoon ever you seen; and indeed, Mr. Flurry, it's what we were all sayin', it was a great pity your honour was not there for the likin' you had for Driscoll."

As he spoke the last word there was an outburst of singing and cheering from a car-load of people who had just pulled up at the door. Flurry listened, leaned back in his chair, and began to laugh.

"It scarcely strikes one as a comic incident," said Leigh Kelway, very coldly to me; "in fact, it seems to me that the police ought—"

"Show me Slipper!" bawled a voice in the shop; "show me that dirty little undherlooper till I have his blood! Hadn't I the race won only for he souring the mare on me! What's that you say? I tell ye he did! He left seven slaps on her with the handle of a hay-rake—"

There was in the room in which we were sitting a second door, leading to the back yard, a door consecrated to the unobtrusive visits of so-called "Sunday travellers." Through it Slipper faded away like a dream, and, simultaneously, a tall young man, with a face like a red-hot potato tied up in a bandage, squeezed his way from the shop into the room.

"Well, Driscoll," said Flurry, "since it wasn't the teeth of the rake he left on the mare, you needn't be talking!"

Leigh Kelway looked from one to the other with a wilder expression in his eye than I had thought it capable of. I read in it a resolve to abandon Ireland to her fate.

At eight o'clock we were still waiting for the car that we had been assured should be ours directly it returned from the races. At half-past eight we had adopted the only possible course that remained, and had accepted the offers of lifts on the laden cars that were returning to Skebawn, and I presently was gratified by the spectacle of my friend Leigh Kelway wedged between a roulette table and its proprietor on one side of a car, with Driscoll and Slipper, mysteriously reconciled and excessively drunk, seated, locked in each other's arms, on the other. Flurry and I, somewhat similarly placed, followed on two other cars. I was scarcely surprised when I was informed that the melancholy white animal in the shafts of the leading car was Owld Bocock's much-enduring steeplechaser.

The night was very dark and stormy, and it is almost superfluous to say that no one carried lamps; the rain poured upon us, and through wind and wet Owld Bocock's mare set the pace at a rate that showed she knew from bitter experience what was expected from her by gentlemen who had spent the evening in a public-house; behind her the other two tired horses followed closely, incited to emulation by shouting, singing, and a liberal allowance of whip. We were a good ten miles from Skebawn, and never had the road seemed so long. For mile after mile the half-seen low walls slid past us, with occasional plunges into caverns of darkness under trees. Sometimes from a wayside cabin a dog would dash out to bark at us as we rattled by; sometimes our cavalcade swung aside to pass, with yells and counter-yells, crawling carts filled with other belated race-goers.

I was nearly wet through, even though I received considerable shelter from a Skebawn publican, who slept heavily and irrepressibly on my shoulder. Driscoll, on the leading car, had struck up an approximation to the "Wearing of the Green," when a wavering star appeared on the road ahead of us. It grew momently larger; it came towards us apace. Flurry, on the car behind me, shouted suddenly—

"That's the mail car, with one of the lamps out! Tell those fellows ahead to look out!"

But the warning fell on deaf ears.

> "When laws can change the blades of grass
>   From growing as they grow—"

howled five discordant voices, oblivious of the towering proximity of the star.

A Bianconi mail car is nearly three times the size of an ordinary outside car, and when on a dark night it advances, Cyclops-like, with but one eye, it is difficult for even a sober driver to calculate its bulk. Above the sounds of melody there arose the thunder of heavy wheels, the splashing trample of three big horses, then a crash and a turmoil of shouts. Our cars pulled up just in time, and I tore myself from the embrace of my publican to go to Leigh Kelway's assistance.

The wing of the Bianconi had caught the wing of the smaller car, flinging Owld Bocock's mare on her side and throwing her freight head-long on top of her, the heap being surmounted by the roulette table. The driver of the mail car unshipped his solitary lamp and turned it on the disaster. I saw that Flurry had already got hold of Leigh Kelway by the heels, and was dragging him from under the others. He struggled up hatless, muddy, and gasping, with Driscoll hanging on by his neck, still singing the "Wearing of the Green."

A voice from the mail car said incredulously, *"Leigh Kelway!"* A spec-tacled face glared down upon him from under the dripping spikes of an umbrella.

It was the Right Honourable the Earl of Waterbury, Leigh Kelway's chief, returning from his fishing excursion.

Meanwhile Slipper, in the ditch, did not cease to announce that "Divil so pleasant an afthernoon ever ye seen as what was in it!"

THE ONLY SON OF AOIFE

Isabella Augusta, Lady Gregory

THE time Cuchulain came back from Alban, after he had learned the use of arms under Scathach, he left Aoife, the queen he had overcome in battle, with child.

And when he was leaving her, he told her what name to give the child, and he gave her a gold ring, and bade her keep it safe till the child grew to be a lad, and till his thumb would fill it; and he bade her to give it to him then, and to send him to Ireland, and he would know he was his son by that token. She promised to do so, and with that Cuchulain went back to Ireland.

It was not long after the child was born, word came to Aoife that Cuchulain had taken Emer to be his wife in Ireland. When she heard that, great jealousy came on her, and great anger, and her love for Cuchulain was turned to hatred; and she remembered her three champions that he had killed, and how he had overcome herself, and she determined in her mind that when her son would come to have the strength of a man, she would get her revenge through him. She told Conlaoch her son nothing of this, but brought him up like any king's son; and when he was come to sensible years, she put him under the teaching of Scathach, to be taught the use of arms and the art of war. He turned out as apt a scholar as his father, and it was not long before he had learnt all Scathach had to teach.

Then Aoife gave him the arms of a champion, and bade him go to Ireland, but first she laid three commands on him: the first never to give way to any living person, but to die sooner than be made turn back; the second, not to refuse a challenge from the greatest champion alive, but to fight him at all risks, even if he was sure to lose his life; the third, not to tell his name on any account, though he might be threatened with death

112

for hiding it. She put him under *geasa,* that is, under bonds, not to do these things.

Then the young man, Conlaoch, set out, as it was not long before his ship brought him to Ireland, and the place he landed at was Baile's Strand, near Dundealgan.

It chanced that at that time Conchubar, the High King, was holding his court there, for it was a convenient gathering-place for his chief men, and they were settling some business that belonged to the government of that district.

When word was brought to Conchubar that there was a ship come to the strand, and a young lad in it armed as if for fighting, and armed men with him, he sent one of the chief men of his household to ask his name, and on what business he was come.

The messenger's name was Cuinaire, and he went down to the strand, and when he saw the young man he said: "A welcome to you, young hero from the east, with the merry face. It is likely, seeing you come armed as if for fighting, you are gone astray on your journey; but as you are come to Ireland, tell me your name and what your deeds have been, and your victories in the eastern bounds of the world."

"As to my name," said Conlaoch, "it is of no great account; but whatever it is, I am under bonds not to tell it to the stoutest man living."

"It is best for you to tell it at the king's desire," said Cuinaire, "before you get your death through refusing it, as many a champion from Alban and from Britain has done before now." "If that is the order you put on us when we land here, it is I will break it," said Conlaoch, "and no one will obey it any longer from this out."

So Cuinaire went back and told the king what the young lad had said. Then Conchubar said to his people: "Who will go out into the field, and drag the name and the story out of this young man?" "I will go," said Conall, for his hand was never slow in fighting. And he went out, and found the lad angry and destroying, handling his arms, and they attacked one another with a great noise of swords and shouts, and they were gripped together, and fought for a while, and then Conall was overcome, and the great name and the praise that was on Conall, it was on the head of Conlaoch it was now.

Word was sent then to where Cuchulain was, in pleasant, bright-faced Dundealgan. And the messenger told him the whole story, and he said: "Conall is lying humbled, and it is slow the help is in coming; it is a welcome there would be before the Hound."

Cuchulain rose up then and went to where Conlaoch was, and he still handling his arms. And Cuchulain asked him his name and said: "It would be well for you, young hero of unknown name, to loosen yourself from this knot, and not to bring down my hand upon you, for it will be hard for you to escape death." But Conlaoch said: "If I put you down in the fight, the way I put down your comrade, there will be a great name on me; but if I draw back now, there will be mockery on me, and it will be said I was afraid of the fight. I will never give in to any man to tell the name, or to give an account of myself. But if I was not held with a command," he said, "there is no man in the world I would sooner give it to than to yourself, since I saw your face. But do not think, brave champion of Ireland, that I will let you take away the fame I have won, for nothing."

With that they fought together, and it is seldom such a battle was seen, and all wondered that the young lad could stand so well against Cuchulain.

So they fought a long while, neither getting the better of the other, but at last Cuchulain was charged so hotly by the lad that he was forced to give way, and although he had fought so many good fights, and killed so many great champions, and understood the use of arms better than any man living, he was pressed very hard.

And he called for the Gae Bulg, and his anger came on him, and the flames of the hero-light began to shine about his head, and by that sign Conlaoch knew him to be Cuchulain, his father. And just at that time he was aiming his spear at him, and when he knew it was Cuchulain, he threw his spear crooked that it might pass beside him. But Cuchulain threw his spear, the Gae Bulg, at him with all his might, and it struck the lad in the side and went into his body, so that he fell to the ground.

And Cuchulain said: "Now, boy, tell your name and what you are, for it is short your life will be, for you will not live after that wound."

And Conlaoch showed the ring that was on his hand, and he said: "Come here where I am lying on the field, let my men from the east come round me. I am suffering for revenge. I am Conlaoch, son of the Hound, heir of dear Dundealgan; I was bound to this secret in Dun Scathach, the secret in which I have found my grief."

And Cuchulain said: "It is a pity your mother not to be here to see you brought down. She might have stretched out her hand to stop the spear that wounded you." And Conlaoch said: "My curse be on my mother, for it was she put me under bonds; it was she sent me here to try my strength against yours." And Cuchulain said: "My curse be on your mother, the woman that is full of treachery; it is through her harmful thoughts these tears have been brought on us." And Conlaoch said: "My name was never forced from my mouth till now; I never gave an account of myself to any man under the sun. But, O Cuchulain of the sharp sword, it was a pity you not to know me the time I threw the slanting spear behind you in the fight."

And then the sorrow of death came upon Conlaoch, and Cuchulain took his sword and put it through him, sooner than leave him in the pain and the punishment he was in.

And then great trouble and anguish came on Cuchulain, and he made this complaint:

"It is a pity it is, O son of Aoife, that ever you came into the province of Ulster, that you ever met with the Hound of Cuailgne.

"If I and my fair Conlaoch were doing feats of war on the one side, the men of Ireland from sea to sea would not be equal to us together. It is no wonder I to be under grief when I see the shield and the arms of Conlaoch. A pity it is there is no one at all, a pity there are not hundreds of men on whom I could get satisfaction for his death.

"If it was the king himself had hurt your fair body, it is I would have shortened his days.

"It is well for the House of the Red Branch, and for the heads of its fair army of heroes, it was not they that killed my only son.

"It is well for Laegaire of Victories it is not from him you got your heavy pain.

"It is well for the heroes of Conall they did not join in the killing of you; it is well that travelling across the plain of Macha they did not fall in with me after such a fight.

"It is well for the tall, well-shaped Forbuide; well for Dubthach, your Black Beetle of Ulster.

"It is well for you, Cormac Conloingeas, your share of arms gave no help, that it is not from your weapons he got his wound, the hard-skinned shield or the blade.

"It is a pity it was not one of the plains of Munster, or in Leinster of the sharp blades, or at Cruachan of the rough fighters, that struck down my comely Conlaoch.

"It is a pity it was not in the country of the Cruithne, of the fierce Fians, you fell in a heavy quarrel, or in the country of the Greeks, or in some other place of the world, you died, and I could avenge you.

"Or in Spain, or in Sorcha, or in the country of the Saxons of the free armies; there would not then be this death in my heart.

"It is very well for the men of Alban it was not they that destroyed your fame; and it is well for the men of the Gall.

"Och! It is bad that it happened; my grief! it is on me is the misfortune, O Conlaoch of the Red Spear, I myself to have spilled your blood.

"I to be under defeat, without strength. It is a pity Aoife never taught you to know the power of my strength in the fight.

"It is no wonder I to be blinded after such a fight and such a defeat.

"It is no wonder I to be tired out, and without the sons of Usnach beside me.

"Without a son, without a brother, with none to come after me; without Conlaoch, without a name to keep my strength.

"To be without Naoise, without Ainnle, without Ardan; is it not with me is my fill of trouble?

"I am the father that killed his son, the fine green branch; there is no hand or shelter to help me.

"I am a raven that has no home; I am a boat going from wave to wave; I am a ship that has lost its rudder; I am the apple left on the tree; it is little I thought of falling from it; grief and sorrow will be with me from this time."

Then Cuchulain stood up and faced all the men of Ulster. "There is trouble on Cuchulain," said Conchubar; "he is after killing his own son, and if I and all my men were to go against him, by the end of the day he would destroy every man of us. Go now," he said to Cathbad, the Druid, "and bind him to go down to Baile's Strand, and to give three days fighting against the waves of the sea, rather than to kill us all."

So Cathbad put an enchantment on him, and bound him to go down. And when he came to the strand, there was a great white stone before him, and he took his sword in his right hand, and he said: "If I had the head of the woman that sent her son to his death, I would split it as I split this stone." And he made four quarters of the stone.

Then he fought with the waves three days and three nights, till he fell from hunger and weakness, so that some men said he got his death there. But it was not there he got his death, but on the plain of Muirthemne.

HOME SICKNESS

George Moore

HE told the doctor he was due in the bar-room at eight o'clock in the morning; the bar-room was in a slum in the Bowery; and he had only been able to keep himself in health by getting up at five o'clock and going for long walks in the Central Park.

"A sea voyage is what you want," said the doctor. "Why not go to Ireland for two or three months? You will come back a new man."

"I'd like to see Ireland again."

And then he began to wonder how the people at home were getting on. The doctor was right. He thanked him, and three weeks afterwards he landed in Cork.

As he sat in the railway carriage he recalled his native village—he could see it and its lake, and then the fields one by one, and the roads. He could see a large piece of rocky land—some three or four hundred acres of headland stretching out into the winding lake. Upon this headland the peasantry had been given permission to build their cabins by former owners of the Georgian house standing on the pleasant green hill. The present owners considered the village a disgrace, but the villagers paid high rents for their plots of ground, and all the manual labour that the Big House required came from the village: the gardeners, the stable helpers, the house and the kitchen maids.

He had been thirteen years in America, and when the train stopped at his station, he looked round to see if there were any changes in it. It was just the same blue limestone station-house as it was thirteen years ago. The platform and the sheds were the same, and there were five miles of road from the station to Duncannon. The sea voyage had done him good, but five miles were too far for him to-day; the last time he had walked the road, he had walked it in an hour and a half, carrying a heavy bundle on a stick.

He was sorry he did not feel strong enough for the walk; the evening was fine, and he would meet many people coming home from the fair, some of whom he had known in his youth, and they would tell him where he could get a clean lodging. But the carman would be able to tell him that; he called the car that was waiting at the station, and soon he was answering questions about America. But Bryden wanted to hear of those who were still living in the old country, and after hearing the stories of many people he had forgotten, he heard that Mike Scully, who had been away in a situation for many years as a coachman in the King's County, had come back and built a fine house with a concrete floor. Now there was a good loft in Mike Scully's house, and Mike would be pleased to take in a lodger.

Bryden remembered that Mike had been in a situation at the Big House; he had intended to be a jockey, but had suddenly shot up into a fine tall man, and had had to become a coachman instead. Bryden tried to recall the face, but he could only remember a straight nose, and a somewhat dusky complexion. Mike was one of the heroes his childhood, and his youth floated before him, and he caught glimpses of himself, something that was more than a phantom and less than a reality. Suddenly his reverie was broken: the carman pointed with his whip, and Bryden saw a tall, finely-built, middle-aged man coming through the gates, and the driver said:—

"There's Mike Scully."

Mike had forgotten Bryden even more completely than Bryden had forgotten him, and many aunts and uncles were mentioned before he began to understand.

"You've grown into a fine man, James," he said, looking at Bryden's great width of chest. "But you are thin in the cheeks, and you're sallow in the cheeks too."

"I haven't been very well lately—that is one of the reasons I have come back; but I want to see you all again."

Bryden paid the carman, wished him "God-speed," and he and Mike divided the luggage between them, Mike carrying the bag and Bryden the bundle, and they walked round the lake, for the townland was at the back of the demesne; and while they walked, James proposed to pay Mike ten shillings a week for his board and lodging.

He remembered the woods thick and well-forested; now they were windworn, the drains were choked, and the bridge leading across the lake inlet was falling away. Their way led between long fields where herds of cattle were grazing; the road was broken—Bryden wondered how the villagers drove their carts over it, and Mike told him that the landlord could not keep it in repair, and he would not allow it to be kept in repair out of the rates, for then it would be a public road, and he did not think there should be a public road through his property.

At the end of many fields they came to the village, and it looked a desolate place, even on this fine evening, and Bryden remarked that the county did not seem to be as much lived in as it used to be. It was at once strange and familiar to see the chickens in the kitchen; and, wishing to re-knit himself to the old habits, he begged of Mrs. Scully not to drive them out, saying he did not mind them. Mike told his wife that Bryden was born in Duncannon, and when he mentioned Bryden's name she gave him her hand, after wiping it in her apron, saying he was heartily welcome, only she was afraid he would not care to sleep in a loft.

"Why wouldn't I sleep in a loft, a dry loft! You're thinking a good deal of America over here," said he, "but I reckon it isn't all you think it. Here you work when you like and you sit down when you like; but when you have had a touch of blood-poisoning as I had, and when you have seen young people walking with a stick, you think that there is something to be said for old Ireland."

"Now won't you be taking a sup of milk? You'll be wanting a drink after travelling," said Mrs. Scully.

And when he had drunk the milk Mike asked him if he would like to go inside or if he would like to go for a walk.

"Maybe it is sitting down you would like to be."

And they went into the cabin, and started to talk about the wages a man could get in America, and the long hours of work.

And after Bryden had told Mike everything about America that he thought would interest him, he asked Mike about Ireland. But Mike did not seem to be able to tell him much that was of interest. They were all very poor—poorer, perhaps, than when he left them.

"I don't think anyone except myself has a five pound note to his name."

Bryden hoped he felt sufficiently sorry for Mike. But after all Mike's life and prospects mattered little to him. He had come back in search of health; and he felt better already; the milk had done him good, and the bacon and cabbage in the pot sent forth a savoury odour. The Scullys were very kind, they pressed him to make a good meal; a few weeks of country air and food, they said, would give him back the health he had lost in the Bowery; and when Bryden said he was longing for a smoke, Mike said there was no better sign than that. During his long illness he had never wanted to smoke, and he was a confirmed smoker.

It was comfortable to sit by the mild peat fire watching the smoke of their pipes drifting up the chimney, and all Bryden wanted was to be let alone; he did not want to hear of anyone's misfortunes, but about nine o'clock a number of villagers came in, and their appearance was depressing. Bryden remembered one or two of them—he used to know them very well when he was a boy; their talk was as depressing as their appearance, and he could feel no interest whatever in them. He was not moved when he heard that Higgins the stone-mason was dead; he was not affected when he heard that Mary Kelly, who used to go to do the laundry at the Big House, had married; he was only interested when he heard she had gone to America. No, he had not met her there, America is a big place. Then one of the peasants asked him if he remembered Patsy Carabine, who used to do the gardening at the Big House. Yes, he remembered Patsy well. Patsy was in the poor-house. He had not been able to do any work on account of his arm; his house had fallen in; he had given up his holding and gone into the poor-house. All this was very sad, and to avoid hearing any further unpleasantness, Bryden began to tell them about America. And they sat round listening to him; but all the talking was on his side; he wearied of it; and looking round the group he recognised a ragged hunchback with grey hair; twenty years ago he was a young hunchback, and, turning to him, Bryden asked him if he were doing well with his five acres.

"Ah, not much. This has been a bad season. The potatoes failed; they were watery—there is no diet in them."

These peasants were all agreed that they could make nothing out of their farms. Their regret was that they had not gone to America when they were young; and after striving to take an interest in the fact that O'Connor had lost a mare and foal worth forty pounds Bryden began to wish himself back in the slum. And when they left the house he wondered if every evening would be like the present one. Mike piled fresh sods on the fire, and he hoped it would show enough light in the loft for Bryden to undress himself by.

The cackling of some geese in the road kept him awake, and the loneliness of the country seemed to penetrate to his bones, and to freeze the marrow in them. There was a bat in the loft—a dog howled in the distance—and then he drew the clothes over his head. Never had he been so unhappy, and the sound of Mike breathing by his wife's side in the kitchen added to his nervous terror. Then he dozed a little; and lying on his back he dreamed he was awake, and the men he had seen sitting round the fireside that evening seemed to him like spectres come out of some unknown region of morass and reedy tarn. He stretched out his hands for his clothes, determined to fly from this house, but remembering the lonely road that led to the station he fell back on his pillow. The geese still cackled, but he was too tired to be kept awake any longer. He seemed to have been asleep only a few minutes when he heard Mike calling him. Mike had come half way up the ladder and was telling him that breakfast was ready. "What kind of breakfast will he give me?" Bryden asked himself as he pulled on his clothes. There were tea and hot griddle cakes for breakfast, and there were fresh eggs; there was sunlight in the kitchen and he liked to hear Mike tell of the work he was going to do in the fields. Mike rented a farm of about fifteen acres, at least ten of it was grass; he grew an acre of potatoes and some corn, and some turnips for his sheep. He had a nice bit of meadow, and he took down his scythe, and as he put the whetstone in his belt Bryden noticed a second scythe, and he asked Mike if he should go down with him and help him to finish the field.

"You haven't done any mowing this many a year; I don't think you'd be of much help. You'd better go for a walk by the lake, but you may come in the afternoon if you like and help to turn the grass over."

Bryden was afraid he would find the lake shore very lonely, but the magic of returning health is the sufficient distraction for the convalescent, and the morning passed agreeably. The weather was still and sunny. He could hear the ducks in the reeds. The hours dreamed themselves away, and it became his habit to go to the lake every morning. One morning he met the landlord, and they walked together, talking of the country, of what it had been, and the ruin it was slipping into. James Bryden told him that ill health had brought him back to Ireland; and the landlord lent him his boat, and Bryden rowed about the islands, and resting upon his oars he looked at the old castles, and remembered the prehistoric raiders that the landlord had told him about. He came across the stones to which the lake dwellers had tied their boats, and these signs of ancient Ireland were pleasing to Bryden in his present mood.

As well as the great lake there was a smaller lake in the bog where the villagers cut their turf. This lake was famous for its pike, and the landlord allowed Bryden to fish there, and one evening when he was looking for a frog with which to bait his line he met Margaret Dirken driving home the cows for the milking. Margaret was the herdsman's daughter, and she lived in a cottage near the Big House; but she came up to the village whenever there was a dance, and Bryden had found himself opposite to her in the reels. But until this evening he had had little opportunity of speaking to her, and he was glad to speak to someone, for the evening was lonely, and they stood talking together.

"You're getting your health again," she said. "You'll soon be leaving us."

"I'm in no hurry."

"You're grand people over there; I hear a man is paid four dollars a day for his work."

"And how much," said James, "has he to pay for his food and for his clothes?"

Her cheeks were bright and her teeth small, white and beautifully even; and a woman's soul looked at Bryden out of her soft Irish eyes. He was troubled and turned aside, and catching sight of a frog looking at him out of a tuft of grass he said:—

"I have been looking for a frog to put upon my pike line."

The frog jumped right and left, and nearly escaped in some bushes, but he caught it and returned with it in his hand.

"It is just the kind of frog a pike will like," he said. "Look at its great white belly and its bright yellow back."

And without more ado he pushed the wire to which the hook was fastened through the frog's fresh body, and dragging it through the mouth he passed the hooks through the hind legs and tied the line to the end of the wire.

"I think," said Margaret, "I must be looking after my cows; it's time I got them home."

"Won't you come down to the lake while I set my line?"

She thought for a moment and said:—

"No, I'll see you from here."

He went down to the reedy tarn, and at his approach several snipe got up, and they flew above his head uttering sharp cries. His fishing-rod was a long hazel stick, and he threw the frog as far as he could into the lake. In doing this he roused some wild ducks; a mallard and two ducks go up, and they flew towards the larger lake. Margaret watched them; they flew in a line with an old castle; and they had not disappeared from view when Bryden came towards her, and he and she drove the cows home together that evening.

They had not met very often when she said, "James, you had better not come here so often calling to me."

"Don't you wish to me to come?"

"Yes, I wish you to come well enough, but keeping company is not the custom of the country, and I don't want to be talked about."

"Are you afraid the priest would speak against us from the altar?"

"He has spoken against keeping company, but it is not so much what the priest says, for there is no harm in talking."

"But if you are going to be married there is no harm in walking out together."

"Well, not so much, but marriages are made differently in these parts; there is not much courting here."

And next day it was known in the village that James was going to marry Margaret Dirken.

His desire to exel the boys in dancing had aroused much gaiety in the parish, and for some time past there had been dancing in every house where there was a floor fit to dance upon; and if the cottager had no money to pay for a barrel of beer, James Bryden, who had money, sent him a barrel, so that Margaret might get her dance. She told him that they sometimes crossed over into another parish where the priest was not so averse to dancing, and James wondered. And next morning at Mass he wondered at their simple fervour. Some of them held their hands above their heads as they prayed, and all this was very new and very old to James Bryden. But the obedience of these people to their priest surprised him. When he was a lad they had not been so obedient, or he had forgotten their obedience; and he listened in mixed anger and wonderment to the priest who was scolding his parishioners, speaking to them by name, saying that he had heard there was dancing going on in their homes. Worse than that, he said he had seen boys and girls loitering about the roads, and the talk that went on was of one kind—love. He said that newspapers containing love-stories were finding their way into the people's houses, stories about love, in which there was nothing elevating or ennobling. The people listened, accepting the priest's opinion without question. And their submission was pathetic. It was the submission of a primitive people clinging to religious authority, and Bryden contrasted the weakness and incompetence of the people about him with the modern restlessness and cold energy of the people he had left behind him.

One evening, as they were dancing, a knock came to the door, and the piper stopped playing, and the dancers whispered:—

"Some one has told on us; it is the priest."

And the awe-stricken villagers crowded round the cottage fire, afraid to open the door. But the priest said that if they did not open the door he would put his shoulder to it and force it open. Bryden went towards the door, saying he would allow no one to threaten him, priest or no priest, but Margaret caught his arm and told him that if he said anything to the priest, the priest would speak against them from the altar, and they would be shunned by the neighbours. It was Mike Scully who went to the door and let the priest in, and he came in saying they were dancing their souls into hell.

"I've heard of your goings on," he said—"of your beer-drinking and dancing. I will not have it in my parish. If you want that sort of thing you had better go to America."

"If that is intended for me, sir, I will go back to-morrow. Margaret can follow."

"It isn't the dancing, it's the drinking I'm opposed to," said the priest, turning to Bryden.

"Well, no one has drunk too much, sir," said Bryden.

"But you'll sit here drinking all night," and the priest's eyes went towards the corner where the women had gathered, and Bryden felt that the priest looked on the women as more dangerous than the porter. "It's after midnight," he said, taking out his watch.

By Bryden's watch it was only half-past eleven, and while they were arguing about the time Mrs. Scully offered Bryden's umbrella to the priest, for in his hurry to stop the dancing the priest had gone out without his; and, as if to show Bryden that he bore him no ill-will, the priest accepted the loan of the umbrella, for he was thinking of the big marriage fee that Bryden would pay him.

"I shall be badly off for the umbrella to-morrow," Bryden said, as soon as the priest was out of the house. He was going with his father-in-law to a fair. His father-in-law was learning him how to buy and sell cattle. And his father-in-law was saying that the country was mending, and that a man might become rich in Ireland if he only had a little capital. Bryden had the capital, and Margaret had an uncle on the other side of the lake who would leave her all he had, that would be fifty pounds, and never in the village of Duncannon had a young couple begun life with so much prospect of success as would James Bryden and Margaret Dirken.

Some time after Christmas was spoken of as the best time for the marriage; James Bryden said that he would not be able to get his money out of America before the spring. The delay seemed to vex him, and he seemed anxious to be married, until one day he received a letter from America, from a man who had served in the bar with him. This friend wrote to ask Bryden if he were coming back. The letter was no more than a passing wish to see Bryden again. Yet Bryden stood looking at it, and everyone wondered what could be in the letter. It seemed momentous, and they hardly believed him when he said it was from a friend who wanted to know if his health were better. He tried to forget the letter, and he looked at the worn fields, divided by walls of loose stones, and a great longing came upon him.

The smell of the Bowery slum had come across the Atlantic, and had found him out in this western headland; and one night he awoke from a dream in which he was hurling some drunken customer through the open doors into the darkness. He had seen his friend in his white duck jacket throwing drink from glass into glass amid the din of voices and strange accents; he had heard the clang of money as it was swept into the till, and his sense sickened for the bar-room. But how should he tell Margaret Dirken that he could not marry her? She had built her life upon this marriage. He could not tell he that he would not marry her . . . yet he must go. He felt as if he were being hunted; the thought that he must tell Margaret that he could not marry her hunted him day after day as a weasel hunts a rabbit. Again and again he went to meet her with the intention of telling her that he did not love her, that their lives were not for one another, that it had all been a mistake, and that happily he had found out it was a mistake soon enough. But Margaret, as if she guessed what he was about to speak of, threw her arms about him and begged him to say he loved her, and that they would be married at once. He agreed that he loved her, and that they would be married at once. But he had not left her many minutes before the feeling came upon him that he could not marry her—that he must go away. The smell of the bar-room hunted him down. Was it for the sake of the money that he might make there that he wished to go back? No, it was not the money. What then? His eyes fell on the bleak country, on the little fields divided by bleak walls; he remembered the pathetic ignorance of the people, and it was these things that he could not endure. It was the priest who came to forbid the dancing. Yes, it was the priest. As he stood looking at the line of the hills the bar-room seemed by him. He heard the politicians, and the excitement of politics was in his blood again. He must go away from this place—he must get back to the bar-room. Looking up he saw the scanty orchard, and he hated the spare road that led to the village, and he hated the little hill at the top of which the village began, and he hated more than all other places the house where he was to live with Margaret Dirken—if he married her. He could see it from where he stood—by the edge of the lake, with twenty acres of pasture land about it, for the landlord had given up part of his demesne land to them.

He caught sight of Margaret, and he called to her to come through the stile.

"I have just had a letter from America."

"About the money?" she said.

"Yes, about the money. But I shall have to go over there."

He stood looking at her, seeking for words; and she guessed from his embarrassment that he would say to her that he must go to America before they were married.

"Do you mean, James, you will have to go at once?"

"Yes," he said, "at once. But I shall come back in time to be married in August. It will only mean delaying our marriage a month."

They walked on a little way talking; every step he took James felt that he was a step nearer the Bowery slum. And when they came to the gate Bryden said:—

"I must hasten or I shall miss the train."

"But," she said, "you are not going now—you are not going to-day?"

"Yes, this morning. It is seven miles. I shall have to hurry not to miss the train."

And then she asked him if he would ever come back.

"Yes," he said, "I am coming back."

"If you are coming back, James, why not let me go with you?"

"You could not walk fast enough. We should miss the train."

"One moment, James. Don't make me suffer; tell me the truth. You are not coming back. Your clothes—where shall I send them?"

He hurried away, hoping he would come back. He tried to think that he liked the country he was leaving, that it would be better to have a farmhouse and live there with Margaret Dirken than to serve drinks behind a counter in the Bowery. He did not think he was telling her a lie when he said he was coming back. Her offer to forward his clothes touched his heart, and at the end of the road he stood and asked himself if he should go back to her. He would miss the train if he waited another minute, and he ran on. And he would have missed the train if he had not met a car. Once he was on the car he felt himself safe—the country was already behind him. The train and the boat at Cork were mere formulæ; he was already in America.

The moment he landed he felt the thrill of home that he had not found in his native village, and he wondered how it was that the smell of the bar seemed more natural than the smell of the fields, and the roar of crowds more welcome than the silence of the lake's edge. However, he offered up a thanksgiving for his escape, and entered into negotiations for the purchase of the bar-room.

* * *

He took a wife, she bore him sons and daughters, the bar-room prospered, property came and went; he grew old, his wife died, he retired from business, and reached the age when a man begins to feel there are not many years in front of him, and that all he has had to do in life has been done. His children married, lonesomeness began to creep about him; in the evening, when he looked into the fire-light, a vague, tender reverie floated up, and Margaret's soft eyes and name vivified the dusk. His wife and children passed out of mind, and it seemed to him that a memory was the only real thing he possessed, and the desire to see Margaret again grew intense. But she was an old woman, she had married, maybe she was dead. Well, he would like to be buried in the village where he was born.

There is an unchanging, silent life within every man that none knows but himself, and his unchanging, silent life was his memory of Margaret Dirken. The bar-room was forgotten and all that concerned it, and the things he saw most clearly were the green hillside, and the bog lake and the rushes about it, and the greater lake in the distance, and behind it the blue lines of wandering hills.

THE BLIND MAN

James Stephens

HE was one who would have passed by the Sphinx without seeing it. He did not believe in the necessity for sphinxes, or in their reality, for that matter—they did not exist for him. Indeed, he was one to whom the Sphinx would not have been visible. He might have eyed it and noted a certain bulk of grotesque stone, but nothing more significant.

He was sex-blind, and, so, peculiarly limited by the fact that he could not appreciate women. If he had been pressed for a theory or metaphysic of womanhood he would have been unable to formulate any. Their presence he admitted, perforce: their utility was quite apparent to him on the surface, but, subterraneously, he doubted both their existence and their utility. He might have said perplexedly—Why cannot they do whatever they have to do without being always in the way? He might have said—Hang it, they are everywhere, and what good are they doing? They bothered him, they destroyed his ease when he was near them, and they spoke a language which he did not understand and did not want to understand. But as his limitations did not press on him neither did they trouble him. He was not sexually deficient, and he did not dislike women; he simply ignored them, and was only really at home with men. All the crudities which we enumerate as masculine delighted him—simple things, for, in the gender of abstract ideas, vice is feminine, brutality is masculine, the female being older, vastly older than the male, much more competent in every way, stronger, even in her physique, than he, and, having little baggage of mental or ethical preoccupations to delay her progress, she is still the guardian of evolution, requiring little more from man than to be stroked and petted for a while.

He could be brutal at times. He liked to get drunk at seasonable periods. He would cheerfully break a head or a window, and would bandage the one damage or pay for the other with equal skill and pleasure. He liked to tramp rugged miles swinging his arms and whistling as he went, and he could sit for hours by the side of a ditch thinking thoughts without words—an easy and a pleasant way of thinking, and one which may lead to something in the long run.

Even his mother was an abstraction to him. He was kind to her so far as doing things went, but he looked over her, or round her, and marched away and forgot her.

Sex-blindedness carries with it many other darknesses. We do not know what masculine thing is projected by the feminine consciousness, and civilisation, even life itself, must stand at a halt until that has been discovered or created; but art is the female projected by the male: science is the male projected by the male—as yet a poor thing, and to remain so until it has become art; that is, has become fertilised and so more psychological than mechanical. The small part of science which came to his notice (inventions, machinery, etc.) was easily and delightedly comprehended by him. He could do intricate things with a knife and a piece of string, or a hammer and a saw; but a picture, a poem, a statue, a piece of music—these left him as uninterested as they found him: more so, in truth, for they left him bored and dejected.

His mother came to dislike him, and there were many causes and many justifications for her dislike. She was an orderly, busy, competent woman, the counterpart of endless millions of her sex, who liked to understand what she saw or felt, and who had no happiness in reading riddles. To her he was at times an enigma, and at times again a simpleton. In both aspects he displeased and embarrassed her. One has one's sense of property, and in him she could not put her finger on anything that was hers. We demand continuity, logic in other words, but between her son and herself there was a gulf fixed, spanned by no bridge whatever; there was complete isolation; no boat plied between them at all. All the kindly human things which she loved were unintelligible to him, and his coarse pleasures or blunt evasions distressed and bewildered her. When she spoke to him he gaped or yawned; and yet she did not speak on weighty matters, just the necessary small-change of existence—somebody's cold, somebody's dress, somebody's marriage or death. When she addressed him on sterner subjects, the ground, the weather, the crops, he looked at her as if she were a baby, he listened with stubborn resentment, and strode away a confessed boor. There was no contact anywhere between them, and he was a slow exasperation to her—What can we do with that which is ours and not ours? either we own a thing or we do not, and, whichever way it goes, there is some end to it; but certain enigmas are illegitimate and are so hounded from decent cogitation.

She could do nothing but dismiss him, and she could not even do that, for there he was at the required periods, always primed with the wrong reply to any question, the wrong aspiration, the wrong conjecture; a perpetual trampler on mental corns, a person for whom one could do nothing but apologise.

They lived on a small farm, and almost the entire work of the place was done by him. His younger brother assisted, but that assistance could have easily been done without. If the cattle were sick, he cured them almost by instinct. If the horse was lame or wanted a new shoe, he knew precisely what to do in both events. When the time came for ploughing, he gripped the handles and drove a furrow which was as straight and as economical as any furrow in the world. He could dig all day long and be happy; he gathered in the harvest as another would gather in a bride; and, in the intervals between these occupations, he fled to the nearest publichouse and wallowed among his kind.

He did not fly away to drink; he fled to be among men—Then he awakened. His tongue worked with the best of them, and adequately too. He could speak weightily on many things—boxing, wrestling, hunting, fishing, the seasons, the weather, and the chances of this and the other man's crops. He had deep knowledge about brands of tobacco and the peculiar virtues of many different liquors. He knew birds and beetles and worms; how a weasel would behave in extraordinary circumstances; how to train every breed of horse and dog. He recited goats from the cradle to the grave, could tell the name of any tree from its leaf; knew how a bull could be coerced, a cow cut up, and what plasters were good for a broken head. Sometimes, and often enough, the talk would chance on women, and then he laughed as heartily as any one else, but he was always relieved when the conversation trailed to more interesting things.

His mother died and left the farm to the younger instead of the elder son; an unusual thing to do, but she did detest him. She knew her younger son very well. He was foreign to her in nothing. His temper ran parallel with her own, his tastes were hers, his ideas had been largely derived from her, she could track them at any time and make or demolish him. He would go to a dance or a picnic and be as exhilarated as she was, and would discuss the matter afterwards. He could speak with some cogency on the shape of this and that female person, the hat of such an one, the disagreeableness of tea at this house and the goodness of it at the other. He could even listen to one speaking without going to sleep at the fourth word. In all he was a decent, quiet lad who would become a father the exact replica of his own, and whose daughters would resemble his mother as closely as two peas resemble their green ancestors—So she left him the farm.

Of course, there was no attempt to turn the elder brother out. Indeed, for some years the two men worked quietly together and prospered and were contented; then, as was inevitable, the younger brother got married, and the elder had to look out for a new place to live in, and to work in—things had become difficult.

It is very easy to say that in such and such circumstances a man should do this and that well-pondered thing, but the courts of logic have as yet the most circumscribed jurisdiction. Just as statistics can prove anything and be quite wrong, so reason can sit in its padded chair issuing pronouncements which are seldom within measurable distance of any reality. Everything is true only in relation to its centre of thought. Some people think with their heads—their subsequent actions are as logical and unpleasant as are those of the other sort who think only with their blood, and this latter has its irrefutable logic also. He thought in this subterranean fashion, and if he had thought in the other the issue would not have been any different.

Still, it was not an easy problem for him, or for any person lacking initiative—a sexual characteristic. He might have emigrated, but his roots were deeply struck in his own place, so the idea never occurred to him; furthermore, our thoughts are often no deeper than our pockets, and one wants money to move anywhere. For any other life than that of farming he had no training and small desire. He had no money and he was a farmer's son. Without money he could not get a farm; being a farmer's son he could not sink to the degradation of a day labourer; logically he could sink, actually he could not without endangering his own centres and verities—so he also got married.

He married a farm of about ten acres, and the sun began to shine on him once more; but only for a few days. Suddenly the sun went away from the heavens; the moon disappeared from the silent night; the silent night itself fled afar, leaving in its stead a noisy, dirty blackness through which one slept or yawned as one could. There was the farm, of course—one could go there and work; but the freshness went out of the very ground; the crops lost their sweetness and candour; the horses and cows disowned him; the goats ceased to be his friends—It was all up with him. He did not whistle any longer. He did not swing his shoulders as he walked, and, although he continued to smoke, he did not look for a particular green bank whereon he could sit quietly flooded with those slow thoughts that had no words.

For he discovered that he had not married a farm at all. He had married a woman—a thin-jawed, elderly slattern, whose sole beauty was her farm. How her jaws worked! The processions and congregations of words that fell and dribbled and slid out of them! Those jaws were never quiet, and in spite of all he did not say anything. There was not anything to say, but much to do from which he shivered away in terror. He looked at her sometimes through the muscles of his arms, through his big, strong hands, through fogs and fumes and singular, quiet tumults that raged within him. She lessoned him on the things he knew so well, and she was always wrong. She lectured him on those things which she did know, but the unending disquisition, the perpetual repetition, the foolish, empty emphasis, the dragging weightiness of her tongue made him repudiate her knowledge and hate it as much as he did her.

Sometimes, looking at her, he would rub his eyes and yawn with fatigue and wonder—There she was! A something enwrapped about with petticoats. Veritably alive. Active as an insect! Palpable to the touch! And what was she doing to him? Why did she do it? Why didn't she go away? Why didn't she die? What sense was there in the making of such a creature that clothed itself like a bolster, without any freedom or entertainment or shapeliness?

Her eyes were fixed on him and they always seemed to be angry; and her tongue was uttering rubbish about horses, rubbish about cows, rubbish about hay and oats. Nor was this the sum of his weariness. It was not alone that he was married; he was multitudinously, egregiously married. He had married a whole family, and what a family—

Her mother lived with her, her eldest sister lived with her, her youngest sister lived with her—And these were all swathed about with petticoats and shawls. They had no movement. Their feet were like those of no creature he had ever observed. One could hear the flip-flap of their slippers all over the place, and at all hours. They were down-at-heel, draggle-tailed, and futile. There was no workmanship about them. They were as unfinished, as unsightly as a puddle on a road. They insulted his eyesight, his hearing, and his energy. They had lank hair that slapped about them like wet seaweed, and they were all talking, talking, talking.

The mother was of an incredible age. She was senile with age. Her cracked cackle never ceased for an instant. She talked to the dog and the cat; she talked to the walls of the room; she spoke out through the window to the weather; she shut her eyes in a corner and harangued the circumambient darkness. The eldest sister was as silent as a deep ditch and as ugly. She slid here and there with her head on one side like an inquisitive hen watching one curiously, and was always doing nothing with an air of futile employment. The youngest was a semi-lunatic who prattled and prattled without ceasing, and was always catching one's sleeve, and laughing at one's face.—And everywhere those flopping, wriggling petticoats were appearing and disappearing. One saw slack hair whisking by the corner of one's eye. Mysteriously, urgently, they were coming and going and coming again, and never, never being silent.

More and more he went running to the public-house. But it was no longer to be among men, it was to get drunk. One might imagine him sitting there thinking those slow thoughts without words. One might predict that the day would come when he would realise very suddenly, very clearly, all that he had been thinking about, and, when this urgent, terrible thought had been translated into its own terms of action, he would be quietly hanged by the neck until he was as dead as he had been before he was alive.

THE DEAD

James Joyce

LILY, the caretaker's daughter, was literally run off her feet. Hardly had she brought one gentleman into the little pantry behind the office on the ground floor and helped him off with his overcoat than the wheezy hall-door bell clanged again and she had to scamper along the bare hallway to let in another guest. It was well for her she had not to attend to the ladies also. But Miss Kate and Miss Julia had thought of that and had converted the bathroom upstairs into a ladies' dressing-room. Miss Kate and Miss Julia were there, gossiping and laughing and fussing, walking after each other to the head of the stairs, peering down over the banisters and calling down to Lily to ask her who had come.

It was always a great affair, the Misses Morkan's annual dance. Everybody who knew them came to it, members of the family, old friends of the family, the members of Julia's choir, any of Kate's pupils that were grown up enough, and even some of Mary Jane's pupils too. Never once had it fallen flat. For years and years it had gone off in splendid style, as long as anyone could remember; ever since Kate and Julia, after the death of their brother Pat, had left the house in Stoney Batter and taken Mary Jane, their only niece, to live with them in the dark, gaunt house on Usher's Island, the upper part of which they had rented from Mr. Fulham, the corn-factor on the ground floor. That was a good thirty years ago if it was a day. Mary Jane, who was then a little girl in short clothes, was now the main prop of the household, for she had the organ in Haddington Road. She had been through the Academy and gave a pupils' concert every year in the upper room of the Antient Concert Rooms. Many of her pupils belonged to the better-class families on the Kingstown and Dalkey line. Old as they were, her aunts also did their share. Julia, though she was quite grey, was still the leading soprano in Adam and Eve's, and Kate, being too feeble to go about much, gave music lessons to beginners on the old square piano in the back room. Lily, the caretaker's daughter, did housemaid's work for them. Though their life was modest, they believed in eating well; the best of everything: diamond-bone sirloins, three-shilling tea and the best bottled stout. But Lily seldom made a mistake in the orders, so that she got on well with her three mistresses. They were fussy, that was all. But the only thing they would not stand was back answers.

Of course, they had good reason to be fussy on such a night. And then it was long after ten o'clock and yet there was no sign of Gabriel and his wife. Besides they were dreadfully afraid that Freddy Malins might turn up screwed. They would not wish for worlds that any of Mary Jane's pupils should see him under the influence; and when he was like that it was sometimes very hard to manage him. Freddy Malins always came late, but they wondered what could be keeping Gabriel: and that was what brought them every two minutes to the banisters to ask Lily had Gabriel or Freddy come.

"O, Mr. Conroy," said Lily to Gabriel when she opened the door for him, "Miss Kate and Miss Julia thought you were never coming. Good-night, Mrs. Conroy."

"I'll engage they did," said Gabriel, "but they forget that my wife here takes three mortal hours to dress herself."

He stood on the mat, scraping the snow from his goloshes, while Lily led his wife to the foot of the stairs and called out:

"Miss Kate, here's Mrs. Conroy."

Kate and Julia came toddling down the dark stairs at once. Both of them kissed Gabriel's wife, said she must be perished alive, and asked was Gabriel with her.

"Here I am as right as the mail, Aunt Kate! Go on up. I'll follow," called out Gabriel from the dark.

He continued scraping his feet vigorously while the three women went upstairs, laughing, to the ladies' dressing-room. A light fringe of snow lay like a cape on the shoulders of his overcoat and like toecaps on the toes of his goloshes; and, as the buttons of his overcoat slipped with a squeaking noise through the snow-stiffened frieze, a cold, fragrant air from out-of-doors escaped from crevices and folds.

"Is it snowing again, Mr. Conroy?" asked Lily.

She had preceded him into the pantry to help him off with his overcoat. Gabriel smiled at the three syllables she had given his surname and glanced at her. She was a slim, growing girl, pale in complexion and with hay-coloured hair. The gas in the pantry made her look still paler. Gabriel had known her when she was a child and used to sit on the lowest step nursing a rag doll.

"Yes, Lily," he answered, "and I think we're in for a night of it."

He looked up at the pantry ceiling, which was shaking with the stamping and shuffling of feet on the floor above, listened for a moment to the piano and then glanced at the girl, who was folding his overcoat carefully at the end of a shelf.

"Tell me, Lily," he said in a friendly tone, "do you still go to school?"

"O no, sir," she answered. "I'm done schooling this year and more."

"O, then," said Gabriel gaily, "I suppose we'll be going to your wedding one of these fine days with your young man, eh?"

The girl glanced back at him over her shoulder and said with great bitterness:

"The men that is now is only all palaver and what they can get out of you."

Gabriel coloured, as if he felt he had made a mistake and, without looking at her, kicked off his goloshes and flicked actively with his muffler at his patent-leather shoes.

He was a stout, tallish young man. The high colour of his cheeks pushed upwards even to his forehead, where it scattered itself in a few formless patches of pale red; and on his hairless face there scintillated restlessly the polished lenses and the bright gilt rims of the glasses which screened his delicate and restless eyes. His glossy black hair was parted in the middle and brushed in a long curve behind his ears where it curled slightly beneath the groove left by his hat.

When he had flicked lustre into his shoes he stood up and pulled his waistcoat down more tightly on his plump body. Then he took a coin rapidly from his pocket.

"O Lily," he said, thrusting it into her hands, "it's Christmas-time, isn't it? Just . . . here's a little. . . ."

He walked rapidly towards the door.

"O no, sir!" cried the girl, following him. "Really, sir, I wouldn't take it."

"Christmas-time! Christmas-time!" said Gabriel, almost trotting to the stairs and waving his hand to her in deprecation.

The girl, seeing that he had gained the stairs, called out after him:

"Well, thank you, sir."

He waited outside the drawing-room door until the waltz should finish, listening to the skirts that swept against it and to the shuffling of feet. He was still discomposed by the girl's bitter and sudden retort. It had cast a gloom over him which he tried to dispel by arranging his cuffs and the bows of his tie. He then took from his waistcoat pocket a little paper and glanced at the headings he had made for his speech. He was undecided about the lines from Robert Browning, for he feared they would be above the heads of his hearers. Some quotation that they would recog-

nise from Shakespeare or from the Melodies would be better. The indelicate clacking of the men's heels and the shuffling of their soles reminded
him that their grade of culture differed from his. He would only make
himself ridiculous by quoting poetry to them which they could not
understand. They would think that he was airing his superior education.
He would fail with them just as he had failed with the girl in the pantry.
He had taken up a wrong tone. His whole speech was a mistake from first
to last, an utter failure.

Just then his aunts and his wife came out of the ladies' dressing-room.
His aunts were two small, plainly dressed old women. Aunt Julia was an
inch or so the taller. Her hair, drawn low over the tops of her ears, was
grey; and grey also, with darker shadows, was her large flaccid face.
Though she was stout in build and stood erect, her slow eyes and parted
lips gave her the appearance of a woman who did not know where she
was or where she was going. Aunt Kate was more vivacious. Her face,
healthier than her sister's, was all puckers and creases, like a shrivelled red
apple, and her hair, braided in the same old-fashioned way, had not lost
its ripe nut colour.

They both kissed Gabriel frankly. He was their favourite nephew, the
son of their dead elder sister, Ellen, who had married T. J. Conroy of the
Port and Docks.

"Gretta tells me you're not going to take a cab back to Monkstown
to-night, Gabriel," said Aunt Kate.

"No," said Gabriel, turning to his wife, "we had quite enough of that
last year, hadn't we? Don't you remember, Aunt Kate, what a cold Gretta
got out of it? Cab windows rattling all the way, and the east wind blowing in after we passed Merrion. Very jolly it was. Gretta caught a dreadful cold."

Aunt Kate frowned severely and nodded her head at every word.

"Quite right, Gabriel, quite right," she said. "You can't be too careful."

"But as for Gretta there," said Gabriel, "she'd walk home in the snow
if she were let."

Mrs. Conroy laughed.

"Don't mind him, Aunt Kate," she said. "He's really an awful bother,
what with green shades for Tom's eyes at night and making him do the
dumb-bells, and forcing Eva to eat the stirabout. The poor child! And
she simply hates the sight of it! . . . O, but you'll never guess what he
makes me wear now!"

She broke out into a peal of laughter and glanced at her husband,
whose admiring and happy eyes had been wandering from her dress to
her face and hair. The two aunts laughed heartily, too, for Gabriel's solici-
tude was a standing joke with them.

"Goloshes!" said Mrs. Conroy. "That's the latest. Whenever it's wet underfoot I must put on my goloshes. To-night even, he wanted me to put them on, but I wouldn't. The next thing he'll buy me will be a diving suit."

Gabriel laughed nervously and patted his tie reassuringly, while Aunt Kate nearly doubled herself, so heartily did she enjoy the joke. The smile soon faded from Aunt Julia's face and her mirthless eyes were directed towards her nephew's face. After a pause she asked:

"And what are goloshes, Gabriel?"

"Goloshes, Julia!" exclaimed her sister. "Goodness me, don't you know what goloshes are? You wear them over your . . . over your boots, Gretta, isn't it?"

"Yes," said Mrs. Conroy. "Guttapercha things. We both have a pair now. Gabriel says everyone wears them on the continent."

"O, on the continent," murmured Aunt Julia, nodding her head slowly.

Gabriel knitted his brows and said, as if he were slightly angered:

"It's nothing very wonderful, but Gretta thinks it very funny because she says the word reminds her of Christy Minstrels."

"But tell me, Gabriel," said Aunt Kate, with brisk tact. "Of course, you've seen about the room. Gretta was saying . . ."

"O, the room is all right," replied Gabriel. "I've taken one in the Gresham."

"To be sure," said Aunt Kate, "by far the best thing to do. And the children, Gretta, you're not anxious about them?"

"O, for one night," said Mrs. Conroy. "Besides, Bessie will look after them."

"To be sure," said Aunt Kate again. "What a comfort it is to have a girl like that, one you can depend on! There's that Lily, I'm sure I don't know what has come over her lately. She's not the girl she was at all."

Gabriel was about to ask his aunt some questions on this point, but she broke off suddenly to gaze after her sister, who had wandered down the stairs and was craning her neck over the banisters.

"Now, I ask you," she said almost testily, "where is Julia going? Julia! Julia! Where are you going?"

Julia, who had gone halfway down one flight, came back and announced blandly:

"Here's Freddy."

At the same moment a clapping of hands and a final flourish of the pianist told that the waltz had ended. The drawing-room door was opened from within and some couples came out. Aunt Kate drew Gabriel aside hurriedly and whispered into his ear:

"Slip down, Gabriel, like a good fellow and see if he's all right, and don't let him up if he's screwed. I'm sure he's screwed. I'm sure he is."

Gabriel went to the stairs and listened over the banisters. He could hear two persons talking in the pantry. Then he recognised Freddy Malins' laugh. He went down the stairs noisily.

"It's such a relief," said Aunt Kate to Mrs. Conroy, "that Gabriel is here. I always feel easier in my mind when he's here. . . . Julia, there's Miss Daly and Miss Power will take some refreshment. Thanks for your beautiful waltz, Miss Daly. It made lovely time."

A tall wizen-faced man, with a stiff grizzled moustache and swarthy skin, who was passing out with his partner, said:

"And may we have some refreshment, too, Miss Morkan?"

"Julia," said Aunt Kate summarily, "and here's Mr. Browne and Miss Furlong. Take them in, Julia, with Miss Daly and Miss Power."

"I'm the man for the ladies," said Mr. Browne, pursing his lips until his moustache bristled and smiling in all his wrinkles. "You know, Miss Morkan, the reason they are so fond of me is——"

He did not finish his sentence, but, seeing that Aunt Kate was out of earshot, at once led the three young ladies into the back room. The middle of the room was occupied by two square tables placed end to end, and on these Aunt Julia and the caretaker were straightening and smoothing a large cloth. On the sideboard were arrayed dishes and plates, and glasses and bundles of knives and forks and spoons. The top of the closed square piano served also as a sideboard for viands and sweets. At a smaller sideboard in one corner two young men were standing, drinking hop-bitters.

Mr. Browne led his charges thither and invited them all, in jest, to some ladies' punch, hot, strong and sweet. As they said they never took anything strong, he opened three bottles of lemonade for them. Then he asked one of the young men to move aside, and, taking hold of the decanter, filled out for himself a goodly measure of whisky. The young men eyed him respectfully while he took a trial sip.

"God help me," he said, smiling, "it's the doctor's orders."

His wizened face broke into a broader smile, and the three young ladies laughed in musical echo to his pleasantry, swaying their bodies to and fro, with nervous jerks of their shoulders. The boldest said:

"O, now, Mr. Browne, I'm sure the doctor never ordered anything of the kind."

Mr. Browne took another sip of his whisky and said, with sidling mimicry:

"Well, you see, I'm like the famous Mrs. Cassidy, who is reported to have said: 'Now, Mary Grimes, if I don't take it, make me take it, for I feel I want it.'"

His hot face had leaned forward a little too confidentially and he had assumed a very low Dublin accent so that the young ladies, with one instinct, received his speech in silence. Miss Furlong, who was one of Mary Jane's pupils, asked Miss Daly what was the name of the pretty waltz she had played; and Mr. Browne, seeing that he was ignored, turned promptly to the two young men who were more appreciative.

A red-faced young woman, dressed in pansy, came into the room, excitedly clapping her hands and crying:

"Quadrilles! Quadrilles!"

Close on her heels came Aunt Kate, crying:

"Two gentlemen and three ladies, Mary Jane!"

"O, here's Mr. Bergin and Mr. Kerrigan," said Mary Jane. "Mr. Kerrigan, will you take Miss Power? Miss Furlong, may I get you a partner, Mr. Bergin. O, that'll just do now."

"Three ladies, Mary Jane," said Aunt Kate.

The two young gentlemen asked the ladies if they might have the pleasure, and Mary Jane turned to Miss Daly.

"O, Miss Daly, you're really awfully good, after playing for the last two dances, but really we're so short of ladies to-night."

"I don't mind in the least, Miss Morkan."

"But I've a nice partner for you, Mr. Bartell D'Arcy, the tenor. I'll get him to sing later on. All Dublin is raving about him."

"Lovely voice, lovely voice!" said Aunt Kate.

As the piano had twice begun the prelude to the first figure Mary Jane led her recruits quickly from the room. They had hardly gone when Aunt Julia wandered slowly into the room, looking behind her at something.

"What is the matter, Julia?" asked Aunt Kate anxiously. "Who is it?"

Julia, who was carrying in a column of table-napkins, turned to her sister and said, simply, as if the question had surprised her:

"It's only Freddy, Kate, and Gabriel with him."

In fact right behind her Gabriel could be seen piloting Freddy Malins across the landing. The latter, a young man of about forty, was of Gabriel's size and build, with very round shoulders. His face was fleshy and pallid, touched with colour only at the thick hanging lobes of his ears and at the wide wings of his nose. He had coarse features, a blunt nose, a convex and receding brow, tumid and protruded lips. His heavy-lidded eyes and the disorder of his scanty hair made him look sleepy. He was laughing heartily in a high key at a story which he had been telling Gabriel on the stairs and at the same time rubbing the knuckles of his left fist backwards and forwards into his left eye.

"Good-evening, Freddy," said Aunt Julia.

Freddy Malins bade the Misses Morkan good-evening in what seemed an offhand fashion by reason of the habitual catch in his voice and then, seeing that Mr. Browne was grinning at him from the sideboard, crossed the room on rather shaky legs and began to repeat in an undertone the story he had just told to Gabriel.

"He's not so bad, is he?" said Aunt Kate to Gabriel.

Gabriel's brows were dark but he raised them quickly and answered: "O, no, hardly noticeable."

"Now, isn't he a terrible fellow!" she said. "And his poor mother made him take the pledge on New Year's Eve. But come on, Gabriel, into the drawing-room."

Before leaving the room with Gabriel she signalled to Mr. Browne by frowning and shaking her forefinger in warning to and fro. Mr. Browne nodded in answer and, when she had gone, said to Freddy Malins:

"Now, then, Teddy, I'm going to fill you out a good glass of lemon-ade just to buck you up."

Freddy Malins, who was nearing the climax of his story, waved the offer aside impatiently but Mr. Browne, having first called Freddy Malins' attention to a disarray in his dress, filled out and handed him a full glass of lemonade. Freddy Malins' left hand accepted the glass mechanically, his right hand being engaged in the mechanical readjustment of his dress. Mr. Browne, whose face was once more wrinkling with mirth, poured out for himself a glass of whisky while Freddy Malins exploded, before he had well reached the climax of his story, in a kink of high-pitched bronchitic laughter and, setting down his untasted and overflowing glass, began to rub the knuckles of his left fist backwards and forwards into his left eye, repeating words of his last phrase as well as his fit of laughter would allow him.

* * *

Gabriel could not listen while Mary Jane was playing her Academy piece, full of runs and difficult passages, to the hushed drawing-room. He liked music but the piece she was playing had no melody for him and he doubted whether it had any melody for the other listeners, though they had begged Mary Jane to play something. Four young men, who had come from the refreshment-room to stand in the doorway at the sound of the piano, had gone away quietly in couples after a few minutes. The only persons who seemed to follow the music were Mary Jane herself, her hands racing along the key-board or lifted from it at the pauses like those of a priestess in momentary imprecation, and Aunt Kate standing at her elbow to turn the page.

Gabriel's eyes, irritated by the floor, which glittered with beeswax under the heavy chandelier, wandered to the wall above the piano. A pic-ture of the balcony scene in *Romeo and Juliet* hung there and beside it was a picture of the two murdered princes in the Tower which Aunt Julia had worked in red, blue and brown wools when she was a girl. Probably in the school they had gone to as girls that kind of work had been taught for one year. His mother had worked for him as a birthday present a waistcoat of purple tabinet, with little foxes' heads upon it, lined with brown satin and having round mulberry buttons. It was strange that his mother had had no musical talent though Aunt Kate used to call her the brains carrier of the Morkan family. Both she and Julia had always seemed a little proud of their serious and matronly sister. Her photograph stood before the pierglass. She held an open book on her knees and was pointing out something in it to Constantine who, dressed in a man-o'-war suit, lay at her feet. It was she who had chosen the names of her sons for she was very sensible of the dignity of family life. Thanks to her, Constantine was now senior curate in Balbriggan and, thanks to her, Gabriel himself had taken his degree in the Royal University. A shadow passed over his face as he remembered her sullen opposition to his marriage. Some slighting phrases she had used still rankled in his memory; she had once spoken of Gretta as being country cute and that was not true of Gretta at all. It was Gretta who had nursed her during all her last long illness in their house at Monkstown.

He knew that Mary Jane must be near the end of her piece for she was playing again the opening melody with runs of scales after every bar and while he waited for the end the resentment died down in his heart. The piece ended with a trill of octaves in the treble and a final deep octave in the bass. Great applause greeted Mary Jane as, blushing and rolling up her music nervously, she escaped from the room. The most vigorous clapping came from the four young men in the doorway who had gone away to the refreshment-room at the beginning of the piece but had come back when the piano had stopped.

Lancers were arranged. Gabriel found himself partnered with Miss Ivors. She was a frank-mannered talkative young lady, with a freckled face and prominent brown eyes. She did not wear a low-cut bodice and the large brooch which was fixed in the front of her collar bore on it an Irish device and motto.

When they had taken their places she said abruptly:

"I have a crow to pluck with you."

"With me?" said Gabriel.

She nodded her head gravely.

"What is it?" asked Gabriel, smiling at her solemn manner.

"Who is G. C.?" answered Miss Ivors, turning her eyes upon him.

Gabriel coloured and was about to knit his brows, as if he did not understand, when she said bluntly:

"O, innocent Amy! I have found out that you write for *The Daily Express*. Now, aren't you ashamed of yourself?"

"Why should I be ashamed of myself?" asked Gabriel, blinking his eyes and trying to smile.

"Well, I'm ashamed of you," said Miss Ivors frankly. "To say you'd write for a paper like that. I didn't think you were a West Briton."

A look of perplexity appeared on Gabriel's face. It was true that he wrote a literary column every Wednesday in *The Daily Express,* for which he was paid fifteen shillings. But that did not make him a West Briton surely. The books he received for review were almost more welcome than the paltry cheque. He loved to feel the covers and turn over the pages of newly printed books. Nearly every day when his teaching in the college was ended he used to wander down the quays to the second-hand booksellers, to Hickey's on Bachelor's Walk, to Webb's or Massey's on Aston's Quay, or to O'Clohissey's in the by-street. He did not know how to meet her charge. He wanted to say that literature was above politics. But they were friends of many years' standing and their careers had been parallel, first at the University and then as teachers: he could not risk a grandiose phrase with her. He continued blinking his eyes and trying to smile and murmured lamely that he saw nothing political in writing reviews of books.

When their turn to cross had come he was still perplexed and inattentive. Miss Ivors promptly took his hand in a warm grasp and said in a soft friendly tone:

"Of course, I was only joking. Come, we cross now."

When they were together again she spoke of the University question and Gabriel felt more at ease. A friend of hers had shown her his review of Browning's poems. That was how she had found out the secret: but she liked the review immensely. Then she said suddenly:

"O, Mr. Conroy, will you come for an excursion to the Aran Isles this summer? We're going to stay there a whole month. It will be splendid out in the Atlantic. You ought to come. Mr. Clancy is coming, and Mr. Kilkelly and Kathleen Kearney. It would be splendid for Gretta too if she'd come. She's from Connacht, isn't she?"

"Her people are," said Gabriel shortly.

"But you will come, won't you?" said Miss Ivors, laying her warm hand eagerly on his arm.

"The fact is," said Gabriel, "I have just arranged to go——"

"Go where?" asked Miss Ivors.

"Well, you know, every year I go for a cycling tour with some fellows and so——"

"But where?" asked Miss Ivors.

"Well, we usually go to France or Belgium or perhaps Germany," said Gabriel awkwardly.

"And why do you go to France and Belgium," said Miss Ivors, "instead of visiting your own land?"

"Well," said Gabriel, "it's partly to keep in touch with the languages and partly for a change."

"And haven't you your own language to keep in touch with—Irish?" asked Miss Ivors.

"Well," said Gabriel, "if it comes to that, you know, Irish is not my language."

Their neighbours had turned to listen to the cross-examination. Gabriel glanced right and left nervously and tried to keep his good humour under the ordeal which was making a blush invade his forehead.

"And haven't you your own land to visit," continued Miss Ivors, "that you know nothing of, your own people, and your own country?"

"O, to tell you the truth," retorted Gabriel suddenly, "I'm sick of my own country, sick of it!"

"Why?" asked Miss Ivors.

Gabriel did not answer for his retort had heated him.

"Why?" repeated Miss Ivors.

They had to go visiting together and, as he had not answered her, Miss Ivors said warmly:

"Of course, you've no answer."

Gabriel tried to cover his agitation by taking part in the dance with great energy. He avoided her eyes for he had seen a sour expression on her face. But when they met in the long chain he was surprised to feel his hand firmly pressed. She looked at him from under her brows for a moment quizzically until he smiled. Then, just as the chain was about to start again, she stood on tiptoe and whispered into his ear:

"West Briton!"

When the lancers were over Gabriel went away to a remote corner of the room where Freddy Malins' mother was sitting. She was a stout feeble old woman with white hair. Her voice had a catch in it like her son's and she stuttered slightly. She had been told that Freddy had come and that he was nearly all right. Gabriel asked her whether she had had a good crossing. She lived with her married daughter in Glasgow and came to Dublin on a visit once a year. She answered placidly that she had had a beautiful crossing and that the captain had been most attentive to her. She spoke also of the beautiful house her daughter kept in Glasgow, and of all the friends they had there. While her tongue rambled on Gabriel tried to banish from his mind all memory of the unpleasant incident with Miss Ivors. Of course the girl or woman, or whatever she was, was an enthusiast but there was a time for all things. Perhaps he ought not to have answered her like that. But she had no right to call him a West Briton before people, even in joke. She had tried to make him ridiculous before people, heckling him and staring at him with her rabbit's eyes.

He saw his wife making her way towards him through the waltzing couples. When she reached him she said into his ear:

"Gabriel, Aunt Kate wants to know won't you carve the goose as usual. Miss Daly will carve the ham and I'll do the pudding."

"All right," said Gabriel.

"She's sending in the younger ones first as soon as this waltz is over so that we'll have the table to ourselves."

"Were you dancing?" asked Gabriel.

"Of course I was. Didn't you see me? What row had you with Molly Ivors?"

"No row. Why? Did she say so?"

"Something like that. I'm trying to get that Mr. D'Arcy to sing. He's full of conceit, I think."

"There was no row," said Gabriel moodily, "only she wanted me to go for a trip to the west of Ireland and I said I wouldn't."

His wife clasped her hands excitedly and gave a little jump.

"O, do go, Gabriel," she cried. "I'd love to see Galway again."

"You can go if you like," said Gabriel coldly.

She looked at him for a moment, then turned to Mrs. Malins and said: "There's a nice husband for you, Mrs. Malins."

While she was threading her way back across the room Mrs. Malins, without adverting to the interruption, went on to tell Gabriel what beautiful places there were in Scotland and beautiful scenery. Her son-in-law brought them every year to the lakes and they used to go fishing. Her son-in-law was a splendid fisher. One day he caught a beautiful big fish and the man in the hotel cooked it for their dinner.

Gabriel hardly heard what she said. Now that supper was coming near he began to think again about his speech and about the quotation. When he saw Freddy Malins coming across the room to visit his mother Gabriel left the chair free for him and retired into the embrasure of the window. The room had already cleared and from the back room came the clatter of plates and knives. Those who still remained in the drawing-room seemed tired of dancing and were conversing quietly in little groups. Gabriel's warm trembling fingers tapped the cold pane of the window. How cool it must be outside! How pleasant it would be to walk out alone, first along by the river and then through the park! The snow would be lying on the branches of the trees and forming a bright cap on the top of the Wellington Monument. How much more pleasant it would be there than at the supper-table!

He ran over the headings of his speech: Irish hospitality, sad memories, the Three Graces, Paris, the quotation from Browning. He repeated to himself a phrase he had written in his review: "One feels that one is listening to a thought-tormented music." Miss Ivors had praised the review. Was she sincere? Had she really any life of her own behind all her propagandism? There had never been any ill-feeling between them until that night. It unnerved him to think that she would be at the supper-table, looking up at him while he spoke with her critical quizzing eyes. Perhaps she would not be sorry to see him fail in his speech. An idea came into his mind and gave him courage. He would say, alluding to Aunt Kate and Aunt Julia: "Ladies and Gentlemen, the generation which is now on the wane among us may have had its faults but for my part I think it had certain qualities of hospitality, of humour, of humanity, which the new and very serious and hypereducated generation that is growing up around us seems to me to lack." Very good: that was one for Miss Ivors. What did he care that his aunts were only two ignorant old women?

A murmur in the room attracted his attention. Mr. Browne was advancing from the door, gallantly escorting Aunt Julia, who leaned upon his arm, smiling and hanging her head. An irregular musketry of applause escorted her also as far as the piano and then, as Mary Jane seated herself on the stool, and Aunt Julia, no longer smiling, half turned so as to pitch her voice fairly into the room, gradually ceased. Gabriel recognised the prelude. It was that of an old song of Aunt Julia's— *Arrayed for the Bridal*. Her voice, strong and clear in tone, attacked with great spirit the runs which embellish the air and though she sang very rapidly she did not miss even the smallest of the grace notes. To follow the voice, without looking at the singer's face, was to feel and share the excitement of swift and secure flight. Gabriel applauded loudly with all the others at the close of the song and loud applause was borne in from the invisible supper-table. It sounded so genuine that a little colour struggled into Aunt Julia's face as she bent to replace in the music-stand the old leather-bound song-book that had her initials on the cover. Freddy Malins, who had listened with his head perched sideways to hear her better, was still applauding when everyone else had ceased and talking animatedly to his mother who nodded her head gravely and slowly in acquiescence. At last, when he could clap no more, he stood up suddenly and hurried across the room to Aunt Julia whose hand he seized and held in both his hands, shaking it when words failed him or the catch in his voice proved too much for him.

"I was just telling my mother," he said, "I never heard you sing so well, never. No, I never heard your voice so good as it is to-night. Now! Would you believe that now? That's the truth. Upon my word and honour that's the truth. I never heard your voice sound so fresh and so . . . so clear and fresh, never."

Aunt Julia smiled broadly and murmured something about compliments as she released her hand from his grasp. Mr. Browne extended his open hand towards her and said to those who were near him in the manner of a showman introducing a prodigy to an audience:

"Miss Julia Morkan, my latest discovery!"

He was laughing very heartily at this himself when Freddy Malins turned to him and said:

"Well, Browne, if you're serious you might make a worse discovery. All I can say is I never heard her sing half so well as long as I am coming here. And that's the honest truth."

"Neither did I," said Mr. Browne. "I think her voice has greatly improved."

Aunt Julia shrugged her shoulders and said with meek pride:

"Thirty years ago I hadn't a bad voice as voices go."

"I often told Julia," said Aunt Kate emphatically, "that she was simply thrown away in that choir. But she never would be said by me."

She turned as if to appeal to the good sense of the others against a refractory child while Aunt Julia gazed in front of her, a vague smile of reminiscence playing on her face.

"No," continued Aunt Kate, "she wouldn't be said or led by anyone, slaving there in that choir night and day, night and day. Six o'clock on Christmas morning! And all for what?"

"Well, isn't it for the honour of God, Aunt Kate?" asked Mary Jane, twisting round on the piano-stool and smiling.

Aunt Kate turned fiercely on her niece and said:

"I know all about the honour of God, Mary Jane, but I think it's not at all honourable for the pope to turn out the women out of the choirs that have slaved there all their lives and put little whipper-snappers of boys over their heads. I suppose it is for the good of the Church if the pope does it. But it's not just, Mary Jane, and it's not right."

She had worked herself into a passion and would have continued in defence of her sister for it was a sore subject with her but Mary Jane, seeing that all the dancers had come back, intervened pacifically:

"Now, Aunt Kate, you're giving scandal to Mr. Browne who is of the other persuasion."

Aunt Kate turned to Mr. Browne, who was grinning at this allusion to his religion, and said hastily:

"O, I don't question the pope's being right. I'm only a stupid old woman and I wouldn't presume to do such a thing. But there's such a thing as common everyday politeness and gratitude. And if I were in Julia's place I'd tell that Father Healey straight up to his face . . ."

"And besides, Aunt Kate," said Mary Jane, "we really are all hungry and when we are hungry we are all very quarrelsome."

"And when we are thirsty we are also quarrelsome," added Mr. Browne.

"So that we had better go to supper," said Mary Jane, "and finish the discussion afterwards."

On the landing outside the drawing-room Gabriel found his wife and Mary Jane trying to persuade Miss Ivors to stay for supper. But Miss Ivors, who had put on her hat and was buttoning her cloak, would not stay. She did not feel in the least hungry and she had already overstayed her time.

"But only for ten minutes, Molly," said Mrs. Conroy. "That won't delay you."

"To take a pick itself," said Mary Jane, "after all your dancing."

"I really couldn't," said Miss Ivors.

"I am afraid you didn't enjoy yourself at all," said Mary Jane hopelessly.

"Ever so much, I assure you," said Miss Ivors, "but you really must let me run off now."

"But how can you get home?" asked Mrs. Conroy.

"O, it's only two steps up the quay."

Gabriel hesitated a moment and said:

"If you will allow me, Miss Ivors, I'll see you home if you are really obliged to go."

But Miss Ivors broke away from them.

"I won't hear of it," she cried. "For goodness' sake go in to your suppers and don't mind me. I'm quite well able to take care of myself."

"Well, you're the comical girl, Molly," said Mrs. Conroy frankly.

"*Beannacht libh,*" cried Miss Ivors, with a laugh, as she ran down the staircase.

Mary Jane gazed after her, a moody puzzled expression on her face, while Mrs. Conroy leaned over the banisters to listen for the hall-door. Gabriel asked himself was he the cause of her abrupt departure. But she did not seem to be in ill humour: she had gone away laughing. He stared blankly down the staircase.

At the moment Aunt Kate came toddling out of the supper-room, almost wringing her hands in despair.

"Where is Gabriel?" she cried. "Where on earth is Gabriel? There's everyone waiting in there, stage to let, and nobody to carve the goose!"

"Here I am, Aunt Kate!" cried Gabriel, with sudden animation, "ready to carve a flock of geese, if necessary."

A fat brown goose lay at one end of the table and at the other end, on a bed of creased paper strewn with sprigs of parsley, lay a great ham, stripped of its outer skin and peppered over with crust crumbs, a neat paper frill round its shin and beside this was a round of spiced beef. Between these rival ends ran parallel lines of side-dishes: two little minsters of jelly, red and yellow; a shallow dish full of blocks of blancmange and red jam, a large green leaf-shaped dish with a stalk-shaped handle, on which lay bunches of purple raisins and peeled almonds, a companion dish on which lay a solid rectangle of Smyrna figs, a dish of custard topped with grated nutmeg, a small bowl full of chocolates and sweets wrapped in gold and silver papers and a glass vase in which stood some tall celery stalks. In the centre of the table there stood, as sentries to a fruit-stand which upheld a pyramid of oranges and American apples, two squat old-fashioned decanters of cut glass, one containing port and the other dark sherry. On the closed square piano a pudding in a huge yellow dish lay in waiting and behind it were three squads of bottles of stout and ale and minerals, drawn up according to the colours of their uniforms, the first two black, with brown and red labels, the third and smallest squad white, with transverse green sashes.

Gabriel took his seat boldly at the head of the table and, having looked to the edge of the carver, plunged his fork firmly into the goose. He felt quite at ease now for he was an expert carver and liked nothing better than to find himself at the head of a well-laden table.

"Miss Furlong, what shall I send you?" he asked. "A wing or a slice of the breast?"

"Just a small slice of the breast." .

"Miss Higgins, what for you?"

"O, anything at all, Mr. Conroy."

While Gabriel and Miss Daly exchanged plates of goose and plates of ham and spiced beef Lily went from guest to guest with a dish of hot floury potatoes wrapped in a white napkin. This was Mary Jane's idea and she had also suggested apple sauce for the goose but Aunt Kate had said that plain roast goose without any apple sauce had always been good enough for her and she hoped she might never eat worse. Mary Jane waited on her pupils and saw that they got the best slices and Aunt Kate and Aunt Julia opened and carried across from the piano bottles of stout and ale for the gentlemen and bottles of minerals for the ladies. There was a great deal of confusion and laughter and noise, the noise of orders and counter-orders, of knives and forks, of corks and glass-stoppers. Gabriel began to carve second helpings as soon as he had finished the first round without serving himself. Everyone protested loudly so that he compromised by taking a long draught of stout for he had found the carving hot work. Mary Jane settled down quietly to her supper but Aunt Kate and Aunt Julia were still toddling round the table, walking on each other's heels, getting in each other's way and giving each other unheeded orders. Mr. Browne begged of them to sit down and eat their suppers and so did Gabriel but they said there was time enough, so that, at last, Freddy Malins stood up and, capturing Aunt Kate, plumped her down on her chair amid general laughter.

When everyone had been well served Gabriel said, smiling:

"Now, if anyone wants a little more of what vulgar people call stuffing let him or her speak."

A chorus of voices invited him to begin his own supper and Lily came forward with three potatoes which she had reserved for him.

"Very well," said Gabriel amiably, as he took another preparatory draught, "kindly forget my existence, ladies and gentlemen, for a few minutes."

He set to his supper and took no part in the conversation with which the table covered Lily's removal of the plates. The subject of talk was the opera company which was then at the Theatre Royal. Mr. Bartell D'Arcy, the tenor, a dark-complexioned young man with a smart moustache, praised very highly the leading contralto of the company but Miss Furlong thought she had a rather vulgar style of production. Freddy Malins said there was a negro chieftain singing in the second part of the Gaiety pantomime who had one of the finest tenor voices he had ever heard.

"Have you heard him?" he asked Mr. Bartell D'Arcy across the table.

"No," answered Mr. Bartell D'Arcy carelessly.

"Because," Freddy Malins explained, "now I'd be curious to hear your opinion of him. I think he has a grand voice."

"It takes Teddy to find out the really good things," said Mr. Browne familiarly to the table.

"And why couldn't he have a voice too?" asked Freddy Malins sharply. "Is it because he's only a black?"

Nobody answered this question and Mary Jane led the table back to the legitimate opera. One of her pupils had given her a pass for *Mignon*. Of course it was very fine, she said, but it made her think of poor Georgina Burns. Mr. Browne could go back farther still, to the old Italian companies that used to come to Dublin—Tietjens, Ilma de Murzka, Campanini, the great Trebelli Giuglini, Ravelli, Aramburo. Those were the days, he said, when there was something like singing to be heard in Dublin. He told too of how the top gallery of the old Royal used to be packed night after night, of how one night an Italian tenor had sung five encores to *Let me like a Soldier fall,* introducing a high C every time, and of how the gallery boys would sometimes in their enthusiasm unyoke the horses from the carriage of some great *prima donna* and pull her themselves through the streets to her hotel. Why did they never play the grand old operas now, he asked, *Dinorah, Lucrezia Borgia?* Because they could not get the voices to sing them: that was why."

"O, well," said Mr. Bartell D'Arcy, "I presume there are as good singers to-day as there were then."

"Where are they?" asked Mr. Browne defiantly.

"In London, Paris, Milan," said Mr. Bartell D'Arcy warmly. "I suppose Caruso, for example, is quite as good, if not better than any of the men you have mentioned."

"Maybe so," said Mr. Browne. "But I may tell you I doubt it strongly."

"O, I'd give anything to hear Caruso sing," said Mary Jane.

"For me," said Aunt Kate, who had been picking a bone, "there was only one tenor. To please me, I mean. But I suppose none of you ever heard of him."

"Who was he, Miss Morkan?" asked Mr. Bartell D'Arcy politely.

"His name," said Aunt Kate, "was Parkinson. I heard him when he was in his prime and I think he had then the purest tenor voice that was ever put into a man's throat."

"Strange," said Mr. Bartell D'Arcy. "I never even heard of him."

"Yes, yes, Miss Morkan is right," said Mr. Browne. "I remember hearing of old Parkinson but he's too far back for me."

"A beautiful, pure, sweet, mellow English tenor," said Aunt Kate with enthusiasm.

Gabriel having finished, the huge pudding was transferred to the table. The clatter of forks and spoons began again. Gabriel's wife served out spoonfuls of the pudding and passed the plates down the table. Midway down they were held up by Mary Jane, who replenished them with raspberry or orange jelly or with blancmange and jam. The pudding was of Aunt Julia's making and she received praises for it from all quarters. She herself said that it was not quite brown enough.

"Well, I hope, Miss Morkan," said Mr. Browne, "that I'm brown enough for you because, you know, I'm all brown."

All the gentlemen, except Gabriel, ate some of the pudding out of compliment to Aunt Julia. As Gabriel never ate sweets the celery had been left for him. Freddy Malins also took a stalk of celery and ate it with his pudding. He had been told that celery was a capital thing for the blood and he was just then under doctor's care. Mrs. Malins, who had been silent all through the supper, said that her son was going down to Mount Melleray in a week or so. The table then spoke of Mount Melleray, how bracing the air was down there, how hospitable the monks were and how they never asked for a penny-piece from their guests.

"And do you mean to say," asked Mr. Browne incredulously, "that a chap can go down there and put up there as if it were a hotel and live on the fat of the land and then come away without paying anything?"

"O, most people give some donation to the monastery when they leave," said Mary Jane.

"I wish we had an institution like that in our Church," said Mr. Browne candidly.

He was astonished to hear that the monks never spoke, got up at two in the morning and slept in their coffins. He asked what they did it for.

"That's the rule of the order," said Aunt Kate firmly.

"Yes, but why?" asked Mr. Browne.

Aunt Kate repeated that it was the rule, that was all. Mr. Browne still seemed not to understand. Freddy Malins explained to him, as best he could, that the monks were trying to make up for the sins committed by all the sinners in the outside world. The explanation was not very clear for Mr. Browne grinned and said:

"I like that idea very much but wouldn't a comfortable spring bed do them as well as a coffin?"

"The coffin," said Mary Jane, "is to remind them of their last end."

As the subject had grown lugubrious it was buried in a silence of the table during which Mrs. Malins could be heard saying to her neighbour in an indistinct undertone:

"They are very good men, the monks, very pious men."

The raisins and almonds and figs and apples and oranges and choco-lates and sweets were now passed about the table and Aunt Julia invited all the guests to have either port or sherry. At first Mr. Bartell D'Arcy refused to take either but one of his neighbours nudged him and whis-pered something to him upon which he allowed his glass to be filled. Gradually as the last glasses were being filled the conversation ceased. A pause followed, broken only by the noise of the wine and by unsettlings of chairs. The Misses Morkan, all three, looked down at the tablecloth. Someone coughed once or twice and then a few gentlemen patted the table gently as a signal for silence. The silence came and Gabriel pushed back his chair and stood up.

The patting at once grew louder in encouragement and then ceased altogether. Gabriel leaned his ten trembling fingers on the tablecloth and smiled nervously at the company. Meeting a row of upturned faces he raised his eyes to the chandelier. The piano was playing a waltz tune and he could hear the skirts sweeping against the drawing-room door. People, perhaps, were standing in the snow on the quay outside, gazing up at the lighted windows and listening to the waltz music. The air was pure there. In the distance lay the park where the trees were weighted with snow. The Wellington Monument wore a gleaming cap of snow that flashed westward over the white field of Fifteen Acres.

He began:

"Ladies and Gentlemen,

"It has fallen to my lot this evening, as in years past, to perform a very pleasing task but a task for which I am afraid my poor powers as a speaker are all too inadequate."

"No, no!" said Mr. Browne.

"But, however that may be, I can only ask you to-night to take the will for the deed and to lend me your attention for a few moments while I endeavour to express to you in words what my feelings are on this occasion.

"Ladies and Gentlemen, it is not the first time that we have gathered together under this hospitable roof, around this hospitable board. It is not the first time that we have been the recipients—or perhaps, I had better say, the victims—of the hospitality of certain good ladies."

He made a circle in the air with his arm and paused. Everyone laughed or smiled at Aunt Kate and Aunt Julia and Mary Jane who all turned crimson with pleasure. Gabriel went on more boldly:

"I feel more strongly with every recurring year that our country has no tradition which does it so much honour and which it should guard so jealously as that of its hospitality. It is a tradition that is unique as far as my experience goes (and I have visited not a few places abroad) among the modern nations. Some would say, perhaps, that with us it is rather a failing than anything to be boasted of. But granted even that, it is, to my mind, a princely failing, and one that I trust will long be cultivated among us. Of one thing, at least, I am sure. As long as this one roof shelters the good ladies aforesaid—and I wish from my heart it may do so for many and many a long year to come—the tradition of genuine warm-hearted courteous Irish hospitality, which our forefathers have handed down to us and which we in turn must hand down to our descendants, is still alive among us."

A hearty murmur of assent ran round the table. It shot through Gabriel's mind that Miss Ivors was not there and that she had gone away discourteously: and he said with confidence in himself:

"Ladies and Gentlemen,

"A new generation is growing up in our midst, a generation actuated by new ideas and new principles. It is serious and enthusiastic for these new ideas and its enthusiasm, even when it is misdirected, is, I believe, in the main sincere. But we are living in a sceptical and, if I may use the phrase, a thought-tormented age: and sometimes I fear that this new generation, educated or hypereducated as it is, will lack those qualities of humanity, of hospitality, of kindly humour which belonged to an older day. Listening to-night to the names of all those great singers of the past it seemed to me, I must confess, that we were living in a less spacious age. Those days might, without exaggeration, be called spacious days: and if they are gone beyond recall let us hope, at least, that in gatherings such as this we shall still speak of them with pride and affection, still cherish in our hearts the memory of those dead and gone great ones whose fame the world will not willingly let die."

"Hear, hear!" said Mr. Browne loudly.

"But yet," continued Gabriel, his voice falling into a softer inflection, "there are always in gatherings such as this sadder thoughts that will recur to our minds: thoughts of the past, of youth, of changes, of absent faces that we miss here to-night. Our path through life is strewn with many such sad memories: and were we to brood upon them always we could not find the heart to go on bravely with our work among the living. We have all of us living duties and living affections which claim, and rightly claim, our strenuous endeavours.

"Therefore, I will not linger on the past. I will not let any gloomy moralising intrude upon us here to-night. Here we are gathered together for a brief moment from the bustle and rush of our everyday routine. We are met here as friends, in the spirit of good-fellowship, as colleagues, also to a certain extent, in the true spirit of *camaraderie,* and as the guests of— what shall I call them?—the Three Graces of the Dublin musical world."

The table burst into applause and laughter at this allusion. Aunt Julia vainly asked each of her neighbours in turn to tell her what Gabriel had said.

"He says we are the Three Graces, Aunt Julia," said Mary Jane.

Aunt Julia did not understand but she looked up, smiling, at Gabriel, who continued in the same vein:

"Ladies and Gentlemen,

"I will not attempt to play to-night the part that Paris played on another occasion. I will not attempt to choose between them. The task would be an invidious one and one beyond my poor powers. For when I view them in turn, whether it be our chief hostess herself, whose good heart, whose too good heart, has become a byword with all who know her, or her sister, who seems to be gifted with perennial youth and whose singing must have been a surprise and a revelation to us all to-night, or, last but not least, when I consider our youngest hostess, talented, cheerful, hard-working and the best of nieces, I confess, Ladies and Gentlemen, that I do not know to which of them I should award the prize."

Gabriel glanced down at his aunts and, seeing the large smile on Aunt Julia's face and the tears which had risen to Aunt Kate's eyes, hastened to his close. He raised his glass of port gallantly, while every member of the company fingered a glass expectantly, and said loudly:

"Let us toast them all three together. Let us drink to their health, wealth, long life, happiness and prosperity and may they long continue to hold the proud and self-won position which they hold in their profession and the position of honour and affection which they hold in our hearts."

All the guests stood up, glass in hand, and turning towards the three seated ladies, sang in unison, with Mr. Browne as leader:

"For they are jolly gay fellows,
For they are jolly gay fellows,
For they are jolly gay fellows,
Which nobody can deny."

Aunt Kate was making frank use of her handkerchief and even Aunt Julia seemed moved. Freddy Malins beat time with his pudding-fork and the singers turned towards one another, as if in melodious conference, while they sang with emphasis:

"Unless he tells a lie,
Unless he tells a lie,"

Then, turning once more towards their hostesses, they sang:

"For they are jolly gay fellows,
For they are jolly gay fellows,
For they are jolly gay fellows,
Which nobody can deny."

The acclamation which followed was taken up beyond the door of the supper-room by many of the other guests and renewed time after time, Freddy Malins acting as officer with his fork on high.

★ ★ ★

The piercing morning air came into the hall where they were standing so that Aunt Kate said:

"Close the door, somebody. Mrs. Malins will get her death of cold."

"Browne is out there, Aunt Kate," said Mary Jane.

"Browne is everywhere," said Aunt Kate, lowering her voice.

Mary Jane laughed at her tone.

"Really," she said archly, "he is very attentive."

"He has been laid on here like the gas," said Aunt Kate in the same tone, "all during the Christmas."

She laughed herself this time good-humouredly and then added quickly:

"But tell him to come in, Mary Jane, and close the door. I hope to goodness he didn't hear me."

At that moment the hall-door was opened and Mr. Browne came in from the doorstep, laughing as if his heart would break. He was dressed in a long green overcoat with mock astrakhan cuffs and collar and wore on his head an oval fur cap. He pointed down the snow-covered quay from where the sound of shrill prolonged whistling was borne in.

"Teddy will have all the cabs in Dublin out," he said.

Gabriel advanced from the little pantry behind the office, struggling into his overcoat and, looking round the hall, said:

"Gretta not down yet?"

"She's getting on her things, Gabriel," said Aunt Kate.

"Who's playing up there?" asked Gabriel.

"Nobody. They're all gone."

"O no, Aunt Kate," said Mary Jane. "Bartell D'Arcy and Miss O'Callaghan aren't gone yet."

"Someone is fooling at the piano anyhow," said Gabriel.

Mary Jane glanced at Gabriel and Mr. Browne and said with a shiver:

"It makes me feel cold to look at you two gentlemen muffled up like that. I wouldn't like to face your journey home at this hour."

"I'd like nothing better this minute," said Mr. Browne stoutly, "than a rattling fine walk in the country or a fast drive with a good spanking goer between the shafts."

"We used to have a very good horse and trap at home," said Aunt Julia sadly.

"The never-to-be-forgotten Johnny," said Mary Jane, laughing.

Aunt Kate and Gabriel laughed too.

"Why, what was wonderful about Johnny?" asked Mr. Browne.

"The late lamented Patrick Morkan, our grandfather, that is," explained Gabriel, "commonly known in his later years as the old gentleman, was a glue-boiler."

"O, now, Gabriel," said Aunt Kate, laughing, "he had a starch mill."

"Well, glue or starch," said Gabriel, "the old gentleman had a horse by the name of Johnny. And Johnny used to work in the old gentleman's mill, walking round and round in order to drive the mill. That was all very well; but now comes the tragic part about Johnny. One fine day the old gentleman thought he'd like to drive out with the quality to a military review in the park."

"The Lord have mercy on his soul," said Aunt Kate compassionately.

"Amen," said Gabriel. "So the old gentleman, as I said, harnessed Johnny and put on his very best tall hat and his very best stock collar and drove out in grand style from his ancestral mansion somewhere near Back Lane, I think."

Everyone laughed, even Mrs. Malins, at Gabriel's manner and Aunt Kate said:

"O, now, Gabriel, he didn't live in Back Lane, really. Only the mill was there."

"Out from the mansion of his forefathers," continued Gabriel, "he drove with Johnny. And everything went on beautifully until Johnny came in sight of King Billy's statue: and whether he fell in love with the horse King Billy sits on or whether he thought he was back again in the mill, anyhow he began to walk round the statue."

Gabriel paced in a circle round the hall in his goloshes amid the laughter of the others.

"Round and round he went," said Gabriel, "and the old gentleman, who was a very pompous old gentleman, was highly indignant. 'Go on, sir! What do you mean, sir? Johnny! Johnny! Most extraordinary conduct! Can't understand the horse!'"

The peals of laughter which followed Gabriel's imitation of the incident was interrupted by a resounding knock at the hall-door. Mary Jane ran to open it and let in Freddy Malins. Freddy Malins, with his hat well back on his head and his shoulders humped with cold, was puffing and steaming after his exertions.

"I could only get one cab," he said.

"O, we'll find another along the quay," said Gabriel.

"Yes," said Aunt Kate. "Better not keep Mrs. Malins standing in the draught."

Mrs. Malins was helped down the front steps by her son and Mr. Browne and, after many manoeuvres, hoisted into the cab. Freddy Malins clambered in after her and spent a long time settling her on the seat, Mr. Browne helping him with advice. At last she was settled comfortably and Freddy Malins invited Mr. Browne into the cab. There was a good deal of confused talk, and then Mr. Browne got into the cab. The cabman settled his rug over his knees, and bent down for the address. The confusion grew greater and the cabman was directed differently by Freddy Malins and Mr. Browne, each of whom had his head out through a window of the cab. The difficulty was to know where to drop Mr. Browne along the route, and Aunt Kate, Aunt Julia and Mary Jane helped the discussion from the doorstep with cross-directions and contradictions and abundance of laughter. As for Freddy Malins he was speechless with laughter. He popped his head in and out of the window every moment to the great danger of his hat, and told his mother how the discussion was progressing, till at last Mr. Browne shouted to the bewildered cabman above the din of everybody's laughter:

"Do you know Trinity College?"

"Yes, sir," said the cabman.

"Well, drive bang up against Trinity College gates," said Mr. Browne, "and then we'll tell you where to go. You understand now?"

"Yes, sir," said the cabman.

"Make like a bird for Trinity College."

"Right, sir," said the cabman.

The horse was whipped up and the cab rattled off along the quay amid a chorus of laughter and adieus.

Gabriel had not gone to the door with the others. He was in a dark part of the hall gazing up the staircase. A woman was standing near the top of the first flight, in the shadow also. He could not see her face but he could see the terra-cotta and salmon-pink panels of her skirt which the shadow made appear black and white. It was his wife. She was leaning on the banisters, listening to something. Gabriel was surprised at her stillness and strained his ear to listen also. But he could hear little save the noise of laughter and dispute on the front steps, a few chords struck on the piano and a few notes of a man's voice singing.

He stood still in the gloom of the hall, trying to catch the air that the voice was singing and gazing up at his wife. There was grace and mystery in her attitude as if she were a symbol of something. He asked himself what is a woman standing on the stairs in the shadow, listening to distant music, a symbol of. If he were a painter he would paint her in that attitude. Her blue felt hat would show off the bronze of her hair against the darkness and the dark panels of her skirt would show off the light ones. *Distant Music* he would call the picture if he were a painter.

The hall-door was closed; and Aunt Kate, Aunt Julia and Mary Jane came down the hall, still laughing.

"Well, isn't Freddy terrible?" said Mary Jane. "He's really terrible."

Gabriel said nothing but pointed up the stairs towards where his wife was standing. Now that the hall-door was closed the voice and the piano could be heard more clearly. Gabriel held up his hand for them to be silent. The song seemed to be in the old Irish tonality and the singer seemed uncertain both of his words and of his voice. The voice, made plaintive by distance and by the singer's hoarseness, faintly illuminated the cadence of the air with words expressing grief:

> "O, the rain falls on my heavy locks
> And the dew wets my skin,
> My babe lies cold . . ."

"O," exclaimed Mary Jane. "It's Bartell D'Arcy singing and he wouldn't sing all the night. O, I'll get him to sing a song before he goes."

"O, do, Mary Jane," said Aunt Kate.

Mary Jane brushed past the others and ran to the staircase, but before she reached it the singing stopped and the piano was closed abruptly.

"O, what a pity!" she cried. "Is he coming down, Gretta?"

Gabriel heard his wife answer yes and saw her come down towards them. A few steps behind her were Mr. Bartell D'Arcy and Miss O'Callaghan.

"O, Mr. D'Arcy," cried Mary Jane, "it's downright mean of you to break off like that when we were all in raptures listening to you."

"I have been at him all the evening," said Miss O'Callaghan, "and Mrs. Conroy, too, and he told us he had a dreadful cold and couldn't sing."

"O, Mr. D'Arcy," said Aunt Kate, "now that was a great fib to tell."

"Can't you see that I'm as hoarse as a crow?" said Mr. D'Arcy roughly.

He went into the pantry hastily and put on his overcoat. The others, taken aback by his rude speech, could find nothing to say. Aunt Kate wrinkled her brows and made signs to the others to drop the subject. Mr. D'Arcy stood swathing his neck carefully and frowning.

"It's the weather," said Aunt Julia, after a pause.

"Yes, everybody has colds," said Aunt Kate readily, "everybody."

"They say," said Mary Jane, "we haven't had snow like it for thirty years; and I read this morning in the newspapers that the snow is general all over Ireland."

"I love the look of snow," said Aunt Julia sadly.

"So do I," said Miss O'Callaghan. "I think Christmas is never really Christmas unless we have the snow on the ground."

"But poor Mr. D'Arcy doesn't like the snow," said Aunt Kate, smiling.

Mr. D'Arcy came from the pantry, fully swathed and buttoned, and in a repentant tone told them the history of his cold. Everyone gave him advice and said it was a great pity and urged him to be very careful of his throat in the night air. Gabriel watched his wife, who did not join in the conversation. She was standing right under the dusty fanlight and the flame of the gas lit up the rich bronze of her hair, which he had seen her drying at the fire a few days before. She was in the same attitude and seemed unaware of the talk about her. At last she turned towards them and Gabriel saw that there was colour on her cheeks and that her eyes were shining. A sudden tide of joy went leaping out of his heart.

"Mr. D'Arcy," she said, "what is the name of that song you were singing?"

"It's called *The Lass of Aughrim*," said Mr. D'Arcy, "but I couldn't remember it properly. Why? Do you know it?"

"*The Lass of Aughrim*," she repeated. "I couldn't think of the name."

"It's a very nice air," said Mary Jane. "I'm sorry you were not in voice to-night."

"Now, Mary Jane," said Aunt Kate, "don't annoy Mr. D'Arcy. I won't have him annoyed."

Seeing that all were ready to start she shepherded them to the door, where good-night was said:

"Well, good-night, Aunt Kate, and thanks for the pleasant evening."

"Good-night, Gabriel. Good-night, Gretta!"

"Good-night, Aunt Kate, and thanks ever so much. Good-night, Aunt Julia."

"O, good-night, Gretta, I didn't see you."

"Good-night, Mr. D'Arcy. Good-night, Miss O'Callaghan."

"Good-night, Miss Morkan."

"Good-night, again."

"Good-night, all. Safe home."

"Good-night. Good-night."

The morning was still dark. A dull, yellow light brooded over the houses and the river; and the sky seemed to be descending. It was slushy underfoot; and only streaks and patches of snow lay on the roofs, on the parapets of the quay and on the area railings. The lamps were still burning redly in the murky air and, across the river, the palace of the Four Courts stood out menacingly against the heavy sky.

She was walking on before him with Mr. Bartell D'Arcy, her shoes in a brown parcel tucked under one arm and her hands holding her skirt up from the slush. She had no longer any grace of attitude, but Gabriel's eyes were still bright with happiness. The blood went bounding along his veins; and the thoughts went rioting through his brain, proud, joyful, tender, valorous.

She was walking on before him so lightly and so erect that he longed to run after her noiselessly, catch her by the shoulders and say something foolish and affectionate into her ear. She seemed to him so frail that he longed to defend her against something and then to be alone with her. Moments of their secret life together burst like stars upon his memory. A heliotrope envelope was lying beside his breakfast-cup and he was caressing it with his hand. Birds were twittering in the ivy and the sunny web of the curtain was shimmering along the floor: he could not eat for happiness. They were standing on the crowded platform and he was placing a ticket inside the warm palm of her glove. He was standing with her in the cold, looking in through a grated window at a man making bottles in a roaring furnace. It was very cold. Her face, fragrant in the cold air, was quite close to his; and suddenly he called out to the man at the furnace:

"Is the fire hot, sir?"

But the man could not hear with the noise of the furnace. It was just as well. He might have answered rudely.

A wave of yet more tender joy escaped from his heart and went coursing in warm flood along his arteries. Like the tender fire of stars moments of their life together, that no one knew of or would ever know of, broke upon and illumined his memory. He longed to recall to her those moments, to make her forget the years of their dull existence together and remember only their moments of ecstasy. For the years, he felt, had not quenched his soul or hers. Their children, his writing, her household cares had not quenched all their souls' tender fire. In one letter that he had written to her then he had said: "Why is it that words like these seem to me so dull and cold? Is it because there is no word tender enough to be your name?"

Like distant music these words that he had written years before were borne towards him from the past. He longed to be alone with her. When the others had gone away, when he and she were in the room in the hotel, then they would be alone together. He would call her softly:

"Gretta!"

Perhaps she would not hear at once: she would be undressing. Then something in his voice would strike her. She would turn and look at him. . . .

At the corner of Winetavern Street they met a cab. He was glad of its rattling noise as it saved him from conversation. She was looking out of the window and seemed tired. The others spoke only a few words, pointing out some building or street. The horse galloped along wearily under the murky morning sky, dragging his old rattling box after his heels, and Gabriel was again in a cab with her, galloping to catch the boat, galloping to their honeymoon.

As the cab drove across O'Connell Bridge Miss O'Callaghan said:

"They say you never cross O'Connell Bridge without seeing a white horse."

"I see a white man this time," said Gabriel.

"Where?" asked Mr. Bartell D'Arcy.

Gabriel pointed to the statue, on which lay patches of snow. Then he nodded familiarly to it and waved his hand.

"Good-night, Dan," he said gaily.

When the cab drew up before the hotel, Gabriel jumped out and, in spite of Mr. Bartell D'Arcy's protest, paid the driver. He gave the man a shilling over his fare. The man saluted and said:

"A prosperous New Year to you, sir."

"The same to you," said Gabriel cordially.

She leaned for a moment on his arm in getting out of the cab and while standing at the curbstone, bidding the others good-night. She leaned lightly on his arm, as lightly as when she had danced with him a few hours before. He had left proud and happy then, happy that she was his, proud of her grace and wifely carriage. But now, after the kindling again of so many memories, the first touch of her body, musical and strange and perfumed, sent through him a keen pang of lust. Under cover of her silence he pressed her arm closely to his side; and, as they stood at the hotel door, he felt that they had escaped from their lives and duties, escaped from home and friends and run away together with wild and radiant hearts to a new adventure.

An old man was dozing in a great hooded chair in the hall. He lit a candle in the office and went before them to the stairs. They followed

him in silence, their feet falling in soft thuds on the thickly carpeted
stairs. She mounted the stairs behind the porter, her head bowed in the
ascent, her frail shoulders curved as with a burden, her skirt girt tightly
about her. He could have flung his arms about her hips and held her still,
for his arms were trembling with desire to seize her and only the stress
of his nails against the palms of his hands held the wild impulse of his
body in check. The porter halted on the stairs to settle his guttering candle. They halted, too, on the steps below him. In the silence Gabriel
could hear the falling of the molten wax into the tray and the thumping
of his own heart against his ribs.

The porter led them along a corridor and opened a door. Then he set
his unstable candle down on a toilet-table and asked at what hour they
were to be called in the morning.

"Eight," said Gabriel.

The porter pointed to the tap of the electric-light and began a muttered apology, but Gabriel cut him short.

"We don't want any light. We have light enough from the street. And
I say," he added, pointing to the candle, "you might remove that handsome article, like a good man."

The porter took up his candle again, but slowly, for he was surprised
by such a novel idea. Then he mumbled good-night and went out.
Gabriel shot the lock to.

A ghastly light from the street lamp lay in a long shaft from one window to the door. Gabriel threw his overcoat and hat on a couch and
crossed the room towards the window. He looked down into the street
in order that his emotion might calm a little. Then he turned and leaned
against a chest of drawers with his back to the light. She had taken off
her hat and cloak and was standing before a large swinging mirror,
unhooking her waist. Gabriel paused for a few moments, watching her,
and then said:

"Gretta!"

She turned away from the mirror slowly and walked along the shaft of
light towards him. Her face looked so serious and weary that the words
would not pass Gabriel's lips. No, it was not the moment yet.

"You looked tired," he said.

"I am a little," she answered.

"You don't feel ill or weak?"

"No, tired: that's all."

She went on to the window and stood there, looking out. Gabriel
waited again and then, fearing that diffidence was about to conquer him,
he said abruptly:

"By the way, Gretta!"

"What is it?"

"You know that poor fellow Malins?" he said quickly.

"Yes. What about him?"

"Well, poor fellow, he's a decent sort of chap, after all," continued Gabriel in a false voice. "He gave me back that sovereign I lent him, and I didn't expect it, really. It's a pity he wouldn't keep away from that Browne, because he's not a bad fellow, really."

He was trembling now with annoyance. Why did she seem so abstracted? He did not know how he could begin. Was she annoyed, too, about something? If she would only turn to him or come to him of her own accord! To take her as she was would be brutal. No, he must see some ardour in her eyes first. He longed to be master of her strange mood.

"When did you lend him the pound?" she asked, after a pause.

Gabriel strove to restrain himself from breaking out into brutal language about the sottish Malins and his pound. He longed to cry to her from his soul, to crush her body against his, to overmaster her. But he said:

"O, at Christmas, when he opened that little Christmas-card shop in Henry Street."

He was in such a fever of rage and desire that he did not hear her come from the window. She stood before him for an instant, looking at him strangely. Then, suddenly raising herself on tiptoe and resting her hands lightly on his shoulders, she kissed him.

"You are a very generous person, Gabriel," she said.

Gabriel, trembling with delight at her sudden kiss and at the quaintness of her phrase, put his hands on her hair and began smoothing it back, scarcely touching it with his fingers. The washing had made it fine and brilliant. His heart was brimming over with happiness. Just when he was wishing for it she had come to him of her own accord. Perhaps her thoughts had been running with his. Perhaps she had felt the impetuous desire that was in him, and then the yielding mood had come upon her. Now that she had fallen to him so easily, he wondered why he had been so diffident.

He stood, holding her head between his hands. Then, slipping one arm swiftly about her body and drawing her towards him, he said softly:

"Gretta, dear, what are you thinking about?"

She did not answer nor yield wholly to his arm. He said again, softly:

"Tell me what it is, Gretta. I think I know what is the matter. Do I know?"

She did not answer at once. Then she said in an outburst of tears:

"O, I am thinking about that song, *The Lass of Aughrim*."

She broke loose from him and ran to the bed and, throwing her arms across the bed-rail, hid her face. Gabriel stood stock-still for a moment in astonishment and then followed her. As he passed in the way of the cheval-glass he caught sight of himself in full length, his broad, well-filled shirt-front, the face whose expression always puzzled him when he saw it in a mirror, and his glimmering gilt-rimmed eyeglasses. He halted a few paces from her and said:

"What about the song? Why does that make you cry?"

She raised her head from her arms and dried her eyes with the back of her hand like a child. A kinder note than he had intended went into his voice.

"Why, Gretta?" he asked.

"I am thinking about a person long ago who used to sing that song."

"And who was the person long ago?" asked Gabriel, smiling.

"It was a person I used to know in Galway when I was living with my grandmother," she said.

The smile passed away from Gabriel's face. A dull anger began to gather again at the back of his mind and the dull fires of his lust began to glow angrily in his veins.

"Someone you were in love with?" he asked ironically.

"It was a young boy I used to know," she answered, "named Michael Furey. He used to sing that song, *The Lass of Aughrim*. He was very delicate."

Gabriel was silent. He did not wish her to think that he was interested in this delicate boy.

"I can see him so plainly," she said, after a moment. "Such eyes as he had: big, dark eyes! And such an expression in them—an expression!"

"O, then, you are in love with him?" said Gabriel.

"I used to go out walking with him," she said, "when I was in Galway."

A thought flew across Gabriel's mind.

"Perhaps that was why you wanted to go to Galway with that Ivors girl?" he said coldly.

She looked at him and asked in surprise:

"What for?"

Her eyes made Gabriel feel awkward. He shrugged his shoulders and said:

"How do I know? To see him, perhaps."

She looked away from him along the shaft of light towards the window in silence.

"He is dead," she said at length. "He died when he was only seventeen. Isn't it a terrible thing to die so young as that?"

"What was he?" asked Gabriel, still ironically.

"He was in the gasworks," she said.

Gabriel felt humiliated by the failure of his irony and by the evocation of this figure from the dead, a boy in the gasworks. While he had been full of memories of their secret life together, full of tenderness and joy and desire, she had been comparing him in her mind with another. A shameful consciousness of his own person assailed him. He saw himself as a ludicrous figure, acting as a pennyboy for his aunts, a nervous, well-meaning sentimentalist, orating to vulgarians and idealising his own clownish lusts, the pitiable fatuous fellow he had caught a glimpse of in the mirror. Instinctively he turned his back more to the light lest she might see the shame that burned upon his forehead.

He tried to keep up his tone of cold interrogation, but his voice when he spoke was humble and indifferent.

"I suppose you were in love with this Michael Furey, Gretta," he said.

"I was great with him at that time," she said.

Her voice was veiled and sad. Gabriel, feeling now how vain it would be to try to lead her whither he had purposed, caressed one of her hands and said, also sadly:

"And what did he die of so young, Gretta? Consumption, was it?"

"I think he died for me," she answered.

A vague terror seized Gabriel at this answer, as if, at that hour when he had hoped to triumph, some impalpable and vindictive being was coming against him, gathering forces against him in its vague world. But he shook himself free of it with an effort of reason and continued to caress her hand. He did not question her again, for he felt that she would tell him of herself. Her hand was warm and moist: it did not respond to his touch, but he continued to caress it just as he had caressed her first letter to him that spring morning.

"It was in the winter," she said, "about the beginning of the winter when I was going to leave my grandmother's and come up here to the convent. And he was ill at the time in his lodgings in Galway and wouldn't be let out, and his people in Oughterard were written to. He was in decline, they said, or something like that. I never knew rightly."

She paused for a moment and sighed.

"Poor fellow," she said. "He was very fond of me and he was such a gentle boy. We used to go out together, walking, you know, Gabriel, like the way they do in the country. He was going to study singing only for his health. He had a very good voice, poor Michael Furey."

"Well; and then?" asked Gabriel.

"And then when it came to the time for me to leave Galway and come up to the convent he was much worse and I wouldn't be let see him so I wrote him a letter saying I was going up to Dublin and would be back in the summer, and hoping he would be better then."

She paused for a moment to get her voice under control, and then went on:

"Then the night before I left, I was in my grandmother's house in

Nuns' Island, packing up, and I heard gravel thrown up against the window. The window was so wet I couldn't see, so I ran downstairs as I was and slipped out the back into the garden and there was the poor fellow at the end of the garden, shivering."

"And did you not tell him to go back?" asked Gabriel.

"I implored of him to go home at once and told him he would get his death in the rain. But he said he did not want to live. I can see his eyes as well as well! He was standing at the end of the wall where there was a tree."

"And did he go home?" asked Gabriel.

"Yes, he went home. And when I was only a week in the convent he died and he was buried in Oughterard, where his people came from. O, the day I heard that, that he was dead!"

She stopped, choking with sobs, and, overcome by emotion, flung herself face downward on the bed, sobbing in the quilt. Gabriel held her hand for a moment longer, irresolutely, and then, shy of intruding on her grief, let it fall gently and walked quietly to the window.

She was fast asleep.

Gabriel, leaning on his elbow, looked for a few moments unresentfully on her tangled hair and half-open mouth, listening to her deep-drawn breath. So she had had that romance in her life: a man had died for her sake. It hardly pained him now to think how poor a part he, her husband, had played in her life. He watched her while she slept, as though he and she had never lived together as man and wife. His curious eyes rested long upon her face and on her hair: and, as he thought of what she must have been then, in that time of her first girlish beauty, a strange, friendly pity for her entered his soul. He did not like to say even to himself that her face was no longer beautiful, but he knew that it was no longer the face for which Michael Furey had braved death.

Perhaps she had not told him all the story. His eyes moved to the chair over which she had thrown some of her clothes. A petticoat string dangled to the floor. One boot stood upright, its limp upper fallen down: the fellow of it lay upon its side. He wondered at his riot of emotions of an hour before. From what had it proceeded? From his aunt's supper, from his own foolish speech, from the wine and dancing, the merry-making when saying good-night in the hall, the pleasure of the walk along the river in the snow. Poor Aunt Julia! She, too, would soon be a shade with the shade of Patrick Morkan and his horse. He had caught that haggard look upon her face for a moment when she was singing *Arrayed for the Bridal*. Soon, perhaps, he would be sitting in that same drawing-room, dressed in black, his silk hat on his knees. The blinds would be drawn down and Aunt Kate would be sitting beside him, crying and blowing her nose and telling him how Julia had died. He would cast about in his mind for some words that might console her, and would find only lame and useless ones. Yes, yes: that would happen very soon.

The air of the room chilled his shoulders. He stretched himself cautiously along under the sheets and lay down beside his wife. One by one, they were all becoming shades. Better pass boldly into that other world, in the full glory of some passion, than fade and wither dismally with age. He thought of how she who lay beside him had locked in her heart for so many years that image of her lover's eyes when he had told her that he did not wish to live.

Generous tears filled Gabriel's eyes. He had never felt like that himself towards any woman, but he knew that such a feeling must be love. The tears gathered more thickly in his eyes and in the partial darkness he imagined he saw the form of a young man standing under a dripping tree. Other forms were near. His soul had approached that region where dwell the vast hosts of the dead. He was conscious of, but could not apprehend, their wayward and flickering existence. His own identity was fading out into a grey impalpable world: the solid world itself, which these dead had one time reared and lived in, was dissolving and dwindling.

A few light taps upon the pane made him turn to the window. It had begun to snow again. He watched sleepily the flakes, silver and dark, falling obliquely against the lamplight. The time had come for him to set out on his journey westward. Yes, the newspapers were right: snow was general all over Ireland. It was falling on every part of the dark central plain, on the treeless hills, falling softly upon the Bog of Allen and, farther westward, softly falling into the dark mutinous Shannon waves. It was falling, too, upon every part of the lonely churchyard on the hill where Michael Furey lay buried. It lay thickly drifted on the crooked crosses and headstones, on the spears of the little gate, on the barren thorns. His soul swooned slowly as he heard the snow falling faintly through the universe and faintly falling, like the descent of their last end, upon all the living and the dead.

THE PLOUGHING OF LEACA-NA-NAOMH

Daniel Corkery

WITH which shall I begin—man or place? Perhaps I had better first tell of the man; of him the incident left so withered that no sooner had I laid eyes on him than I said: Here is one whose blood at some terrible moment of his life stood still, stood still and never afterwards regained its quiet, old-time ebb-and-flow. A word or two then about the place—a sculped-out shell in the Kerry mountains, an evil-looking place, green-glaring like a sea when a storm has passed. To connect man and place together, even as they worked one with the other to bring the tragedy about, ought not then to be so difficult.

I had gone into those desolate treeless hills searching after the traces of an old-time Gaelic family that once were lords of them. But in this mountainy glen I forgot my purpose almost as soon as I entered it.

In that round-ended valley—they call such a valley a coom—there was but one farmhouse, and Considine was the name of the householder— Shawn Considine, the man whose features were white with despair; his haggard appearance reminded me of what one so often sees in war-ravaged Munster—a ruined castle-wall hanging out above the woods, a grey spectre. He made me welcome, speaking slowly, as if he was not used to such amenities. At once I began to explain my quest. I soon stumbled; I felt that his thoughts were far away. I started again. A daughter of his looked at me—Nora was her name—looked at me with meaning; I could not read her look aright. Haphazardly I went through old family names and recalled old-world incidents; but with no more success. He then made to speak; I could catch only broken phrases, repeated again and again. "In the presence of God." "In the Kingdom of God." "All gone for ever." "Let them rest in peace"—(I translate from the Irish). Others, too, there were of which I could make nothing. Suddenly I went silent.

His eyes had begun to change. They were not becoming fiery or angry—that would have emboldened me, I would have blown on his anger; a little passion, even an outburst of bitter temper would have troubled me but little if in its sudden revelation I came on some new fact or even a new name in the broken story of that ruined family. But no; not fiery but cold and terror-stricken were his eyes becoming. Fear was rising in them like dank water. I withdrew my gaze, and his daughter ventured on speech:

"If you speak of the cattle, noble person, or of the land, or of the new laws, my father will converse with you; but he is dark about what happened long ago." Her eyes were even more earnest than her tongue—they implored the pity of silence.

So much for the man. A word now about the place where his large but neglected farmhouse stood against a bluff of rock. To enter that evil-looking green-mountained glen was like entering the jaws of some slimy, cold-blooded animal. You felt yourself leaving the sun, you shrunk together, you hunched yourself as if to bear an ugly pressure. In the far-back part of it was what is called in the Irish language a *leaca*—a slope of land, a lift of land, a bracket of land jutting out from the side of a mountain. This leaca, which the daughter explained was called Leaca-na-Naomh—the Leaca of the Saints—was very remarkable. It shone like a gem. It held the sunshine as a field holds its crop of golden wheat. On three sides it was pedestalled by the sheerest rock. On the fourth side it curved up to join the parent mountain-flank. Huge and high it was, yet height and size took some time to estimate, for there were mountains all around it. When you had been looking at it for some time you said aloud: "That leaca is high!" When you had stared for a longer time you said: "That leaca is immensely high—and huge!" Still the most remarkable thing about it was the way it held the sunshine. When all the valley had gone into the gloom of twilight—and this happened in the early afternoon—the leaca was still at mid-day. When the valley was dark with night and the lamps had been long alight in the farmhouse, the leaca had still the red gleam of sunset on it. It hung above the misty valley like a velarium—as they used to call that awning-cloth which hung above the emperor's seat in the amphitheatre.

"What is it called, do you say?" I asked again.

"Leaca-na-Naomh," she replied.

"Saints used to live on it?"

"The Hermits," she answered, and sighed deeply.

Her trouble told me that that leaca had to do with the fear that was burrowing like a mole in her father's heart. I would test it. Soon afterwards the old man came by, his eyes on the ground, his lips moving.

"That leaca," I said, "what do you call it?"

He looked up with a startled expression. He was very white; he couldn't abide my steady gaze.

"Nora," he cried, raising his voice suddenly and angrily, "cas isteach iad, cas isteach iad!" He almost roared at the gentle girl.

"Turn in—what?" I said, roughly, "the cattle are in long ago."

"'Tis right they should," he answered, leaving me.

Yes, this leaca and this man had between them moulded out a tragedy, as between two hands.

Though the sun had gone still I sat staring at it. It was far off, but whatever light remained in the sky had gathered to it. I was wondering at its clear definition among all the vague and misty mountain-shapes when a voice, quivering with age, high and untuneful, addressed me:

"'Twould be right for you to see it when there's snow on it."

"Ah!"

"'Tis blinding!" The voice had changed so much as his inner vision strengthened that I gazed up quickly at him. He was a very old man, somewhat fairy-like in appearance, but he had the eyes of a boy! These eyes told me he was one who had lived imaginatively. Therefore I almost gripped him lest he should escape; from him would I learn of Leaca-na-Naomh. Shall I speak of him as a vassal of the house, or as a tatter of the family, or as a spall of the rough landscape? He was native to all three. His homespun was patched with patches as large and as straight-cut as those you'd see on a fisherman's sail. He was, clothes and all, the same colour as the aged lichen of the rocks; but his eyes were as fresh as dew.

Gripping him, as I have said, I searched his face, as one searches a poem for a hidden meaning.

"When did it happen, this dreadful thing?" I said.

He was taken off his guard. I could imagine, I could almost feel his mind struggling, summoning up an energy sufficient to express his idea of how as well as when the thing happened. At last he spoke deliberately.

"When the master,"—I knew he meant the householder—"was at his best, his swiftest and strongest in health, in riches, in force and spirit." He hammered every word.

"Ah!" I said; and I noticed the night had begun to thicken, fitly I thought, for my mind was already making mad leaps into the darkness of conjecture. He began to speak a more simple language:

"In those days he was without burden or ailment—unless maybe every little biteen of land between the rocks that he had not as yet brought under the plough was a burden. This, that, yonder, all those fine fields that have gone back again into heather and furze, it was he made them. There's sweat in them! But while he bent over them in the little dark days of November, dropping his sweat, he would raise up his eyes and fix them on the leaca. *That* would be worth all of them, and worth more than double all of them if it was brought under the plough."

"And why not?" I said.

"Plough the bed of the saints?"

"I had forgotten."

"You are not a Gael of the Gaels maybe?"

"I had forgotten; continue; it grows chilly."

"He had a serving-man; he was a fool; they were common in the country then; they had not been as yet herded into asylums. He was a fool; but a true Gael. That he never forgot; except once."

"Continue."

"He had also a sire horse, Griosach he called him, he was so strong, so high and princely."

"A plough horse?"

"He had never been harnessed. He was the master's pride and boast. The people gathered on the hillsides when he rode him to Mass. You looked at the master; you looked at the horse; the horse knew the hillsides were looking at him. He made music with his hoofs, he kept his eyes to himself, he was so proud."

"What of the fool?"

"Have I spoken of the fool?"

"Yes, a true Gael."

"'Tis true, that word. He was as strong as Griosach. He was what no one else was: he was a match for Griosach. The master petted the horse. The horse petted the master. Both of them knew they went well together. But Griosach the sire horse feared Liam Ruadh the fool; and Liam Ruadh the fool feared Griosach the sire horse. For neither had as yet found out that he was stronger than the other. They would play together like two strong boys, equally matched in strength and daring. They would wrestle and throw each other. Then they would leave off; and begin again when they had recovered their breath.

"Yes," I said, "the master, the horse Griosach, the fool Liam—now, the Leaca, the Leaca."

"I have brought in the leaca. It will come in again, now! The master was one day standing at a gap for a long time; there was no one near him. Liam Ruadh came near him. 'It is not lucky to be so silent as that,' he said. The master raised his head and answered:

"'The Leaca for wheat.'

"The fool nearly fell down in a sprawling heap. No one had ever heard of anything like that.

"'No,' he said like a child.

"'The Leaca for wheat,' the master said again, as if there was someone inside him speaking.

"'The fool was getting hot and angry.

"'The Leaca for prayer!' he said.

"'The Leaca for wheat,' said the master, a third time.

"When the fool heard him he gathered himself up and roared—a loud 'O-oh!' it went around the hills like sudden thunder; in the little breath he had left he said: 'The Leaca for prayer!'

"The master went away from him; who could tell what might have happened?

"The next day the fool was washing a sheep's diseased foot—he had the struggling animal held firm in his arms when the master slipped behind him and whispered in his ear:

"'The Leaca for wheat.'

"Before the fool could free the animal the master was gone. He was a wild, swift man that day. He laughed. It was that self-same night he went into the shed where Liam slept and stood a moment looking at the large face of the fool working in his dreams. He watched him like that a minute. Then he flashed the lantern quite close into the fool's eyes so as to dazzle him, and he cried out harshly, 'The Leaca for wheat,' making his voice appear far off, like a trumpet-call, and before the fool could understand where he was, or whether he was asleep or awake, the light was gone and the master was gone.

"Day after day the master put the same thought into the fool's ear. And Liam was becoming sullen and dark. Then one night long after we were all in our sleep we heard a wild crash. The fool had gone to the master's room. He found the door bolted. He put his shoulder to it. The door went in about the room, and the arch above it fell in pieces around the fool's head—all in the still night.

"'Who's there? What is it?' cried the master, starting up in his bed.

"'Griosach for the plough!' said the fool.

"No one could think of Griosach being hitched to a plough. The master gave him no answer. He lay down in his bed and covered his face. The fool went back to his straw. Whenever the master now said 'The Leaca for wheat' the fool would answer 'Griosach for the plough.'

"The tree turns the wind aside, yet the wind at last twists the tree. Like wind and tree master and fool played against each other, until at last they each of them had spent their force.

"'I will take Griosach and Niamh and plough the leaca,' said the fool; it was a hard November day.

"'As you wish,' said the master. Many a storm finishes with a little sob of wind. Their voices were now like a little wind.

"The next night a pair of smiths were brought into the coom all the way from Aunascawl. The day after the mountains were ringing with their blows as the ploughing-gear was overhauled. Without rest or laughter or chatter the work went on, for Liam was at their shoulders, and he hardly gave them time to wipe their sweaty hair. One began to sing:"'Tis my grief on Monday now,' but Liam struck him one blow and stretched him. He returned to his work quiet enough after that. We saw the fool's anger rising. We made way for him; and he was going back and forth the whole day long; in the evening his mouth began to froth and his tongue to blab. We drew away from him; wondering what he was thinking of. The master himself began to grow timid; he hadn't a word in him; but he kept looking up at us from under his brow as if he feared we would turn against him. Sure we wouldn't; wasn't he our master—even what he did?

"When the smiths had mounted their horses that night to return to Aunascawl one of them stooped down to the master's ear and whispered: 'Watch him, he's in a fever.'

"'Who?'

"'The fool.' That was a true word.

"Some of us rode down with the smiths to the mouth of the pass, and as we did so snow began to fall silently and thickly. We were glad; we thought it might put back the dreadful business of the ploughing. When we returned towards the house we were talking. But a boy checked us.

"'Whisht!' he said.

"We listened. We crept beneath the thatch of the stables. Within we heard the fool talking to the horses. We knew he was putting his arms around their necks. When he came out, he was quiet and happy-looking. We crouched aside to let him pass. Then we told the master.

"'Go to your beds,' he said, coldly enough.

"We played no cards that night; we sang no songs; we thought it too long until we were in our dark beds. The last thing we thought of was the snow falling, falling, falling on Leaca-na-Naomh and on all the mountains. There was not a stir or a sigh in the house. Everyone feared to hear his own bed creak. And at last we slept.

"What awoke me? I could hear voices whispering. There was fright in them. Before I could distinguish one word from another I felt my neck creeping. I shook myself. I leaped up. I looked out. The light was blinding. The moon was shining on the slopes of new snow. There was none falling now; a light, thin wind was blowing out of the lovely stars.

"Beneath my window I saw five persons standing in a little group, all clutching one another like people standing in a flooded river. They were very still; they would not move even when they whispered. As I wondered to see them so fearfully clutching one another a voice spoke in my room:

"'For God's sake, Stephen, get ready and come down.'

"'Man, what's the matter with ye?'

"'For God's sake come down.'

"'Tell me, tell me!'

"'How can I? Come down!'

"I tried to be calm; I went out and made for that little group, putting my hand against my eyes, the new snow was so blinding.

"'Where's the master?' I said.

"'There!' They did not seem to care whether or not I looked at the master.

"He was a little apart; he was clutching a jut of rock as if the land was slipping from his feet. His cowardice made me afraid. I was hard put to control my breath.

"'What are ye, are ye all staring at?' I said.

"'Leaca-na——'—the voice seemed to come from over a mile away, yet it was the man beside me had spoken.

"I looked. The leaca was a dazzling blaze, it was true, but I had often before seen it as a bright and wonderful. I was puzzled.

"'Is it the leaca ye're all staring——' I began; but several of them silently lifted up a hand and pointed towards it. I could have stared at them instead; whether or not it was the white moonlight that was on them, they looked like men half-frozen, too chilled to speak. But I looked where those outstretched hands silently bade me. Then I, too, was struck dumb and became one of that icy group, for I saw a little white cloud moving across Leaca, a feathery cloud, and from the heart of it there came every now and then a little flash of fire, a spark. Sometimes, too, the little cloud would grow thin, as if it were scattering away, at which times it was a moving shadow we saw. As I blinked at it I felt my hand groping about to catch something, to catch someone, to make sure of myself; for the appearance of everything, the whiteness, the stillness, and then that moving cloud whiter than everything else, whiter than anything in the world, and so like an angel's wing moving along the leaca, frightened me until I felt like fainting away. To make things worse, straight from the little cloud came down a whisper, a long, thin, clear, silvery cry: 'Griosach! Ho-o-o-oh! Ho-o-o-oh!' a ploughing cry. We did not move; we kept our silence: everyone knew that that cry was going through everyone else as through himself, a stroke of coldness. Then I understood why the master was hanging on to a rock; he must have heard the cry before anyone else. It was terrible, made so thin and silvery by the distance; and yet it was a cry of joy—the fool had conquered Griosach!

"I do not know what wild thoughts had begun to come into my head when one man in the group gasped out 'Now!' and then another, and yet another. Their voices were breath, not sound. Then they all said 'Ah!' and I understood the fear that had moved their tongues. I saw the little cloud pause a moment on the edge of the leaca, almost hang over the edge, and then begin to draw back from it. The fool had turned his team on the verge and was now ploughing up against the hill.

"'O-o-h,' said the master, in the first moment of relief; it was more like a cry of agony. He looked round at us with ghastly eyes; and our eyeballs turned towards his, just as cold and fixed. Again that silvery cry floated down at us 'Griosach! Ho-o-o-oh!' And again the stroke of coldness passed through every one of us. The cry began to come more frequently, more triumphantly, for now again the little cloud was ploughing down the slope, and its pace had quickened. It was making once more for that edge beneath which was a sheer fall of hundreds of feet.

"Behind us, suddenly, from the direction of the thatched stables came a loud and high whinny—a call to a mate. It was so unexpected, and we were all so rapt up in what was before our eyes, that it shook us, making us spring from one another. I was the first to recover.

"'My God,' I said, 'that's Niamh, that's Niamh!'

"The whinny came again; it was Niamh surely.

"'What is he ploughing with, then? What has he with Griosach?'

"A man came running from the stables; he was trying to cry out: he could hardly be heard:

"'Griosach and Lugh! Griosach and Lugh!'

"Lugh was another sire horse; and the two sires would eat each other; they always had ill-will for each other. The master was staring at us.

"''Tisn't Lugh?' he said, with a gurgle in his voice.

"No one could answer him. We were thinking if the mare's cry reached the sires their anger would blaze up and no one could hold them; but why should Liam have yoked such a team?

"'Hush! hush!' said a woman's voice.

"We at once heard a new cry; it came down from the leaca:

"'Griosach, Back! Back!' It was almost inaudible, but we could feel the swiftness and terror in it. 'Back! Back!' came down again. 'Back, Griosach, back!'

"'They're fighting, they're fighting—the sires!' one of our horse-boys yelled out—the first sound above a breath that had come from any of us, for he was fonder of Lugh than of the favourite Griosach, and had forgotten everything else. And we saw that the little cloud was almost at a stand-still; yet that it was disturbed; sparks were flying from it; and we heard little clanking sounds, very faint, coming from it. They might mean great leaps and rearings.

"Suddenly we saw the master spring from that rock to which he had been clinging as limp as a leaf in autumn, spring from it with great life and roar up towards the leaca:

"'Liam! Liam! Liam Ruadh!' He turned to us, 'Shout, boys, and break his fever,' he cried, 'Shout, shout!'

"We were glad of that.

"'Liam! Liam! Liam Ruadh!' we roared.

"'My God! My God!' we heard as we finished. It was the master's voice; he then fell down. At once we raised our voices again; it would keep us from seeing or hearing what was happening on the leaca.

"'Liam! Liam! Liam Ruadh!'

"There was wild confusion.

"'Liam! Liam! Liam! Ruadh! Ruadh! Ruadh!' the mountains were singing back to us, making the confusion worse. We were twisted about—one man staring at the ground, one at the rock in front of his face, another at the sky high over the leaca, and one had his hand stretched out like a sign-post on a hilltop, I remember him best; none of us were looking at the leaca itself. But we were listening and listening, and at last they died, the echoes, and there was a cold silence, cold, cold. Then we heard old Diarmuid's passionless voice begin to pray:

"'Abhaile ar an sioruidheacht go raibh a anam.' 'At home in Eternity may his soul——.' We turned round, one by one, without speaking a word, and stared at the leaca. It was bare! The little cloud was still in the air—a white dust, ascending. Along the leaca we saw two thin shadowy lines—they looked as if they had been drawn in very watery ink on its dazzling surface. Of horses, plough, and fool there wasn't a trace. They had gone over the edge while we roared."

"Noble person, as they went over I'm sure Liam Ruadh had one fist at Lugh's bridle, and the other at Griosach's, and that he was swinging high in the air between them. Our roaring didn't break his fever, say that it didn't, noble person? But don't question the master about it. I have told you all!"

* * *

"I will leave this place to-night," I said.

"It is late, noble person."

"I will leave it now, bring me my horse."

That is why I made no further inquiries in that valley as to the fate of that old Gaelic family that were once lords of those hills. I gave up the quest. Sometimes a thought comes to me that Liam Ruadh might have been the last of an immemorial line, no scion of which, if God had left him his senses, would have ploughed the Leaca of the Saints, no, not even if it were to save him from begging at fairs and in public houses.

THE WEAVER'S GRAVE

Seumas O'Kelly

A Story of Old Men

I

MORTIMER Hehir, the weaver, had died, and they had come in search of his grave to Cloon na Morav, the Meadow of the Dead. Meehaul Lynskey, the nail-maker, was first across the stile. There was excitement in his face. His long warped body moved in a shuffle over the ground. Following him came Cahir Bowes, the stone-breaker, who was so beaten down from the hips forward, that his back was horizontal as the back of an animal. His right hand held a stick which propped him up in front, his left hand clutched his coat behind, just above the small of the back. By these devices he kept himself from toppling head over heels as he walked. Mother earth was drawing the brow of Cahir Bowes by magnetic force, and Cahir Bowes was resisting her fatal kiss to the last. And just now there was animation in the face he raised from its customary contemplation of the ground. Both old men had the air of those who had been unexpectedly let loose. For a long time they had lurked somewhere in the shadows of life, the world having no business for them, and now, suddenly, they had been remembered and called forth to perform an office which nobody else on earth could perform. The excitement in their faces as they crossed over the stile into Cloon na Morav expressed a vehemence in their belated usefulness. Hot on their heels came two dark, handsome, stoutly-built men, alike even to the cord that tied their corduroy trousers under their knees, and, being grave-diggers, they carried flashing spades. Last of all, and after a little delay, a firm white hand

176

was laid on the stile, a dark figure followed, the figure of a woman whose palely sad face was picturesquely, almost dramatically, framed in a black shawl which hung from the crown of the head. She was the widow of Mortimer Hehir, the weaver, and she followed the others into Cloon na Morav, the Meadow of the Dead.

To glance at Cloon na Morav as you went by on the hilly road, was to get an impression of a very old burial-ground; to pause on the road and look at Cloon na Morav was to become conscious of its quiet situation, of winds singing down from the hills in a chant for the dead; to walk over to the wall and look at the mounds inside was to provoke quotations from Gray's Elegy; to make the Sign of the Cross, lean over the wall, observe the gloomy lichened background of the wall opposite, and mark the things that seemed to stray about, like yellow snakes in the grass, was to think of Hamlet moralising at the graveside of Ophelia, and hear him establish the identity of Yorick. To get over the stile and stumble about inside, was to forget all these things and to know Cloon na Morav for itself. Who could tell the age of Cloon na Morav? The mind could only swoon away into mythology, paddle about in the dotage of paganism, the toothless infancy of Christianity. How many generations, how many septs, how many clans, how many families, how many people, had gone into Cloon na Morav? The mind could only take wing on the romances of mathematics. The ground was billowy, grotesque. Several partially suppressed insurrections—a great thirsting, worming, pushing, and shouldering under the sod—had given it character. A long tough growth of grass wired it from end to end; Nature, by this effort, endeavouring to control the strivings of the more daring of the insurgents of Cloon na Morav. No path here; no plan or map or register existed; if there ever had been one or the other it had been lost. Invasions and wars and famines and feuds had swept the ground and left it. All claims to interment had been based on powerful traditional rights. These rights had years ago come to an end—all save in a few outstanding cases, the rounding up of a spent generation. The overflow from Cloon na Morav had already set a new cemetery on its legs a mile away, a cemetery in which limestone headstones and Celtic crosses were springing up like mushrooms, advertising the triviality of a civilisation of men and women, who, according to their own epitaphs, had done exactly the two things they could not very well avoid doing: they had all, their obituary notices said, been born and they had all died. Obscure quotations from Scripture were sometimes added by way of apology. There was an almost unanimous expression of forgiveness to the Lord for what had happened to the deceased. None of this lack of humour in Cloon na Morav. Its monuments were comparatively few, and such of them as it had not swallowed were well within the general atmosphere. No obituary notice in the place was

complete; all were either wholly or partially eaten up by the teeth of
time. The monuments that had made a stout battle for existence were
pathetic in their futility. The vanity of the fashionable of dim ages made
one weep. Who on earth could have brought in the white marble slab to
Cloon na Morav? It had grown green with shame. Perhaps the lettering,
once readable upon it, had been conscientiously picked out in gold. The
shrieking winds and the fierce rains of the hills alone could tell. Plain
heavy stones, their shoulders rounded with a chisel, presumably to give
them some off-handed resemblance to humanity, now swooned at fantastic angles from their settings, as if the people to whose memory they
had been dedicated had shouldered them away as an impertinence. Other
slabs lay in fragments on the ground, filling the mind with thoughts of
Moses descending from Mount Sinai and waxing angry at sight of his
followers dancing about false gods, casting the stone tables containing the
Commandments to the ground, breaking them in pieces—the most
tragic destruction of a first edition that the world has known. Still other
heavy square dark slabs, surely creatures of a pagan imagination, were laid
flat down on numerous short legs, looking sometimes like representations
of monstrous black cockroaches, and again like tables at which the guests
of Cloon na Morav might sit down, goblin-like, in the moonlight, when
nobody was looking. Most of the legs had given way and the tables lay
overturned, as if there had been a quarrel at cards the night before. Those
that had kept their legs exhibited great cracks or fissures across their
backs, like slabs of dark ice breaking up. Over by the wall, draped in its
pattern of dark green lichen, certain families of dim ages had made an
effort to keep up the traditions of the Eastern sepulchres. They had
showed an aristocratic reluctance to take to the common clay in Cloon
na Morav. They had built low casket-shaped houses against the gloomy
wall, putting an enormously heavy iron door with ponderous iron
rings—like the rings on a pier by the sea—at one end, a tremendous
lock—one wondered what Goliath kept the key—finally cementing the
whole thing up and surrounding it with spiked iron railings. In these
contraptions very aristocratic families locked up their dead as if they
were dangerous wild animals. But these ancient vanities only heightened
the general democracy of the ground. To prove a traditional right to a
place in its community was to have the bond of your pedigree sealed.
The act of burial in Cloon na Morav was in itself an epitaph. And it was
amazing to think that there were two people still over the sod who had
such a right—one Mortimer Hehir, the weaver, just passed away, the
other Malachi Roohan, a cooper, still breathing. When these two sur-
vivors of a great generation got tucked under the sward of Cloon na
Morav its terrific history would, for all practical purposes, have ended.

II

Meehaul Lynskey, the nailer, hitched forward his bony shoulders and cast his eyes over the ground—eyes that were small and sharp, but unaccustomed to range over wide spaces. The width and the wealth of Cloon na Morav were baffling to him. He had spent his long life on the look-out for one small object so that he might hit it. The colour that he loved was the golden glowing end of a stick of burning iron; wherever he saw that he seized it in a small sconce at the end of a long handle, wrenched it off by a twitch of the wrist, hit it with a flat hammer several deft taps, dropped it into a vessel of water, out of which it came a cool and perfect nail. To do this thing several hundred times six days in the week, and pull the chain of a bellows at short intervals, Meehaul Lynskey had developed an extraordinary dexterity of sight and touch, a swiftness of business that no mortal man could exceed, and so long as he had been pitted against nail-makers of flesh and blood he had more than held his own; he had, indeed, even put up a tremendous but an unequal struggle against the competition of nail-making machinery. Accustomed as he was to concentrate on a single, glowing, definite object, the complexity and disorder of Cloon na Morav unnerved him. But he was not going to betray any of these professional defects to Cahir Bowes, the stonebreaker. He had been sent there as an ambassador by the caretaker of Cloon na Morav, picked out for his great age, his local knowledge, and his good character, and it was his business to point out to the twin grave-diggers, sons of the caretaker, the weaver's grave, so that it might be opened to receive him. Meehaul Lynskey had a knowledge of the place, and was quite certain as to a great number of grave sites, while the caretaker, being an official without records, had a profound ignorance of the whole place.

Cahir Bowes followed the drifting figure of the nail-maker over the ground, his face hitched up between his shoulders, his eyes keen and gray, glint-like as the mountains of stones he had in his day broken up as road material. Cahir, no less than Meehaul, had his knowledge of Cloon na Morav and some of his own people were buried here. His sharp, clear eyes took in the various mounds with the eye of a prospector. He, too, had been sent there as an ambassador, and as between himself and Meehaul Lynskey he did not think there could be any two opinions; his knowledge was superior to the knowledge of the nailer. Whenever Cahir Bowes met a loose stone on the grass quite instinctively he turned it over with his stick, his sharp old eyes judging its grain with a professional swiftness. Then he cracked at it with his stick, as if the stick were a hammer, and the stone, attacked on its most vulnerable spot, would fall to pieces like glass. In stones Cahir Bowes saw not sermons but seams. Even the headstones he tapped significantly with the ferrule of his stick, for Cahir Bowes had an artist's passion for his art, though his art was far from creative. He was one of the great destroyers, the reducers, the makers of chaos, a powerful and remorseless critic of the Stone Age.

The two old men wandered about Cloon na Morav, in no hurry whatever to get through with their business. After all they had been a long time pensioned off, forgotten, neglected, by the world. The renewed sensation of usefulness was precious to them. They knew that when this business was over they were not likely to be in request for anything in this world again. They were ready to oblige the world, but the world would have to allow them their own time. The world, made up of the two grave-diggers and the widow of the weaver, gathered all this without any vocal proclamation. Slowly, mechanically as it were, they followed the two ancients about Cloon na Morav. And the two ancients wandered about with the labour of age and the hearts of children. They separated, wandered about silently as if they were picking up old acquaintances, stumbling upon forgotten things, gathering up the threads of days that were over, reviving their memories, and then drew together, beginning to talk slowly, almost casually, and all their talk was of the dead, of the people who lay in the ground about them. They warmed to it, airing their knowledge, calling up names and complications of family relationships, telling stories, reviving all virtues, whispering at past vices, past vices that did not sound like vices at all, for the long years are great mitigators and run in splendid harness with the coyest of all the virtues, Charity. The whispered scandals of Cloon na Morav were seen by the twin grave-diggers and the widow of the weaver through such a haze of antiquity that they were no longer scandals but romances. The rake and the drab, seen a good way down the avenue, merely look picturesque. The grave-diggers rested their spades in the ground, leaning on the handles in exactly the same graveyard pose, and the pale widow stood in the background, silent, apart, patient, and, like all dark, tragic looking women, a little mysterious.

The stonebreaker pointed with his quivering stick at the graves of the people whom he spoke about. Every time he raised that forward support one instinctively looked, anxious and fearful, to see if the clutch were secure on the small of the back. Cahir Bowes had the sort of shape that made one eternally fearful for his equilibrium. The nailer, who, like his friend the stonebreaker, wheezed a good deal, made short, sharp gestures, and always with the right hand; the fingers were hooked in such a way, and he shot out the arm in such a manner, that they gave the illusion that he held a hammer and that it was struck out over a very hot fire. Every time Meehaul Lynskey made this gesture one expected to see sparks flying.

"Where are we to bury the weaver?" one of the grave-diggers asked at last.

Both old men laboured around to see where the interruption, the impertinence, had come from. They looked from one twin to the other, with gravity, indeed anxiety, for they were not sure which was which, or if there was not some illusion in the resemblance, some trick of youth to baffle age.

"Where are we to bury the weaver?" the other twin repeated, and the strained look on the old men's faces deepened. They were trying to fix in their minds which of the twins had interrupted first and which last. The eyes of Meehaul Lynskey fixed on one twin with the instinct of his trade, while Cahir Bowes ranged both and eventually wandered to the figure of the widow in the background, silently accusing her of impatience in a matter about which it would be indelicate for her to show haste.

"We can't stay here for ever," said the first twin.

It was the twin upon whom Meehaul Lynskey had fastened his small eyes, and sure of his man this time, Meehaul Lynskey hit him.

"There's many a better man than you," said Meehaul Lynskey, "that will stay here for ever." He swept Cloon na Morav with the hooked fingers.

"Them that stays in Cloon na Morav for ever," said Cahir Bowes with a wheezing energy, "have nothing to be ashamed of—nothing to be ashamed of. Remember that, young fellow."

Meehaul Lynskey did not seem to like the intervention, the help, of Cahir Bowes. It was a sort of implication that he had not—*he,* mind you—had not hit the nail properly on the head.

"Well, where are we to bury him, anyway?" said the twin, hoping to profit by the chagrin of the nailer—the nailer who, by implication, had failed to nail.

"You'll bury him," said Meehaul Lynskey, "where all belonging to him is buried."

"We come," said the other twin, "with some sort of intention of that kind." He drawled out the words, in imitation of the old men. The skin relaxed on his handsome dark face and then bunched in puckers of humour about the eyes; Meehaul Lynskey's gaze, wandering for once, went to the handsome dark face of the other twin and the skin relaxed and then bunched in puckers of humour about *his* eyes, so that Meehaul Lynskey had an unnerving sensation that these young grave-diggers were purposely confusing him.

"You'll bury him," he began with some vehemence, and was amazed to find Cahir Bowes again taking the words out of his mouth, snatching the hammer out of his hand, so to speak.

"—where you're told to bury him," Cahir Bowes finished for him.

Meehaul Lynskey was so hurt that his long slanting figure moved away down the graveyard, then stopped suddenly. He had determined to do a dreadful thing. He had determined to do a thing that was worse than kicking a crutch from under a cripple's shoulder; that was like stealing the holy water out of a room where a man lay dying. He had determined to ruin the last day's amusement on this earth for Cahir Bowes and himself by prematurely and basely disclosing the weaver's grave!

"Here," called back Meehaul Lynskey, "is the weaver's grave, and here you will bury him."

All moved down to the spot, Cahir Bowes going with extraordinary spirit, the ferrule of his terrible stick cracking on the stones he met on the way.

"Between these two mounds," said Meehaul Lynskey, and already the twins raised their twin spades in a sinister movement, like swords of lancers flashing at a drill.

"Between these two mounds," said Meehaul Lynskey, "is the grave of Mortimer Hehir."

"Hold on!" cried Cahir Bowes. He was so eager, so excited, that he struck one of the grave-diggers a whack of his stick on the back. Both grave-diggers swung about to him as if both had been hurt by the one blow.

"Easy there," said the first twin.

"Easy there," said the second twin.

"Easy yourselves," cried Cahir Bowes. He wheeled about his now quivering face on Meehaul Lynskey.

"What is it you're saying about the spot between the mounds?" he demanded.

"I'm saying," said Meehaul Lynskey vehemently, "that it's the weaver's grave."

"What weaver?" asked Cahir Bowes.

"Mortimer Hehir," replied Meehaul Lynskey. "There's no other weaver in it."

"Was Julia Rafferty a weaver?"

"What Julia Rafferty?"

"The midwife, God rest her."

"How could she be a weaver if she was a midwife?"

"Not a one of me knows. But I'll tell you what I do know and know rightly; that it's Julia Rafferty is in that place and no weaver at all."

"Amn't I tell you it's the weaver's grave?"

"And amn't I telling you it's not?"

"That I may be as dead as my father but the weaver was buried there."

"A bone of a weaver was never sunk in it as long as weavers was weavers. Full of Raffertys it is."

"Alive with weavers it is."

"Heavenlyful Father, was the like ever heard: to say that a grave was alive with dead weavers."

"It's full of them—full as a tick."

"And the clean grave that Mortimer Hehir was never done boasting about—dry and sweet and deep and no way bulging at all. Did you see the burial of his father ever?"

"I did, in troth, see the burial of his father—forty year ago if it's a day."

"Forty year ago—it's fifty-one year come the sixteenth of May. It's well I remember it and it's well I have occasion to remember it, for it was the day after that again that myself ran away to join the soldiers, my aunt hot foot after me, she to be buying me out the week after, I a high-spirited fellow morebetoken."

"Leave the soldiers out of it and leave your aunt out of it and stick to the weaver's grave. Here in this place was the last weaver buried, and I'll tell you what's more. In a straight line with it is the grave of——"

"A straight line, indeed! Who but yourself, Meehaul Lynskey, ever heard of a straight line in Cloon na Morav? No such thing was ever wanted or ever allowed in it."

"In a straight direct line, measured with a rule——"

"Measured with crooked, stumbling feet, maybe feet half reeling in drink."

"Can't you listen to me now?"

"I was aways a bad warrant to listen to anything except sense. Yourself ought to be the last man in the world to talk about straight lines, you with the sight scattered in your head, with the divil of sparks flying under your eyes."

"Don't mind me sparks now, nor me sight neither, for in a straight measured line with the weaver's grave was the grave of the Cassidys."

"What Cassidys?"

"The Cassidys that herded for the O'Sheas."

"Which O'Sheas?"

"O'Shea Ruadh of Cappakelly. Don't you know anyone at all, or is it gone entirely your memory is?"

"Cappakelly *inagh!* And who cares a whistle about O'Shea Ruadh, he or his seed, breed and generations? It's a rotten lot of landgrabbers they were."

"Me hand to you on that. Striving ever they were to put their red paws on this bit of grass and that perch of meadow."

"Hungry in themselves even for the cut-away bog."

"And Mortimer Hehir a decent weaver, respecting every man's wool."

"His forehead pallid with honesty over the yarn and the loom."

"If a bit broad-spoken when he came to the door for a smoke of the pipe."

"Well, there won't be a mouthful of clay between himself and O'Shea Ruadh now."

"In the end what did O'Shea Ruadh get after all his striving?"

"I'll tell you that. He got what land suits a blind fiddler."

"Enough to pad the crown of the head and tap the sole of the foot! Now you're talking."

"And the devil a word out of him now no more than anyone else in Cloon na Morav."

"It's easy talking to us all about land when we're packed up in our timber boxes."

"As the weaver was when he got sprinkled with the holy water in that place."

"As Julia Rafferty was when they read the prayers over her in that place, she a fine, buxom, cheerful woman in her day, with great skill in her business."

"Skill or no skill, I'm telling you she's not there, wherever she is."

"I suppose you want me to take her up in my arms and show her to you?"

"Well, then, indeed, Cahir, I do not. 'Tisn't a very handsome pair you would make at all, you not able to stand much more hardship than Julia herself."

From this there developed a slow, laboured, aged dispute between the two authorities. They moved from grave to grave, pitting memory against memory, story against story, knocking down reminiscence with reminiscence, arguing in a powerful intimate obscurity that no outsider could hope to follow, blasting knowledge with knowledge, until the whole place seemed strewn with the corpses of their arguments. The two grave-diggers followed them about in a grim silence; impatience in their movements, their glances; the widow keeping track of the grand tour with a miserable feeling, a feeling, as site after site was rejected, that the tremendous exclusiveness of Cloon na Morav would altogether push her dead man, the weaver, out of his privilege. The dispute ended, like all epics, where it began. Nothing was established, nothing settled. But the two old men were quite exhausted, Meehaul Lynskey sitting down on the back of one of the monstrous cockroaches, Cahir Bowes leaning against a tombstone that was half-submerged, its end up like the stern of a derelict at sea. Here they sat glaring at each other like a pair of grim vultures.

The two grave-diggers grew restive. Their business had to be done. The weaver would have to be buried. Time pressed. They held a consultation apart. It broke up after a brief exchange of views, a little laughter.

"Meehaul Lynskey is right," said one of the twins.

Meehaul Lynskey's face lit up. Cahir Bowes looked as if he had been slapped on the cheeks. He moved out from his tombstone.

"Meehaul Lynskey is right," repeated the other twin. They had decided to break up the dispute by taking sides. They raised their spades and moved to the site which Meehaul Lynskey had urged upon them.

"Don't touch that place," Cahir Bowes cried, raising his stick. He was measuring the back of the grave-digger again when the man spun round upon him, menace in his handsome dark face.

"Touch me with that stick," he cried, "and I'll——,"

Some movement in the background, some agitation in the widow's shawl, caused the grave-digger's menace to dissolve, the words to die in his mouth, a swift flush mounting the man's face. A faint smile of grati-tude swept the widow's face like a flash. It was as if she had cried out, "Ah, don't touch the poor old, cranky fellow! you might hurt him." And it was as if the grave-digger had cried back: "He has annoyed me greatly, but I don't intend to hurt him. And since you say so with your eyes I won't even threaten him."

Under pressure of the half threat, Cahir Bowes shuffled back a little way, striking an attitude of feeble dignity, leaning out on his stick while the grave-diggers got to work.

"It's the weaver's grave, surely," said Meehaul Lynskey.

"If it is," said Cahir Bowes, "remember his father was buried down seven feet. You gave in to that this morning."

"There was no giving in about it," said Meehaul Lynskey. "We all know that one of the wonders of Cloon na Morav was the burial of the last weaver seven feet, he having left it as an injunction on his family. The world knows he went down the seven feet."

"And remember this," said Cahir Bowes, "that Julia Rafferty was buried no seven feet. If she is down three feet it's as much as she went."

Sure enough, the grave-diggers had not dug down more than three feet of ground when one of the spades struck hollowly on unhealthy timber. The sound was unmistakable and ominous. There was silence for a moment. Then Cahir Bowes made a sudden short spurt up a mound beside him, as if he were some sort of mechanical animal wound up, his horizontal back quivering. On the mound he made a super-human effort to straighten himself. He got his ears and his blunt nose into a consider-able elevation. He had not been so upright for twenty years. And raising his weird countenance, he broke into a cackle that was certainly meant to be a crow. He glared at Meehaul Lynskey, his emotion so great that his eyes swam in a watery triumph.

Meehaul Lynskey had his eyes, as was his custom, upon one thing, and that thing was the grave, and especially the spot on the grave where the spade had struck the coffin. He looked stunned and fearful. His eyes slowly withdrew their gimletlike scrutiny from the spot, and sought the triumphant crowing figure of Cahir Bowes on the mound.

Meehaul Lynskey looked as if he would like to say something, but no words came. Instead he ambled away, retired from the battle, and standing apart, rubbed one leg against the other, above the back of the ankles, like some great insect. His hooked fingers at the same time stroked the bridge of his nose. He was beaten.

"I suppose it's not the weaver's grave," said one of the grave-diggers. Both of them looked at Cahir Bowes.

"Well, you know it's not," said the stonebreaker. "It's Julia Rafferty you struck. She helped many a one into the world in her day, and it's poor recompense to her to say she can't be at rest when she left it." He turned to the remote figure of Meehaul Lynskey and cried: "Ah-ha, well you may rub your ignorant legs. And I'm hoping Julia will forgive you this day's ugly work."

In silence, quickly, with reverence, the twins scooped back the clay over the spot. The widow looked on with the same quiet, patient, mysterious silence. One of the grave-diggers turned on Cahir Bowes.

"I suppose you know where the weaver's grave is?" he asked.

Cahir Bowes looked at him with an ancient tartness, then said: "You suppose!"

"Of course, you know where it is."

Cahir Bowes looked as if he knew where the gates of heaven were, and that he might—or might not—enlighten an ignorant world. It all depended! His eyes wandered knowingly out over the meadows beyond the graveyard. He said:

"I do know where the weaver's grave is."

"We'll be very much obliged to you if you show it to us."

"Very much obliged," endorsed the other twin.

The stonebreaker, thus flattered, led the way to a new site, one nearer to the wall, where were the plagiarisms of the Eastern sepulchres. Cahir Bowes made little journeys about, measuring so many steps from one place to another, mumbling strange and unintelligible information to himself, going through an extraordinary geometrical emotion, striking the ground hard taps with his stick.

"Glory be to the Lord!" cried Meehaul Lynskey, "he's like the man they had driving the water for the well in the quarry field, he whacking the ground with his magic hazel wand."

Cahir Bowes made no reply. He was too absorbed in his own emotion. A little steam was beginning to ascend from his brow. He was moving about the ground like some grotesque spider weaving an invisible web.

"I suppose now," said Meehaul Lynskey, addressing the marble monument, "that as soon as Cahir hits the right spot one of the weavers will turn about below. Or maybe he expects one of them to whistle up at him out of the ground. That's it; devil a other! When we hear the whistle we'll all know for certain where to bury the weaver."

Cahir Bowes was contracting his movements, so that he was now circling about the one spot, like a dog going to lie down.

Meehaul Lynskey drew a little closer, watching eagerly, his grim yellow face, seared with yellow marks from the fires of his workshop, tightened up in a sceptical pucker. His half-muttered words were bitter with an aged sarcasm. He cried:

"Say nothing; he'll get it yet, will the man of knowledge, the know-all, Cahir Bowes! Give him time. Give him until this day twelvemonth. Look at that for a right-about-turn of the left heel. Isn't the nimbleness of that young fellow a treat to see? Are they whistling to you from below, Cahir? Is it dancing to the weaver's music you are? That's it, devil a other."

Cahir Bowes was mapping out a space on the grass with his stick. Gradually it took, more or less, the outline of a grave site. He took off his hat and mopped his steaming brow with a red handkerchief, saying:

"There is the weaver's grave."

"God in Heaven!" cried Meehaul Lynskey, "will you look at what he calls the weaver's grave? I'll say nothing at all. I'll hold my tongue. I'll shut up. Not one word will I say about Alick Finlay, the mildest man that ever lived, a man full of religion, never at the end of his prayers! But, sure, it's the saints of God that get the worst of it in this world, and if Alick escaped during life, faith he's in for it now, with the pirates and the body-snatchers of Cloon na Morav on top of him."

A corncrake began to sing in the nearby meadow, and his rasping notes sounded like a queer accompaniment to the words of Meehaul Lynskey. The grave-diggers, who had gone to work on the Cahir Bowes site, laughed a little, one of them looking for a moment at Meehaul Lynskey, saying:

"Listen to that damned old corncrake in the meadow! I'd like to put a sod in his mouth."

The man's eye went to the widow. She showed no emotion one way or the other, and the grave-digger got back to his work. Meehaul Lynskey, however, wore the cap. He said:

"To be sure! I'm to sing dumb. I'm not to have a word out of me at all. Others can rattle away as they like in this place, as if they owned it. The ancient good old stock is to be nowhere and the scruff of the hills let rampage as they will. That's it, devil a other. Castles falling and dunghills rising! Well, God be with the good old times and the good old mannerly people that used to be in it, and God be with Alick Finlay, the holiest——"

A sod of earth came through the air from the direction of the grave, and, skimming Meehaul Lynskey's head, dropped somewhere behind. The corncrake stopped his notes in the meadow, and Meehaul Lynskey stood statuesque in a mute protest, and silence reigned in the place while the clay sang up in a swinging rhythm from the grave.

Cahir Bowes, watching the operations with intensity, said:

"It was nearly going astray on me."

Meehaul Lynskey gave a little snort. He asked:

"What was?"

"The weaver's grave."

"Remember this: the last weaver is down seven feet. And remember this: Alick Finlay is down less than Julia Rafferty."

He had no sooner spoken when a fearful thing happened. Suddenly out of the soft cutting of the earth a spade sounded harsh on tinware, there was a crash, less harsh, but painfully distinct, as if rotten boards were falling together, then a distinct subsidence of the earth. The work stopped at once. A moment's fearful silence followed. It was broken by a short, dry laugh from Meehaul Lynskey. He said:

"God be merciful to us all! That's the latter end of Alick Finlay."

The two grave-diggers looked at each other. The shawl of the widow in the background was agitated. One twin said to the other:

"This can't be the weaver's grave."

The other agreed. They all turned their eyes upon Cahir Bowes. He was hanging forward in a pained strain, his head quaking, his fingers twitching on his stick. Meehaul Lynskey turned to the marble monument and said with venom:

"If I was guilty I'd go down on my knees and beg God's pardon. If I didn't I'd know the ghost of Alick Finlay, saint as he was, would leap upon me and guzzle me—for what right would I have to set anybody at him with driving spades when he was long years in the grave?"

Cahir Bowes took no notice. He was looking at the ground, searching about, and slowly, painfully, began his web-spinning again. The grave-diggers covered in the ground without a word. Cahir Bowes appeared to get lost in some fearful maze of his own making. A little whimper broke from him now and again. The steam from his brow thickened in the air, and eventually he settled down on the end of a headstone, having got the worst of it. Meehaul Lynskey sat on another stone facing him, and they glared, sinister and grotesque, at each other.

"Cahir Bowes," said Meehaul Lynskey, "I'll tell you what you are, and then you can tell me what I am."

"Have it whatever way you like," said Cahir Bowes. "What is it that I am?"

"You're a gentleman, a grand oul' stone-breaking gentleman. That's what you are, devil a other!"

The wrinkles on the withered face of Cahir Bowes contracted, his eyes stared across at Meehaul Lynskey, and two yellow teeth showed between his lips. He wheezed:

"And do you know what you are?"

"I don't."

"You're a nailer, that's what you are, a damned nailer."

They glared at each other in a quaking, grim silence.

And it was at this moment of collapse, of deadlock, that the widow spoke for the first time. At the first sound of her voice one of the twins perked his head, his eyes going to her face. She said in a tone as quiet as her whole behaviour:

"Maybe I ought to go up to the Tunnel Road and ask Malachi Roohan where the grave is."

They had all forgotten the oldest man of them all, Malachi Roohan. He would be the last mortal man to enter Cloon na Morav. He had been the great friend of Mortimer Hehir, the weaver, in the days that were over, and the whole world knew that Mortimer Hehir's knowledge of Cloon na Morav was perfect. Maybe Malachi Roohan would have learned a great deal from him. And Malachi Roohan, the cooper, was so long bed-ridden that those who remembered him at all thought of him as a man who had died a long time ago.

"There's nothing else for it," said one of the twins, leaving down his spade, and immediately the other twin laid his spade beside it.

The two ancients on the headstones said nothing. Not even *they* could raise a voice against the possibilities of Malachi Roohan, the cooper. By their terrible aged silence they gave consent, and the widow turned to walk out of Cloon na Morav. One of the grave-diggers took out his pipe. The eyes of the other followed the widow, he hesitated, then walked after her. She became conscious of the man's step behind her as she got upon the stile, and turned her palely sad face upon him. He stood awkwardly, his eyes wandering, then said:

"Ask Malachi Roohan where the grave is, the exact place."

It was to do this the widow was leaving Cloon na Morav; she had just announced that she was going to ask Malachi Roohan where the grave was. Yet the man's tone was that of one who was giving her extraordinary acute advice. There was a little half-embarrassed note of confidence in his tone. In a dim way the widow thought that, maybe, he had accompanied her to the stile in a little awkward impulse of sympathy. Men were very curious in their ways sometimes. The widow was a very well-mannered woman, and she tried to look as if she had received a very valuable direction. She said:

"I will. I'll put that question to Malachi Roohan."

And then she passed out over the stile.

III

The widow went up the road, and beyond it struck the first of the houses of the nearby town. She passed through faded streets in her quiet gait, moderately grief-stricken at the death of her weaver. She had been his fourth wife, and the widowhoods of fourth wives had not the rich abandon, the great emotional cataclysm of first, or even second, widowhoods. It is a little chastened in its poignancy. The widow had a nice feeling that it would be out of place to give way to any of the characteristic manifestations of normal widowhood. She shrank from drawing attention to the fact that she had been a fourth wife. People's memories become so extraordinarily acute to family history in times of death! The widow did not care to come in as a sort of dramatic surprise in the gossip of the people about the weaver's life. She had heard snatches of such gossip at the wake the night before. She was beginning to understand why people love wakes and the intimate personalities of wakehouses. People listen to, remember, and believe what they hear at wakes. It is more precious to them than anything they ever hear in school, church, or playhouse. It is hardly because they get certain entertainment at the wake. It is more because the wake is a grand review of family ghosts. There one hears all the stories, the little flattering touches, the little unflattering bitternesses, the traditions, the astonishing records, of the clans. The woman with a memory speaking to the company from a chair beside a laid-out corpse carries more authority than the bishop allocuting from his chair. The wake is realism. The widow had heard a great deal at the wake about the clan of the weavers, and noted, without expressing any emotion, that she had come into the story not like other women, for anything personal to her own womanhood—for beauty, or high spirit, or temper, or faithfulness, or unfaithfulness—but simply because she was a fourth wife, a kind of curiosity, the back-wash of Mortimer Hehir's romances. The widow felt a remote sense of injustice in all this. She had said to herself that widows who had been fourth wives deserved more sympathy than widows who had been first wives, for the simple reason that fourth widows had never been, and could never be, first wives! The thought confused her a little, and she did not pursue it, instinctively feeling that if she did accept the conventional view of her condition she would only crystallize her widowhood into a grievance that nobody would try to understand, and which would, accordingly, be merely useless. And what was the good of it, anyhow? The widow smoothed her dark hair on each side of her head under her shawl.

She had no bitter and no sweet memories of the weaver. There was nothing that was even vivid in their marriage. She had no complaints to make of Mortimer Hehir. He had not come to her in any fiery love impulse. It was the marriage of an old man with a woman years younger. She had recognised him as an old man from first to last, a man who had already been thrice through a wedded experience, and her temperament, naturally calm, had met his half-stormy, half-petulant character without suffering any sort of shock. The weaver had tried to keep up to the illusion of a perennial youth by dyeing his hair, and marrying one wife as soon as possible after another. The fourth wife had come to him late in life. She had a placid understanding that she was a mere flattery to the weaver's truculent egoism.

These thoughts, in some shape or other, occupied, without agitating, the mind of the widow as she passed, a dark shadowy figure through streets that were clamorous in their quietudes, painful in their lack of all the purposes for which streets have ever been created. Her only emotion was one which she knew to be quite creditable to her situation: a sincere desire to see the weaver buried in the grave to which the respectability of his family and the claims of his ancient house fully and fairly entitled him to. The proceedings in Cloon na Morav had been painful, even tragical, to the widow. The weavers had always been great authorities and zealous guardians of the ancient burial place. This function had been traditional and voluntary with them. This was especially true of the last of them, Mortimer Hehir. He had been the greatest of all authorities on the burial places of the local clans. His knowledge was scientific. He had been the grand savant of Cloon na Morav. He had policed the place. Nay, he had been its tyrant. He had over and over again prevented terrible mistakes, complications that would have appalled those concerned if they had not been beyond all such concerns. The widow of the weaver had often thought that in his day Mortimer Hehir had made his solicitation for the place a passion, unreasonable, almost violent. They said that all this had sprung from a fear that had come to him in his early youth that through some blunder an alien, an inferior, even an enemy, might come to find his way into the family burial place of the weavers. This fear had made him what he was. And in his later years his pride in the family burial place became a worship. His trade had gone down, and his pride had gone up. The burial ground in Cloon na Morav was the grand proof of his aristocracy. That was the coat-of-arms, the estate, the mark of high breeding, in the weavers. And now the man who had minded everybody's grave had not been able to mind his own. The widow thought that it was one of those injustices which blacken the reputation of the whole earth. She had felt, indeed, that she had been herself slack not to have learned long ago the lie of this precious grave from the weaver himself; and that he himself had been slack in not properly instructing her. But that was the way in this miserable world! In his passion for classifying the rights of others, the weaver had obscured his own. In his long and

entirely successful battle in keeping alien corpses out of his own aristocratic pit he had made his own corpse alien to every pit in the place. The
living high priest was the dead pariah of Cloon na Morav. Nobody could
now tell except, perhaps, Malachi Roohan, the precise spot which he had
defended against the blunders and confusions of the entire community, a
dead-forgetting, indifferent, slack lot!

  The widow tried to recall all she had ever heard the weaver say about
his grave, in the hope of getting some clue, something that might be better than the scandalous scatter-brained efforts of Meehaul Lynskey and
Cahir Bowes. She remembered various detached things that the weaver,
a talkative man, had said about his grave. Fifty years ago since that grave
had been last opened, and it had then been opened to receive the remains
of his father. It had been thirty years previous to that since it had taken
in his father, that is, the newly dead weaver's father's father. The weavers
were a long-lived lot, and there were not many males of them; one son
was as much as any one of them begot to pass to the succession of the
loom; if there were daughters they scattered, and their graves were con-
tinents apart. The three wives of the late weaver were buried in the new
cemetery. The widow remembered that the weaver seldom spoke of
them, and took no interest in their resting-place. His heart was in Cloon
na Morav and the sweet, dry, deep aristocratic bed he had there in reserve
for himself. But all his talk had been generalization. He had never, that
the widow could recall, said anything about the site, about the signs and
measurements by which it could be identified. No doubt it had been well
known to many people, but they had all died. The weaver had never
realised what their slipping away might mean to himself. The position of
the grave was so intimate to his own mind that it never occurred to him
that it could be obscure to the minds of others. Mortimer Hehir had
passed away like some learned and solitary astronomer who had discovered a new star, hugging its beauty, its exclusiveness, its possession to his
heart, secretly rejoicing how its name would travel with his own through
heavenly space for all time—and forgetting to mark its place among the
known stars grouped upon his charts. Meehaul Lynskey and Cahir Bowes
might now be two seasoned astronomers of venal knowledge looking for
the star which the weaver, in his love for it, had let slip upon the mighty
complexity of the skies.

  The thing that is clearest to the mind of a man is often the thing that
is most opaque to the intelligence of his bosom companion. A saint may
walk the earth in the simple belief that all the world beholds his glowing halo; but all the world does not; if it did the saint would be stoned.
And Mortimer Hehir had been as innocently proud of his grave as a saint
might be ecstatic of his halo. He believed that when the time came he
would get a royal funeral—a funeral fitting to the last of the line of great

Cloon na Morav weavers. Instead of that they had no more idea of where to bury him than if he had been a wild tinker of the roads.

The widow, thinking of these things in her own mind, was about to sigh when, behind a window pane, she heard the sudden bubble of a roller canary's song. She had reached, half absent-mindedly, the home of Malachi Roohan, the cooper.

IV

The widow of the weaver approached the door of Malachi Roohan's house with an apologetic step, pawing the threshold a little in the manner of peasant women—a mannerism picked up from shy animals—before she stooped her head and made her entrance.

Malachi Roohan's daughter withdrew from the fire a face which reflected the passionate soul of a cook. The face cooled as the widow disclosed her business.

"I wouldn't put it a-past my father to have knowledge of the grave," said the daughter of the house, adding, "the Lord a mercy on the weaver."

She led the widow into the presence of the cooper.

The room was small and low and stuffy, indifferently served with light by an unopenable window. There was the smell of old age, of decay, in the room. It brought almost a sense of faintness to the widow. She had the feeling that God had made her to move in the ways of old men—passionate, cantankerous, egoistic old men—old men for whom she was always doing something, always remembering things, from missing buttons to lost graves.

Her eyes sought the bed of Malachi Roohan with an unemotional, quietly sceptical gaze. But she did not see anything of the cooper. The daughter leaned over the bed, listened attentively, and then very deftly turned down the clothes, revealing the bust of Malachi Roohan. The widow saw a weird face, not in the least pale or lined, but ruddy, with a mahogany bald head, a head upon which the leathery skin—for there did not seem any flesh—hardly concealed the stark outlines of the skull. From the chin there strayed a grey beard, the most shaken and whipped-looking beard that the widow had ever seen; it was, in truth, a very miracle of a beard, for one wondered how it had come there, and having come there, how it continued to hang on, for there did not seem anything to which it could claim natural allegiance. The widow was as much astonished at this beard as if she saw a plant growing in a pot without soil. Through its gaps she could see the leather of the skin, the bones of a neck, which was indeed a neck. Over this head and shoulders the cooper's daughter bent and shouted into a crumpled ear. A little spasm of life stirred in the mummy. A low, mumbling sound came from the bed. The widow was already beginning to feel that, perhaps, she had done wrong in remembering that the cooper was still extant. But what else could she have done? If the weaver was buried in a wrong grave she did not believe that his soul would ever rest in peace. And what could be more dreadful than a soul wandering on the howling winds of the earth? The weaver would grieve, even in heaven, for his grave, grieve, maybe, as bitterly as a saint might grieve who had lost his halo. He was a passionate old man, such an old man as would have a turbulent spirit. He would surely——. The widow stifled the thoughts that flashed into her mind. She was no more superstitious than the rest of us, but——. These vague and terrible fears, and her moderately decent sorrow, were alike banished from her mind by what followed. The mummy on the bed came to life. And, what was more, he did it himself. His daughter looked on with the air of one whose sensibilities had become blunted by a long familiarity with the various stages of his resurrections. The widow gathered that the daughter had been well drilled; she had been taught how to keep her place. She did not tender the slightest help to her father as he drew himself together on the bed. He turned over on his side, then on his back, and stealthily began to insinuate his shoulder blades on the pillow, pushing up his weird head to the streak of light from the little window. The widow had been so long accustomed to assist the aged that she made some involuntary movement of succour. Some half-seen gesture by the daughter, a sudden lifting of the eyelids on the face of the patient, disclosing a pair of blue eyes, gave the widow instinctive pause. She remained where she was, aloof like the daughter of the house. And as she caught the blue of Malachi Roohan's eyes it broke upon the widow that here in the essence of the cooper there lived a spirit of extraordinary independence. Here, surely, was a man who had been accustomed to look out for himself, who resented attentions, even in these days of his flickering consciousness. Up he wormed his shoulder blades, his mahogany skull, his leathery skin, his sensational eyes, his miraculous beard, to the light and to the full view of the visitor. At a certain stage of the resurrection—when the cooper had drawn two long, stringy arms from under the clothes—his daughter made a drilled movement forward, seeking something in the bed. The widow saw her discover the end of a rope, and this she placed in the hands of her indomitable father. The other end of the rope was fastened to the iron rail of the foot of the bed. The sinews of the patient's hands clutched the rope, and slowly, wonderfully, magically, as it seemed to the widow, the cooper raised himself to a sitting posture in the bed. There was dead silence in the room except for the laboured breathing of the performer. The eyes of the widow blinked. Yes, there was that ghost of a man hoisting himself up from the dead on a length of rope, reversing the usual procedure. By that length of rope did the cooper hang on to life, and the effort of life. It represented his connection with the world, the world which had forgotten him, which marched past his window outside without knowing the stupendous thing that went on in his room. There he was, sitting up in the bed, restored to view by his own unaided efforts, holding his grip on life to the last. It cost him something to do it, but he did it. It would take him longer and longer every day to grip along that length of rope; he would fail ell by ell, sinking back to the last helplessness on his rope, descending into eternity as a vessel is lowered on a rope into a dark, deep well. But there he was now, still able for his work, unbeholding to all, self-dependent and alive, looking a little vaguely with his blue eyes at the widow of the weaver. His daughter swiftly and quietly propped pillows at his back, and she did it with the air of one who was allowed a special privilege.

"Nan!" called the old man to his daughter.

The widow, cool-tempered as she was, almost jumped on her feet. The voice was amazingly powerful. It was like a shout, filling the little room with vibrations. For four things did the widow ever after remember Malachi Roohan—for his rope, his blue eyes, his powerful voice, and his magic beard. They were thrown on the background of his skeleton in powerful relief.

"Yes, Father," his daughter replied, shouting into his ear. He was apparently very deaf. This infirmity came upon the widow with a shock. The cooper was full of physical surprises.

"Who's this one?" the cooper shouted, looking at the widow. He had the belief that he was delivering an aside.

"Mrs. Hehir."

"Mrs. Hehir—what Hehir would she be?"

"The weaver's wife."

"The weaver? Is it Mortimer Hehir?"

"Yes, Father."

"In troth I know her. She's Delia Morrissey, that married the weaver; Delia Morrissey that he followed to Munster, a raving lunatic with the dint of love."

A hot wave of embarrassment swept the widow. For a moment she thought the mind of the cooper was wandering. Then she remembered that the maiden name of the weaver's first wife was, indeed, Delia Morrissey. She had heard it, by chance, once or twice.

"Isn't it Delia Morrissey herself we have in it??" the old man asked.

The widow whispered to the daughter:

"Leave it so."

She shrank from a difficult discussion with the spectre in the bed on the family history of the weaver. A sense of shame came to her that she

could be the wife to a contemporary of this astonishing old man holding on to the life rope.

"I'm out!" shouted Malachi Roohan, his blue eyes lighting suddenly.
"Delia Morrissey died. She was one day eating her dinner and a bone
stuck in her throat. The weaver clapped her on the back, but it was all to
no good. She choked to death before his eyes on the floor. I remember
that. And the weaver himself near died of grief after. But he married secondly. Who's this he married secondly, Nan?"

Nan did not know. She turned to the widow for enlightenment. The
widow moistened her lips. She had to concentrate her thoughts on a subject which, for her own peace of mind, she had habitually avoided. She
hated genealogy. She said a little nervously:

"Sara MacCabe."

The cooper's daughter shouted the name into his ear.

"So you're Sally MacCabe, from Looscaun, the one Mortimer took off
the blacksmith? Well, well, that was a great business surely, the pair of
them hot-tempered men, and your own beauty going to their heads like
strong drink."

He looked at the widow, a half-sceptical, half-admiring expression
flickering across the leathery face. It was such a look as he might have
given to Dervorgilla of Leinster, Deirdre of Uladh, or Helen of Troy.

The widow was not the notorious Sara MacCabe from Looscaun; that
lady had been the second wife of the weaver. It was said they had led a
stormy life, made up of passionate quarrels and partings, and still more
passionate reconciliations, Sara MacCabe from Looscaun not having
quite forgotten, or wholly neglected, the blacksmith after her marriage
to the weaver. But the widow again only whispered to the cooper's
daughter:

"Leave it so."

"What way is Mortimer keeping?" asked the old man.

"He's dead," replied the daughter.

The fingers of the old man quivered on the rope.

"Dead? Mortimer Hehir dead?" he cried. "What in the name of God
happened him?"

Nan did not know what happened him. She knew that the widow
would not mind, so, without waiting for a prompt, she replied:

"A weakness came over him, a sudden weakness."

"To think of a man being whipped off all of a sudden like that!" cried
the cooper. "When that's the way it was with Mortimer Hehir what one
of us can be sure at all? Nan, none of us is sure! To think of the weaver,
with his heart as strong as a bull, going off in a little weakness! It's the
treacherous world we live in, the treacherous world, surely. Never another
yard of tweed will be put up on his old loom! Morty, Morty, you were a

good companion, a great warrant to walk the hills, whistling the tunes, pleasant in your conversation and as broad-spoken as the Bible."

"Did you know the weaver well, Father?" the daughter asked.

"Who better?" he replied. "Who drank more pints with him than what myself did? And indeed it's to his wake I'd be setting out, and it's under his coffin my shoulder would be going, if I wasn't confined to my rope."

He bowed his head for a few moments. The two women exchanged a quick, sympathetic glance.

The breathing of the old man was the breathing of one who slept. The head sank lower.

The widow said:

"You ought to make him lie down. He's tired."

The daughter made some movement of dissent; she was afraid to interfere. Maybe the cooper could be very violent if roused. After a time he raised his head again. He looked in a new mood. He was fresher, more wide awake. His beard hung in wisps to the bedclothes.

"Asking him about the grave," the widow said.

The daughter hesitated for a moment, and in that moment the cooper looked up as if he had heard, or partially heard. He said:

"If you wait a minute now I'll tell you what the weaver was." He stared for some seconds at the little window.

"Oh, we'll wait," said the daughter, and turning to the widow, added, "Won't we, Mrs. Hehir?"

"Indeed we will wait," said the widow.

"The weaver," said the old man suddenly, "was a dream."

He turned his head to the women to see how they had taken it.

"Maybe," said the daughter, with a little touch of laughter, "Maybe Mrs. Hehir would not give in to that."

The widow moved her hands uneasily under the shawl. She stared a little fearfully at the cooper. His blue eyes were clear as lake water over white sand.

"Whether she gives in to it, or whether she doesn't give in to it," said Malachi Roohan, "it's a dream Mortimer Hehir was. And his loom, and his shuttles, and his warping bars, and his bobbin, and the threads that he put upon the shifting racks, were all a dream. And the only thing he ever wove upon his loom was a dream."

The old man smacked his lips, his hard gums whacking. His daughter looked at him with her head a little to one side.

"And what's more," said the cooper, "every woman that ever came into his head, and every wife he married, was a dream. I'm telling you that, Nan, and I'm telling it to you of the weaver. His life was a dream, and his death is a dream. And his widow there is a dream. And all the world is a dream. Do you hear me, Nan, this world is all a dream?"

"I hear you very well, Father," the daughter sang in a piercing voice.

The cooper raised his head with a jerk, and his beard swept forward, giving him an appearance of vivid energy. He spoke in a voice like a trumpet blast:

"And I'm a dream!"

He turned his blue eyes on the widow. An unnerving sensation came to her. The cooper was the most dreadful old man she had ever seen, and what he was saying sounded the most terrible thing she had ever listened to. He cried:

"The idiot laughing in the street, the King looking at his crown, the woman turning her head to the sound of a man's step, the bells ringing in the belfry, the man walking his land, the weaver at his loom, the cooper handling his barrel, the Pope stooping for his red slippers— they're all a dream. And I'll tell you why they're a dream: because this world was meant to be a dream."

"Father," said the daughter, "you're talking too much. You'll over-reach yourself."

The old man gave himself a little pull on the rope. It was his gesture of energy, a demonstration of the fine fettle he was in. He said:

"You're saying that because you don't understand me."

"I understand you very well."

"You only think you do. Listen to me now, Nan. I want you to do something for me. You won't refuse me?"

"I will not refuse you, Father; you know very well I won't."

"You're a good daughter to me, surely, Nan. And do what I tell you now. Shut close your eyes. Shut them fast and tight. No fluttering of the lids now."

"Very well, Father."

The daughter closed her eyes, throwing up her face in the attitude of one blind. The widow was conscious of the woman's strong, rough features, something good-natured in the line of the large mouth. The old man watched the face of his daughter with excitement. He asked:

"What is it that you see now, Nan?"

"Nothing at all, Father."

"In troth you do. Keep them closed tight and you'll see it."

"I see nothing only——"

"Only what? Why don't you say it?"

"Only darkness, Father."

"And isn't that something to see? Isn't it easier to see darkness than to see light? Now, Nan, look into the darkness."

"I'm looking, Father."

"And think of something—anything at all—the stool before the kitchen fire outside."

"I'm thinking of it."

"And do you remember it?"

"I do well."

"And when you remember it what do you want to do—sit on it, maybe?"

"No, Father."

"And why wouldn't you want to sit on it?"

"Because—because I'd like to see it first, to make sure."

The old man gave a little crow of delight. He cried:

"There it is! You want to make sure that it is there, although you remember it well. And that is the way with everything in this world. People close their eyes and they are not sure of anything. They want to see it again before they believe. There is Nan, now, and she does not believe in the stool before the fire, the little stool she's looking at all her life, that her mother used to set her on before the fire when she was a small child. She closes her eyes, and it is gone! And listen to me now, Nan—if you had a man of your own and you closed your eyes you wouldn't be too sure he was the man you remembered, and you'd want to open your eyes and look at him to make sure he was the man you knew before the lids dropped on your eyes. And if you had children about you and you turned your back and closed your eyes and tried to remember them you'd want to look at them to make sure. You'd be no more sure of them than you are now of the stool in the kitchen. One flash of the eyelids and everything in this world is gone."

"I'm telling you, Father, you're talking too much."

"I'm not talking half enough. Aren't we all uneasy about the world, the things in the world that we can only believe in while we're looking at them? From one season of our life to another haven't we a kind of belief that some time we'll waken up and find everything different? Didn't you ever feel that, Nan? Didn't you think things would change, that the world would be a new place altogether, and that all that was going on around us was only a business that was doing us out of something else? We put up with it while the little hankering is nibbling at the butt of our hearts for the something else! All the men there be who believe that some day The Thing will happen, that they'll turn round the corner and waken up in the new great Street!"

"And sure," said the daughter, "maybe they are right, and maybe they will waken up."

The old man's body was shaken with a queer spasm of laughter. It began under the clothes on the bed, worked up his trunk, ran along his stringy arms, out into the rope, and the iron foot of the bed rattled. A look of extraordinarily malicious humour lit up the vivid face of the cooper. The widow beheld him with fascination, a growing sense of alarm. He might say anything. He might do anything. He might begin to sing some fearful song. He might leap out of bed.

"Nan," he said, "do you believe you'll swing round the corner and waken up?"

"Well," said Nan, hesitating a little, "I do."

The cooper gave a sort of peacock crow again. He cried:

"Och! Nan Roohan believes she'll waken up! Waken up from what? From a sleep and from a dream, from this world! Well, if you believe that, Nan Roohan, it shows you know what's what. You know what the thing around you, called the world, is. And it's only dreamers who can hope to waken up—do you hear me, Nan; it's only dreamers who can hope to waken up."

"I hear you," said Nan.

"The world is only a dream, and a dream is nothing at all! We all want to waken up out of the great nothingness of this world."

"And, please God, we will," said Nan.

"You can tell all the world from me," said the cooper, "that it won't."

"And why won't we, Father?"

"Because," said the old man, "we ourselves are the dream. When we're over the dream is over with us. That's why."

"Father," said the daughter, her head again a little to one side, "you know a great deal."

"I know enough," said the cooper shortly.

"And maybe you could tell us something about the weaver's grave. Mrs. Hehir wants to know."

"And amn't I after telling you all about the weaver's grave? Amn't I telling you it is all a dream?"

"You never said that, Father. Indeed you never did."

"I said everything in this world is a dream, and the weaver's grave is in this world, below in Cloon na Morav."

"Where in Cloon na Morav? What part of it, Father? That is what Mrs. Hehir wants to know. Can you tell her?"

"I can tell her," said Malachi Roohan. "I was at his father's burial. I remember it above all burials, because that was the day the handsome girl, Honor Costello, fell over a grave and fainted. The sweat broke out on young Donohoe when he saw Honor Costello tumbling over the grave. Not a marry would he marry her after that, and he sworn to it by the kiss of her lips. 'I'll marry no woman that fell on a grave,' says Donohoe. 'She'd maybe have a child by me with turned-in eyes or a twisted limb.' So he married a farmer's daughter, and the same morning Honor Costello married a cattle drover. Very well, then. Donohoe's wife had no child at all. She was a barren woman. Do you hear me, Nan? A barren woman she was. And such childer as Honor Costello had by the drover! Yellow hair they had, heavy as seaweed, the skin of them clear as the wind, and limbs as clean as a whistle. It was said the drover was of the blood of the Danes, and it broke out in Honor Costello's family!"

"Maybe," said the daughter, "they were Vikings."

"What are you saying?" cried the old man testily. "Ain't I telling you it's Danes they were. Did anyone ever hear a greater miracle?"

"No one ever did," said the daughter, and both women clicked their tongues to express sympathetic wonder at the tale.

"And I'll tell you what saved Honor Costello," said the cooper. "When she fell in Cloon na Morav she turned her cloak inside out."

"What about the weaver's grave, Father? Mrs. Hehir wants to know."

The old man looked at the widow; his blue eyes searched her face and her figure; the expression of satirical admiration flashed over his features. The nostrils of the nose twitched. He said:

"So that's the end of the story! Sally MacCabe, the blacksmith's favourite, wants to know where she'll sink the weaver out of sight! Great battles were fought in Looscaun over Sally MacCabe! The weaver thought his heart would burst, and the blacksmith damned his soul for the sake of Sally MacCabe's idle hours."

"Father," said the daughter of the house, "let the dead rest."

"Ay," said Malachi Roohan, "let the foolish dead rest. The dream of Looscaun is over. And now the pale woman is looking for the black weaver's grave. Well, good luck to her!"

The cooper was taken with another spasm of grotesque laughter. The only difference was that this time it began by the rattling of the rail of the bed, travelled along the rope, down his stringy arms dying out somewhere in his legs in the bed. He smacked his lips, a peculiar harsh sound, as if there was not much meat to it.

"Do I know where Mortimer Hehir's grave is?" he said ruminatingly. "Do I know where me rope is?"

"Where is it, then?" his daughter asked. Her patience was great.

"I'll tell you that," said the cooper. "It's under the elm tree of Cloon na Morav. That's where it is surely. There was never a weaver yet that did not find rest under the elm tree of Cloon na Morav. There they all went as surely as the buds came on the branches. Let Sally MacCabe put poor Morty there; let her give him a tear or two in memory of the days that his heart was ready to burst for her, and believe you me no ghost will ever haunt her. No dead man ever yet came back to look upon a woman!"

A furtive sigh escaped the widow. With her handkerchief she wiped a little perspiration from both sides of her nose. The old man wagged his head sympathetically. He thought she was the long dead Sally MacCabe lamenting the weaver! The widow's emotion arose from relief that the mystery of the grave had at last been cleared up. Yet her dealings with old men had taught her caution. Quite suddenly the memory of the handsome dark face of the grave-digger who had followed her to the stile came back to her. She remembered that he said something about "the exact position of the grave." The widow prompted yet another question:

"What position under the elm tree?"

The old man listened to the question; a strained look came into his face.

"Position of what?" he asked.

"Of the grave."

"Of what grave?"

"The weaver's grave."

Another spasm seized the old frame, but this time it came from no aged merriment. It gripped his skeleton and shook it. It was as if some invisible powerful hand had suddenly taken him by the back of the neck and shaken him. His knuckles rattled on the rope. They had an appalling sound. A horrible feeling came to the widow that the cooper would fall to pieces like a bag of bones. He turned his face to his daughter. Great tears had welled into the blue eyes, giving them an appearance of childish petulance, then of acute suffering.

"What are you talking to me of graves for?" he asked, and the powerful voice broke. "Why will you be tormenting me like this? It's not going to die I am, is it? Is it going to die I am, Nan?"

The daughter bent over him as she might bend over a child. She said:

"Indeed, there's great fear of you. Lie down and rest yourself. Fatigued out and out you are."

The grip slowly slackened on the rope. He sank back, quite helpless, a little whimper breaking from him. The daughter stooped lower, reaching for a pillow that had fallen in by the wall. A sudden sharp snarl sounded from the bed, and it dropped from her hand.

"Don't touch me!" the cooper cried. The voice was again restored, powerful in its command. And to the amazement of the widow she saw him again grip along the rope and rise in the bed.

"Amn't I tired telling you not to touch me?" he cried. "Have I any business talking to you at all? Is it gone my authority is in this house?"

He glared at his daughter, his eyes red with anger, like a dog crouching in his kennel, and the daughter stepped back, a wry smile on her large mouth. The widow stepped back with her, and for a moment he held the women with their backs to the wall by his angry red eyes. Another growl and the cooper sank back inch by inch on the rope. In all her experience of old men the widow had never seen anything like this old man; his resurrections and his collapse. When he was quite down the daughter gingerly put the clothes over his shoulders and then beckoned the widow out of the room.

The widow left the house of Malachi Roohan, the cooper, with the feeling that she had discovered the grave of an old man by almost killing another.

V

The widow walked along the streets, outwardly calm, inwardly confused. Her first thought was "the day is going on me!" There were many things still to be done at home; she remembered the weaver lying there, quiet at last, the candles lighting about him, the brown habit over him, a crucifix in his hands—everything as it should be. It seemed ages to the widow since he had really fallen ill. He was very exacting and peevish all that time. His death agony had been protracted, almost melodramatically violent. A few times the widow had nearly run out of the house, leaving the weaver to fight the death battle alone. But her commonsense, her good nerves, and her religious convictions, had stood to her, and when she put the pennies on the weaver's eyes she was glad she had done her duty to the last. She was glad now that she had taken the search for the grave out of the hands of Meehaul Lynskey and Cahir Bowes; Malachi Roohan had been a sight, and she would never forget him, but he had known what nobody else knew. The widow, as she ascended a little upward sweep of the road to Cloon na Morav, noted that the sky beyond it was more vivid, a red band of light having struck across the grey blue, just on the horizon. Up against this red background was the dark outline of landscape, and especially Cloon na Morav. She kept her eyes upon it as she drew nearer. Objects that were vague on the landscape began to bulk up with more distinction.

She noted the back wall of Cloon na Morav, its green lichen more vivid under the red patch of the skyline. And presently, above the green wall, black against the vivid sky, she saw elevated the bulk of one of the black cockroaches. On it were perched two drab figures, so grotesque, so still, that they seemed part of the thing itself. One figure was sloping out from the end of the tombstone so curiously that for a moment the widow thought it was a man who had reached down from the table to see what was under it. At the other end of the table was a slender warped figure, and as the widow gazed upon it she saw a sign of animation. The head and face, bleak in their outlines, were raised up in a gesture of despair. The face was turned flush against the sky, so much so that the widow's eyes instinctively sought the sky too. Above the slash of red, in the west, was a single star, flashing so briskly and so freshly that it might

have never shone before. For all the widow knew, it might have been a
young star frolicking in the heavens with all the joy of youth. Was that,
she wondered, what the old man, Meehaul Lynskey, was gazing at. He
was very, very old, and the star was very, very young! Was there some
protest in the gesture of the head he raised to that thing in the sky; was
there some mockery in the sparkle of the thing of the sky for the face of
the man? Why should a star be always young, a man aged so soon?
Should not a man be greater than a star? Was it this Meehaul Lynskey
was thinking? The widow could not say, but something in the thing
awed her. She had the sensation of one who surprises a man in some act
that lifts him above the commonplaces of existences. It was as if Meehaul
Lynskey were discovered prostrate before some altar, in the throes of a
religious agony. Old men were, the widow felt, very, very strange, and she
did not know that she would ever understand them. As she looked at the
bleak head of Meehaul Lynskey, up against the vivid patch of the sky, she
wondered if there could really be something in that head which would
make him as great as a star, immortal as a star? Suddenly Meehaul
Lynskey made a movement. The widow saw it quite distinctly. She saw
the arm raised, the hand go out, with its crooked fingers in one, two,
three quick, short taps in the direction of the star. The widow stood to
watch, and the gesture was so familiar, so homely, so personal that it was
quite understandable to her. She knew then that Meehaul Lynskey was
not thinking of any great things at all. He was only a nailer! And seeing
the Evening Star sparkle in the sky he had only thought of his workshop,
of the bellows, the irons, the fire, the sparks, and the glowing iron which
might be made into a nail while it was hot! He had in imagination seized
a hammer and made a blow across interstellar space at Venus! All the
beauty and youth of the star frolicking on the pale sky above the slash of
vivid redness had only suggested to him the making of yet another nail!
If Meehaul Lynskey could push up his scarred yellow face among the
stars of the sky he would see in them only the sparks of his little smithy.

Cahir Bowes was, the widow thought, looking down at the earth, from
the other end of the tombstone, to see if there were any hard things there
which he could smash up. The old men had their backs turned upon
each other. Very likely they had another discussion since, which ended
in this attitude of mutual contempt. The widow was conscious again of
the unreasonableness of old men, but not much resentful of it. She was
too long accustomed to them to have any great sense of revolt. Her emotion, if it could be called an emotion, was a settled, dull toleration of all
their little bigotries.

She put her hand on the stile for the second time that day, and again
raised her palely sad face over the graveyard of Cloon na Morav. As she
did so she had the most extraordinary experience of the whole day's

sensations. It was such a sensation as gave her at once a wonderful sense of the reality and the unreality of life. She paused on the stile, and had a clear insight into something that had up to this moment been obscure. And no sooner had the thing become definite and clear than a sense of the wonder of life came to her. It was all very like the dream Malachi Roohan had talked about.

In the pale grass, under the vivid colours of the sky, the two grave-diggers were lying on their backs, staring silently up at the heavens. The widow looked at them as she paused on the stile. Her thoughts of these men had been indifferent, subconscious, up to this instant. They were handsome young men. Perhaps if there had been only one of them the widow would have been more attentive. The dark handsomeness did not seem the same thing when repeated. Their beauty, if one could call it beauty, had been collective, the beauty of flowers, of dark, velvety pansies, the distinctive marks of one faithfully duplicated on the other. The good looks of one had, to the mind of the widow, somehow nullified the good looks of the other. There was too much borrowing of Peter to pay Paul in their well-favoured features. The first grave-digger spoiled the illusion of individuality in the second grave-digger. The widow had not thought so, but she would have agreed if anybody whispered to her that a good-looking man who wanted to win favour with a woman should never have so complete a twin brother. It would be possible for a woman to part tenderly with a man, and, if she met his image and likeness around the corner, knock him down. There is nothing more powerful, but nothing more delicate in life than the values of individuality. To create the impression that humanity was a thing which could be turned out like a coinage would be to ruin the whole illusion of life. The twin grave-diggers had created some sort of such impression, vague, and not very insistent, in the mind of the widow, and it had made her lose any special interest in them. Now, however, as she hesitated on the stile, all this was swept from her mind at a stroke. That most subtle and powerful of all things, personality, sprang silently from the twins and made them, to the mind of the widow, things as far apart as the poles. The two men lay at length, and exactly the same length and bulk, in the long, grey grass. But, as the widow looked upon them, one twin seemed conscious of her presence, while the other continued his absorption in the heavens above. The supreme twin turned his head, and his soft, velvety brown eyes met the eyes of the widow. There was welcome in the man's eyes. The widow read that welcome as plainly as if he had spoken his thoughts. The next moment he had sprung to his feet, smiling. He took a few steps forward, then, self-conscious, pulled up. If he had only jumped up and smiled the widow would have understood. But those few eager steps forward and then that stock stillness! The other twin rose reluctantly, and as he did so the widow was conscious of even physical differences in the brothers. The eyes were not the same. No such velvety soft lights were in the eyes of the second one. He was more sheepish. He was more phlegmatic. He was only a plagiarism of the original man! The widow wondered how she had not seen all this before. The resemblance between the twins was only skin deep. The two old men, at the moment the second twin rose, detached themselves slowly, almost painfully, from their tombstone, and all moved forward to meet the widow. The widow, collecting her though, piloted her skirts modestly about her legs as she got down from the narrow stonework of the stile and stumbled into the contrariness of Cloon na Morav. A wild sense of satisfaction swept her that she had come back the bearer of useful information.

"Well," said Meehaul Lynskey, "did you see Malachi Roohan?" The widow looked at his scorched, sceptical, yellow face, and said:

"I did."

"Had he any word for us?"

"He had. He remembers the place of the weaver's grave." The widow looked a little vaguely about Cloon na Morav.

"What does he say?"

"He says it's under the elm tree."

There was silence. The stone-breaker swung about on his legs, his head making a semi-circular movement over the ground, and his sharp eyes were turned upward, as if he were searching the heavens for an elm tree. The nailer dropped his underjaw and stared tensely across the ground, blankly, patiently, like a fisherman on the edge of the shore gazing over an empty sea. The grave-digger turned his head away shyly, like a boy, as if he did not want to see the confusion of the widow; the man was full of the most delicate mannerisms. The other grave-digger settled into a stolid attitude, then the skin bunched up about his brown eyes in puckers of humour. A miserable feeling swept the widow. She had the feeling that she stood on the verge of some collapse.

"Under the elm tree," mumbled the stone-breaker.

"That's what he said," added the widow. "Under the elm tree of Cloon na Morav."

"Well," said Cahir Bowes, "when you find the elm tree you'll find the grave."

The widow did not know what an elm tree was. Nothing had ever happened in life as she knew it to render any special knowledge of trees profitable, and therefore desirable. Trees were good; they made nice firing when chopped up; timber, and all that was fashioned out of timber, came from trees. This knowledge the widow had accepted as she had accepted all the other remote phenomena of the world into which she had been born. But that trees should have distinctive names, that they should have family relationships seemed to the mind of the widow only an unnecessary complication of the affairs of the universe. What good was it? She could understand calling fruit trees fruit trees and all other kind simply trees. But that one should be an elm and another an ash, that there should be name after name, species after species, giving them peculiarities and personalities, was one of the things that the widow did not like. And at this moment, when the elm tree of Malachi Roohan had raised a fresh problem in Cloon na Morav, the likeness of old men to old trees—their crankiness, their complexity, their angles, their very barks, bulges, gnarled twistiness, and kinks—was very close, and brought a sense of oppression to the sorely-tried brain of the widow.

"Under the elm tree," repeated Meehaul Lynskey. "The elm tree of Cloon na Morav." He broke into an aged cackle of a laugh. "If I was any good at all at making a rhyme I'd make one about that elm tree, devil a other but I would."

The widow looked around Cloon na Morav, and her eyes, for the first time in her life, were consciously searching for trees. If there were numerous trees there she could understand how easy it might be for Malachi Roohan to make a mistake. He might have mistaken some other sort of tree for an elm—the widow felt that there must be plenty of other trees very like an elm. In fact, she reasoned that other trees, do their best, could not help looking like an elm. There must be thousands and millions of people like herself in the world who pass through life in the belief that a certain kind of tree was an elm when, in reality, it may be an ash or an oak or a chestnut or a beech, or even a poplar, a birch, or a yew. Malachi Roohan was never likely to allow anybody to amend his knowledge of an elm tree. He would let go his rope in the belief that there was an elm tree in Cloon na Morav, and that under it was the weaver's grave—that is, if Malachi Roohan had not, in some ghastly aged kink, invented the thing. The widow, not sharply, but still with an appreciation of the thing, grasped that a dispute about trees would be the very sort of dispute in which Meehaul Lynskey and Cahir Bowes would, like the very old men that they were, have revelled. Under the impulse of the message she had brought from the cooper they would have launched out into another powerful struggle from tree to tree in Cloon na Morav; they would again have strewn the place with the corpses of slain arguments, and in the net result they would not have been able to establish anything either about elm trees or about the weaver's grave. The slow, sad gaze of the widow for trees in Cloon na Morav brought to her, in these circumstances, both pain and relief. It was a relief that Meehaul Lynskey and Cahir Bowes could not challenge each other to a battle of trees; it was a pain that the tree of Malachi Roohan was nowhere in sight. The widow could see for herself that there was not any sort of a tree in Cloon na

Morav. The ground was enclosed upon three sides by walls, on the fourth by a hedge of quicks. Not even old men could transform a hedge into an elm tree. Neither could they make the few struggling briars clinging about the railings of the sepulchres into anything except briars. The elm tree of Malachi Roohan was now non-existent. Nobody would ever know whether it had or had not ever existed. The widow would as soon give the soul of the weaver to the howling winds of the world as go back and interview the cooper again on the subject.

"Old Malachi Roohan," said Cahir Bowes with tolerant decision, "is doting."

"The nearest elm tree I know," said Meehaul Lynskey, "is half a mile away."

"The one above at Carragh?" questioned Cahir Bowes.

"Ay, beside the mill."

No more was to be said. The riddle of the weaver's grave was still the riddle of the weaver's grave. Cloon na Morav kept its secret. But, nevertheless, the weaver would have to be buried. He could not be housed indefinitely. Talking courage from the harrowing aspects of the deadlock, Meehaul Lynskey went back, plump and courageously to his original allegiance.

"The grave of the weaver is there," he said, and he struck out his hooked fingers in the direction of the disturbance of the sod which the grave-diggers had made under pressure of his earlier enthusiasm.

Cahir Bowes turned on him with a withering, quavering glance.

"Aren't you afraid that God would strike you where you stand?" he demanded.

"I'm not—not a bit afraid," said Meehaul Lynskey. "It's the weaver's grave."

"You say that," cried Cahir Bowes, "after what we all saw and what we all heard?"

"I do," said Meehaul Lynskey, stoutly. He wiped his lips with the palm of his hand, and launched out into one of his arguments, arguments, as usual, packed with particulars.

"I saw the weaver's father lowered in that place. And I'll tell you, what's more, it was Father Owen MacCarthy that read over him, he a young red-haired curate in this place at the time, long before ever he became parish priest of Benelog. There was I, standing in this exact spot, a young man, too, with a light moustache, holding me hat in me hand, and there one side of me—maybe five yards from the marble stone of the Keernahans—was Patsy Curtin that drank himself to death after, and on the other side of me was Honor Costello, that fell on the grave and married the cattle drover, a big, loose-shouldered Dane."

Patiently, half absent-mindedly, listening to the renewal of the dispute, the widow remembered the words of Malachi Roohan, and his story of Honor Costello, who fell on the grave over fifty years ago. What memories these old men had! How unreliable they were, and yet flashing out astounding corroborations of each other. Maybe there was something in what Meehaul Lynskey was saying. Maybe—but the widow checked her thoughts. What was the use of it all? This grave could not be the weaver's grave; it had been grimly demonstrated to them all that it was full of stout coffins. The widow, with a gesture of agitation, smoothed her hair down the gentle slope of her head under the shawl. As she did so her eyes caught the eyes of the grave-digger; he was looking at her! He withdrew his eyes at once, and began to twitch the ends of his dark moustache with his fingers.

"If," said Cahir Bowes, "this be the grave of the weaver, what's Julia Rafferty doing in it? Answer me that, Meehaul Lynskey."

"I don't know what's she doing in it, and what's more, I don't care. And believe you my word, many a queer thing happened in Cloon na Morav that had no right to happen in it. Julia Rafferty, maybe, isn't the only one that is where she had no right to be."

"Maybe she isn't," said Cahir Bowes, "but it's there she is, anyhow, and I'm thinking it's there she's likely to stay."

"If she's in the weaver's grave," cried Meehaul Lynskey, "what I say is, out with her!"

"Very well, then, Meehaul Lynskey. Let you yourself be the powerful man to deal with Julia Rafferty. But remember this, and remember it's my word, that touch one bone in this place and you touch all."

"No fear at all have I to right a wrong. I'm no backslider when it comes to justice, and justice I'll see done among the living and the dead."

"Go ahead, then, me hearty fellow. If Julia herself is in the wrong place somebody else must be in her own place, and you'll be following one rightment with another wrongment until in the end you'll go mad with the tangle of dead men's wrongs. That's the end that's in store for you, Meehaul Lynskey."

Meehaul Lynskey spat on his fist and struck out with the hooked fingers. His blood was up.

"That I may be as dead as my father!" he began in a traditional oath, and at that Cahir Bowes gave a little cry and raised his stick with a battle flourish. They went up and down the dips of the ground, rising and falling on the waves of their anger, and the widow stood where she was, miserable and downhearted, her feet growing stone cold from the chilly dampness of the ground. The twin, who did not now count, took out his pipe and lit it, looking at the old men with a stolid gaze. The twin who now counted walked uneasily away, bit an end off a chunk of tobacco, and came to stand in the ground in a line with the widow, looking on with her several feet away; but again the widow was conscious of the man's growing sympathy.

"They're a nice pair of boyos, them two old lads," he remarked to the widow. He turned his head to her. He was very handsome.

"Do you think they will find it?" she asked. Her voice was a little nervous, and the man shifted on his feet, nervously responsive.

"It's hard to say," he said. "You'd never know what to think. Two old lads, the like of them, do be very tricky."

"God grant they'll get it," said the widow.

"God grant," said the grave-digger.

But they didn't. They only got exhausted as before, wheezing and coughing, and glaring at each other as they sat down on two mounds.

The grave-digger turned to the widow.

She was aware of the nice warmth of his brown eyes.

"Are you waking the weaver again tonight?" he asked.

"I am," said the widow.

"Well, maybe some person—some old man or woman from the country—may turn up and be able to tell where the grave is. You could make inquiries."

"Yes," said the widow, but without any enthusiasm, "I could make inquiries."

The grave-digger hesitated for a moment, and said more sympathetically, "We could all, maybe, make inquiries." There was a softer personal note, a note of adventure, in the voice.

The widow turned her head to the man and smiled at him quite frankly.

"I'm beholding to you," she said and then added with a little wounded sigh, "Everyone is very good to me."

The grave-digger twirled the ends of his moustache.

Cahir Bowes, who had heard, rose from his mound and said briskly, "I'll agree to leave it at that." His air was that of one who had made an extraordinary personal sacrifice. What was he really thinking was that he would have another great day of it with Meehaul Lynskey in Cloon na Morav to-morrow. He'd show that oul' fellow, Lynskey, what stuff Boweses were made of.

"And I'm not against it," said Meehaul Lynskey. He took the tone of one who was never to be outdone in magnanimity. He was also thinking of another day of effort to-morrow, a day that would, please God, show the Boweses what the Lynskeys were like.

With that the party came straggling out of Cloon na Morav, the two old men first, the widow next, the grave-diggers waiting to put on their coats and light their pipes.

There was a little upward slope on the road to the town, and as the two old men took it the widow thought they looked very spent after their day. She wondered if Cahir Bowes would ever be able for that hill. She would give him a glass of whiskey at home, if there was any left in the bottle. Of the two, and as limp and slack as his body looked, Meehaul Lynskey appeared the better able for the hill. They walked together, that is to say, abreast, but they kept almost the width of the road between each other, as if this gulf expressed the breach of friendship between them on the head of the dispute about the weaver's grave. They had been making liars of each other all day, and they would, please God, make liars of each other all day to-morrow. The widow, understanding the meaning of this hostility, had a faint sense of amusement at the contrariness of old men. How could she tell what was passing in the head which Cahir Bowes hung, like a fuchsia drop, over the road? How could she know of the strange rise and fall of the thoughts, the little frets, the tempers, the faint humours, which chased each other there? Nobody—not even Cahir Bowes himself—could account for them. All the widow knew was that Cahir Bowes stood suddenly on the road. Something had happened in his brain, some old memory cell long dormant had become nascent, had a stir, a pulse, a flicker of warmth, of activity, and swiftly as a flash of lightning in the sky, a glow of lucidity lit up his memory. It was as if a searchlight had suddenly flooded the dark corners of his brain. The immediate physical effect on Cahir Bowes was to cause him to stand stark still on the road, Meehaul Lynskey going ahead without him. The widow saw Cahir Bowes pivot on his heels, his head, at the end of the horizontal body, swinging round like the movement of a hand on a run-away clock. Instead of pointing up the hill homeward the head pointed down the hill and back to Cloon na Morav. There followed the most extraordinary movements—shufflings, gyrations—that the widow had ever seen. Cahir Bowes wanted to run like mad away down the road. That was plain. And Cahir Bowes believed that he was running like mad away down the road. That was also evident. But what he actually did was to make little jumps on his feet, his stick rattling the ground in front, and each jump did not bring him an inch of ground. He would have gone more rapidly in his normal shuffle. His efforts were like a terrible parody of the springs of a kangaroo. And Cahir Bowes, in a voice that was now more a scream than a cackle, was calling out unintelligible things. The widow, looking at him, paused in wonder, then over her face there came a relaxation, a colour, her eyes warmed, her expression lost its settled pensiveness, and all her body was shaken with uncontrollable laughter. Cahir Bowes passed her on the road in his fantastic leaps, his abortive buck-jumps, screaming and cracking his stick on the ground, his left hand still gripped tightly behind, a powerful brake on the small of his back.

Meehaul Lynskey turned back and his face was shaken with an aged emotion as he looked after the stone-breaker. Then he removed his hat and blessed himself.

"The cross of Christ between us and harm," he exclaimed. "Old Cahir Bowes has gone off his head at last. I thought there was something up with him all day. It was easily known there was something ugly working in his mind."

The widow controlled her laughter and checked herself, making the sign of the Cross on her forehead, too. She said:

"God forgive me for laughing and the weaver with the habit but fresh upon him."

The grave-digger who counted was coming out somewhat eagerly over the stile, but Cahir Bowes, flourishing his stick, beat him back again and then himself re-entered Cloon na Morav. He stumbled over the grass, now rising on a mound, now disappearing altogether in a dip of the ground, travelling in a giddy course like a hooker in a storm; again, for a long time, he remained submerged, showing, however, the eternal stick, his periscope, his indication to the world that he was about his business. In a level piece of ground, marked by stones with large mottle white marks upon them, he settled and cried out to all, and calling God to witness, that this surely was the weaver's grave. There was scepticism, hesitation, on the part of the grave-diggers, but after some parley, and because Cahir Bowes was so passionate, vehement, crying and shouting, dribbling water from the mouth, showing his yellow teeth, pouring sweat on his forehead, quivering on his legs, they began to dig carefully in the spot. The widow, at this, re-arranged the shawl on her head and entered Cloon na Morav, conscious, as she shuffled over the stile, that a pair of warm brown eyes were, for a moment, upon her movements and then withdrawn. She stood a little way back from the digging and waited the result with a slightly more accelerated beating of the heart. The twins looked as if they were ready to strike something unexpected at any moment, digging carefully, and Cahir Bowes hung over the place, cackling and crowing, urging the men to swifter work. The earth sang up out of the ground, dark and rich in colour, gleaming like gold, in the deepening twilight in the place. Two feet, three feet, four feet of earth came up, the spades pushing through the earth in regular and powerful pushes, and still the coast was clear. Cahir Bowes trembled with excitement on his stick. Five feet of a pit yawned in the ancient ground. The spade work ceased. One of the grave-diggers looked up at Cahir Bowes and said:

"You hit the weaver's grave this time right enough. Not another grave in the place could be as free as this."

The widow sighed a quick little sigh and looked at the face of the other grave-digger, hesitated, then allowed a remote smile of thankful-

ness to flit across her palely sad face. The eyes of the man wandered away
over the darkening spaces of Cloon na Morav.

"I got the weaver's grave surely," cried Cahir Bowes, his old face full
of a weird animation. If he had found the Philosopher's Stone he would
only have broken it. But to find the weaver's grave was an accomplish-
ment that would help him into a wisdom before which all his world
would bow. He looked around triumphantly and said:

"Where is Meehaul Lynskey now; what will the people be saying at all
about his attack on Julia Rafferty's grave? Julia will haunt him, and I'd
sooner have anyone at all haunting me than the ghost of Julia Rafferty.
Where is Meehaul Lynskey now? Is it ashamed to show his liary face he
is? And what talk had Malachi Roohan about an elm tree? Elm tree,
indeed! If it's trees that is troubling him now let him climb up on one of
them and hang himself from it with his rope! Where is that old fellow,
Meehaul Lynskey, and his rotten head? Where is he, I say? Let him come
in here now to Cloon na Morav until I be showing him the weaver's
grave, five feet down and not a rib or a knuckle in it, as clean and beautiful as the weaver ever wished it. Come in here, Meehaul Lynskey, until
I hear the lies panting again in your yellow throat."

He went in his extraordinary movement over the ground, making for
the stile all the while talking.

Meehaul Lynskey had crouched behind the wall outside when Cahir
Bowes led the diggers to the new site, his old face twisted in an attentive, almost agonizing emotion. He stood peeping over the wall, saying to
himself:

"Whisht, will you! Don't mind that old madman. He hasn't it at all.
I'm telling you he hasn't it. Whisht, will you! Let him dig away. They'll
hit something in a minute. They'll level him when they find out. His
brain has turned. Whist, now, will you, and I'll have that rambling old
lunatic, Cahir Bowes, in a minute. I'll leap in on him. I'll charge him
before the world. I'll show him up. I'll take the gab out of him. I'll lac-
erate him. I'll lambaste him. Whisht, will you!"

But as the digging went on and the terrible cries of triumph arose
inside Meehaul Lynskey's knees knocked together. His head bent level to
the wall, yellow and grimacing, nerves twitching across it, a little yellow
froth gathering at the corners of the mouth. When Cahir Bowes came
beating for the stile Meehaul Lynskey rubbed one leg with the other, a
little below the calf, and cried brokenly to himself:

"God in Heaven, he has it! He has the weaver's grave."

He turned about and slunk along in the shadow of the wall up the hill,
panting and broken. By the time Cahir Bowes had reached the stile
Meehaul Lynskey's figure was shadowily dipping down over the crest of

the road. A sharp cry from Cahir Bowes caused him to shrink out of sight like a dog at whom a weapon had been thrown.

The eyes of the grave-digger who did not now count followed the figure of Cahir Bowes as he moved to the stile. He laughed a little in amusement, then wiped his brow. He came up out of the grave. He turned to the widow and said:

"We're down five feet. Isn't that enough in which to sink the weaver? Are you satisfied?"

The man spoke to her without any pretence at fine feeling. He addressed her as a fourth wife should be addressed. The widow was conscious but unresentful of the man's manner. She regarded him calmly and without any resentment. On his part there was no resentment either, no hypocrisy, no make-believe. Her unemotional eyes followed his action as he stuck his spade into the loose mould on the ground. A cry from Cahir Bowes distracted the man, he laughed again, and before the widow could make a reply he said:

"Old Cahir is great value. Come down until we hear him handling the nailer."

He walked away down over the ground.

The widow was left alone with the other grave-digger. He drew himself up out of the pit with a sinuous movement of the body which the widow noted. He stood without a word beside the pile of heaving clay and looked across at the widow. She looked back at him and suddenly the silence became full of unspoken words, of flying, ringing emotions. The widow could see the dark green wall, above it the band of still deepening red, above that the still more pallid grey sky, and directly over the man's head the gay frolicking of the fresh star in the sky. Cloon na Morav was flooded with a deep, vague light. The widow scented the fresh wind about her, the cool fragrance of the earth, and yet a warmth that was strangely beautiful. The light of the man's dark eyes were visible in the shadow which hid his face. The pile of earth beside him was like a vague shape of miniature bronze mountains. He stood with a stillness which was tense and dramatic. The widow thought that the world was strange, the sky extraordinary, the man's head against the red sky a wonder, a poem, above it the sparkle of the great young star. The widow knew that they would be left together like this for one minute, a minute which would be as a flash and as eternity. And she knew now that sooner or later this man would come to her and that she would welcome him. Below at the stile the voice of Cahir Bowes was cackling in its aged notes. Beyond this the stillness was the stillness of heaven and earth. Suddenly a sense of faintness came to the widow. The whole place swooned before her eyes. Never was this world so strange, so like the dream that Malachi Roohan had talked about. A movement in the figure of the man beside the heap of bronze had come to her as as warning, a fear, and a delight. She moved herself a little in response, made a step backward. The next instant she saw the figure of the man spring across the open black mouth of the weaver's grave to her.

A faint sound escaped her and then his breath was hot on her face, his mouth on her lips.

Half a minute later Cahir Bowes came shuffling back, followed by the twin.

"I'll bone him yet," said Cahir Bowes. "Never you fear I'll make that old nailer face me. I'll show him up at the weaver's wake to-night!"

The twin laughed behind him. He shook his head at his brother, who was standing a pace away from the widow. He said:

"Five feet."

He looked into the grave and then looked at the widow, saying:

"Are you satisfied?"

There was silence for a second or two, and when she spoke the widow's voice was low but fresh, like the voice of a young girl. She said:

"I'm satisfied."

THE PEDLAR'S REVENGE

Liam O'Flaherty

OLD Paddy Moynihan was dead when the police appeared on the scene of the accident. He lay stretched out on his back at the bottom of the deep ravine below the blacksmith's house. His head rested on a smooth granite stone and his hands were crossed over his enormous stomach. His battered old black hat was tied on to his skull with a piece of twine that passed beneath his chin. Men and boys from the village stood around him in a circle, discussing the manner of his death in subdued tones. Directly overhead, women and girls leaned in a compact group over the low stone wall of the blacksmith's yard. They were all peering down into the shadowy depths of the ravine at the dim shape of the dead man, with their mouths wide open and a fixed look of horror in their eyes.

Sergeant Toomey made a brief inspection of the corpse and then turned to Joe Finnerty, the rate collector.

"Tommy Murtagh told me," he said, "that it was you . . ."

"Yes," said Finnerty. "It was I sent Tommy along to fetch you. I told him to get a priest as well, but no priest came."

"Both the parish priest and the curate are away on sick calls at the moment," said the sergeant.

"In any case," said Finnerty, "there was little that a priest could do for him. The poor old fellow remained unconscious from the moment he fell until he died."

"Did you see him fall?" said the sergeant.

"I did," said Finnerty. "I was coming down the road when I caught sight of him on the blacksmith's wall there above. He was very excited. He kept shouting and brandishing his stick. "The Pedlar poisoned me," he said. He kept repeating that statement in a sing-song shout, over and over again, like a whinging child. Then he got to his feet and moved for-

216

ward, heading for the road. He had taken only half a step, though, when he seemed to get struck by some sort of colic. He dropped his stick, clutched his stomach with both hands and staggering backwards, bent almost double, to sit down again on the wall. The next thing I knew, he was going head over heels into the ravine, backwards, yelling like a stuck pig. Upon my soul! His roaring must have been heard miles away."

"It was a terrific yell, all right," said Peter Lavin, the doctor's servant. "I was mowing down there below in the meadow when I heard it. I raised my head like a shot and saw old Paddy go through the air. Great God! He looked as big as a house. He turned somersault twice before he passed out of my sight, going on away down into the hole. I heard the splash, though, when he struck the ground, like a heavy sack dropped into the sea from a boat's deck."

He pointed towards a deep wide dent in the wet ground to the right and said:

"That was where he landed, sergeant."

The sergeant walked over and looked at the hollow. The whole ground was heavily laden with water that flowed from the mossy face of the cliff. Three little boys had stuck a rolled dock-leaf into a crevice and they were drinking in turn at the thin jet of water that came from the bright green funnel.

"Why did he think he was poisoned?" said the sergeant.

"I've no idea," said Finnerty. "It's certain, in any case, that he had swallowed something that didn't agree with him. The poor fellow was in convulsions with pain just before he fell."

The sergeant looked up along the sheer face of the cliff at a thick cluster of ivy that grew just beneath the overarching brow. A clutch of young sparrows were chirping plaintively for food from their nest within the ivy.

"According to him," the sergeant said, as he walked back to the corpse, "The Pedlar was responsible for whatever ailed him."

"That's right," said Finnerty. "He kept repeating that The Pedlar had poisoned him, over and over again. I wouldn't pay much attention to that, though, The Pedlar and himself were deadly enemies. They have accused one another of every crime in the calendar scores of times."

"'Faith, I saw him coming out of The Pedlar's house a few hours ago," said Anthony Gill. "He didn't look like a poisoned man at that time. He had a broad smile on his face and he was talking to himself, as he came shuffling down along the road towards me. I asked him where he was going in such a great hurry and he told me to mind my own business. I looked back after he had passed and saw him go into Pete Maloney's shop."

"I was there when he came in," said Bartly Timoney. "He was looking for candles."

"Candles?" said the sergeant.

"He bought four candles," Timoney said. "He practically ran out of the shop with them, mumbling to himself and laughing. Begob, like Anthony there said, he seemed to be in great form at the time."

"Candles?" said the sergeant again. "Why should he be in such a great hurry to buy candles?"

"Poor man!" said Finnerty. "He was very old and not quite right in the head. Lord have mercy on him, he's been half-mad these last two years, ever since he lost his wife. Ah! The poor old fellow is better off dead than the way he was, living all alone in his little cottage, without anybody to feed him and keep him clean."

The sergeant turned to Peter Lavin and said:

"Did the doctor come back from town yet?"

"He won't be back until this evening," Lavin said. "He's waiting over for the result of the operation on Tom Kelly's wife."

"All right, lads," the sergeant said. "We might as well see about removing poor old Moynihan."

"That's easier said than done," said Anthony Gill. "We weighed him a few weeks ago in Quinn's scales against three sacks of flour to settle a bet. Charley Ridge, the lighthouse keeper, bet a pound note that he was heavier than three sacks of flour and Tommy Perkins covered the pound, maintaining that he would fall short of that weight. The lighthouse keeper lost, but it was only by a whisker. I never saw anything go so close. There were only a few ounces in the difference. Well! Three sacks of flour weigh three hundred and thirty-six pounds. How are we going to carry that much dead weight out of this hole?"

"The simplest way, sergeant," said Guard Hynes, "would be to get a rope and haul him straight up to the blacksmith's yard."

Everybody agreed with Hynes.

"I've got a lot of gear belonging to my boat up at the house," said Bartly Timoney. "I'll go and get a strong rope."

He began to clamber up the side of the ravine.

"Bring a couple of slings as well," the sergeant called after him. "They'll keep him steady."

All the younger men followed Timoney, in order to give a hand with the hauling.

"There may be heavier men than old Moynihan," said Finnerty to those that remained below with the corpse, "but he was the tallest and the strongest man seen in his part of the country within living memory. He was six feet inches in his bare feet and there was no known limit to his strength. I've seen him toss a full-grown bullock without hardly any effort at all, in the field behind Tom Daly's pub at Gortmor. Then he drank the three gallons of porter that he won for doing it, as quickly as you or I would drink three pints."

"He was a strong man, all right," said Gill. "You could heap a horse's load on to his back and he'd walk away with it, as straight as a rod, calmly smoking his pipe."

"Yet he was as gentle as a child," said Lavin, "in spite of his strength. They say that he never struck anybody in his whole life."

"Many is the day he worked on my land," said Sam Clancy, "and I'll agree that he was as good as ten men. He could keep going from morning to night without slacking pace. However, it was the devil's own job giving him enough to eat. The side of a pig, or even a whole sheep, would make no more than a good snack for him. The poor fellow told me that he suffered agonies from hunger. He could never get enough to eat. It must have been absolute torture for him, when he got too old to work and had to live on the pension."

Timoney came back and threw down two slings, over the low wall where the women and girls were gathered. Then he let down the end of a stout rope. Sergeant Toomey made one sling fast about Moynihan's upper chest and the other about his knees. Then he passed the end of the rope through the slings and knotted it securely.

"Haul away now," he said to Timoney.

The two old sparrows fluttered back and forth across the ravine, uttering shrill cries, when they saw the corpse drawn up slowly along the face of the cliff. The fledglings remained silent in obedience to these constantly repeated warnings, until old Moynihan's dangling right hand brushed gently against the ivy outside their nest. The light sound being like that made by the bodies of their parents, when entering with food, they broke into a frenzied chatter. Thereupon, the old birds became hysterical with anxiety. The mother dropped a piece of worm from her beak. Then she and her cock hurled themselves at old Moynihan's head, with all their feathers raised. They kept attacking him fiercely, with beak and claw, until he was drawn up over the wall into the yard.

When the corpse was stretched out on the blacksmith's cart, Sergeant Toomey turned to the women that were there and said:

"It would be an act of charity for ye to come and get him ready for burial. He has nobody of his own to wash and shave him."

"In God's name," they said, "we'll do whatever is needed."

They all followed the men that were pushing the cart up the road towards the dead man's cottage.

"Listen," the sergeant said to Finnerty, as they walked along side by side. "Didn't The Pedlar bring old Moynihan to court at one time over the destruction of a shed."

"He did, 'faith," said Finnerty, "and he was awarded damages, too, by District Justice Roche."

"How long ago was that?" the sergeant said.

"It must be over twenty years," said Finnerty.

"A long time before I came here," said the sergeant. "I never heard the proper details of the story."

"It was only a ramshackle old shed," said Finnerty, "where The Pedlar used to keep all the stuff that he collected around the countryside, rags and old iron and bits of ancient furniture and all sorts of curiosities that had been washed ashore from wrecked ships. Moynihan came along one day and saw The Pedlar's ass tied to the iron staple in the door-jamb of the shed. Lord have mercy on the dead, he was very fond of playing childish pranks, like all simple-minded big fellows. So he got a turnip and stuck it on to the end of his stick. Then he leaned over the wall of The Pedlar's backyard and began to torment the ass, drawing the unfortunate animal on and on after the turnip. The ass kept straining at its rope until the door-jamb was dragged out of the wall. Then the wall collapsed and finally the whole shed came down in a heap. The Pedlar was away at the time and nobody saw the damage being done except old Moynihan himself. The poor fellow would have got into no trouble if he had kept his mouth shut. Instead of doing so, it was how he ran down into the village and told everybody what had happened. He nearly split his sides laughing at his own story. As a result of his confessions, he very naturally didn't have a foot to stand on when the case came up before the court."

The dead man's cottage looked very desolate. The little garden in front was overgrown with weeds. There were several large holes in the roof. The door was broken. The windows were covered with sacking. The interior was in a shocking state of filth and disorder.

"He'll have to stay on the cart," said Sergeant Toomey, after he had inspected the two rooms, "until there is a proper place to lay him out like a christian."

He left Guard Hynes in charge of the body and then set off with Joe Finnerty to The Pedlar's cottage.

"I couldn't find the candles," he said on the way. "Neither could I find out exactly what he had for his last meal. His little pot and his frying pan were on the hearth, having evidently been used to prepare whatever he ate. There was a small piece of potato skin at the bottom of the pot, but the frying pan was licked as clean as a new pin. God only knows what he fried on it."

"Poor old Paddy!" said Finnerty. "He had been half-starved for a long time. He was going around like a dog, scavenging for miserable scraps in shameful places. Yet people gave him sufficient food to satisfy the appetite of any ordinary person, in addition to what he was able to buy with his pension money."

The Pedlar's cottage was only a few yards away from Moynihan's sordid hovel, to which its neatness offered a very striking contrast. It was really very pretty, with its windows painted dark blue and its walls spotlessly white and the bright May sunlight sparkling on its slate roof. The garden was well stocked with fruit trees and vegetables and flowers, all dressed in a manner that bore evidence to the owner's constant diligence and skill. It also contained three hives of honey-bees which made a pleasant clamour as they worked among the flowers. The air was charged with a delicious perfume, which was carried up by the gentle breeze from the different plants and flowers.

The Pedlar hailed the two men as they were approaching the house along a narrow flagged path that ran through the centre of the garden.

"Good day," he said to them. "What's goin' on over at Paddy Moynihan's house? I heard a cart and a lot of people arrive there."

He was sitting on a three-legged stool to the right of the open doorway. His palsied hands moved up and down, constantly, along the blackthorn stick that he held erect between his knees. His legs were also palsied. The metalled heels of his boots kept beating a minute and almost inaudible tattoo on the broad smooth flagstone beneath his stool. He was very small and so stooped that he was bent almost double. His boots, his threadbare black suit, his white shirt and his black felt hat were all very neat; like his house and his garden. Indeed, he was immaculately clean from head to foot, except for his wrinkled little face. It was in great part covered with stubbly grey hair, that looked more like an animal's fur than a proper human beard.

"It was old Paddy Moynihan himself," said the sergeant in a solemn tone, "that they brought home on the cart."

The Pedlar laughed drily in his throat, making a sound that was somewhat like the bleating of a goat, plaintive and without any merriment.

"Ho! Ho! Did the shameless scoundrel get drunk again?" he said in a thin high-pitched voice. 'Two months ago, he got speechless in Richie Tallon's pub with two sheep-jobbers from Castlegorm. He had to be taken home on Phil Manion's ass-cart. There wasn't room for the whole of him on the cart. Two lads had to follow along behind, holding up the lower parts of his legs."

"Old Paddy is dead," the sergeant said in a stern tone.

The Pedlar became motionless for a few moments on hearing this news, with his shrewd blue eyes looking upwards at the sergeant's face from beneath his bushy grey eyebrows. Then his heels began once more to beat their minute tattoo and his fingers moved tremulously along the surface of the blackthorn stick, up and down, as if it were a pipe from which they were drawing music.

"I'll ask God to have mercy on his soul," he said coldly, "but I won't say that I'm sorry to hear he's dead. Why should I? To tell you the honest truth, the news that you bring lifts a great weight off my mind. How did he die?"

He again laughed drily in his throat, after the sergeant had told him the manner of old Moynihan's death. His laughter now sounded gay.

"It must have been his weight that killed him," he said, "for John Delaney, a carpenter that used to live in Srulane long ago, fell down at that very same place without hurting himself in the least. It was a terrible night, about forty years ago. Delaney was coming home alone from a funeral at Tirnee, where he had gone to make the coffin. As usual, he was dead drunk, and never let a word out of him as he fell. He stayed down there in the hole for the rest of that night and all next day. He crawled out of it at nightfall, as right as rain. That same Delaney was the king of all drunkards. I remember one time he fell into a coffin he was making for an old woman at . . ."

"I must warn you," Sergeant Toomey interrupted, "that Paddy Moynihan made certain allegations against you, in the presence of Joe Finnerty here, shortly before he died. They were to the effect that you had . . ."

"Ho! Ho! Bad cess to the scoundrel!" The Pedlar interrupted in turn. "He's been making allegations against me all his life. He's been tormenting me, too. God forgive me! I've hated that man since I was a child."

"You've hated him all that time?" said the sergeant.

"We were the same age," said The Pedlar. "I'll be seventy-nine next month. I'm only a few weeks older than Paddy. We started going to school on the very same day. He took a violent dislike to me from the first moment he laid eyes on me. I was born stooped, just the same as I am now. I was delicate into the bargain and they didn't think I'd live. When I was seven or eight years old, I was no bigger than a dwarf. On the other hand, Paddy Moynihan was already a big hefty block of a lad. He was twice the size of other boys his own age. He tortured me in every way that he could. His favourite trick was to sneak up behind me and yell into my ear. You know what a powerful voice he had as a grown man. Well! It was very nearly as powerful when he was a lad. His yell was deep and rumbling, like the roar of an angry bull. I always fell down in a fit whenever he sneaked up behind me and yelled into my ear."

"That was no way to treat a delicate lad," said the sergeant in a sympathetic tone. "It was no wonder that you got to hate him."

"Don't believe a word of what he's telling you," said Finnerty to the sergeant. "Paddy Moynihan never did anything of the sort."

The Pedlar again became motionless for a few seconds, as he looked at Finnerty's legs. Then he resumed his dance and turned his glance back to the sergeant's face.

"He did worse things to me," he said. "He made the other scholars stand around me in a ring and beat my bare feet with little pebbles. He used to laugh at the top of his voice while he watched them do it. If I tried to break out of the ring, or sat down on the ground and put my feet under me, he'd threaten me with worse torture. "Stand there," he'd say, "or I'll keep shouting into your ear until you die." Of course, I'd rather let them go on beating me than have him do the other thing. Oh! God! The shouting in my ear was a terrible torture. I used to froth at the mouth so much, when I fell down, that they thought for a long time I had epilepsy."

"You old devil!" cried Finnerty angrily. "You should be ashamed of yourself for telling lies about the dead."

"Let him have his say," the sergeant said to Finnerty. "Every man has a right to say what he pleases on his own threshold."

"He had no right to speak ill of the dead, all the same," said Finnerty, "especially when there isn't a word of truth in what he says. Sure, it's well known that poor old Paddy Moynihan, Lord have mercy on him, wouldn't hurt a fly. There was no more harm in him than in a babe unborn."

"Take it easy, Joe," said the sergeant. "There are two sides to every story."

Then he turned to The Pedlar and added:

"'Faith, you had cause to hate Moynihan, all right. No wonder you planned to get revenge on him."

"I was too much afraid of him at that time," said The Pedlar, "to think of revenge. Oh! God! He had the life nearly frightened out of me. He and his gang used to hunt me all the way home from school, throwing little stones at me and clods of dirt. "Pedlar, Pedlar, Pedlar," they'd shout and they coming after me."

"Musha, bad luck to you," said Finnerty, "for a cunning old rascal, trying to make us believe it was Paddy Moynihan put the scholars up to shouting "Pedlar" after you. Sure, everybody in the parish has shouted "Pedlar" after a Counihan at one time or other and thought nothing of it. Neither did the Counihans. Why should they? They've all been known as "The Pedlars" from one generation to another, every mother's son of them."

The sergeant walked over to the open doorway and thrust his head into the kitchen.

"Leave the man alone," he said to Finnerty.

The fireplace, the dressers that were laden with beautiful old brown delft-ware and the flagged floor were all spotlessly clean and brightly polished.

"Ah! Woe!" The Pedlar cried out in a loud voice, as he began to rock himself like a lamenting woman. "The Counihans are all gone except myself and I'll soon be gone, too, leaving no kith or kin behind me. The day of the wandering merchant is now done. He and his ass will climb no more up from the sea along the stony mountain roads, bringing lovely bright things from faraway cities to the wild people of the glens. Ah! Woe! Woe!"

"If you were that much afraid of Moynihan," said the sergeant, as he walked back from the doorway to The Pedlar's stool, "it must have been the devil's own job for you to get revenge on him."

The Pedlar stopped rocking himself and looked up sideways at the sergeant, with a very cunning smile on his little bearded face.

"It was easy," he whispered in a tone of intense pleasure, "once I had learned his secret."

"What secret did he have?" said the sergeant.

"He was a coward," said The Pedlar.

"A coward!" cried Finnerty. "Paddy Moynihan a coward!"

"Keep quiet, Joe," said the sergeant.

"I was nineteen years of age at the time," said The Pedlar, "and in such a poor state of health that I was barely able to walk. Yet I had to keep going. My mother, Lord have mercy on her, had just died after a long sickness, leaving me alone in the world with hardly a penny to my name. I was coming home one evening from Ballymullen, with a load of goods in my ass's creels, when Moynihan came along and began to torment me. "Your load isn't properly balanced," he said. "It's going to overturn." Then he began to pick up loose stones from the road and put them into the creels, first into one and then into the other, pretending that he was trying to balance the load. I knew very well what he had in mind, but I said nothing. I was speechless with fright. Then he suddenly began to laugh and he took bigger stones from the wall and threw them into the creels, one after the other. Laughing at the top of his voice, he kept throwing in more and more stones, until the poor ass fell down under the terrible weight. That was more than I could bear. In spite of my terror, I picked up a stone and threw it at him. It wasn't much of a stone and I didn't throw it hard, but it struck him in the cheek and managed to draw blood. He put up his hand and felt the cut. Then he looked at his fingers. "Lord God!" he said in a weak little voice. "Blood is coming from my cheek. I'm cut." Upon my soul, he let a terrible yell out of him and set off down the road towards the village as fast as he could, with his hand to his cheek and he screaming like a frightened girl. As for me, 'faith, I raised up my ass and went home happy that evening. There was a little bird singing in my heart, for I knew that Moynihan would never again be able to torture me."

"Right enough," said the sergeant, "you had him in your power after that. You had only to decide . . ."

"Best of all, though," The Pedlar interrupted excitedly, "was when I found out that he was mortally afraid of bees. Before that, he was able to steal all my fruit and vegetables while I was out on the roads. It was no use keeping a dog. The sight of him struck terror into the fiercest dog there ever was."

"You wicked old black spider!" said Finnerty. "Why do you go on telling lies about the dead?"

"Keep quiet, Joe," said the sergeant. "Let him finish his story!"

"All animals loved Moynihan," said Finnerty, "because he was gentle with them. They knew there was no harm in him. Children loved him, too. Indeed, every living creature was fond of the poor old fellow except this vindictive little cripple, who envied his strength and his good nature and his laughter. It was his rollicking laughter, above all else, that aroused the hatred of this cursed little man."

"So you got bees," the sergeant said to The Pedlar.

"I bought three hives," The Pedlar said, "and put them here in the garden. That did the trick. Ho! Ho! The ruffian has suffered agonies on account of those bees, especially since the war made food scarce in the shops. Many is the good day's sport I've had, sitting here on my stool, watching him go back and forth like a hungry wolf, with his eyes fixed on the lovely fruit and vegetables that he daren't touch. Even so, I'm glad to hear he's dead."

"You are?" said Sergeant Toomey.

"It takes a load off my mind," The Pedlar said.

"It does?" said the sergeant.

"Lately," said The Pedlar, "I was beginning to get afraid of him again. He was going mad with hunger. You can't trust a madman. In spite of his cowardice, he might attack me in order to rob my house and garden."

"Was that why you decided to poison him?" said the sergeant.

The Pedlar started violently and became motionless, with his upward-glancing eyes fixed on the sergeant's chest. He looked worried for a moment. Then his bearded face became suffused with a cunning smile and his palsied limbs resumed their uncouth dance. The metalled heels of his boots now made quite a loud and triumphant sound as they beat upon the flagstone.

"You are a clever man, Sergeant Toomey," he whispered in a sneering tone, "but you'll never be able to prove that I'm guilty of having caused Paddy Moynihan's death."

"He was in your house today," said the sergeant.

"He was," said The Pedlar.

"Did you give him anything?" said the sergeant.

"I gave him nothing," said The Pedlar.

"You might as well tell the truth," said the sergeant. "When the doctor comes back this evening, we'll know exactly what old Moynihan had for his last meal."

"I can tell you that myself," said The Pedlar.

"You can?" said the sergeant.

"He burst into my kitchen," said The Pedlar, "while I was frying a few potatoes with some of the bacon fat that I collect in a bowl. "Where did you get the bacon?" he said. He loved bacon and he was furious because there was none to be had in the shops. "I have no bacon," I said. "You're a liar," said he. "I can smell it." I was afraid to tell him the truth, for fear he might ransack the house and find my bowl of bacon fat. Then he'd kill me if I tried to prevent him from marching off with it. So I told him it was candles I was frying with potatoes. God forgive me, I was terribly frightened by the wild look in his eyes. So I told him the first thing that came into my head, in order to get him out of the house. "Candles!" he said. "In that case, I'll soon be eating fried potatoes myself." Then he ran out of the house. I locked the door as soon as he had gone. Not long afterwards, he came back and tried to get in, but I pretended not to hear him knocking. "You old miser!" he shouted, as he gave the door a terrible kick that nearly took it off its hinges. "I have candles myself now. I'll soon be as well fed as you are." He kept laughing to himself as he went away. That was the last I saw or heard of him."

"You think he ate the candles?" said the sergeant.

"I'm certain of it," said The Pedlar. "He'd eat anything."

The sergeant folded his arms across his chest and stared at The Pedlar in silence for a little while. Then he shook his head.

"May God forgive you!" he said.

"Why do you say that?" The Pedlar whispered softly.

"You are a very clever man," said the sergeant. "There is nothing that the law can do to a man as clever as you, but you'll have to answer for your crime to Almighty God on the Day of Judgement all the same."

Then he turned to Finnerty and said sharply:

"Come on, Joe. Let's get out of here."

Finnerty spat on the ground at The Pedlar's feet.

"You terrible man!" he said. "You wicked dwarf! You'll roast in hell for all eternity in payment for your crime."

Then he followed the sergeant down along the narrow flagged path that divided the garden.

"Ho! Ho!" The Pedlar cried in triumph as he stared after them. "Ho! Ho! My lovelies! Isn't it great to hear the mighty of this earth asking for

God's help to punish the poor? Isn't it great to see the law of the land crying out to God for help against the weak and the persecuted."

He broke into a peal of mocking laughter, which he suddenly cut short.

"Do ye hear me laugh out loud?" he shouted after them. "No man heard me laugh like this in all my life before. I'm laughing out loud, because I fear neither God nor man. This is the hour of my delight. It is, 'faith. It's the hour of my satisfaction."

He continued to laugh at intervals, on a shrill high note, while the two men went down the flagged path to the gate and then turned right along the road that led back to Moynihan's sordid cottage.

"Ho! Ho!" he crowed between the peals of laughter. "I have a lovely satisfaction now for all my terrible shame and pain and sorrow. I can die in peace."

The metalled heels of his boots now beat a frantic tattoo upon the flagstones and his palsied hands continued to move back and forth over the surface of his blackthorn stick, as if it were a pipe from which they were drawing music.